THE
STORM WITCH

VIOLETTE MALAN

THE STORM WITCH

A Novel of Dhulyn and Parno

DAW BOOKS, INC.
DONALD A. WOLLHEIM, FOUNDER
375 Hudson Street, New York, NY 10014
ELIZABETH R. WOLLHEIM
SHEILA E. GILBERT
PUBLISHERS
www.dawbooks.com

First Printing, September 2009

1 2 3 4 5 6 7 8 9

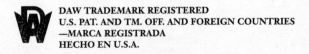

For Paul

Acknowledgments

As always, my first thanks go to the two people without whom there would be no reason to thank anyone else, my agent, Joshua Bilmes, and my editor, Sheila Gilbert. My thanks also go to my cousin José Ignacio Díaz Hellín, and Alberto Domingues Saenz, the chefs extraordinaire of Restorante Restoval in Badajoz, Spain, for the feast fit for a king. There are a whole bunch of people who are involved with helping me to promote my work, in one way or another. My first thanks go to my brother, Oscar Malan, and his wonderful wife Joanna (another chef extraordinaire) who host my book launches in his bookstore, Novel Idea, with Joanna's wonderful nibbles to help draw in the crowds. Special thanks to Melanie Babcock at Print 3 for all her help with my bookmarks and posters. Also to Chris Szabo of Bakka Phoenix Books, and from Chapters, Barbara Bell, Dan Millings, and especially Jessica Strider, who got married this year.

The right to have a character named after her was purchased at silent auction by Trudy Primeau. You'll notice I played with the spelling a bit, Trudy. Say hi to Megz for me.

One

PARNO LIONSMANE PULLED the hood of his cloak down over his forehead and hunched his shoulders against the rain. Here it was, practically high summer, what his Partner Dhulyn Wolfshead would call the Grass Moon, and the rain was coming down as though it was already well past Harvest Moon. He caught Dhulyn's eye as they sidestepped the flow of water running down the center of the narrow cobbled lane. She was frowning, and he knew that more than the weather troubled her.

"Cheer up," he told her. "A few more days at most, and the whole misunderstanding will be cleared up."

His Partner nodded, but almost as if she wasn't listening. Dhulyn was Senior to him—though she was younger, she had been longer in the Mercenary Brotherhood, having come to it as a child—and *that* was part of the problem.

"It's only the Tarkin of Hellik's court they are sending to," he added, "not all the way to Imrion."

This time Dhulyn looked at him as she nodded, and Parno smiled to himself. "I would not have thought it so difficult to find a Brother Senior to me in a city as large as Lesonika," she said. "I thought this would all be over by now."

Both looked up as thunder rumbled.

"A good thing we left the horses, after all," Dhulyn said. She dodged a fountain of water pouring from a greatly overworked overhead gutter. They'd come down from the port of Broduk on the *Catseye*, the typical wide-beamed, single-masted ship of the Midland Sea, with both their warhorses and their packhorse in makeshift stalls on the deck. Just now Dhulyn had decided that all the beasts would be happier in the warm, dry stable provided by the Mercenary House. And the crew of the *Catseye* would be happier as well. Captain Huelra didn't often ship horses—in fact, Parno was fairly certain Dhulyn Wolfshead was the only person Huelra would trust with horses aboard his ship.

"It could be worse," Parno said now.

"How?"

"It could be snowing."

Parno didn't like the way Dhulyn shook her head without even a token smile. He knew her well enough to make a good guess at her thoughts. If there could be such rain—with thunder—in the Grass Moon, why *not* snow? As it was, the hay was flattened in the fields, and oats and young barley would be washed out or stunted if the weather didn't improve soon. Which meant a poor harvest, which meant trouble. Parno brightened. Which generally meant work for the Brotherhood.

The streets inclined more sharply as they approached the harbor where the *Catseye* was moored, but even so the water was over their ankles more than once before they reached the comparatively dryer docks. Here, at least, the volume of water had somewhere to go—into the sea. Lesonika had a deep harbor, and in addition to half a score of the smaller Midland Sea vessels like the *Catseye*, one of the tall, three-masted, ocean-faring ships was also moored there.

Dhulyn slowed almost to a halt, turning her head to stare at the tall ship as they passed it, her normally bright cavalry cloak hanging in sodden folds and darkened to a dull red by the rain. Parno's own cloak, just as good a mix of inglera fleece and wool, slapped wetly around his calves as the wind took it.

"I thought so," she called out to him as he reached her side, her rough silk voice just audible over the pelting rain. "Those *were* Long Ocean Traders at the Mercenary House. Did you see them?"

"The ones in the scaly vests?" he said. "What could they want with our Brothers?"

"Delivering fressian drugs, perhaps."

Parno pursed his lips in a silent whistle, taking a longer look. If his Partner was right, and the ship was carrying even a few casks of fresa, fresnoyn, or fresnant, he was looking at more money than he'd seen in many a moon.

There were sailors out even in this weather, seeing to the mooring lines. The tide was beginning to ebb, Parno saw, and the amount of water flowing from the town into the boat basin—enormous as it was to the city dwellers—would make no difference to the sea level; lines still had to be adjusted, anchors checked. Everywhere there were bare masts, but the usual harbor sounds of creaking stays, shrouds, and halyards could not be heard over the drumming of the water and the rising noise of the wind.

"Demons and perverts," Parno cursed as a spray of water caught him fully in the face. Dhulyn's laughter did not help. They ran the final few paces to the *Catseye* and pounded up the gangplank. The usual sentry was missing, but given the rain and the wind, Parno was not surprised.

There was no glow of light from around the door of Captain Huelra's tiny cabin, and Dhulyn turned immediately toward the entrance to the hold. Their own sleeping quarters were below, their hammocks strung up along with those of the sailors, and Parno hesitated only a moment before following her. A cup of the captain's brandy would have been welcome, but the dry clothing in their packs below beckoned even more strongly. And if it came to that, Parno thought grinning, there was a newly purchased flask of Berdanan brandy hanging at his own hip.

Not that someone else's brandy didn't always taste better.

Dhulyn heaved back the hatch and dropped straight into the hold, ignoring the ladder placed to one side. She moved immediately to the right, leaving Parno a clear space to follow her. He rolled his eyes—even here, Dhulyn would follow the Brotherhood's Common Rule and enter the room as though staging an attack—but he followed her precisely, landing lightly, knees slightly bent, blinking in the lantern light, his right hand on the hilt of his sword, his left on his knife.

And froze.

"Carefully, Paledyn. No sudden moves, if you please." The thickly accented voice came from a dark-haired, heavily mustached man holding the spiked end of a *garwon* to Captain Huelra's head. Huelra sat, wrists and ankles bound, on an upturned cask of the cook's milled flour. Two candle lanterns, one on the floor and one hanging from a hook on the mast, cast double shadows over the scene. Parno gritted his teeth and resisted the urge to look at Dhulyn. He hadn't seen a *garwon* since his Schooling. Long, thin, and fiercely sharp, it was used by divers as an underwater hand weapon. The point actually rested on the skin of Huelra's temple, and could be through the comparatively thin bone and into the man's brain before either Parno or Dhulyn could move. And that did not take into account the young woman with her arbalest already cranked back and pointed at Dhulyn Wolfshead, or the half-dozen others, armed and standing farther back in the shifting shadows.

Parno noted automatically that both the mustached man and the woman were bareheaded, though both wore the oddly patterned scaly vests that he'd seen at the Mercenary House. Long Ocean Traders. He couldn't be sure about the others, though he thought at least one more also wore mail. Parno smiled. As usual, Dhulyn had been right to take precautions—better careful than cursing, that's what she always said. Anyone else would have come down the ladder the normal way, and been caught with their backs to the enemy.

He leaned against the ladder behind him and lifted his hands away from his weapons, knowing without looking that Dhulyn had already done the same. By no means were they out of options, but with that *garwon* at Huelra's temple, a straightforward attack was low on their list.

"You *are* Paledyn? What is called here the Mercenary Brotherhood?" The same man spoke again.

"We are." Without moving her hands, Dhulyn tossed her head and the hood of her wet cloak fell back to reveal her Mercenary badge, the blue and green of the tattoo across her temples and above her ears bright even in this light. Parno still was not used to seeing her with her hair so short, just a damp cloud the color of old blood around her face. Parno shook his own hood off.

"I am Dhulyn Wolfshead," his Partner said. "Called the Scholar. I was Schooled by Dorian the Black Traveler. I have fought at Sadron, Arcosa, and Bhexyllia." And Limona, thought Parno, though perhaps she was right not to mention that particular battle until the Mercenary House here in Lesonika had ruled on the consequences of it. "I fight with my Partner, Parno Lionsmane," Dhulyn concluded.

"And I am that Parno Lionsmane with whom she fights," Parno added. "Called the Chanter and Schooled by Nerysa Warhammer of Tourin."

There was a moment—just a moment—when the eyes of the arbalest woman had shifted, glancing at Dhulyn's badge, but the man holding the *garwon* on Huelra never moved.

"Come with us," the *garwon* holder said. "Now. If not, we kill your friend."

"Or," Dhulyn answered in her most reasonable tone. "We can wait until your wrist gets tired and then kill *you*."

The skeptical snort that sounded from the shadows came from the third man on the left. Parno automatically calculated distance and angle. Dhulyn did not take her eyes from the *garwon*.

"Crew of the *Catseye* are aboard our ship," the man continued in the same even tone. "You don't come, or we don't return," he shrugged. "They'll be killed."

Parno had to admit he was impressed. The mustached man spoke as though he was commenting on the weather. There weren't many who could be threatened by a Mercenary Brother and not even change color—no matter how many armed men stood in the shadows behind them.

"Huelra, is this true?"

"Wolfshead, it is. You'd been gone a few hours—and half my crew on shore leave after you—when these came on board under a trading flag, may their ship have plank worm. Why should I doubt them?" Huelra looked as though he'd like to spit, but couldn't turn his head. "They took us handily, curse their keel, and they took my crew away. That much I saw before they hauled me down here."

Parno could see that under Huelra's fear and rage was a measure of embarrassment at being so easily caught. He'd probably been flattered that the Long Ocean Traders had approached him at all.

Dhulyn smiled her wolf's smile, her lip turning back from the small scar that marked it. "If we didn't care about Huelra," she said to the trader, "we'd hardly care about his crew." This time the man blinked, and Parno stifled a smile of his own.

"It isn't necessary to hold people hostage to hire us," she added. "You might simply offer us money."

The man slowly shook his head, without moving his eyes from Dhulyn's face.

Demons and perverts, Parno thought. This was taking too long. "I'm going to take my cloak off," he said. "It's wet, and it's cold. I've brandy here in this flask, and I see no reason I shouldn't drink some. We understand that if we don't cooperate you'll kill Huelra's people. Tell us why we should stop you."

Now the man was round-eyed with surprise—though still not afraid. He turned his head, almost enough to look at the young women holding the arbalest. "You're Paledyn," he said finally. "Mercenary Brothers. People won't die when you can save them."

Interesting. Not untrue, in and of itself, just interesting the man should say so.

"Dhulyn Wolfshead is Senior Brother," Parno said. "Here and now, it is she who will decide who lives and who dies. So we might as well relax, while she's listening to your request." Parno moved his hands to the clasp of his cloak and let the sodden garment fall to the floor, where he kicked it to one side. Dhulyn was already tossing hers toward the spot where their packs were tied securely against sliding should the ship roll. This time the man did glance quickly at the woman behind him, as he lowered his *garwon*. The woman herself relaxed, but Parno noticed that she did not release the crank on the arbalest.

"Come," Dhulyn said, the merest edge of impatience in her voice. "Tell us what you require of us." Parno opened the flask of brandy, took a swallow, and tossed it to Dhulyn. She caught it neatly in her left hand, but held it without taking a drink. That made three times they had moved without anyone using a weapon. If they could keep this up, this could finish with them all drinking together.

"Malfin Cor of the Long Ocean Nomads." The man had lowered his weapon, but he had not put it down, and he still had his hand on Huelra's shoulder. "Our ship is *Wavetreader*, and this my sister-captain, Darlara Cor." The woman inclined her head.

"Offer to hire and you say no? Then what?" the woman Darlara spoke up. "Our time, and our funds, running out. You *must* cross the Long Ocean with us—"

"If not," Malfin Cor said. "We kill Captain Huelra and his crew, burn *Catseye*."

Parno raised his eyebrows. *That* point had already been made. This did not seem like the kind of shrewd and subtle trading the Nomads had the reputation for. He waited, expecting Dhulyn to make a countersuggestion of her own, but she had fallen silent, and perfectly still. She seemed not even to notice the slight motion of the *Catseye* under her feet. Parno took the chance of looking directly at her. What he saw almost made him reach toward his sword once more. Dhulyn's face was as still as a statue, and what little natural color she had was drained away. But what shocked Parno most was the almost invisible trembling of her lower lip.

"But why must it be Mercenary Brothers you take?" When she finally spoke, even her voice seemed pale.

The two exchanged quick glances again. "Been told it must be, *will* be, it was *Seen*."

Dhulyn's knuckles went white as her grip on the brandy flask tightened. *Blooded demons*, Parno thought. A Seer. These Nomads had been sent by a Seer. He started to relax. He and Dhulyn had been trying to find a Seer for moons now. If these Nomads had been sent by one . . .

"Paledyn we must bring," the man was saying. "Spokesmen between our people and our enemies. Spokesmen *they* will trust."

"Let me guess." Dhulyn's rough-silk voice was sour. "You need such paragons because your enemies no longer trust you to deal honorably with them?" Parno blinked. His Partner must have some reason to ignore the mention of Seers.

The two Captains Cor inclined their heads in unison, apparently unfazed by the implication. "Never been much meeting of souls between us," the woman Darlara said. "They're landsters, and we're of the Crayx."

"Even so, things looked to be getting better, with new negotiators, trade going up, but now . . ." Malfin Cor shook his head. "That's stopped. Won't even speak to us."

"You think you can force *us* to trick them for you?" Dhulyn took a swig of the brandy.

"No! Need you to deal honorably with them. Wish you to negotiate in good faith."

Dhulyn looked down at the flask in her hand, and back up at the Nomad captains. "May I suggest that kidnapping us by threatening to kill our friends may not be the best way for you to begin."

Malfin Cor took in a deep breath and released it slowly, as if he was trying to keep his temper. "Paledyn—Mercenaries, we've tried all other ways. Say we should offer money—very well, what will you take?"

Ah, he's got us there, Parno thought. He'd be having fun, if Dhulyn wasn't so pale, and so still.

Dhulyn was still hesitating. "There are other Mercenary Brothers here in Lesonika. Let me find you one of those," she finally said. "We have a matter for judgment in our House here, a matter of our Brotherhood, and we are not free to take employment until it is resolved."

Now Parno thought he understood Dhulyn's behavior. They were bound by all their oaths of Brotherhood to await the summons of their House. Kedneara the late Queen of Tegrian had asked for a judgment of outlawry against them—mistakenly, of course, but she'd died before being able to withdraw it. They had sworn documents from the present Queen, but if they missed this judgment, if their documents were not presented, it could very well result in outlawry for them.

And the Mercenary Brotherhood was the only home Dhulyn Wolfshead had ever known. No surprise that she was ignoring the reference to a Seer, and considering—even if only for a moment—letting Huelra and his people die rather than lose it. After all, death was what lay in store for all of them. Eventually.

But Captain Malfin Cor was shaking his head. "Must leave with this tide—now, in fact. Who knows how long it might take to find others." He lifted his hand as Dhulyn started to speak again. "It's not *we* can't wait. It's the Crayx."

"I begin to see why they have problems negotiating with these others," Parno said, under his breath.

Dhulyn nodded, but slowly. "We could agree, and then kill you all."

Parno forced his eyebrows to remain at their normal level. *That* was a negotiating tactic he'd never heard her use before.

Another snort of laughter came out of the shadows behind Captain Darlara Cor. Before the sound died away, Parno's hand flicked out, and the hilt of his heaviest dagger bounced off the forehead of the third man to the left. There was a THUNK as the man fell to his knees and pitched forward into the flickering light of the lanterns.

"You were saying?" Dhulyn's rough voice sounded courteous and soft in the sudden silence.

Blinking, Malfin Cor cleared his throat. "You would not," he said. "You are Paledyn." This time he did not sound quite so sure. "You would swear not to."

Dhulyn sighed and Parno caught her glance, lifting his left eyebrow in answer to her look. They would be bound, no question of it. For a Mercenary Brother there was no such thing as a forced oath. They would die rather than swear one. That was their Common Rule.

"And what prevents you from killing your hostages in any case?" Parno said. "Once we've agreed and we're at sea? I only ask since you admit that you can't be trusted."

Captain Malfin Cor bit his lower lip. "Of course," he said nodding, "that would free you from *your* oaths."

A creak of rope made them all look up.

"Wolfshead." Their friend Captain Huelra's voice was tight, but there was nothing else, no plea for himself or his crew. His throat moved as he swallowed. Huelra had no say here, no control over the events around him; so, like a sensible man, he stayed quiet . . . and trusted to his gods.

Well, his gods were looking after him tonight, that was certain.

"How if I came with you myself, and my Partner remained here."

"Dhulyn!"

Even as the words left her mouth, Dhulyn knew what Parno's reaction would be. But it was too late to call them back, and whatever else happened, short of breaking the oaths of the Common Rule—short of breaking the oaths of their Partnership, to which her suggestion came perilously close—she must do whatever she could to keep Parno off the Long Ocean ship.

Without telling him why.

"Without me," she said to him now, "the Mercenary House can rule quickly, they need not wait for a Brother Senior to me. You can explain what has happened here, and I will return as quickly as I can." She turned with lifted eyebrows to Malfin Cor and his sister-captain.

"As soon as our business is finished," he said.

"No." Parno's voice startled her, she had never heard him speak so sharply before. "We are Partnered," he said. "I will not—I cannot—be left behind."

"I am Senior—" Dhulyn began.

"In Battle," Parno said, touching his forehead with the tips of his fingers.

Dhulyn held off, but there was only one answer, and her Partner knew it. "Or in Death," she answered him lifting her own hand to answer his salute. She clenched her teeth against the words she could *not* say. Another rope creaked overhead, or perhaps the same one, and she cleared her throat.

"Let Huelra and his crew go," she said, her heart tight in her chest.

"Now. Free them, and we come with you." What was her alternative? Let them die? And when her Partner asked her why she'd let that happen—because he would ask her, no question—what answer could she give him? That she could not tell him why, that it was all part of the one thing she had promised never to tell him?

"Wolfshead." The tone in Huelra's voice was now completely different. Evidently, he had not been so very certain what their answer would be.

"Huelra," she said. She wondered if anyone else noticed the tightness in her voice. "You must be our advocate to our House. The documents they have already, but you must go, explain to them what has happened, and ask them to wait their judgment." She swallowed. "Ask them to look after our horses."

"It will be done, Wolfshead. Depend on me."

Dhulyn kept her attention on the last few items she was removing from their largest pack. They'd had to abandon much of their gear—not counting weapons, of course—after the battle of Limona, and even after restocking in Beolind there wasn't much. They had moved their packs only after having seen Huelra's crew restored to the *Catseye*, and the cabin they'd been given on the *Wavetreader*—Co-captain Darlara's own, as it turned out—was more than spacious. Or it would be, if Parno wasn't hovering over her like a schoolmaster looming over a student. She kept her hands busy and her eyes down. Not that it did her any good.

"*What* were you thinking?"

"Not now, my soul."

But he persisted, as she'd known he would. "How could you say you would go alone? Demons and perverts, we're Partnered, *why* would you say such a thing?"

Because you are going to die out there, she thought, her lips pressed tight. Because she'd known ever since she'd first touched him that Parno was going to die at sea. Her Vision had shown her the storm, and the deck tilting, and the wall of water that would sweep her Partner over the side. And she had promised never to tell him how he would die. Never.

"I was worried about the hearing," she said finally. "I lost my head."

Parno crouched down next to her, blocking her light, and put his hand on her shoulder. "And the Seer? You felt we must stay, and yet you wanted to go." Here he was, finding excuses for her.

"Now is not a good time to be touching me," she said from between clenched teeth.

Parno lifted his hand immediately and edged back. "Did *you* have a Vision? Is *that* what this is all about?" he said, lowering his voice.

Dhulyn froze, her hands caught flattening the pack for folding, her lower lip between her teeth. Partners did not lie to each other, as a rule. Was there any part of the truth that could serve?

"Yes," she said finally. "I've Seen that a sea voyage will prove to be unlucky for us."

Parno sat back on his heels, blowing out his cheeks. "Well, then." He rubbed at the beard stubble on his chin. "Still, what could you do? Let them kill Huelra and his people? A large price to buy our way out of some bad luck." He stood up and edged around her to where the heavy silk bag holding his pipes lay on the cabin's small table.

"Let's not worry too much, in any case," he said. "With your Sight so chancy as it is, it may be nothing more than the sea illness. Do you want to try using the vera tiles?"

Dhulyn shook her head. She closed the latch on the locker underneath the lower bunk and sat back on her heels, delaying the moment that he would expect her to turn toward him.

"Let it wait a day or two," she said. "My woman's time is coming. And it may be best if our hosts don't know of my Mark."

Parno nodded, rubbing at his face once more. He'd have to let his beard grow again, she thought. It was hard to shave at sea unless you'd had plenty of practice. Her heart lurched again. Practice he wasn't going to get.

"It doesn't sound as though they have a problem with this Seer they've mentioned. Especially since they're doing what she asked. Still, chances are they're more familiar with the commoner ones, Menders, Finders, Healers."

"And if, unlike me, the Seer they know has been fully trained . . ."

Parno nodded. "They'll have the usual expectations."

They would, the same as any reasonable person. That she See for them, look into the future. And she would have to explain once again that her Sight was erratic, that she'd never been trained to use it properly, that her glimpses of the future were not as useful as people might think.

Very few ever believed her.

"Fine, then. Let's hide your Mark from the Nomads," Parno said. "At least until we have some idea of what they actually know about the Marked, and how they feel about them."

Dhulyn looked up at him. Parno was frowning, his eyes focused on the middle distance. Funny how he still thought of the Marked as "them," she thought. But, of course, to him she was his Partner first, and a Seer second.

"Still, it can't do any harm for us to check the tiles, just for ourselves, try to head off this bad luck you're talking about." He held up his hands as she opened her mouth. "I know what you're going to say. Unreliable. But we know much more about your Sight now than we did before. If your woman's time *is* near, *and* you use the tiles, that gives us the best possible chance of accuracy. After all, we know what to expect, it won't be the first Vision we've dealt with."

Dhulyn took a deep breath and consciously willed her hands to loosen from the fists she'd made. She was sorely tempted to tell him and be done with it, lest the short time they had left be spoiled by evasions and half-truths. But she'd sworn, hadn't she, when they'd first Partnered and she'd told Parno that she was Marked. Sworn it would be the one thing she would never tell him. The one secret that would free her to tell him everything—anything—else.

She'd done all she could to keep him off the deep seas, the Long Ocean here in the east, the larger Round Ocean in the Great King's realm far to the west. Even here, in the Midland Sea, she'd made sure they only took coastal vessels such as Captain Huelra's *Catseye*.

And she'd done what she could to keep them from this voyage as well. *Had* she done the right thing? *Could* she have left Huelra and his crew to die? Was following the honorable path of the Common Rule *really* worth Parno's life? Tradition said that one Partner did not survive the death of the other, but that hadn't even entered her thoughts until now. She looked up, but her Partner was focused on his pipes, checking the air bag for soundness. It was Parno she wanted to save, not herself. But if she acted dishonorably, if she broke the Common Rule, what kind of life was she saving for them?

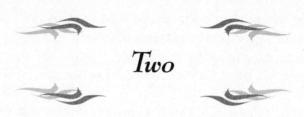

Two

DHULYN WOLFSHEAD TRIED to focus her attention on the book in her hands, but not even the poems of the great The-onyn offered her any escape from her thoughts. She had hardly slept. The sound of water shushing under the hull should have been soothing, a reminder of her days of Schooling aboard the *Black Traveler*, but the sound was wrong somehow, jarring. And as for Parno's breathing, every familiar sigh filled her with reproach. Finally, as soon as there was light enough in the sky, she'd let herself out of their cabin and found a spot where she would be out of the way of the crew on watch but there'd be light enough to read.

Dhulyn wrinkled her nose. A sharp, almost spicy smell overlaid the familiar and expected odors of brine, ozone, oiled decks, and bodies too long washed in salt water. She massaged her temples with the tips of her fingers. Perhaps it was the strange smell causing her headache. And perhaps pigs would become Racha birds. She'd found a coil of rope to sit on, her back against the high rail, in a sheltered spot not far from the man at the wheel, though out of his line of sight. Her sword was hooked to her belt, and her best throwing dagger hung in its thin harness under her vest, between her shoulder blades. She badly missed the knives she would normally carry in her boot tops, but without proper deck shoes, she'd chosen to go barefoot.

The unusual rain had lasted through the night, stopping at sun-rise. The wind seemed light for the speed they were making, but she'd seen no sign of oars. The watch had just changed, and Dhulyn was well aware of the looks and sideways glances of the few whose duties brought them on deck at this hour, though none of them ventured near her. She couldn't be sure what caused the interest, that she was a Mercenary Brother, or that she was reading. She had lowered her eyes once more to her book when a whisper of sound automatically made her slow her breathing and concentrate, reaching out with all her senses. A shadow fell on the page in front of her.

"You are in my light, Captain Malfin Cor," she said without lifting her eyes.

"Seem very comfortable there. Right in thinking you've been on ships before, Dhulyn?" She was getting the feel of the accent, she thought, but that unusual dropping of pronouns . . .

She closed Theonyn's book on the index finger of her right hand. "My name is pronounced 'Dillin,' " she reminded him. "But only my Brothers may call me that. You must call me Wolfshead, or Scholar. And my Partner is Lionsmane, or Chanter."

She leaned back, propping her elbow on a crosspiece of wood. This was the first opportunity she'd had to see the captain in unobstructed light. He was just a finger's width or two shorter than she was herself—and she was tall for a woman—and dressed in the same dark clothing as the rest of his crew, though his loose trousers and simple shirt looked to be of costlier fabric. Like his sister-captain, and one or two of the senior crew including the man at the wheel, Malfin Cor wore a vest—almost a cuirass—made of a peculiar thick leather that would have resembled the skin of a fish, except the scales were much too large. Dhulyn's nostrils widened. The armor also seemed to be the source of the odd smell. Rather than boots, or a town man's shoes, he wore sailor's clogs on his bare feet. The easier to kick them off if he went into the water, Dhulyn remembered from her own Schooling.

Only the captain's chin was clean-shaven. His mustache joined his sideburns, and his braid, she noticed as he turned his head away from her to watch the progress of a very young boy up the forward mast, was reinforced with leather thongs and long enough to reach all the way down his back, and wrap around his waist to form a belt. Dhulyn resisted the urge to touch her own hair, still barely long enough to fall into her eyes. She looked around her. Not everyone she could see had the same hairstyle as the captain, but certainly all who wore one of the odd leather cuirasses.

Dhulyn blew out a silent sigh. Malfin Cor was showing no inclination to move from her side. While it was she who drove the bargains, it was usually Parno who undertook the job of making conversation with clients.

"Last night you called us 'Paledyn,' " she said. "I have heard a similar word among the Berdani, but it is not much used in general."

"More a word of the Mortaxa than ours." Malfin Cor leaned his hip against the rail, folding his arms. "Mortaxa tales and songs tell of warriors and sages of paramount honor and fair dealing, the Hands, in this world, of the Slain God." He gestured toward Dhulyn's hairline. "Known by their shaven and tattooed heads. When we first carried tales of the Mercenary Brotherhood back across Long Ocean, the Mortaxa believed you must be descendants of that order."

Dhulyn nodded. It could be. It was widely held in the Scholars' Libraries that the Mercenary Brotherhood, the Jaldean Priesthood, and the Scholars themselves had been formed by the last of the Caids who had the old knowledge, before that race had died out. The Caids were supposed to have occupied the whole world—small wonder, then, if similar tales and writings were found everywhere.

Dhulyn straightened, blinking. Perhaps there were books there, across the Long Ocean; books that were unknown in the continent of Boravia. They had been in such a hurry to catch the ebbing tide the night before that there had been no discussion of payment or fees. She wondered now if perhaps they could be paid in books. She glanced down at the worn inseam of her linen trousers. Well, perhaps only partly in books.

Her breath caught and she squeezed shut her eyes. For a moment it seemed her heart stopped beating. How was it possible that she'd forgotten? They wouldn't be paid at all. Things wouldn't get that far.

"Something's amiss?" Malfin Cor was looking at her with furrowed brows.

Blood. She'd need to control her face better than this. She closed her book completely and slipped it under her sword sash at the small of her back.

"You say the Mortaxa have this belief, yet it was you who were sure we would not leave Huelra and his crew to die."

Malfin Cor shrugged. "Desperation makes a man grasp at anything. There's none of us among the Crayx haven't heard the stories of the Paledyn, and many have seen the Mercenary Brotherhood. But saw last night not all feel the same way. Plus there's some begrudge having to use this voyage to come fetch you, and may try to show you how much."

"No one can grudge our presence here more than we do ourselves, Malfin Cor." Dhulyn could hear the sincerity in her own voice, and apparently the captain could, too, for he nodded and looked away.

Pain throbbed behind Dhulyn's right eye, and was answered by a sudden but familiar spasm of a muscle in her lower back, the herald of her woman's time, no doubt of it. *Sun and Moon*, just what she needed when she had to be at her sharpest.

"Tell me more about the Mortaxa," she said. Much as she would have liked to ignore the captain, his crew, and the whole blooded ship, some instinct told her to act as naturally as the circumstances would allow. If this were any other job, she would be asking questions, gathering information, formulating plans. "And all you know," she added, "of your dispute with them."

"It's a few days longer than the turning of the moon to cross Long Ocean, Dhulyn Wolfshead. Plenty of time to talk."

Nice if that were true. She shook her head, and added a roll of the eyes for effect. "You really don't know much about diplomacy and negotiation, do you?" she said. "First, *you've* asked for *my* help, so don't think to tell me how to give it to you. Second, there is no such thing as too much time to prepare."

"As you say, Paledyn." He swept her a bow with the suggestion of a smile on his lips. "But wait until your Partner joins us. As soon tell the tale but once, and my sister should be with us."

Dhulyn hesitated, this time making sure her face kept its expression of skeptical interest. Need Parno hear any of this? As she was still formulating her answer, the door to their cabin at the far end of the main deck swung open, and her Partner sauntered out, one hand tucked into his belt, and the other resting negligently on his sword hilt, head cocked as if he were strolling through some capital city's main square. Dhulyn smiled. Parno's amber colored eyes were bright and alert, and except for his bare feet—he'd been on shipboard before, and knew better than to wear his boots—he was fully dressed in trousers, shirt, and leather jerkin. In addition to his regular sword, a short sword and dagger were conspicuous on his belts. His golden hair was unusually dull in the light of the overcast sky.

Parno Lionsmane spotted Dhulyn across the stretch of deck that separated the mid and aft cabins. He smiled. He should have known she'd found the one spot where she could sit down, be in no one's way, keep her eye on most of the crew—and still be the first thing he'd see when he opened their cabin door. Still grinning, Parno made his way across the deck to where Dhulyn sat, taking care not to lurch or stagger. There weren't many of the crew up and about, but it wouldn't do to let anyone see a Mercenary Brother off-balance. He trotted up the gangway and nodded to the captain, a shortened parody of the bow his House's Scholar had taught him as a child.

"You didn't wake me," he said to his Partner when he was close enough to be heard without raising his voice. "No *Shora* this morning?"

Again, that look passed over Dhulyn's face, the paling of her skin, the parting of her lips, accompanied by a shiver as if of frozen grief. And then rapid blinking, and an even more rapid return to a normal expression, except for her lack of color. Could she be having a Vision? But Parno had never seen that look before now, and Dhulyn had been having Visions all the time he'd known her.

"What?" she said, giving him the smile she saved only for him. "I wake you up, you complain; I don't wake you up, you complain. Either way," she shrugged. "The captain's about to tell us why they need us."

"Darlara's in our cabin. Perhaps could join her," the Nomad said. "Devin, hot water?"

A small boy looked over from his post at the steersman's side, flashing a quick smile as he dashed forward toward the galley.

After giving the order, Malfin Cor stood to one side and held out his hand with a flourish, an invitation to take the gangway to the lower deck. There, under and to the right of where the wheel man stood gazing out into the far distance, was a doorway, and a cabin slightly larger than the one they had been given. Parno looked at Dhulyn. She looked back at him. Parno touched his fingertips to his forehead in the Mercenary salute.

"After you, Captain," he said. "We insist." As far as he was concerned they were here by force, job or no job, and until they found out more about the circumstances of their being here, even their client had to be treated with caution.

Parno lifted his eyebrows as they followed Cor into his cabin. He'd wager that the untidiness was not habitual, but reflected Co-captain Darlara's hasty relocation the night before. Like their own, the cabin was longer than it was wide, with bunk beds along the inner wall—the lower one with folded clothing and a jumble of land shoes on it—and two square casement windows on the outer, seaward wall more highly placed than would have been considered normal in a room built on land. What they could see of the floor showed tightly fitted tongue-and-groove planks of a dark red hardwood, though Parno suspected there would be drainage holes somewhere along the edges of the floor, or the bottom of the exterior wall, to allow any water that entered the cabin to escape.

The captains motioned them to take seats at a bench along one side of a large central table—both benches and table, Parno noticed as he slid himself in, made of seasoned pine and bolted to the floor. Dhulyn remained standing for a moment longer, looking at a set of floor-to-ceiling shelves built into the wall between the windows. Each shelf had a rail that would help keep its contents in place as the ship moved, and while most of them contained objects of daily use, metal dishes and mugs, small wooden containers and even a few glasses, there was also a small selection of rolled maps and books—which explained Dhulyn's interest.

When Dhulyn reached out her hand, however, it was not to touch the books, as Parno expected, but one of several small ceramic pots attached to the sides of the shelves, where the plants they held could take advantage of the light coming through the thick glass of the windows.

"Tansy," said Darlara Cor.

"For making tea," added her brother.

The two captains stood together on the far side of the table, the daylight full on their faces. They were the same height—a finger's width or so shorter than Dhulyn—with the same wiry build, and thick, coarse, dark hair. Malfin's mustache made it harder to see, but they also shared the same fine lips, though Darlara's were perhaps a shade fuller, the same high cheekbones and narrow noses.

Their ears were precisely the same shape, and their luminous, almost black eyes were exactly the same distance apart.

"You're twins," Parno said, leaning forward with interest. It was not so obvious with male and female siblings, but he'd seen twins once before. They were rare enough that some made a living traveling with troupes of players or musicians and putting themselves on display.

"Are," they said in unison. "Some landsters are superstitious about twins," added Darlara in her light voice.

"The Mercenary Brotherhood is Schooled to have no prejudice," Dhulyn said. "It's said that twins are often Marked. May I ask . . . ?"

The two captains looked at each other, round-eyed, clearly surprised.

"Many and many twins among Nomads," Malfin answered. "A third of us, I'd say. But never heard of anyone who's Marked."

"Marked among the Mortaxa," Darlara added when it seemed that Dhulyn was about to ask. The two Nomads exchanged so swift a glance that Parno couldn't be certain he actually saw it. "But none among us."

"Not one?" Dhulyn's voice showed surprise, not skepticism. "They're rare, I know. Fewer than three in two hundred, but to have none at all . . . Are *you* superstitious, then, about the Marked?"

"That we're not—ah here's Devin with hot water." Malfin rose at the sound of the knock, and let the boy in. Devin was balanced with unconscious ease, his two hands wrapped around the padded handle of a steaming kettle. Malfin took the kettle from the lad and shooed him out the door when he seemed inclined to stay and stare at the Mercenary Brothers. Parno smiled.

"Peppermint or ginger?" Darlara rose to her feet and went to the shelves to peer into boxes. "Though there's lemon grass here if rather have that."

"No ganje, I suppose?"

Malfin was shaking his head and his sister turned to look at them over her shoulder, a small frown creasing her forehead. "Don't use stimulants," she said.

Of course you don't. Parno kept his sour thought to himself. Just his luck. He'd slept longer than usual, and now found himself feeling groggy.

"Ginger would be fine, if there is enough of it." Dhulyn folded her hands in front of her as Malfin took a tall, round basket as wide across as a dinner plate from a drawer to one side of the bunks. Dhulyn glanced sideways at Parno. They weren't surprised when Malfin took off the lid and revealed a porcelain teapot, of a kind they'd often seen in the lands of the Great King to the West. *Of course,* Parno thought. What served the migrating nomads of the western plains would serve the seagoing nomads just as well. Not only would the basket keep the tea warm, but it would serve as padding should the pot be tossed from the table by an errant wave—or from the back of a runaway horse.

"You were saying, about the Marked," Dhulyn said, as Darlara spooned dried ginger into the pot and Malfin added hot water from the kettle.

"Wouldn't mind a few Marked among us right now, and that's a fact," Malfin said. He put the lid back on the teapot, and closed the basket once again, to allow the tea to steep.

"Those skills, Mender, Finder, Healer—were part of what we traded for with the Mortaxa."

"*Were* part?"

"Yes. About a year ago—"

Dhulyn held up her hand. "Start even farther back. How long have your people been dealing with the Mortaxa? What is the history of your relationship with them?"

The two Cors, brother and sister, looked at each other, identical frowns marking each forehead. Without changing expression, Malfin retrieved a shallow box from the same drawer that had held the teapot, opened it, and offered it to Parno. There were biscuits inside. Parno took one, but Dhulyn shook her head.

"Are shrimp flavored, very good," Darlara said with an air of abstraction, as if she were merely going through the motions of courtesy while thinking about something else. "Our mother's recipe."

"We cannot both eat at the same time," Dhulyn said. "I will wait, to see if Parno becomes ill."

Frowns disappeared as both their faces flushed. "But the tea . . ."

"Comes from the common pot," Dhulyn said. "I can assume you will not poison yourselves in order to poison us."

Now their faces showed white spots of anger. Dhulyn held up her hand, palm toward them. "We'd do this no matter where we were, or who we were eating with," she said. "Even in the court of the Great King to the West. It's our Common Rule. Better careful than cursing."

The two captains looked at each other. Finally, they both shrugged. Malfin put the box of biscuits down on the table, picked out one for himself, and began.

"Nomads have been trading with the landsters for generations—as far back as any record, story, or legend—"

"As far back as the Crayx remember," Darlara added, her formal phrasing giving the words a certain ritual feel. "Which is as far back as time." She lifted the teapot from its basket and poured out four cups, handing the first one to Dhulyn, then one each to Parno and her brother, before taking the last one for herself.

"Like all Nomads, follow the Crayx, each to our own Pod. Seven here in the Long Ocean. Thirteen in the Round, three in the Cold South, three in the Northern Bite. Each with our own trade time and trade center."

"And what is it you trade to them, if you don't mind my asking," Parno said.

Once again that lightning flash of a glance between the two captains. This time Parno knew that Dhulyn had caught it as well.

"Other oceans, other ways," Darlara said with a shrug. "*Mortaxa* had no boats or ships, none that could leave the sight of shore."

Past tense? Parno thought. They *had* no boats.

"So bring them food from the sea. Deep-water fish, seaweed, the birds and shellfish that live in the weed beds, even sponges—all the fruits of the seas and oceans."

"As well as pearls, salt, artifacts of the Caids—"

Here Parno and Dhulyn exchanged a look of their own.

"—and skins, of course." Malfin tapped his scaled vest.

"Not the scaled ones, naturally," Darlara added.

"Naturally," Dhulyn said. Under the table, her foot pressed against Parno's, silencing the question that was about to leave his lips.

"And they'd no Long Ocean vessels, no connection with the Crayx, and so no way to cross the Long Ocean and trade with Boravia," Malfin said, using the term for the land north of the Midland Sea. "Or across the Round Ocean. So those things, too," here Malfin tapped the basket that so clearly came from the Great King's realm. "Those things formed part of our trade goods as well."

"But most, we trade for them, carry their goods—fressian mostly—for a share," Darlara said. "And so we buy our own made goods, clothing, utensils."

"And land-based foods," Malfin added. "Fruits, root vegetables . . ."

"Meat," they said in unison, their tones noticeably wistful.

Dhulyn blinked, reached into the front of her multicolored, patchworked vest and pulled out a stick of sausage, dried and smoked for travel.

"I'm afraid it might be a bit sweaty," she said, holding it out.

Both captains had their hands halfway across the table, eyes shining, before they remembered their manners.

"Thank you, Dhulyn Wolfshead," they said.

"If you've any trade goods with you now," Parno said, "we could stop at Navra before we pass through the Straits. We know trustworthy people there."

Both Malfin and Darlara shook their heads. "Not here to trade," he said. "Just to find Paledyn."

"Would have sent someone more important," Darlara said. "But was our Pod's turn to cross, so we came." She had taken out her knife and scrupulously cut the stick of dried meat in two, giving one half to her brother before she cut a small piece off the part she'd kept for herself. The meat was dry and hard, Parno knew, and they would have to soften the bits in their mouths for a while before they could chew them, but they didn't seem to mind. He took another biscuit from the box in front of him.

"So this is the history of your trade." Dhulyn took a sip of her tea and put the small cup back down on the table in front of her. "You spoke of distrust. Has it been the cause, or the result, of war between you?

This time the look that passed between the two captains was long, and undisguised.

"There've been disputes," Malfin said finally. "How not? But in our time all *we've* seen are fights in taverns and such."

"A blockade here, a boycott there," Darlara said, shrugging. "They're landsters, without Crayx, small surprise there's no open water between us. Times they say we hold back goods, wait until there's desperation to drive up prices, but we come and we go as the Crayx bring and take us. Tell them this, and they don't believe."

"Times they say there's been drought, or flooding, and they drive prices up," Malfin said. "And we don't always believe them."

Darlara snorted and looked quickly to one side. "Still, for generations, there's been trade and profit, even if it didn't come easy. And these past few years, when the Tarxin's son, Tar Xerwin, was spokesman for them, looked like things would get better and better."

Parno nodded, leaning forward on his elbow, and wishing the bench seats had backs. Probably the most common cause of war—as the Mercenary Brotherhood had reason to know—was dispute over trade. And even when the dispute was settled, and treaties and tariffs were formalized, that didn't mean the ones who actually did the trading would always see eye to eye.

"So what changed a year ago?"

"*Dawntreader* Pod went to their regular trade fair in Ketxan City, the capital, good to the day and all, and merchants took goods contracted for but nothing else," Malfin said.

"Nothing else?"

Darlara nodded. "No new trade. Were allowed to anchor in their usual place and put ashore. But there was no fair set up, and were told there wouldn't be. *Dawntreader* asked when next fair would be, told to wait."

"By order of the Tarxin, not the son, mind you, the Tarxin himself. Not worried at first," added Malfin. "Crayx remember, type of thing Mortaxa has done before when wanted to change old treaties, old agreements. *We* thought—"

"*We* don't go to the capital, that's not our route," Darlara interrupted. The first time, Parno realized, the twin captains hadn't spoken in turn. "Ours is Caudix, farther along the coast and a bit north. And at first our trade wasn't affected, but seven months ago, contracts were fulfilled, and our landsters turned us away as well."

"Found out *all* trade, everywhere, stopped. Told us they'd no need to be cheated by us anymore . . ." Malfin's voice died away.

"*Had* you been cheating them?" Dhulyn's voice was matter-of-fact, with no judgment in it. The Mercenary Brotherhood did a great deal of negotiation and bargaining, and Parno knew there was often a very fine line between careful dealing and cheating.

"It's trade, Dhulyn Wolfshead," Malfin said, in unconscious echo of Parno's thoughts. "Each makes the best bargain they can, we and the landsters both. Times *we* feel we've caught the current ahead of them, times *they'd* feel the same."

"The captains of our oldest Pods took our protest to Xalbalil, their Tarxin, who the landsters call the Light of the Sun, and he says, will need new treaties, or maybe no treaties since now will build their own ships," Malfin said. "Breaking most ancient and treasured of agreements."

"So we think, what of it? Still cannot cross the Long Ocean without Crayx," Darlara said.

"And say they don't need us now," Malfin added. "Say have lodestone."

Dhulyn whistled. "I've read about them, but I thought they were old magic of the Caids. Has one been found?"

The two Cors gave identical shrugs. "Wouldn't know. Reminded Mortaxa that Crayx would not accept landster ships, any sent out into the Long Ocean would be destroyed. That is their right by the agreement."

"Then came a storm—"

"Winds and rain—"

"Scattering the Pods, confusing the Crayx," Malfin said.

"The Mortaxa said they wouldn't even treat with us any longer," Darlara finished, "That they couldn't trust us, not now we'd threatened them."

"Many wanted to fight, but the Crayx said try talking again, that there would always be time to fight later."

Parno caught Dhulyn's eye, prepared to share a silent laugh at this familiar, and sensible, attitude, but the smile she gave him was late and stiff.

"Then the Tarxin says their Seers say Paledyn will come with a solution. We're to bring them a Paledyn, or don't come back at all."

Parno glanced again at Dhulyn, holding his breath. She was frowning, her blood-red brows drawn down in a vee. She had not missed the reference to a Seer, that was certain.

"Paledyn." Darlara reached her hand across the table between them. "Just want our rights," she said. "*They* should hold by the ancient treaties, or at least bargain to make new ones, not just toss us aside and try to wreck our ships with storms."

"Wait, wait." Dhulyn patted the air in front of her. "I don't know as much about the far side of the Long Ocean as you do, but surely even there the rain must fall."

"Think *this* weather is natural? The rains here, even here, in the Midland Sea? This is to remind us of our task, since they don't trust us to do it."

"*This* weather? You mean yesterday's rain?" Dhulyn's hand tightened on the cup she had been about to raise to her lips. Her glance met Parno's and he nodded, mindful of the storms of the day before, and the unseasonable winds that had accompanied their sailing in the *Catseye* to Lesonika.

"And more. Wait a moment."

Malfin went to the door of the cabin and opened it. "Devin," he said. "Come here a moment, lad." He turned back to the Mercenaries. "Wait until you see this, Paledyn. Then ask me again about the rain."

The young boy came in and grinned at them again. He had good teeth, Parno noticed. So did they all, now that he came to think of it.

"Show the Mercenary Brothers your ears, lad."

What Parno had taken for a scarf around the boy's head was a length of fine fishnet holding pads of linen over his ears. Both Parno and Dhulyn stood and came around the table to see. Devin tilted his head back, exposing his ears completely. Parno leaned closer. The cartilage at the top of the ears was a dull gray color, as if there was no blood circulating there.

"Can you stop in Navra for a Healer?" Dhulyn's voice was tight and Parno looked at her with surprise.

"No." Malfin shook his head. "Just enough time to get through the Straits as it is."

"*You* know what caused this," Darlara said.

Parno frowned, searching through his memory for the knowledge he felt must be there. He'd seen this type of injury before. The answer was just within his grasp when Dhulyn spoke.

"This is frostbite."

Three

"I TAKE IT YOU DON'T sail into the southernmost seas," Dhulyn said. She took the boy Devin by the chin and tilted his face to catch the light better. There were telltale marks of the killing cold on the firm curve of his left cheek as well, just below the eye, though it seemed the dead skin there would slough off without leaving more behind it than a small scar.

"Never. Frostbite—heard the word, surely—but you *know* it? You've *seen* it?"

Dhulyn nodded. "We're Mercenary Brothers, there's little we haven't seen. If there's to be no Healer, the ears will have to be trimmed of this dead flesh, or the death will spread."

While she was speaking, Dhulyn caught the attention of both captains, questioning them with raised brows, reaching her free hand up the back of her vest for her dagger. Understanding what was wanted, Parno mirrored her position on the boy's other side.

The captains hesitated, eyes narrowing as they considered. When they nodded, Dhulyn and Parno moved, their blades flashing so swiftly that it took the boy Devin a moment to even realize he'd been cut. By then, Dhulyn had taken up the pads of linen and was already pressing them to the boy's ears as Parno retied the bits of netting.

"Anyone else who was affected must be dealt with the same way," Dhulyn said. "Even fingers or toes must be cut, and quickly if the limbs are to be saved."

"Go help Jessika, boy, tell her what Dhulyn Wolfshead has said. Jessika's our Knife," Darlara said, turning to Dhulyn. "She'll see to it now she knows what needs to be done."

The boy nodded and turned to the door, his eyes as round as coins, his grin gone.

"Were crossing when this cold overtook us at the midpoint, some fifteen days from Mortaxa. Ice fell from the sky, and then a wind like a knife for three days." Darlara's eyes were still on the cabin door Devin had closed behind him.

"Knew right away it wasn't natural, any more than this rain," Malfin said.

Dhulyn shivered, and saw the same chill mirrored in Parno's eyes. Unusual for this time of year, that's what everyone had been saying about the rains. But hail? Followed by a killing cold? Unnatural was the proper word.

Darlara nodded at their silence. "Not imagining things, Mercenaries. Live by the weather more than most, and can tell what's natural from what's Mage work. The Mortaxa have a Storm Witch, that's certain."

Dhulyn's hand tightened around her teacup. *Sun and Moon.* A Mage? That's all they needed.

"*Can* you be certain?"

Malfin Cor snorted. "Who else can bring ice and snow in the warm oceans?"

"Or this unnatural rain?" added his sister.

"But why would they?" Parno said. "They've sent you, you say, to find Paledyn. Why attack you on your journey?"

The two captains exchanged another look. "We've wondered," Darlara finally said. "*Did* they send us? Said Paledyn would solve all problems."

"Perhaps don't want conflict solved," Malfin said.

"Maybe just to show us what they can do. That the Witch's power extends so far . . ." Both captains shook their heads, the identical movement almost hypnotizing.

Dhulyn blinked, looked into her empty cup, and held it out as Darlara turned to the teapot. *Say there is a Mage,* she thought, or a Witch, as the Nomads called him. It did not necessarily follow that the man was doing anything more or less than defending his people. And the Nomads admitted they'd made threats.

"Say you let them build their ships," Dhulyn said. "This Storm Witch would leave you be, and you might be able to trade for his services, as you do for the Marked. It would be years, perhaps generations, before the Mortaxa became any real threat to you in terms of trade. In this part of the world there are many traders, and all find profit." Automatically, Dhulyn's Schooled mind fell into the logical paths most useful for negotiation. "If nothing else, you'll have bought their goodwill, and that will buy you time to learn more."

"It's not just the trade," Malfin said. "For the Mortaxa—"

"Or anyone else," interjected Darlara.

"Or anyone else," Malfin agreed, "to build ships and travel on the oceans is an affront to the Crayx. It's *they* have dominion over the oceans, and us their children, no one else."

Dhulyn pursed her lips, keeping her eyes focused once more on her refilled cup. They'd been talking long enough that, insulated basket or no, the ginger tea was losing its heat.

Parno cleared his throat "Is 'Crayx' another word for 'Caid'?" he asked. Dhulyn looked up.

But both Nomads were shaking their heads.

"The Crayx knew them, in their time. Was the Caids granted this domain," Malfin said.

"So ancient is their agreement and binding on all who follow," Darlara agreed. "The Crayx are the guardians of the waters of the world."

"You worship them?"

"Oh, no." Here the Nomads seemed almost to laugh, though they grew serious again at once.

"We're the same people. We belong to them," Darlara said. "And they to us."

"As you two belong to each other."

Well, there was no disputing that. She and Parno *were* Partnered, they *did* belong to each other. But as difficult as the Partnership of Mercenary Brothers was for outsiders to understand, at least they were sitting down together, in the same room. Able to touch, argue, and fight side by side.

Dhulyn glanced at him and saw that Parno was wearing his blandest look, but his left eyebrow was raised. The Mercenary Brotherhood was open-minded about the religious beliefs of others—they had to be. But these "Crayx" were something neither of them had ever heard of.

Malfin slid out from behind the table and stood. "Come," he said, and indicated the door. "Show you."

Dhulyn followed Darlara out of the cabin, letting Malfin and Parno bring up the rear. Darlara glanced up and over her shoulder, nodding at the woman now at the wheel, before acknowledging the mate as he moved toward them across the deck. The sun had gone behind the clouds once again, though the wind had picked up and Dhulyn's finely Schooled balance detected the slight pitch of the deck to port.

The ordinary business of the day had begun while they were in the captains' cabin, and the deck, so empty when the sun had barely risen, was almost crowded with men and women—and children, Dhulyn saw with some surprise until she remembered that these were Nomads, and like the nomads of the land, would travel with their families. All seemed busy. There was movement in and out of the cabins in the central part of the deck, where a young, fair-haired woman who was clearly the Knife was hard at work on the other frostbite victims. Much of the rest of the crew were engaged in the usual work found at all times on all ships, repairing the damage caused by salt on the metalwork, and by wear on ropes and railings. Nearest them, two white-haired men with identical laugh lines were mending a net with fingers made crooked by age, and a middle-aged woman sitting with them was putting a new end on a fraying rope.

Dhulyn slowed, looking around her. What was wrong with what she saw? Of course. There were no lines of apprentices drilling in the *Shora* as there would have been on the ship where she was Schooled. To her right, out of the wind, was a man reading to a group of small children sitting cross-legged at his feet, while a similar group of young people several years older were listening with rapt attention to a man with a *garwon* in his hands.

As if they felt her watching them, the youngest of the children turned to stare at the Mercenaries as they passed, and Dhulyn suppressed a smile as she saw Parno straighten his spine and add a slight swagger to his walk, his hand falling casually to the hilt of his sword. The others, older children and crew alike, studiously avoided looking directly at them, though Dhulyn could feel the glances that were aimed out of the corners of eyes as they followed the two captains to an unoccupied section of the rail.

Malfin leaned out, bracing both hands on the rail, his brow furrowed in concentration as he scanned the water rushing past the hull. Darlara motioned the Mercenaries forward with a gesture, inviting them to join Malfin, as she hung back. With a twitch of her left hand, Dhulyn signaled Parno to take up position at Malfin's right while she stayed back beside Darlara. It wouldn't do to have both of them turn their backs on the crew at the same time.

"Demons and perverts." Parno was using the tone he normally saved for visits to religious shrines—only with less fake courtesy and more genuine awe. "You'd better come see this, my heart." He stepped back from the rail to let her take his place, though he didn't move as far away as she had been. Dhulyn looked over the side.

As she watched, a darkness rose up from the depth of the sea, and took the form of a scaled back. A very large, very long scaled back. Finally, the tail flicked out of the water, somehow giving Dhulyn a sense of playfulness and fun.

"What is it?" She was glad to hear her own voice so steady.

"That is the Crayx."

"Ah. Now I see why your ship has no oars."

A soft "click" made Parno Lionsmane's eyes flutter open. Dhulyn was sitting at their cabin's small table with her back to him, but he had seen her in that position many times—back straight as a lance, head tilted down, fingertips resting on the edge of the table—and knew that she was looking at her vera tiles.

He blinked, just stopping himself from speaking. Looking at her tiles, seeking a Vision, was something Dhulyn hardly ever did on her own. It was always his job to nudge her, persuade her. Parno could tell the moment the Visions began by the change in Dhulyn's breathing, and the shift in the angle of her shoulders as she leaned forward. Still, he made no move to rise from his bunk. Instead, he closed his eyes again and let his own breathing slow. Whatever reason Dhulyn had for hiding this from him, he would let her tell him in her own time.

Finally, Parno heard Dhulyn release her breath in a ragged sigh and begin putting the tiles away, almost soundlessly, into their silk-lined box. He waited until she'd slipped the box back into her pack and nudged his shoulder with her knee before he rolled over, reaching up to rub at his face.

"Bring your sword," she told him from the doorway.

Dhulyn Wolfshead raised her face to the rushing air and took a deep breath, letting it out slowly, mentally chanting the closing words of the Scholar's *Shora*. From up in the Racha's nest she could make out an edge of rosy light on the horizon as the sun began to rise. The pains from her woman's time had kept her wakeful all night, despite the valerian Parno had mixed into a cup of wine for her. Finally she'd gotten up, as quietly as she could, and used a meditation *Shora* to relax enough to try the tiles again. As usual during her woman's time, the Visions had been crisp and focused. She'd Seen a narrow path between rock and crisply trimmed hedges, an unknown Finder bending over a dark blue scrying bowl. But no matter what question she asked, what tile she used as her beginning, she could not change the Vision of Parno that appeared. Nor could she See, as she had done sometimes in the past, any Vision of Parno that might come from a different future, a future in which he did not die in the Long Ocean.

The climb up the rigging to the Racha's nest had loosened the muscles in her lower back, and helped her vent at least some of her frustration. She and Parno had always spoken of her Sight as erratic and unreliable—and so it was, since she could no more guarantee what Vision would come than she could guarantee a given cat would chase a given mouse. But the Visions themselves were clear and truthful, even if she didn't always understand them. And what she did See would come to pass, if steps were not taken to change the circumstances.

But now, if she could not See Parno in any Vision other than the one in which he died, it seemed her days of avoiding this particular future were over.

Movement drew her eyes downward. There he was now. Some instinct made him look immediately upward as he secured the cabin door behind him. His teeth flashed white in the dark gold of his beard and he lifted his fist above his right shoulder, signaling "In Battle."

Dhulyn raised her open hand, fingers spread wide, over her own right shoulder, answering the salute, "In Death."

Parno spoke, but Dhulyn shook her head at him. Between the height and the rushing air, it was impossible to hear him.

Come down, Parno signaled.

She shook her head. *You come up. It's only twenty spans.*

"If I cannot tell you," she said, knowing she was safe to speak. "Then I must never let you guess."

That had been the answer her meditation had shown her. She'd made the right choice yesterday when, talking to Malfin Cor, she'd decided to behave as though this were any normal assignment. Not waking Parno, skipping the morning *Shora*—something that all Mercenary Brothers did every day unless injured—*those* had been mistakes.

If she stepped too far from the path of her normal behavior, if she acted as if nothing—not the job, not the *Shora*, not the Common Rule—mattered anymore, Parno would notice and ask questions. As soon as he realized Dhulyn had Seen it, Parno had made her promise never to tell him how he would die. If she could not keep him alive, she could at least keep her promise.

If only it wasn't *this* death. Dhulyn gripped the narrow rail around the Racha's nest tighter and leaned out, giving Parno as encouraging a grin as she could manage. He was almost halfway up the rigging, but with luck he wouldn't notice anything unnatural about her smile.

"Don't slip and fall, my soul," she called out. Parno didn't look up, but he did make a most rude signal with his left hand. Dhulyn laughed, strangely comforted.

Mercenary Brothers expected to die, their Schooling prepared them for it. But they hoped to die in battle, and preferably at the hands of a worthy opponent. The best death—the one that they all hoped for—was at the hands of another Mercenary Brother.

Not the way Parno would die. Not drowning.

"Oh, my soul, I'm so sorry," she murmured. But not quietly enough.

"Sorry for what?"

"Sorry for this." Dhulyn swung her legs over the side of the Racha's nest, pushed Parno to one side with a foot to his sternum, and fell, catching at the rigging from time to time to slow her descent. It was a game the apprentice mercenaries had often played on the *Black Traveler*. The sound of Parno's cursing followed her all the way down until her bare feet hit the closely fitted planks of the deck.

"Crab *Shora*," she announced as Parno landed beside her, and pulled her second-best sword from its harness at her back. One of the basic twenty-seven *Shoras* that all Mercenary Brothers learned in School, the Crab was designed for right-handed sword and uneven ground. But it was just as well suited to the subtly shifting deck beneath their feet.

Parno's sword flicked out to meet hers. "Come on, then," he said, motioning her forward with beckoning fingers. "Winner gets both breakfasts."

⬧

Where are they Malfin Cor resisted the urge to crane his neck around and search out the nooks and crannies of the ship. Usually, he'd know where anyone on board was without having to look. Having landsters among them changed so many things.

Darlara motioned with her eyes to the left, toward the forward deck. *She's on upper deck, he's in my cabin*

Malfin lowered himself to the pilot's bench next to her. *Best think of it as their cabin* he said.

Darlara nodded, her eyes suddenly spreading wide open. *See their practice this morning* she asked.

Malfin shrugged, resting his elbows on his knees and leaning forward enough to look around his sister to the forward deck. He could just make out the spot of dark red that was Dhulyn Wolfshead's hair.

Seen fighters practice

Not like this, and those that did won't be forgetting it soon

Was it so strange then Without straightening, Mal turned to look at her.

Mal, it was fast Darlara leaned against his shoulder, and Malfin felt a tickle of cold run down his spine as her feelings transferred to him. *Went at each other like were crazed, on the main deck, up and down the rigging and ladders—once she ran balancing on the rail and he doing his best to knock her off* *They were all the time smiling, never a foot put wrong—so fast couldn't always see the blades moving—any minute expected blood to fly* Dar put her hand on his arm. *And, Mal, kept it up until the sun was a span over the edge of the sea, and when finished, were dripping sweat, but breathing easy like sitting in a chair*

Malfin's eyes narrowed. *Could hold their breaths long, you think*

They're landsters, when all's said, but oh, Mal, if you'd seen

Mal considered his sister's thoughts carefully, but there was none of that glow he'd sometimes felt when there was a new man she was interested in. Not that he would have been surprised. Both the Mercenaries were tall even for landsters, and Dar liked them tall. And their coloring was unusual enough to make them exotic to the Nomads. Lionsmane was brown and gold all over, like the animal he was named for, and Wolfshead was pale as a deep-sea pearl, and looked like she'd be just as cool to the touch—except for her hair, red like old blood.

No, what he saw now in Darlara's thoughts wasn't lust, but something closer to awe.

Guess I missed something then

There was only the night watch on deck, your turn tomorrow

I can't wait—look

Darlara sat up and turned to look forward. Parno Lionsmane had come out of the cabin carrying what were clearly pipes in his hands. Dhulyn Wolfshead moved from where she had been sitting, coming halfway down the ladder leading to the forward deck, and speaking to her Partner as she came. He answered, she nodded, sitting down where she was on one of the rungs, and went back to reading her book. Dar looked at her brother and lifted her shoulders in query. He frowned and pointed forward again. Dar looked back, and this time she saw what Mal was drawing to her attention. One or two of the crew were circling, closing in on Parno Lionsmane from other parts of the ship, Goann from the forward hatch, Mikel from the galley underneath where he and Dar were sitting, and what looked like Conford, the new exchange, from one of the cabins amidship. All were keeping Pod silence, so you had to be watching to see anything. There wouldn't be much to notice if you were down on the main deck, but from up here it was obvious.

Trouble he said to his sister.

Mercenary Brother has nothing to worry about she said.

Not even three against one Mal got to his feet and headed for the ladder. *Practice against each other is one thing, a fight with Nomads is another*

But he moved with casual deliberation. Strangers were rare aboard a Nomad ship, the crew would have been unsettled in any case, and the circumstances bringing these particular strangers made things even worse. The crew was itching for a confrontation, and the Mercenaries made as good an excuse as any. And since there was bound to be an incident, better it happened now, under his eye, and not later, perhaps when neither he nor Darlara was by.

And he had to admit he was curious. He'd seen a bit of Lionsmane's speed in the *Catseye*, but so had some of the crew, and now they'd be prepared.

Lionsmane had taken his pipes to the narrow bench, little more than a shelf, that ran along the ship's side under the main deck's rail. The instrument's air bag was partially filled, and he was looking down, attaching first the chanter and then the drones. *Chanter*. That was part of his name, and now Malfin figured he knew why. So if the Wolfshead was called Scholar . . .

Lionsmane took the chanter in his fingers and began the opening notes of a slow dance tune, his elbow squeezing out a rhythm through the drones.

"Hey, pipe-boy, do you dance nice like you play?" That was Conford's voice, heavy with anger, and Mal began to walk faster. Con had only recently come to *Wavetreader* from a Round Ocean ship. And voluntary though an exchange always was, Conford's had been particularly hard. Everything and everyone here was strange to him, and it would take him time to feel that he had a good wind and a fair current. In his mid-twenties, Conford was small and thick-muscled like most Nomads, his grin, seldom seen, showing a space where he was missing a tooth. He wore a *garwon* at his belt—which he had every right to—but was beckoning Parno forward with empty hands.

"Come on, then, show us how well you dance."

Lionsmane didn't even open his eyes, but went on playing. Malfin circled around to ship's starboard, until he was standing to the left of Dhulyn Wolfshead where she sat on the ladder, reading.

"Come on, pipe-boy. Or you gonna get your lady friend to fight for you?"

Other crew were beginning to gather, some elbowing each other, grinning. Josel looked up from the lesson he was chalking on the deck boards and shepherded the children toward the aft hatch, shaking his head as he went.

The Mercenary broke off in mid-note, the drones groaning as he released the air bag. He ignored Conford and looked toward his Partner.

"Dhulyn?"

"You go ahead." The Mercenary woman shrugged one shoulder without lifting her eyes from her book. "I did the last one," she added.

She's Senior, Mal remembered, moving forward until he was next to and below her. *Lionsmane won't act without her nod.*

"Are you sure? He seems to think you beat me this morning."

"I *did* beat you, and look again. That man's not one of the crew who watched us this morning. I think his friends are playing a trick on him."

"I like tricks."

"Well, watch out for your pipes. They won't be easy to replace out here." And she'd still never lifted her eyes from her reading.

Mal was close enough to her to speak without raising his voice. "Not even going to watch?"

"I've seen Parno kill people before."

"Kill?" Mal whirled around and took a pace toward the men. "Hoy, Mercenary, no killing."

"Don't worry, Captain," Conford said. "He won't—hrrrk!"

Malfin didn't see the Lionsmane move, but suddenly the Mercenary was standing next to Conford, who was bent over, hands clutching his stomach, eyes bulging, and the *garwon* at his belt was in the Lionsmane's hand. He tossed it to the Wolfshead, who caught it without looking up. Goann dashed forward, and the Lionsmane spun 'round, rapping her on the bridge of her nose with the chanter he held in his left hand. As Goann jerked back, hands to her face, the Mercenary hooked her feet out from under her and tipped her over into Conford, knocking them both to the deck.

Dhulyn Wolfshead turned a page.

Parno Lionsmane scratched the side of his nose with his chanter. Mikel edged backward, raising his empty hands to waist level. Lionsmane stepped back—slowly—to where his pipes lay next to the rail. He smiled as several others of the crew edged nearer to help Conford and Goann. A couple of the crew were smiling as well, Mal noticed.

"Don't worry, Captain," Dhulyn Wolfshead said, looking up from her book for the first time. "My Partner wouldn't have killed anyone. Probably." She smiled, and a small scar pulled her upper lip back in a snarl. "At least, not with his chanter. Blood's hard to clean from the sound holes."

"*Knew* Conford hadn't watched you practice this morning?" One or two from among the crew who were helping Conford and Goann back to their feet looked thoughtful, sending glances at Parno Lionsmane out of the corner of their eyes. One of the smiling ones thumped Conford on the back. Malfin was relieved to see the young crewman shaking his head with a rueful look. It seemed at least part of the anger he'd brought with him from the *Windwaver* was gone. Lionsmane had returned to his perch at the rail, reattached his chanter and was now playing a much livelier tune, somehow making the pipes sound as though they were laughing.

"Nor the other young woman either."

"Did it deliberately, to show my crew what you can do."

"You said it yourself, Captain. Your people don't know us, don't have the same beliefs in the 'Paledyn' that the Mortaxa have. It would only be a matter of time before someone decided to see just what it means to be a Mercenary Brother."

Mal leaned his left hip against the ladder, inches away from Dhulyn Wolfshead's foot. Let his crew see he was not put off. "Run into this kind of thing before?"

Wolfshead leaned back, her elbows on a rung of the ladder, the book closed on the index finger of her left hand. She looked at him with narrowed eyes, as if she was measuring him.

"There's some everywhere who have never seen a Mercenary Brother fight. The Brotherhood is very old—the Scholars say we go back to the time of the Caids, and it's said that we were once numerous. There are fewer of us now. Half of those who come to be Schooled are turned away, and half of those who are accepted leave—those whom the Schooling does not kill." She looked at him closely. "I've heard it said that one Mercenary Brother against ten ordinary soldiers is a fair fight."

Mal swallowed. "And what do you say?" he said, keeping his tone light.

She smiled her wolf's smile, lifted her shoulders and let them drop. "I say it depends on the Mercenary Brother, and on the soldiers." She looked away, and Mal relaxed. "Nevertheless, our reputation being what it is, there are always idiots who have something they need to prove, and decide that challenging a Mercenary Brother is the way to prove it."

"And do you never kill those idiots?"

"We're not assassins, and we don't kill people just because we can. Now, having said all of this to put you at your ease, Captain, let me tell you also, that not everyone on this ship is a warrior. If we decided to do it, my Partner and I could kill you all, and you would not be able to stop us."

"If you did that, the Crayx would destroy the ship."

"Good to know."
She opened her book.

A GREEN-EYED MAN, HIS DARK HAIR BRUSHED BACK FROM A RECEDING FOREHEAD
HOLDS OUT HIS LEFT HAND. HE HAS AN EXTRA FINGER NEXT TO HIS THUMB . . .

THE STORM RAGES, PUSHING WALLS OF WATER OVER THE RAILS OF THE
WAVETREADER, WASHING OVER DECKS, PUSHING THEM CLOSER AND CLOSER
TO VERTICAL. ONE WAVE FOLLOWS ANOTHER, THERE IS SO MUCH WATER IT IS
IMPOSSIBLE TO BREATHE, ONE COULD DROWN STANDING UPRIGHT, CLINGING
TO THE SHEETS. DHULYN TRIES NOT TO LOOK DOWN TO THE DECK BELOW HER,
KNOWING WHAT SHE'LL SEE, HOPING THAT THIS TIME, IF SHE DOESN'T LOOK,
EVERYTHING WILL CHANGE. BUT NOTHING CHANGES. HER HEAD TILTS, HER EYES
NARROW. PARNO, ALMOST UNRECOGNIZABLE, HIS GOLDEN HAIR DARKENED BY
THE WET. SHE HAS NEVER BEEN ABLE TO TELL WHAT HE IS DOING, MAKING SOME-
THING FAST? HELPING SOMEONE IN THE SHADOWS? THE *WAVETREADER* SHIVERS
AS IF IT HAS STRUCK SOMETHING BELOW THE HULL, AND PARNO IS SWEPT OFF
THE PITCHING SIDE OF THE DECK BY A WAVE TALLER THAN TWO MEN. SHE WAILS,
HER HEART BREAKING, AND LETS GO OF THE ROPE SHE CLINGS TO . . .

A VERY SLIM, DELICATELY-BONED WOMAN WITH SANDY HAIR CROPPED SO
SHORT THAT IT SHOWED HER FINELY SHAPED HEAD SITS IN THE CENTER OF A
ROUND WORKTABLE. HER HAZEL EYES ARE SURROUNDED BY FAINT LINES, AND
LOOK DARK AGAINST HER SKIN LIKE CREAM. SHE WEARS A HIGH-COLLARED
SLEEVELESS BLOUSE IN A MUDDY ORANGE COLOR. THERE ARE FINE LINES, OF
LAUGHTER AND OF CONCENTRATION, AROUND HER MOUTH AND EYES. SHE
IS LOOKING DOWN AT THE LARGE, STRANGELY MARKED PARCHMENTS THAT
COVER THE TABLE ALL AROUND HER. FINALLY, SHE NODS AND LEANS BACK, HER
EYES CLOSED. OVER HER HEAD FORMS A MIST, AND THE DHULYN OF THE VISION
STEPS CLOSER, PUTTING HER HAND ON HER SWORD HILT. THE MIST DARKENS.
A TINY FLASH OF LIGHTNING SEEMS TO BOLT THROUGH IT. THE WOMAN RAISES
HER BARE ARMS UNTIL HER HANDS DISAPPEAR . . .

Dhulyn scooped the vera tiles quickly into their box and shoved it out
of sight just as Parno opened the cabin door.

"Come and tell a tale," he said. "They're tired of dancing and my
throat is parched."

"Nothing ever changes."

Four

"THE CRAYX ARE FAR MORE visible from here," Parno Lionsmane leaned forward, his elbows resting on the light bar of wood that formed the rail of the Racha's nest on the forward mast. He glanced sideways at Malfin Cor, who was gazing out at the horizon. It was late in the afternoon watch, and while Parno hadn't expected to be alone in the lookout, he was surprised it was the co-captain who had joined him.

Parno looked down again, eyes drawn to the sinuous movements just below the water's surface. From here, you could see the whole of the beasts, not just the part that broke water. These were much larger than the *Wavetreader*, much longer than the young one they had glimpsed while they were still in the Midland Sea. Older ones, perhaps? Too large to pass through the Herculat Straits?

Malfin Cor took a deep breath, as if he'd come to some kind of decision. Parno waited, watching the man's face. Instead of speaking, however, he looked down, not at the Crayx, but at the deck of the ship to where Dhulyn sat with the teacher Josel, a small girl child practically in her lap.

Suddenly there was a great jolt, and the ship lurched sideways, as if it had struck a reef. Flung to his left, Parno reached out and caught hold of the railing, automatically looking down in time to see Dhulyn put out one hand to steady herself, the other securing the girl child. As the ship began to right itself, the mast swinging back to upright, there was another jolt, the bar in Parno's hand snapped, and he was thrown outward, plunging down. He twisted in the air, reaching for any part of the rigging that might be close enough to grab, and had just enough time to see that there was nothing beneath him when he struck the water and went under.

Dhulyn looked up when she heard the cry. One man, clinging to a broken bit of rail, was clambering back into the relative safety of the Racha's nest. But not the right man. She saw a flash of gold and brown as her Partner plunged into the water a mere arm's length from the ship's side.

Dhulyn was at the rail in a flash, discarding weapons as she went. She was already barefoot, so no boots would weigh her down. *Sun blast it!* She'd never thought she'd be sorry to have so many bits of metal hidden in her clothing.

There was no outcry, no call of "man overboard!" The crew's sudden bustle had no urgency, no fear in it. She could have sworn there was even some laughter.

Without any order given, crew members were in the rigging, spilling the wind out of the sails. As the ship slowed and began to turn, Dhulyn scanned the surface of the water for any sign of her Partner. Where was he? Had he hit his head? This was not what her Vision had always shown her. Her chest was tight, and her blood beat in her ears. This should *not* be happening.

She stopped hunting for more weapons to discard and swung herself over the rail just as Darlara Cor reached her.

"Look," the Nomad captain said.

One hand still on the rail, her bare feet braced on the outer side of the hull, Dhulyn squinted in the direction Darlara was pointing. If the woman had seen some evidence of Parno . . .

There. A black shadow in the water. Parno's head broke the surface. And then his shoulders. And then . . . he appeared to be kneeling on something.

Silence on the deck. The ship was almost completely dead in the water, floating as smooth and light as though it were docked.

Parno continued to rise until the long head of the Crayx bearing him rose out of the water.

"Sun and Moon shine on us," Dhulyn breathed. She didn't even notice when Darlara grabbed her by the wrist.

"Where is he from? Your Partner? What port?"

"No port." Dhulyn used the captain's arm to help pull herself back onto the deck. "He's from Imrion. Inland," she added, when she saw Darlara's face still blank.

By the time Dhulyn had turned around again, Parno was along-side the ship, and the Crayx was lifting him high enough to reach for the rail himself. She was not the first to the spot, but crew members cleared the way for her as she reached out for Parno, giving him a hand to help him balance as he stepped from the Crayx's head to the rail. Once there, he turned to face the beast, gave his deepest bow, touching the fingertips of his free hand to his forehead.

Dhulyn, steadying her Partner before he could topple into the water once more, raised her own hand to salute the Crayx. Any other time, she would have been fascinated by the beast itself, but now she only caught a glimpse of a long, horsey snout, pale green scales the size of her palm, and disconcertingly large, round eyes as the Crayx waggled its head in acknowledgment of the salutes before sinking once more under the waves.

"Did you see that? Demons and perverts, what a ride!" Parno was grinning, apparently none the worse for his dunking in the water—at least until he saw her face. Dhulyn was quick to force an answering smile to her lips.

"You were never worried, my heart? You know I can swim." He smoothed his wet hair back from his face with both hands.

"You might well have forgotten how," she answered, as indifferently as she could.

Malfin Cor landed on the deck and raced over to them, stepping into the small cleared area that had formed around Dhulyn, Parno, and Darlara.

"Performance over, people. Work waiting, if you please." He was smiling, as were many of the others as the crew moved to obey.

"Saw that?" Dhulyn wasn't sure to whom Malfin was speaking.

"Didn't miss a moment," Darlara said.

"Got good balance, man," Malfin said, thumping Parno on the back. "Who would have thought the Crayx could catch you up without even a braid to hook you by?"

Dhulyn raised her eyebrow in sudden comprehension. *That* was the purpose of the hairstyle worn by so many of the crew of the *Wave-treader*. It had not only cultural, but a very practical significance. If a Nomad went overboard, the Crayx could hook the person by the braid of hair that was so securely attached, to the head on one end, and around the waist at the other.

Suddenly, she felt the shortness of her own hair, carefully oiled to keep it out of her eyes.

"Do the Crayx *always* rescue anyone who falls off the ship?" She tried her best to sound merely curious, and not as though she were asking the most important question in the world.

"Need to be able to sense you," Darlara spoke with eyes narrowed, her gaze on the doorway of the cabin where Parno had gone to change his clothing.

"But if they sense you?"

The woman nodded, visibly gathered her thoughts, and turned back to Dhulyn. "Well, not during a storm, then must stay well away from the ship, in case the fury of the waves slaps them up against us." She shrugged. "Could injure themselves, or break the ship, so of course . . ."

"Not during a storm," Dhulyn said. *Of course.*

The wind had been freshening since sundown, and most of the middle watch were in the rigging, reefing the sails before it became too dangerous to go aloft.

Don't understand it *All this wind and the clouds still above us*

Mean you understand it all too well

Darlara Cor shrugged, knowing her brother could feel the movement, even if there wasn't light enough to see. Even if he weren't looking at her.

Know as well as I what brings this wind, and the rain those clouds tell of Malfin said. *But didn't come out here to look at the sky, not in the middle of my watch, you didn't*

Want to talk of the Mercenary Brothers

Thinking you don't mean both of them *It's Parno Lionsmane's caught your eye, not the woman*

He's Pod-sensed Darlara waited until Mal nodded. *Woman's not* she said. *Luckier for us if she was*

There's something, though, Mal said. *She's not an ordinary landster*

Dar shrugged, willing to concede the point.

So what about the Lionsmane

He should stay with us She looked sideways at him. *I want him*

Mal whistled, but Dar had the feeling he was not as surprised as he made out. *Nothing less* *A sworn Mercenary Brother, and Partnered*

Darlara nodded. *Partnered, well and good, but what's that mean* *Land-sters, Mercenary or no, what do they know of real bonds* *There's more important things* *For one, he's Pod-sensed, his bloodline's useful—more use to us than to himself alone, and with us, managed well, he can have young with as many as he wants*

No way to know he wants any

Easy to find out

Said "for one"

She turned to face her brother, leaning her right elbow on the aft rail. They were standing within sight of the wheel, but Deputy Pilot Liandro Cor was notorious for his concentration, which the gusting winds only increased.

For two, he's a rare fighter, and could teach us all he knows *And for three, he'd be more on our side in the talks with the Mortaxa, couldn't help it*

Dhulyn Wolfshead would have some say there, she's Senior

Still, couldn't hurt

True. Malfin leaned both forearms on the rail next to her. *What if Lionsmane won't be parted from his Partner* *What then*

She could stay, be useful

But Malfin was already shaking his head. *Hard enough to have a senseless one on board for a short time, but for life, near impossible* And how would it be for her, left out, more and more alone* He shook his head again.

I want the Lionsmane I'll part him from her, you'll see* I will, or the Crayx*

They agree

The bloodline, the help, just as important to them

That wasn't a "yes," but Malfin nodded, as Darlara had known he would. He was her twin, after all, as well as her co-captain. What she wanted for the ship and the Pod, he would also. What she wanted for herself, he would help her to get.

Parno Lionsmane stood with his back against the aft rail, where his playing would be less obtrusive for those trying to sleep in their hammocks belowdecks. The notes, carefully chosen to simulate the sounds made by the Crayx, seem to fall away into the dark silence beneath them like a leaf wafting slowly from a tree.

The sound was repeated, two octaves deeper, from the depths below them.

"Say it's easier to hear your thoughts when you play," Darlara said from his left.

"But I can't hear theirs?"

"That will come, given time. And then, if I am sharing at the same time, can also hear mine."

Parno looked at her, but from the seriousness of her face, she was stating only fact. "Interesting," he said, taking refuge in the banal from thoughts he was glad she could not hear. "Let's see what they make of this."

He began playing an old tune that the years had given many flourishes and variations, though he now played the simplest. At first, he sensed nothing else, then, a soft echoing came from the sea, and a resonance in his head as well. The crew nearest them started to tap and then stamp their feet in time to the music. Soon, it seemed that everyone on deck was joining in, and people were even coming out of the hold and the deck cabins to take part, until the *Wavetreader* itself began to shiver in time with the stamping feet, like a huge drum.

Parno concentrated on keeping the pipe's air bag filled to the maximum, and began to pace across the deck, keeping time himself. To each side Crayx surfaced, their wet scales flashing brilliant colors in the morning light.

Dhulyn sat humming in the sun, her back against the wall of the cabins on the central deck. She had a selection of weapons spread around her, like a cobbler surrounded by his tools. It was moist on shipboard, and even the air seemed to taste of salt. Like the crew working on the metal parts of the ship in rotation, Dhulyn would clean and oil some of their weapons every day, until they were on land again.

Malfin Cor approached, nodding to her and rubbing sleep from his eyes. Parno's piping, and the crew's drumming, had awakened even those below. He went to the rail across from her and looked smiling out at the Crayx.

"Did they try to kill him?" Dhulyn asked.

Captain Malfin turned, his eyes widened in shocked astonishment. "The Crayx? *Never*. Never in this world."

"But they did cause my Partner to fall. The ship did not run against rock or reef."

"No. Mean, yes."

Dhulyn took pity on the man. She would get no valuable answers if he kept tripping over his own tongue.

"Yes, they did cause him to fall. No, the ship did not run against anything."

"Well, might say that it ran against the Crayx."

"They're so clumsy, then? Or are there mean spirits among them, as there are sometimes in a herd of horses?"

His silence made her look up from her favorite wrist knife, and she paused, cleaning rag hovering in the air.

"*Horses* are individuals," he said finally. "Crayx are not . . . are not horses," he said. He took his upper lip between his teeth. Looked toward where Parno sat on the rail next to Darlara a few spans away, his feet braced against the narrow bench that ran below it. He was back to noodling on his pipes, pausing with his head at a listening angle, and noodling some more.

Dhulyn glanced back at Captain Mal, took up her wrist knife once more. "They are a flock, you herd them across the sea, they let you ride them. In what way are they not horses?" *And not individuals?*

Malfin pressed his lips into a thin line. Dhulyn waited, bent over her polishing. Either he would tell her, or he would not.

"They're a Pod," he said finally, shrugging. "Might's well say they herd us, as the other way 'round." He fixed his eyes on her face, looking for Sun and Moon only knew what reaction. Dhulyn kept her expression neutral.

"Have their migration routes," he said. "And we follow them."

"That's how you don't get lost crossing the Long Ocean," Dhulyn said, glad as always to add to her store of knowledge. "But you have sails, a rudder. You do navigate on your own."

"It can happen we get separated, and there're harbors where the Crayx can't go. There isn't always one small enough to be comfortable in the Midland Sea, for example."

"And you must sail to find them again."

"Well, yes, though they also find us."

"They see so well? Or can they track you through the water?" Dhulyn held up her hand. "Wait. They sense you. Your sister told me. Do you speak to them?"

"You believe such things are possible?" Malfin's expression was one of skepticism lightly covered with wariness.

"Do you know the Cloud People of the Antedichas Mountains?"

"Seen a few."

"Have you seen a Racha Cloud? Face tattooed with feathers." She tapped the left side of her face to show him where. "Large bird of prey on one shoulder, or flying above them?" Captain Mal nodded. "They are bonded, the Racha and the Cloud. They hear each other's thoughts, feel each other's sensations. The Cloud becomes part bird, and the Racha part human." The skepticism slowly faded from Mal's face, but the wariness had not completely disappeared.

"So," she said. "Are you all bonded, or is it only those of you who wear the scaled vests?"

The captain looked down at himself. "All of us, some more, others less. According to their potential. Those of us who wear the scales have a personal bond to the Pod, won't exchange. The scales, the skins are shed as the Crayx grows older, and larger."

"But how then . . . ?" She indicated Parno with a tilt of her head.

"Because of the music."

Dhulyn followed his glance to Parno. The Crayx were still surfacing and making sounds of their own, sounds her Partner was trying to match with his drones.

"Heard the music and knew, but wanted to be sure."

"Of course." Bumping into the ship—though granted, no one else on board seemed to be worried about that—dumping Parno into the water.

Malfin mistook the nature of her silence. "Nothing to worry you. Even if hadn't confirmed his Pod sense by touching him, could see *and* smell him. *He* wouldn't have been lost."

Dhulyn smiled, consciously stopping short of letting her lips curl back in a snarl. Even if he had a way to know of her private worry, she reminded herself, this was not a completely human person. The Crayx were citizens of a country no one else belonged to, and through their connection, the Nomads would see the world at least partly through the eyes of the Crayx, with whom they had at least as much in common as they had with any human being. Nothing they said or did—or believed—could be taken for granted.

No wonder they had trouble understanding, let alone being understood by, the landlocked Mortaxa. These negotiations would have been very interesting. Very interesting indeed. If only—She stopped that thought. No point in going down that path again.

Dhulyn put down the wrist knife. One of Parno's throwing rings had found its way into her pack and she picked it up, with a frown for the dull spot along one edge. She folded the oily cloth to expose a cleaner patch and glanced at the captain. "Now, what is it *you* want to ask *me?*" she said, smiling again at his startled look.

Malfin cleared his throat, looked toward Parno again, and back at her. "My sister has a mind to bed your man," he said finally. "If you've no objection." His tone ventured on the defiant.

Dhulyn thought she could understand that. Captain Malfin couldn't be sure just how far she accepted what he'd told her—or how far her acceptance of the outsider extended. Dhulyn had no intention of letting him know just how familiar she was with his fears. He knew nothing of what he'd call landsters' attitudes toward each other. He'd have no way of knowing how people looked sideways at her—not because she was a Mercenary Brother, but because her coloring marked her clearly as an Outlander. To say nothing of her other Mark, which couldn't be seen.

On the land, for the most part, the Marked were respected, trusted, relied upon. But there were many people who would nevertheless hesitate to welcome one into the family.

"My objections seem an odd thing for you to be worrying about," was what she said. "Considering how and why we find ourselves on your ship." He found some reassurance in *her* tone, evidently, for the tight muscles around his lips relaxed. "Why is it *you* ask me? Why not your sister?"

"To show the family agrees with her breeding plan, so *I* speak both as brother-and-twin, and as co-captain of the *Wavetreader.*"

"Breeding?" Dhulyn was careful to keep her tone light, interested curiosity only, but she had to loosen her grip on the throwing ring before she cut herself.

"Have to be careful about breeding," Malfin said. "Even exchange between Pods doesn't mix the blood as much as we'd like. When find a landster with Pod sense, it's a good way to add a new bloodline."

"And if a child doesn't have 'Pod sense'?"

Malfin looked at her as though measuring something. "Have havens," he said finally. "Ashore. Different places. Where those children can be safe. Still our kin, Pod sense or no."

Light dawned as Dhulyn realized what Malfin meant. "Landed kin. Where your ships are built, and where you can make repairs that can't be done at sea."

"They are secret, the havens."

Dhulyn smiled. "I will tell no one except Parno Lionsmane."

"Have called yourselves Partners, you and the Lionsmane. Does that mean Darlara is out of luck, or that *you* would claim the child, if there is one?"

" 'Partners are a sword with two edges.' " The words from the Common Rule came easily to her lips, but she knew they wouldn't satisfy the captain. How to explain it? Even Mercenary Brothers who weren't Partnered found it hard to understand. She snorted. Then again, it couldn't be harder to explain than the Crayx.

"We are life Partners, but we're not wed, or mated, or whatever you call that relationship here on the Long Ocean. It means . . . we live and fight together. We would always go into battle on the same side." She paused groping after the words. "There is a ceremony. Afterward . . . when we are in the same room, or near one another, we know it; our hearts may even beat in the same rhythm." She looked away from the captain's eyes. "Every Mercenary hopes to die in battle, on our feet, sword in hand. The best we hope for is to die at the hand of one of our own Brothers who fights for the other side. But Partners will never die at each other's hands." *Not by my hand,* she thought. *Not by my hand.* "It's something like being a twin. Impossible to explain to someone who isn't one, and no need to explain to someone who is."

"Twins don't bed with each other." It was half a question.

Dhulyn smiled and gave him half an answer. "I only said it was something like."

"I would rather give *you* a child." Parno Lionsmane had never said these words aloud, but he got the reaction he expected from his Partner.

Dhulyn smiled the smile she saved only for him and shook her head. "We've been Partnered, what, seven years? If you were likely to give me a child," she pointed out, "it would have happened already."

"You've never Seen anything?" He'd never wanted to ask, but now that they were talking about it, he had to press his advantage. He might not ever have another such excuse. She *had* been behaving oddly the last few days, but he'd put it down to nostalgia, being at sea reminding her of the childhood she'd had on the *Black Traveler* once Dorian the Schooler had rescued her from the slavers.

"Once I thought so. I Saw myself laying out a game of Tailors with a young redheaded girl. Not so dark as I, but not so golden as you."

"And you thought . . ."

"And I thought. But it turned out to be the young woman who is now Queen of Tegrian."

Parno laughed out loud. "You're right. She could have been ours, if we went by coloring alone." He frowned. "I've never fathered a child, that I know of."

"Well, I'm sure I would have noticed if I had ever quickened." She have him such a look of wide-eyed innocence that Parno cuffed her shoulder.

"How is it you think that it never happened?"

"I was given enough potions and drugs in the years between the breaking of the Tribes and the time Dorian rescued me. I always assumed that had something to do with it."

"Shall we ask a Healer, the next time we run across one?" This time Parno thought he might have gone too far. There again was that white stiffness in Dhulyn's face that he'd seen in the hold of the *Catseye*, when they had first met the Nomads. Her eyes narrowed, and she seemed to be looking within.

"We'll still look for a Seer to train you," he assured her, more to break the silence than for any other reason. "That's still our first goal. I'm just saying, if we should happen to meet with a Healer, that's all."

"Yes," she said. Then she cleared her throat and said it again, more naturally this time. "Yes, why not? The next time we run across a Healer, we'll see what can be done."

"After all, you still have your woman's time, that must mean something."

She nodded. "But being that you cannot give me a child," she said. "What are your thoughts about giving Darlara one?"

"I have no objection, in principle." Parno cleared his own throat, half-surprised to find that he did not. "Even if you and I have a child together," he pointed out, "we wouldn't raise it ourselves."

Again, Dhulyn nodded. Most Mercenaries took steps *not* to produce children. Still, the Common Rule gave guidance even for things that rarely happened. Mercenaries who had children with other Mercenaries, not always Partners, never raised the children themselves. There was always one Schooler—at the present time it was Nerysa Warhammer, Parno's own Schooler—who kept a nursery for such children, and sometimes ordinary families were found. The life of a Mercenary Brother did not allow for the rearing of children. Tough and skilled as they were, few Mercenaries lived long enough to be certain of bringing up a child. The time was sure to come when, as Dhulyn always said, the arrow would have your name on it.

"Almost a month to cross the Long Ocean," he said.

"Usually time enough, if a man and a woman are determined."

"My soul—" Parno broke off, then reconsidered. There was one way to check, and Dhulyn would have thought of it long before he did. Her woman's time had passed, but only *just*. Her Sight would be at its clearest. "Would you See for me? Would you use the tiles?"

Parno watched her face closely, nodding to himself when the usual reluctance, the flaring of the nostrils and the twist of the lips that always followed this suggestion didn't come. She still wasn't ready to tell him why she was looking secretly at the tiles. *Goes on much longer, I'll have to ask*, he thought.

Dhulyn pushed herself upright and rounded the table, laying her hand on Parno's shoulder as she passed him. Her small pack was on the lower bunk where she'd pushed it after stowing away the weapons she had cleaned. The ancient, silk-lined olive wood box that held her personal set of vera tiles was in a pocket she'd made along one side. She rounded the table again and sat down opposite Parno, setting the box on the table between them. She searched through the tiles until she'd found Parno's own tile, the Mercenary of Spears, and gave it to him.

"Close your hand around it," she said. "Think of the question you'd like answered."

"How does that help?" he asked. "I don't bear a Mark."

"It does no harm," she said, as she sorted out the Marked tiles, the ones that did not form a part of the ordinary gambler's vera set. The straight line, representing the Finder; the Healer's rectangle, the Seer's circle with a dot in the center, the Mender's triangle, long and narrow like an Imrioni spearhead. The only unique tile, the Lens, was in its own tiny silk bag, drawstrings made from thin braids of Dhulyn's own hair. She set aside one each of the Marked tiles, then made sure all the other sets, the coins, cups, swords, and spears, along with the remaining Marks, were facedown. Placing her hands palms down on the tiles she shuffled them, all the time concentrating on Parno's question.

DHULYN IS STANDING ON THE UPPER AFT DECK, IN FRONT OF THE WHEEL. THERE IS VERY LITTLE WIND, AND IT SEEMS AS THOUGH THE SHIP DOES NOT MOVE. BUT THE CURRENT CARRIES IT, AS IT CARRIES THE CRAYX. A MOVEMENT, AND A TAIL LIFTS LAZILY OUT OF THE WATER, ONE FLUKE OF WHICH IS HOOKED THROUGH THE CHILD'S HARNESS. IN A MOMENT, DHULYN IS CLOSER TO THE RAIL, AND SHE SEES, BELOW THE CHILD, BELOW THE CRAYX, DEEPER THAN SHE SHOULD BE ABLE TO SEE WERE SHE NOT SEEING, SCHOOLS OF FISH, PLANTS FLOATING JUST AT THE EDGE OF WHERE THE LIGHT PENETRATES THE WATER. COMPARED TO THESE OBJECTS, THE SHIP MOVES SWIFTLY, INDEED.

THE CRAYX'S TAIL LIFTS THE CHILD HIGHER, OVER THE RAIL OF THE MAIN DECK, AND DEPOSITS HER, LAUGHING, ON HER STUBBY LEGS. THE CHILD CANNOT MAINTAIN HER BALANCE, AND LANDS WITH A THUD ON HER BACKSIDE. SHE DOES NOT CRY, HOWEVER, BUT TURNS OVER ON HER KNEES AND PREPARES TO STAND UP AGAIN. HER HAIR, STILL SHORT, IS THICK, COARSE, AND A DARK GOLDEN BROWN. HER EYES, WHEN SHE TURNS TO SMILE AT DARLARA WHERE SHE STANDS BY THE RAIL, ARE A WARM AMBER.

DHULYN NODS. SO. DARLARA LIVES, AND THERE WILL BE A CHILD . . .

TWO WOMEN STAND IN A CIRCLE WITH A SHORTER, OLDER MAN. THEY ARE ALL THREE DARK-HAIRED, THOUGH THE MAN'S HAIR IS THINNING, AND ONE WOMAN HAS A PRONOUNCED WIDOW'S PEAK. THEY HOLD HANDS, AND ARE CHANTING, OR SINGING, THOUGH DHULYN CANNOT HEAR THEIR VOICES. THE MAN LIFTS HIS HANDS FREE, AND DHULYN SEES THAT HE HAS SIX FINGERS ON HIS LEFT HAND . . .

THE SLIM WOMAN AGAIN, HER DELICATE CHEEKBONES MORE HARSHLY REVEALED NOW, HER SHORT CAP OF CRISP, SANDY HAIR GRAYING. SHE PEERS INTO THE EYEPIECE OF A LONG CYLINDER ALMOST AS THICK AROUND AS THE WOMAN HERSELF IS. DHULYN CANNOT SEE THE END OF THE CYLINDER; IT PASSES THROUGH THE ROUNDED CEILING OF THE ROOM THE WOMAN STANDS IN. NEXT TO HER IS A TABLE, COVERED WITH CHARTS, AN UNROLLED PARCHMENT HELD OPEN WITH A MUG OF SOME DARK LIQUID AND A PAIR OF CARTOGRAPHER'S COMPASSES. THE WOMAN MAKES AN IMPATIENT SOUND, TURNS TO THE TABLE,

SHUFFLES THE PAPERS AROUND WITH HER LONG FINGERS UNTIL SHE FINDS A SCRAP THAT HAS NO WRITING ON IT, AND MAKES A NOTE BEFORE TURNING BACK TO THE EYEPIECE. . . .

No MORE, DHULYN THINKS, NO MORE. BUT THE VISIONS CONTINUE.

THE FLOOR TILTS AND BECOMES THE DECK OF A SHIP. A STORM RAGES— NO!

"You're green as a grass snake, are you going to be sick?"

"Idiot! Out of the way!"

Five

"**B**UT CAN HEAR YOU *better* when you play."

Parno Lionsmane let the chanter of his pipes fall from his lips. "Which is a fine thing for them, but is doing nothing for me."

"Your mind relaxes with the music," Darlara said.

Parno rubbed the back of his neck with the hand not holding his pipes. He had an idea. "Tell them to be ready."

He set his pipes on the deck in front of him and shut his eyes, taking three deep breaths and letting them out slowly. He let his eyes fall open and fixed them on his chanter, the third sound hole down. Another three breaths. Nothing but the sound hole. A hole was nothing. Absence. No sound and no hole.

Suddenly his throat closed and his stomach dropped as a wave of fear washed over him, pimpling his skin and setting his heart hammering. He blinked, blew out his breath sharply, and looked up. The fear subsided, but his heart still hammered.

"There. Felt that."

"Anything wrong with making me feel happy?" Parno could hear the annoyance in his voice.

"Fear's the easiest to be sure of. Happy feels different for everyone."

Parno nodded. That was undoubtedly true. He leaned over to pick up his pipes, and when he glanced up, Darlara was smiling at him.

"Wouldn't have known you were afraid, if I hadn't known what was coming."

Parno stood up. "I've been afraid before," he said. "I know fear won't hurt me."

Darlara's smile changed, and he found himself smiling back.

Parno was easing the door of the cabin shut, but at a sound from behind him, he relaxed, letting the concentration of the Hunter's *Shora* dissipate. Not even he could walk into Dhulyn's room without awakening her.

"Out of curiosity," she asked, her rough silk voice coming from the dark shadow that was the lower bunk. "Where is Captain Malfin sleeping?"

"When Malfin's on watch, Darlara isn't." Parno sat down on the end of the bench nearest him, the air bag of his pipes letting out a bleat as it pushed against the table's edge.

"I heard you in the night, playing to the Crayx."

There was light enough coming through the shutters that he knew she could see him nodding. "They can hear me, that's certain. And when they answer, I can—almost—hear them. Darlara says that if I stayed here, the Pod sense would awaken fully, eventually."

"And what did you say?"

"I told her that for Mercenaries there is no 'eventually.' "

Dhulyn rolled to sit upright, swinging her legs free of her blankets. "There's that." She pulled up one leg, resting the heel of her foot on the hard wooden edge of the bunk and wrapping her arms around her knee.

Parno considered telling her about the fear, then decided against it. She would find a way to laugh at him about it. "They don't speak, exactly, but I do get glimpses," he told her instead. "They see the world differently."

"Parno, my heart, they live underwater."

Dhulyn got to her feet, pulled her sleep tunic off over her head and reached for her linen trousers and multicolored vest, lying over the bench where she had left them.

He waved her observation away. "But think about what that means. Even in the smallest things." He frowned, searching for an example. "For us, 'down' is only a direction to fall—however carefully we might control the falling. For the Crayx, 'down' is another right, or left, north, or south." He shook his head. "I'm not explaining it well, but better, I think, than it was explained to me."

"It's hard to explain what you take for granted as normal." Dhulyn frowned, reaching around to her left to tie her first sword sash. "Do the Nomads share their thoughts with the Crayx?"

"Just like Racha birds and their Clouds, yes. But there's more. All adult Nomads can see through the Crayx's eyes, and the Crayx through theirs. With the Racha, only the bonded Cloud can hear the bird's thoughts. But while you are with a Crayx, if it shares the thoughts of another, you can share them, too."

"And they share your thoughts?"

"Apparently. Think of it, my soul. To be able to hear another's thoughts, even indirectly, to be able to converse, mind to mind."

"I already know far more than I need to about what *you* think."

Parno laughed and caught the biscuit she threw at him. *All the same,* he thought, *I'd give my best sword to know what* you're *thinking, right now.*

"You'd be able to do this, then, eventually?" Her brows drew together.

"Ah well, I'll learn what I can now, and hope for more on the trip back. These Crayx have other tasks besides teaching me."

There. There it was again. That change in her face, subtler this time, but unmistakable. Ice-gray eyes suddenly dark as she paled, the blood shifting away under her skin. Just now, while they were talking, what he was beginning to think of as the "old" Dhulyn had resurfaced. Animated, curious, already thinking of how to apply this new knowledge of the Crayx to what she knew of the world, of the *Shora*, of the Brotherhood. But now that guarded, shuttered look had returned, her face a mask, with something hidden underneath.

Surely she couldn't believe that he would follow the Crayx, Pod sense or no? Parno pressed his lips together, finding himself annoyed. How many times did he have to prove to her that he was as much a Mercenary Brother as she was? That he wasn't going anywhere, and never would?

A good thing we're Partnered, he thought, half angry, half amused. If any other woman annoyed him this much, he'd have to kill her.

"Come, you know you'll tell me eventually," he finally said. "Whatever the problem is that's worrying you, you can't keep it to yourself forever."

A flash of consternation passed over Dhulyn's face, flecked through with surprise, and then his Partner smiled. "Did you not just tell me that for Mercenaries, there is no 'eventually'?" Almost, *almost* that was her normal tone, her normal expression.

"Not good enough. What stops you—we've changed direction," he said, coming to his feet. Mercenary Brothers could not afford to become disoriented in the heat of battle, and their sense of direction was strong and well trained. They had been traveling more or less northeast, or northeast by east with the wind steady behind them since leaving the Letanian Peninsula and the Herculat Straits—the eastern-most point of the continent that was Boravia—more than half a moon before. Now they were heading almost directly north.

Dhulyn was already at the door to the cabin and Parno followed her out to the main deck where they found the crew assembling in the large open space between the afterdeck and the central cabins. Both captains were standing on the afterdeck, clearly preparing to address the crew.

By now Dhulyn Wolfshead had become accustomed to the way the Nomads reacted to Parno. The nods and small salutes—some, she saw, even touched their fingertips to their foreheads in the Mercenary man-ner. But what made her well-Schooled instincts uneasy was the number of people, of both sexes, who touched Parno as he passed them by.

Luckily, they didn't also touch *her*, or she would have had to do some-thing about it. Dhulyn had quickly realized that, due to their shared Pod sense, the Nomads accepted and included Parno in a way that did not include and accept her. She was used to being excluded—even if she hadn't been a Mercenary Brother, her coloring and height marked her clearly for an Outlander. Even Darlara's increasing air of posses-sion hadn't bothered her—she was used to women who were bedding Parno looking on him as their own. What could be more natural for the period of time the passion lasted? But this was something different. The more Parno was accepted, the more she was excluded. And not just by Darlara.

Something told Dhulyn that it was entirely due to this connection the Nomads had with Parno that space was cleared for them until they reached the front of the group, looking up to where Malfin and Darlara stood together on the aft deck. A light mist was falling, and many of the crew came pulling on rain gear, mostly short capes made from the supple discarded skins of young Crayx. But rainy and cold as it was, all of the crew were present, including children, who stood quietly with their teachers.

Now that she knew what to look for, Dhulyn could see the tell-tale differences in the movements and carriage of some in the crowd that showed there was already some kind of communication going on. Those on watch, for example, were clearly not being relieved, nor were they trying to move closer.

Perhaps it was this feeling of being left out that led Dhulyn, once they were near the front of the group, to touch her forehead to Ana-Paula, who stood to one side of the captains, her hand resting lightly on the big wheel. When not on watch, the chief pilot had revealed that she shared Dhulyn's interest in the games of chance that could be played with vera tiles.

"Speak aloud," Darlara said. "For Mercenaries, and for children."

Dhulyn smiled. This would be the first time she'd been put into the same category as children.

"Helm," Malfin called. "Give us the heading."

"New heading," Ana-Paula said. "North by northwest."

Any ordinary person, perhaps even the crew themselves, would have been ready to wager that no one reacted to the chief pilot's statement. But any Mercenary Brother would have sensed the sudden shifting of mood as dozens of pairs of lungs breathed in, feet were shuffled, throats cleared, and eyes flashed to meet each other.

"North by northwest, it is," Darlara said.

Now there were actual murmurs among the children.

"Most of you will have learned by now that there is another Pod to the north of us, but may not know that is *Skydancer* Pod."

Now the murmurs gained in substance, and even adult voices were raised in tones of excitement as crew members spoke to one another. Dhulyn caught Parno's eye. Casually, very slowly, they moved so as to stand almost back to back.

"Heard right," Darlara said, as if she were answering some remark spoken aloud. "Been seven years since we were in the same current with any of the Dancer Pods, and we'll lose less than a day by turning to share current with them now."

"Any who think our mission can't wait less than a day, speak now, you'll be heard." Malfin looked from side to side and up into the rigging, scanning the crowd for any upheld hand.

"Go ahead, Captains," someone called from the rear. A laugh rippled through the crowd.

"Mikel can't wait," someone else called out. The laughter broke out in earnest.

"Any unmarrieds from the stern watch can exchange," Darlara said, smiling. "And some from the bow watch. You know who you are. As many as three of each gender may go if there are Skydancers willing. Tell me or Malfin before the evening watch begins."

"When will we sight the *Skydancer*?" It was the teacher, Josel, who asked.

"Should see her at dawn."

The assembly broke up, some heading almost immediately belowdecks or into the upper cabins out of the cold and mist, others gathering in twos and threes to discuss the news privately.

One young man remained leaning against the starboard rail, apparently not as interested as the others. Dhulyn recognized the young man Conford, who had been tricked into challenging Parno that first morning.

"Do you disagree with the delay?" she said. "Or are you thinking of making a change?"

"That won't be me," he said, lifting his chin to point out several unmarried crew members who were putting their heads together over by the port rail. "Came only five months ago, myself. Won't exchange again. At least . . . not without leaving children." He looked back at her and Dhulyn sensed there was more to his tale than what he was telling her. "Not everyone can, or will go."

"The captains—"

"Can't," Conford said. "Nor any other who've children too young. Or who might have a relative less than two generations distant with the other Pod. The Crayx keep track, how close the bloodlines." He looked away, and then back at her from under his long, black lashes. "Captain Darlara's hoping to start a whole new line with a Mercenary babe from your Partner."

"We wish her luck," Dhulyn said.

"And you, Dhulyn Wolfshead? Like to start a line of your own?"

"I've no Pod sense," Dhulyn reminded him.

Conford's face stiffened. "Had forgotten. Meant no offense, Mercenary."

"And none taken."

"We didn't see a sign of the southerners that day," Xerwin said, pulling his travel-stained tunic over his head. His friend Naxot was unusually quiet, but it gave Xerwin a chance to practice what he would say in his report to his father the Tarxin. His officers had been left behind with the Battle Wings, manning the forts on the southeastern frontier—not that they'd contradict him, but not putting his men into embarrassing situations was what made Xerwin such a popular commander. "But the *game*, Naxot. Fattest deer I've ever seen. You should come next time, I tell you—"

"Do you think your father would be very angry if I petition to withdraw from my betrothal to your sister?"

Xerwin stiffened, turning to look at Naxot carefully for the first time since he'd arrived in his rooms. The man's face was drawn, and the worry line between his eyebrows was new. *Thank the Caids he's not looking at me*, Xerwin thought. His face was his weak spot, he knew; he still had trouble controlling his expression quickly. Nothing on Naxot's face gave him any clues, so Xerwin decided to treat his friend's words lightly.

"It won't be that much longer," he said. "Surely you can find some court woman willing to amuse you, if that's the problem?" Xerwin deliberately chose the one possibility guaranteed to make his friend blush. Naxot's family were devoted followers of the Slain God, and notoriously orthodox in their social behavior, expecting even their sons to wait for marriage. Not for Naxot the casual encounters which made Xerwin's life more tolerable. Of course, this orthodoxy made Naxot's Noble House excellent allies—the very reason Xerwin had suggested the betrothal in the first place.

But this time the little half-smile of embarrassment that usually followed any teasing along the sexual line failed to form on Naxot's face. This was serious, then.

"My father the Tarxin would be very angry," Xerwin said, judging that bluntness was called for. "Such a request would do more than damage the alliance between our families, it would be an insult he could not overlook. I would not advise your father to approach mine on this subject."

Naxot set aside the breastplate he'd been toying with, staring down at the smoothly tiled white-and-black floor between his feet. "That's why I was hoping you might speak for me."

Xerwin felt his face stiffen into what he thought of as his court mask. "I? I might speak? You wish to break off a betrothal which was made at my suggestion, and you think *I* might speak for you?" Xerwin took a deep breath. It would break Xendra's heart if he let this happen, but at the same time he had to wonder what could make Naxot back away from an alliance equally advantageous to his own family.

"When I proposed this match a year ago, you seemed pleased enough," Xerwin said, aware that a hint of steel sounded in his voice. "Come, Naxot, what's changed you?"

"I haven't changed," Naxot said finally, straightening his shoulders in a way that reminded Xerwin of one of his junior officers bringing him a bad report. "But Tara Xendra has."

Xerwin's hands balled into fists. He could see Naxot's nose smashed and bleeding on the carefully fitted tiles. The pattern began to make his eyes swim. He took a calming breath, keeping his face turned away until he had himself under control. Even if he didn't take his sister's feelings into account, he could not afford to lose the favor of such a powerful family. True, Xendra had been ill, very ill after her accident. For the longest time they feared—but the worst had not happened, thanks to the Healer and the other Marked from the Sanctuary. Xendra was still not quite herself, that was true. But to suggest that there was anything out of the ordinary . . . Xerwin turned back to his friend.

"Xendra's fine," he said. He picked up a bathing robe and pulled it on. "I haven't had a chance to visit her yet, but my advisers tell me her health has continued to improve during my absence on the frontier."

But Naxot lowered his eyes. Just like that junior officer.

Xerwin's advisors had also told him the rumors.

"My sister is not Marked." Xerwin frowned, finding his sword inexplicably in his hand. He put it down, slowly. "You know as well as I that the Sanctuary has examined Xendra and declared she has no Mark. Do you suggest that my sister, daughter of Xalbalil Tarxin, the Light of the Sun, is in some way unworthy of you?"

"I would not care if she were Marked," Naxot said, so simply that Xerwin believed him. "She would still be your sister. But," he shook his head. "It is I who have become unworthy of the Tara Xendra. She is too far above me now."

Xerwin blinked at Naxot's unexpected words. "She has the same rank she's always had." A Tara could not inherit the Tarxinate, but it was not unheard of that the husband of a Tara should become Tarxin himself.

Naxot leaned toward him, eyebrows drawn down. "There may be things even your advisers were not prepared to tell you. The Tarxin, Light of the Sun, has been to see your sister many times in your absence. Each time he comes from her with some new wonder." Naxot's voice dropped to a whisper. "She has explained the magic of the lodestone, and has caused rain to fall."

Xerwin sat down heavily on the bench behind him. What was Naxot saying?

"We are living in the age of miracles." Naxot's voice was thick with awe. "First, Paledyn are reported in the lands across the Long Ocean, and now, Mages arise in our midst. The days of the Caids return."

Xerwin blinked. Naxot's orthodoxy wasn't lip service, he realized. Wasn't—like the Tarxin's—a political expediency.

"It is clear Tara Xendra has an Art," Naxot continued. "The Scholars of my House say that the Witches are Holy Women. Brides of the Slain God. They do not marry, but . . . *bless* only those whom they choose." Naxot blushed deeply. "I cannot . . ." Naxot's voice cracked, and he lowered his eyes. "Such things—I cannot presume."

Xerwin felt the hairs on his arms rise. *Holy Woman.* It couldn't be. Little Xendra? *His* Xendra, who only a few short months ago was begging him to teach her to play *peldar*?

This time it was Xerwin who looked away, as the implication of his friend's words sank in. *Really* sank in. Holy Woman. Storm Witch. This is what had been happening in his absence, and not a word from his so-called advisers, nor from his father, the wily old jackal.

Xerwin licked his lips, drew in a deep breath through his nose, and straightened his shoulders. Naxot was right. The betrothal should be set aside, no doubt. And Xerwin should talk to his sister.

Six

WHEN THE KNOCK CAME, Carcali raised her head with a
jerk. The room spun for a moment before settling down
again. She gripped the edge of the table, blinking and shaking her head. This wasn't her room. Where was her desk? Why didn't
her feet touch the floor? The knock sounded again, and it all came
flooding back. Her room was gone, her whole world—she swallowed
and pushed that thought away.

"Come," she said, and shivered at the sound of the light voice that
piped from her lips. She could get the commanding tone right, but
would she ever become accustomed to the voice?

She rubbed at her still unfamiliar face, looking up as the door swung
open to reveal her senior lady page. The woman had likely functioned
as nurse or governess, but in the months since Carcali had awakened in
this body, Kendraxa had acted less and less like a nurse.

"Have the maps come?" Carcali asked. She picked up the quill pen
that had fallen to one side, resting it against a smoothed chunk of marble where it would not drip on anything important. She was only now
coming to terms with the tools and equipment they used here, and
much valuable time had been wasted before she'd learned about the
Scholars, and then still more convincing those around her that she was
serious about an inquiry to them. It had finally taken an order from the
Tarxin himself for her requests to be acted on.

"Well now, no, my dear. I mean Tara Xendra." Kendraxa fiddled
with the loose ends of her headdress. "The copies are being made, but
it can't be done quickly."

Carcali shut her eyes. She'd forgotten the forsaken things had to be copied by hand. *That* Art had been lost along with the rest of the civilization she'd destroyed. Her nails bit into her palms as her hands formed fists. She *wasn't* going to think about that.

"The Tarxin is waiting for the results of my work," she said.

"The Scholars have their work as well, Tara. Your father the Tarxin, Light of the Sun, understands this."

Carcali wrinkled her nose, unconvinced. The Tarxin hadn't struck her as the kind of man who liked excuses.

"Why *are* you here, then?"

Kendraxa blinked, her eyebrows slightly raised. Carcali bit her lower lip. Again. That was blunter than anyone expected from her, since the Tara she appeared to be was only eleven years old.

"You have visitors," Kendraxa began.

Ice crawled up Carcali's spine. "Not the Healers," she said, skin crawling at the thought of the six-fingered man. "The Tarxin promised . . ." Carcali's voice faded away as her mouth dried up. The Tarxin. The father of the body she was wearing. He'd promised her no more Healers when she told him what she could do. At first, he hadn't believed her, but she'd been able, as frightened as she was, to call clouds to cover the sun. That, and what she'd told him about the lodestone had bought her his promise that the Healers wouldn't make any more attempts to push her out of Xendra's body.

But now, with all this delay—

"Please," she said, trying her hardest to push the fear out of her voice. "Please don't let them in."

"No, my dear, of course not. They can stay outside. It's a petition only, from House Fosola, south of the city. They have had two nights of cold winds, earlier than would be expected at this time of year, and now the winds have died away, they fear a killing frost in the next few days if conditions do not improve." Kendraxa waited and when Carcali didn't reply, she added, "They come with your father's permission."

Carcali's breathing was already returning to normal.

"What do they grow?"

A pause, not very long, perhaps, but long enough that Carcali knew she had done it again. This was something the girl Xendra would have known. She pressed her lips together.

"Peaches, Tara Xendra. Peaches, grapes, and other soft fruit."

"Is it only warmth they need? Not rain?"

"The petition asks for warmth only, Tara Xendra."

"Very well." Carcali was already picturing the crude map of Mortaxa she had in her possession. If she brought the winds up from the west, across the sea, was there enough coastal plain for the moisture to drop before the winds hit the higher ridges? She became aware that Kendraxa was still standing in front of her.

"Was there something else?"

Kendraxa looked at her steadily for a moment, her eyes narrowed, and her mouth in a determined line. Finally, she came closer, clasping her hands together under her bosom. "You *must* rest, my dear. You are looking very thin, and I know you are not eating enough."

Carcali stared, but the older woman did not lower her eyes. Finally, Carcali nodded.

"Once I've dealt with this frost, Kendraxa," she said. "I'll lie down. I promise."

"Shall I close the shutters?"

"I'll take care of it. Thank you, you may go."

The woman smiled stiffly, bowed, and let herself out.

Carcali sat for a few minutes, one hand hovering over the map of Mortaxa before she grabbed the map next to it. She unrolled it carefully, using the weight already on the table to hold it open. She studied it for a few minutes before she nodded. The lands belonging to House Fosola *were* close enough to appear on a map of Ketxan City. That gave her more detail and should make things easier for her.

She rubbed her face, wincing at the feel of unfamiliar cheekbones, unfamiliar lips, skin, hairline. They were asking for just a small fix, a tiny change really, in the big scheme of the climate. But it would be useful, she'd be helping people. And she should be able to do it easily, without full immersion in the weatherspheres. She'd done exactly this kind of thing plenty of times before—even apprentices could do it.

And she *had* to do it, she told herself. Her Art was her way to safety, here in this strange new world.

Carcali began to take slow, deep breaths, feeling the tingle of the Art move through her bones, dance along her muscles until she could feel the hairs lift on her arms. She closed her eyes, let her head fall back, and raised her arms, reaching literally as well as figuratively for the spheres—she brought her arms down abruptly and wrapped them around herself, biting her lip.

It was all right. No problem. She hadn't lost the connection to the body. She just had to be more careful, that was all. She couldn't risk— she *wouldn't* risk.

She refocused her attention on what she was doing.

Spoke the words.

Felt herself lighter, lifting. For a moment, floating, she looked down and saw her body, not her *real* body, but her body now, Xendra's body. *This* was the body she now wore, this dark-haired child, and *this* was the body she was anchored to, and would return to. She forced its imprint on her floating consciousness, solidifying the connection, making sure it wouldn't break.

Delicately, Carcali let herself float, keeping a firm grip on her anchor, on the body. Not the best way to perform the Art, not very accurate, but safer, so much safer, and the only way now that there were no other Weather Artists to help anchor her.

She let her eyes wander, looking for the rich reds and golden oranges that would tell her of warm air. It was farther afield than she would have expected, and full of the gray mist that meant moisture. A great soggy warmth over the sea.

She hesitated, frowning. There were two ships on the surface of the water, the sinuous movements of beasts beneath the surface. She moved closer. These had to be Nomads. No one else had ships. She looked back at the warm mass of air. Without surrendering herself to the weatherspheres, there was no way to be absolutely certain, but she was sure that the ships were far enough away. They'd be safe enough. A little rain, a little wind, nothing they couldn't handle.

Turning, careful of the anchor, like a kite on a breeze, Carcali gathered the chosen currents together, tugging the warmth free of the moisture. Suddenly, she lost control, felt the air mass twisting and spilling away from her. She refocused her attention, and reached for the warmth again, breathing it in, making it more closely a part of herself, building it into a skin around her. Turning, she looked for the place she wished the warmth to be, and found it.

Gently at first, and then with more force, she released what she had gathered, breathing out the warm air, pushing it toward the coastline where western Mortaxa met the Long Ocean, over the islands, across the coastal plain and east to the rolling hills and fruited valleys that needed protection from the frost.

They did not meet the *Skydancer* until after midday. The wind had been freshening and dying away all morning, making the topsails flap and the ropes creak. The sun that had scorched them so badly the day before was hidden behind a sky heavy with haze, making the air, if it were possible, even hotter and the sea a dull gray mass of crumpled pewter. Parno Lionsmane had taken out his pipes, but had set them aside almost at once. Dhulyn had called for a very short *Shora* that daybreak, but they both had very little energy in the breathless heat. They had been sailing northeast, and north again toward the waist of the world.

What wind there was now blew against them, and the *Wavetreader* hove to as soon as the other Pod was sighted. Parno had thought the *Wavetreader* large, but *Skydancer* was half again the smaller ship's size, four-masted, and with at least two more decks. As she bore down on them, Parno glanced around, narrowing his eyes and tightening his grip on the rail when he saw no one, most especially not Dhulyn, seemed at all concerned.

Blooded sailors, he thought. You could never tell whether to be worried or not. It did seem, however, that this was a time of "or not," as it took the other crew only a few moments to spill the winds from their sails and bring the two ships together, riding side by side—though not close enough to board in the manner of pirates. Parno could see the faces of the *Skydancer's* crew clearly, see gold and silver glinting at wrist and throat, almost make out the color of their eyes. They were much the same physical type as the Nomads he already knew, wiry and small, though there seemed to be more variety of skin shading and hair color than on board the *Wavetreader*.

"Can't they get us any closer?" he said to Dhulyn, thinking it must involve some deep seafaring lore he knew nothing of. "At this distance they'll have to put a boat over the side."

"Look down."

Of course. How could he have forgotten. This was more than a meeting between the two crews. Parno scanned the water between the ships and saw Crayx swimming in the open space between the two hulls. Unlike the humans, there was very little variation in color between the two Pods, but somehow Parno knew that he was looking at members of both groups.

#Welcome# #Pleasure#

Parno jerked upright and stepped back from the rail as if avoiding the point of a sword.

"What?" Dhulyn closed her hand around his wrist, her palm cool and dry against his hot skin.

Parno licked his lips. "I heard them just now, they speak to one another."

"And not just to one another, I think." Dhulyn shot a glance over her shoulder.

Parno looked around. The crew of the *Wavetreader* were gathering on deck, crowding the rail and climbing into the rigging the better to see their kin on the other ship.

"No one's saying anything." he said. "No greetings, no questions, nothing."

"The younger children are not here," Dhulyn said.

"Only those over the age of ten were allowed on deck." *And how do I know this?* he thought. There were several of the older youngsters close by them, round-eyed with anticipation. And while a few were waving, and some were wriggling and shoving each other with excitement, none of them were making a sound, neither calling across to the other ship, nor chattering to each other.

Dhulyn was right. It was not just the Crayx speaking to each other. Like a humming in his blood, only just beyond the reach of his own underdeveloped Pod sense, Parno could feel the communication taking place around him.

Movement on the other deck caught his attention as two ruddy-haired men, as alike as matched daggers, bronzed and freckled by the sun, approached the rail of the *Skydancer* just as Darlara and her brother came to the rail not far to Parno's left.

"What do you wager all the ships' captains are twins?" Dhulyn spoke in her nightwatch voice, a thread of sound audible only to him, and then only because they stood close enough to rub shoulders.

"No bet," he answered in the same voice.

Anything louder than the nightwatch whisper might well have been heard, Parno thought, for the ship around them had now fallen eerily silent. Even the children had ceased their fidgeting, and all that could be heard were the sounds of the stays creaking as the wind sang through them, a light slap as small wavelets touched against the hulls.

A sail flapped once and was still. Suddenly the air seemed oppressively hot and damp, and the pressure shifted.

Dhulyn nudged him with her elbow, pointing with her chin. Darlara and Malfin stood each with one hand on the rail, their free hands linked, their eyes open and fixed on the twin captains opposite them. They and all the crew that Parno could see had similar expressions. Not, he was glad to note, the empty-eyed look he'd seen once or twice before when people shared their mental spaces with other creatures, but more like the look of thoughtful concentration that he had seen on the faces of people using their Mark to Find or Mend.

Now and again an emotion flickered across someone's expression, shown by a frown here, a lifted eyebrow there. As the communication continued, there were fewer and fewer smiles.

#Impatience# #Annoyance# #AngerFear#

Parno didn't flinch this time, though he felt himself frown in response to the momentarily glimpsed emotions.

"They communicate simultaneously, all of them at once," Dhulyn said, this time in a more normal voice, as if she felt the same need that he did to disturb the silence.

"It's certainly faster," he replied, hoping that he'd kept the longing and eagerness out of his voice.

She nodded, showing him the ghost of her smile. "Do you think there's time for us to—no, here they come."

It was most obvious in the children. Everyone around them relaxed, and took deep breaths, though they hadn't been noticeably tense. Some of the crew shrugged, and resumed whatever tasks the sighting of the *Skydancer* had interrupted, those on watch back to their posts, parents and minders hurrying to rejoin the younger children. There were looks exchanged, some frightened, some still frowning, a few speculative.

Parno waited, and when Darlara turned from the rail, she looked, as he'd expected, to him. She smiled, but with a small twist to her mouth, as if her news were mixed.

"No exchange?" he asked her, guessing what the main concern would be.

"Oh, no. That'll go as planned."

"And what won't?" Dhulyn said.

Darlara smoothed stray hairs back from her face and sighed. "*Skydancers* say the Mortaxa build their ship still, don't wait for us as agreed."

"And there have been waterspouts in the spawning grounds," Malfin added.

"Though no deaths, thank the Caids, since it's the wrong time of year." Dar gave Parno a sidelong look.

"Maybe warning us, showing us what they *could* do," Malfin said.

"Waterspouts?" Parno wasn't sure he'd heard the word before.

"Great swirling columns of water that rise up out of the ocean and then disappear again."

Parno turned to Dhulyn, watched her gray eyes go ice-cold as comprehension dawned. "Tornadoes," she said, her voice hard. "At sea, the waters would rise," she added. Her normally pale skin had whitened even further, and Parno wondered if she were actually about to faint.

"*Skydancers* say the time to negotiate has passed," Malfin said. He turned to put the sudden wind at his back. If possible, the air seemed even hotter than before.

"Cursed Mortaxa never meant to negotiate in the first place," Darlara said. "Sent us on an errand to keep us quiet and out of the way."

"Maybe so." Malfin shrugged. "But this needs more thought. We've the Paledyn now, after all. Surely the Mortaxa'll have to meet with us."

"Why? Heard what the *Skydancers* said. Cursed Mortaxa don't care what happens to any of us."

But Dhulyn had drawn a little apart, no longer listening. "You don't need us," she said, her rough silk voice gone hollow. "We don't have to be here." She had that stone look again. She looked at Parno. "They didn't need us."

"What of it? It's a bother, no doubt, but we have to be somewhere, what difference where?" Was she still worrying about that hearing back in Lesonika? Or, he wondered as another idea took form, was she now worried about the consequences of his Pod sense?

"You don't understand." She took him by the upper arms as if she were about to shake him. "We didn't have to be here. We didn't have to come!"

It took Parno a second to realize the Dhulyn was shouting, the noise of the wind had risen so high.

Then another voice was shouting, and everyone was looking up to Devin in the Racha's nest, and looking to the east in response to his signal.

There, on the horizon, a narrow band of white sky showed under the blackening cloud that stretched above it, hard-edged as a sword blade. Across that narrow band of whiteness, a thin black thread seemed to join the cloud to the sea.

A bell began to ring on deck, loud enough even to be heard over the noise of the wind.

"Get below." Dhulyn didn't wait for Parno to obey her, she took him by the arm and shoved him toward the nearest open hatch. She didn't want him in the cabin; even that was too close to the rail for comfort. If there remained any way to avoid what she'd Seen coming, this would be her only chance.

"I can help."

"You know nothing about sailing and less about storms at sea." Her skin dimpled at the sudden drop in temperature as the air pressure plummeted.

"The Crayx can help me."

"Gone," Darlara was shouting into the terrible noise. "Can't risk staying here. Even if the spout doesn't get them, they could be smashed against the ships."

Just what Darlara had told her on that first day. The Crayx couldn't help them in a bad storm.

The main and top foresails were being hoisted, despite the force of the wind that threatened to split them, in an attempt to use that very wind to separate the two ships as quickly as possible.

"No exchange after all," Dhulyn said, though no one heard her.

The thread of dark color between the roof of cloud and the sea was thicker now. The waterspout was changing its shape with every moment, like a tremendous snake joining sky and sea. It began to widen at the top where it met the cloud, and spread out at the bottom like the base of a candlestick.

Now the same crew who had hoisted the foresails were reefing them—not tidily as they had always done before, but simply dumping them to the deck and shoving them out of the way. The ship had turned, and they would run with the sea.

Dhulyn's ears popped with the change of air pressure and suddenly she could hear the waterspout itself, a wild, shrill, rustling noise sweeping toward them, the gray waves white with foam under the twirling, swaying, monstrous pillar that came nearer and nearer, dancing across the troubled water.

Out of the corner of her eye Dhulyn saw someone miss a toehold in the rigging and go overboard—between water and wind she could not see who it was. Parno had moved over to the hatch, but was only helping to fasten it down.

A deafening CRACK to starboard, as two of the *Skydancer* masts broke off short, one after another. Almost in the same moment the waterspout was upon her, seeming at once to suck her up into itself as pieces fell.

As the *Wavetreader* was flung up on her beam ends, Dhulyn fell sideways, grabbing as if by instinct at the rope that caught her across the face. She wrapped her arm around it, and, turning her face into the wind, looked for another place to anchor herself—or for someone else to grab on to.

"Parno!" He could not possibly hear her, but he was looking her way, grinning like a madman. *My soul*, she mouthed.

He began to make his way up the slanting deck toward her, half walking, half climbing. Dhulyn braced her feet, and stretched out her arm until her shoulder cracked, as he reached for her hand. He turned his foot on what looked like someone's arm sticking out from under a fold of sail, and was sliding away from her as the wave hit and swept him overboard.

Dhulyn was screaming as she unwrapped her arm from the anchoring rope, screaming as she used it to swing herself over the rail and let go. Screaming as she hit the water and the breath was knocked from her lungs.

In Battle and in Death.

Seven

POUNDING. STEADY, RHYTHMIC. Not a heartbeat. The heart
didn't pound so slowly. Not even with drugs. And it was softer
than a heart, more distant. After a while, Dhulyn Wolfshead
grew aware that movement had stopped. She tried to push that awareness away, to sink back into the black, but even that effort only helped
her come more completely to herself.

She lifted her head.

Immediately, the world around her rose and fell, as if she still tossed
on the waves of the Long Ocean. She turned her head to one side and
was sick, the taste of salt water making her shudder as it tore itself out
of her throat.

She laid her head back on her outstretched arm, blinking, her lashes
stuck together with salt. Her hand shook as she raised it to her mouth,
her arm weighted with fatigue. She did not have enough saliva to spit
on her fingers, realized that was a good thing when she remembered
she'd just vomited, and rubbed at her lashes with the back of her wrist
instead. No change. Was she blind, or was it just darkness? She felt
the grit of sand moving under her shoulder, brushed some off her face.
She pushed, inching herself backward with arms and legs so heavy they
seemed to belong to someone else. Her weakness terrified her, but
then the darkness drew her down once more.

When Dhulyn woke again, the sun was just clearing the horizon,
properly in the west, she noted, as her sense of direction, tortured
by constant movement during the hours—days?—in the water, reasserted itself. She raised her head, pushed herself to sit upright, and
looked down, frowning, as her hand touched something damp. Her

nose wrinkled, and she scrubbed the hand as vigorously as she could—which wasn't very—in a cleaner patch of sand. Apparently, she hadn't pushed herself as far from the small pool of muck and seawater she'd vomited during the night as she'd thought.

"If this is the afterlife, I'm not impressed." Dhulyn winced and put her hand up to her throat, swallowed, and winced again. As swollen and rough as that time she'd had the fever in Medwain. And no sign of lemon or honey to soothe it.

So much for calling for help. But it wasn't help she wanted. Every muscle aching as though she'd had a beating, Dhulyn rolled over until she lay on her back, closed her eyes against the slanting light and took a deep breath in through her nose, letting it out through her mouth. On the third repetition she began to repeat the words of her personal *Shora*, the triggering phrase which would enhance her concentration, her ability to focus on the *Shora* she wanted to use.

But it wouldn't matter which one she used. She already knew what any of the Hunter *Shoras* would tell her. There was nothing near her. No animal, no bird, no human. Not her Partner. Not Parno.

When the shaking stopped, the sun was already much higher in the sky. Still curled in a ball, her head still cradled in her arms. Why wasn't she dead? Tradition among the Mercenary Brotherhood had always led them to believe that no one survived the death of her Partner, and Dhulyn had gone into the water with that thought uppermost in her mind.

So why, then, was she still alive? For a moment, her heart bounded—but then she took herself in hand once more. Sense reasserted itself. She and Parno had gone into the water at almost the same moment. The Crayx were nowhere near. Had he been alive, and able to keep his head out of water, he should have washed up on the same Moon-and-Stars–cursed shore as she had. And he wasn't here.

Just as he hadn't been in any of the futures she had Seen since stepping aboard the *Wavetreader*. No future with Parno in it. Before, she'd often Seen Visions of Parno older, sometimes alone, sometimes with herself. But those futures had all stopped once their feet were on the path that led to this one.

She pushed those thoughts away, willing her mind to focus on anything rather than the yawning empty hole in the middle of her chest. How many Partnered Brothers did she know of, besides Parno and herself? There were many in the tales that made up the basis of the Common Rule. Glorious deaths. There was Dysmos Stareye and Palmond the Handless. Separated by the press of battle, they had nevertheless breathed their last breaths at the same moment. Or so the tale told.

And a fine tale it is, Dhulyn thought. *But I'm alive.*

Fanryn Bloodhand and Thionan Hawkmoon. They'd died together, if not exactly at the same moment. As the one Partner lay dying, the other stood over her, sword in hand until she was herself overrun. That was what being Partnered meant.

Dhulyn sat up, blinking, and resisted the urge to scrub at her face and eyes with her salt-and-sand–encrusted hands. She must find fresh water and soon. Three minutes without air, three days without water, three weeks without food. The trilogy of the Common Rule. And one which still applied to her, no matter what she might wish for.

"Mother Sun." Her lips moved, but Dhulyn was careful not to speak aloud. *Is it your doing that I am here?* Dhulyn rarely questioned the distant gods of her people: Sun, Moon, and Stars. As a rule, her people didn't pray much. Sun, Moon, and Stars were always with you, even when you couldn't see them, her mother once said. They answered all prayers, but not always with the answer you wanted.

"In Battle, or in Death." The Mercenary salute. Was it that simple? Partners died together because most Mercenary Brothers died in battle? Because what was enough to overwhelm one would overwhelm both? Dysmos and Palmond died in battle. As had Fanryn and Thionan. Was Parno gone and she still here because there hadn't been a battle? Must she then wait for her own death to join him once more?

"In Battle *and* in Death." The slightly modified salute between Partnered Mercenaries—and seldom used even by them. That would be where she met Parno again. *So be it.*

She looked toward the sea. That pathway to death had failed her already. Clearly, something more was expected. Something more, presumably, than lying here until dehydration finished the job the sea had not done. Dhulyn pushed herself upright and began her *Shora* ritual again. She would search for water this time, fresh water. Then she'd see what Mother Sun and Father Moon brought to her path.

The spot in the hills where the stream widened into a shallow, reed-edged pool not only provided fresh water, but a couple of the sleepier fish. They were bland eaten raw, with neither salt nor lemon to give flavor, but they were food, and something told Dhulyn that death by starvation would not serve her purpose any more than death by drowning.

Ah! In *Battle*, or in *Death*. Surely, if *she* died in battle, it would be enough to reunite her with Parno. And she knew just what battle would suit her best. Mercenary Brothers did not leave each other unavenged—that was part of the Common Rule as well—and Dhulyn knew where the path to her vengeance lay.

The Storm Witch.

Dhulyn nodded, whistling silently as she began to stretch out each muscle in turn. First, the long muscles of her legs, arms, and back. Then, the shorter muscles of chest, abdomen, neck, hands, feet, and face. Parno had been killed by a waterspout where no such phenomenon should be—caused by that thrice-cursed snail spawn of a Witch. And when the Storm Witch was dead, Dhulyn herself could die and join her Partner.

Dhulyn gave a sigh of contentment and stood up. Now that she was fed and watered, and had rinsed off all the sand and salt in the cool pond, she felt almost her normal self. A pang stabbed her, sharp and cold. She would never feel normal again. She pushed that thought away. *Not now.* She could not afford to indulge her grief, not now that she had plans to make, a goal to reach.

She looked at the tips of her fingers and the pads of her feet. Wrinkled, but even now smoothing out. She could not have been very long in the sea, perhaps only overnight. There was no way to be sure, however, how far that frightening force of wind and wave had carried her. She felt the seams and pockets of her clothing. Sword and long knife had been lost in the water. She felt at the back of her vest, and found the inner pocket torn open and empty. So, she drummed her fingers on her thigh. Except for the lack of shoes and weapons—other than those she was born with—she was in good condition.

Dhulyn glanced up at the sun. Almost at its midday height. She picked up her vest, pulled out the laces, squatted once more at the edge of the water, and pushed the vest under the surface. She sat back on her heels, lifting the dripping vest onto her knees, refolded the sodden garment so it could be worn as a hood, and pulled it on over her head. Better sunburn than sunstroke, she thought. The layers of stitched-in and quilted-over cloth would hold water for a long time before drying out, keeping her head cool as well as protected from the sun. She leaned forward again, pushing her hands into the soft mud along the edge of the water. Some of that would help protect her skin.

But first Dhulyn waded back into the water until she was knee-deep. She took a deep breath, felt herself relax into the Stalking Cat *Shora*, and composed herself in patience, waiting for the telltale shifting of shadows below the surface that would mean fish.

When she'd captured four more of the small fish and cleaned them with the same rock she'd used before, she wrapped them in grass she soaked in the water. Finally, she pulled her linen trousers toward her, drew the waist string completely closed, forming a bag into which she pushed the fish. She set the bag to one side, along with the stone she'd used as a knife, and another, rounder stone that fit well into the palm of her hand. She examined the rocks and scrub grass around her. She had food, weapons, and a covering for her head. No way to carry water except inside her.

Belly tight with liquid, mud liberally applied to shoulders and arms, Dhulyn rose once more to her feet and tied her trousers around her waist by the legs. She'd have to eat the fish fairly quickly as it was. They wouldn't last long in this heat, and she'd want to eat them while they would still provide some moisture.

When she reached the small ridge to the east of the pool Dhulyn stopped and looked around her. The sea was at her left, to the north and west. Should she try farther inland, or keep to the coast? Downstream was what the Common Rule usually advised, but here, downstream would only lead her back to the sea.

Dhulyn cocked her head—and her stomach dropped; her vision darkened for an instant as she realized what she was doing. Parno would not be expressing his opinion, and she would never again sort out her own decision by arguing it over with him. Never again. She pushed those bleaker thoughts away.

"Just you wait," she said aloud, not admitting even to herself whom she was addressing. First, she had to find people. Then, she could die in a civilized manner, killing someone else. But only a particular someone would do. In Battle *and* in Death.

She took a deep breath, let it out with all her force, marked a higher ridge as the edge of the next watershed and started walking.

Carcali sat on her lesser throne next to the Tarxin and tried hard not to fidget. Part of the problem was that the body she wore was much younger than her own, and inclined to fidget, and even after several months of occupancy, her control over it wasn't what she'd like it to be. Especially here and now, where she didn't really understand what was going on, and boredom could so easily set in.

She realized she was frowning and cleared her expression. If she were being honest, she'd have to admit that anxiety rather than boredom was making her fidget. She'd sent away the servant who'd summoned her to this audience, anxious to finish her mapping of nearby weather patterns, only to find someone much more senior at her door, accompanied not so subtly by a man wearing armor and carrying a spear.

"The Tarxin Xalbalil, Light of the Sun, commands your presence immediately," the counselor had said. "You are to begin to learn the needs of the realm." In the crispness of his tone Carcali had recognized, underneath the courtesy that he had to give her as the Tara, a not very well-disguised mix of skepticism, irritable impatience, and a certain amount of resentment about having been the one sent to fetch her.

Aides had hustled her straight to the lesser throne as she entered the chamber and the Tarxin, resplendent in a tunic that seemed to be made from solid gold, hadn't even looked at her as he'd signaled to the pages at the door.

At first she'd been interested; this was the first time she had seen the man in public since she'd awakened in the body of his daughter, and she took advantage of the preliminaries to glance at him out of the corner of her eye. He was short by her own standards, but on the tall side for the Mortaxa. His hair had once been as black, and was still as thick as his daughter's, but much coarser, and very straight. Xendra must have inherited her curls from her mother. Like hers, his skin was a dark, even gold, though his showed the remains of pockmarks, and the signs of frequent shaving.

His throne was made in the shape of a sunburst, and the room was lighted in such a way that anyone not on the dais would have difficulty looking straight at him. Carcali found herself nodding. Brilliant setup, really. Someone on the Tarxin's staff should get full marks for clever promotion.

Once the audience itself began, Carcali found her attention drifting. These were minor petitions, from least nobles trying to buy their way into lesser status, to wealthy traders looking for royal favor, or hoping to have disputes settled by the Tarxin himself. Strange, really, how some things never changed. The amount of time that was spent waiting for people who thought they were more important than you to make decisions about things that weren't important to anyone.

Her mind drifted away to the last time she'd spent a morning waiting like this. The decorations in the long passage of the Artists' Hall had been more subtle, simple touches of color and abstract forms, but the bench she had waited on then was more comfortable than the lesser throne. To be fair, it wasn't that the Artists had kept her waiting, more that she'd arrived for her interview early.

Why was that, exactly? Carcali always tried to be exactly on time . . . oh, yes, *now* she remembered. She'd had a fight with her roommate, Wenora, a real fight, the kind that took you where you didn't really want to go, and she'd left their rooms before either of them said something unforgivable.

Carcali had come up with an plan to solve the crisis that had suspended all classes in the Academy and was keeping all the Artists and even the senior Mages locked away in meditation and vigil. She had expected Wenora to be pleased and excited, and she'd been hurt by her friend's lack of enthusiasm.

"Come on, Car, you're only a Crafter. What makes you think that you can come up with a solution when even the Mages and the Artists are racking their brains?"

"Master Aranwe always says that a good idea can come from anywhere," Carcali had pointed out. "That we shouldn't hold ourselves back by being afraid to say what we think."

"Oh, I see you holding yourself back—never!" There had been nothing but teasing affection in Wenora's smile. "What's your big plan, then?"

"I've written it all out, but basically, they're going about it the wrong way," she said to her friend. "The earth's warming too fast, right? Well instead of trying to patch things up down here, I say we go straight to the source. We should be trying to cool down the sun."

The look on Wenora's face was priceless. "Who could do such a thing?"

"I could do it." Carcali grinned. "It would be easier if I had help, but I'm pretty sure I could do it myself if I had to. Don't you see?" In her eagerness she'd leaned forward, but Wenora remained sitting stiffly upright. "That's why no one else has thought of this. They're used to solving problems with a nudge here and a nudge there. Pooling strengths, gathering resources. They're simply not taking into account what power like mine might be able to do."

A long silence greeted her words.

"That's right," Wenora finally said. "There's only ever been one or two as powerful as you in the whole history of the Art. What a lucky thing you're here to save us all." Carcali was surprised at the bitterness and sarcasm in the other girl's voice. She'd thought they were friends, that Wenora—they'd been roommates since their apprenticeship, for the Art's sake—surely Wenora wasn't jealous of her.

"Wenora." But her roommate was keeping her head turned aside, her lips a thin line in her stiff face.

That was when Carcali had left their rooms and gone to wait in the Artists' Hall. Wenora was scared, that was all. Everyone knew that fear made you stupid, and angry, too. Wenora would get over it, and they'd be friends again.

Finally, the summons had come and she'd followed the lay page into the Council Room. There, as she'd expected, she found the Artists, the Heads of each branch of the Weather Arts. Sue Roh of Earth, Fion Tan, of Air, Bri AnM of Fire and Mar Lene of Water. And Jenn Shan, of course, current Head Artist, and the tie-breaking vote if one should be needed. Luckily, Jenn Shan was also an Artist of Air, something Carcali felt boded well for her chances, since she was a Crafter of that Art herself. There'd be two on her side—or at least two who could follow her arguments more easily.

Carcali sat down in the candidate's chair, where she'd fully expected to be sitting for her Mage's examination in two months' time, if this crisis hadn't put all classes and all examinations on hold. She'd be the youngest qualified Mage in the history of the Academy—once she was finally examined. She crossed her ankles and laid her hands palm down on her thighs. She nodded to Jenn Shan to show that she was ready to begin.

"Your proposal is interesting." The Head Artist placed her hand on the sheaf of papers before her. "It shows your great heart, and your youthful enthusiasm. It pains me to tell you that energy and enthusiasm are not enough."

The blow was so sudden, and so unexpected that Carcali felt as if the Head Artist had borrowed the skills of the Artist of Water and frozen her solid as a lump of ice. She hadn't really expected her plan to be accepted right away—she'd figured that there would have to be some minor adjustments, and she'd been ready to welcome input and suggestions, especially from the Artists.

But to be rejected out of hand. Rejected completely.

"I don't understand," she said, shock giving her the determination to speak. "Is there a flaw in my design?"

"Your design looks feasible, on the surface," Fion Tan, Artist of Air, said. "But the amount of power required . . ." The older man shook his head.

"But I could do it myself if others were unwilling, or unable, to help me—"

"No," Fion Tan shook his head. "You couldn't. That's where your own inexperience is misleading you. You're not ready. You're months away from your examinations, and you would have to pass them, and pass them with the highest distinction, before you could undertake even to help in an action as far-reaching as cooling the sun."

"I *can* do it," Carcali said, hoping she didn't sound merely stubborn. "You know I'm powerful enough."

"Powerful, yes." The Head, Jenn Shan, took back the reins of the discussion. "Disciplined, no. You could not sustain your anchors long enough, and without that, you would lose control over all the forces in your hands. Power without discipline is nothing but a danger to us all."

Fion Tan consulted a notebook he had in front of him. "Discipline has been a problem for you, hasn't it? Not unexpected in an apprentice, especially one with such a great natural ability. The Art isn't easy, and the limits, while necessary, can chafe." He turned a page. "No lesser Academy in your town, I see." He looked up. "You've resisted submitting to discipline all along, haven't you? And not just ours, but even your own."

"That's not true." Carcali's hands had formed into fists.

"Really? Then you have learned all your *Shora*? You're ready to be examined on them now?"

Carcali refused to lower her eyes, even though she felt her cheeks and ears burning.

"Your adviser has spoken to you on this point, has he not?"

Even the calmer, softer voice of the Head Artist couldn't soothe her. *That's* what this was about? She hadn't been practicing her *Shora* like a good little girl? She hadn't been following their precious stodgy old rules?

"You may not be aware that your adviser has needed to speak for you often, pleading your case, asking for more time to persuade you." This was Fion Tan again. "But even he admits that you are argumentative, that you go too much your own way in spite of others." With one hand still holding his notebook open, he tapped his own copy of her plan. "Which this proposal more than amply demonstrates. There are others among your tutors who have been pressing for more severe penalties, perhaps even expulsion from the Academy, since you show little interest in our methods, and our traditions."

"Enough." Calm as it was, Jenn Shan's voice cracked like a whip, and the Artist of Air subsided, closing his notebook. "In the face of the present crisis," Jenn Shan continued, "we lack the time to look into your candidacy, Carcali. Simply put, we cannot agree to your plan. There is no Artist powerful enough to undertake it. And while *your* power is undeniable, your skills are insufficient. The Council has decided. You may go."

Carcali had stood up and left them, turning and marching out of the Council Room with her face burning and her teeth clenched. Her skills were insufficient, were they? Sanctimonious pricks. Rather the world came to an end than try something that wasn't part of their precious traditions. She'd show them.

She'd show them right now.

She had started to run, turning down corridor after familiar corridor until she'd reached her own lab space. There she'd hoisted herself into the Weathersheres Chair and hurriedly strapped herself in, hands trembling. If even one of those stodgy old beasts who called themselves the Artists Council understood her at all, they'd be here stopping her—but no, it would never occur to them that she wouldn't just go chastened back to her room like a good little Crafter. Just showed how smart they *really* were.

Carcali lay back and closed her eyes, taking a deep breath. She felt herself lift, and relaxed into it, let herself spread thin, until she was absorbed, the air her breath, the rain and moisture her blood and fluids. At one with the heat, the cold, and the push of unbelievable pressures. She looked about herself. She was swimming in the swirl of colors that were the currents of the air, like splashes of paint on an ordinary artist's palette. All shades, all colors, every shade and tint—some without names in the human language—and each carrying its own message, its own piece of information.

And there, the hot, bright streak that was the pathway of the sun.

Pain brought Carcali back to the present. She was squeezing her hands so tightly her nails were digging into her palms.

She gradually became aware that the audience was ending, people were stepping back from the throne, and lowering their heads in respect as the Tarxin rose to his feet. At the right moment, Carcali edged forward on the lesser throne and stood up. As the Tarxin turned away, he spoke to one of his attendants.

"Bring the child."

What does he want? Carcali made a conscious effort to breathe more slowly as she stepped in front of the servant. What if he said something about her coming when she was summoned? All right, that would give her the opening she needed to explain to him why studying the maps that had finally arrived was more important than sitting through a meaningless public ceremony—no. Better if she said she'd been caught up and distracted by her work. *Don't antagonize him,* she reminded herself. He was the one keeping the Healers away.

"Daughter." The man's voice was dry and cool, the word had no feeling behind it. Carcali hesitated, unsure whether she was meant to respond. "Do you now find yourself recovered from your ordeal?"

"Yes. Yes, *Father,*" she corrected quickly.

"You are feeling well?"

"Yes, I—" The blow came so quickly Carcali did not see it, could not have ducked or moved out of the way. Her cheek felt hot. Stunned, she was raising her hand to her face when another blow landed. This time she found herself on her knees.

"You will come when I send for you. You will not daydream. You will be attentive and alert. You will not embarrass the throne again. You are showing yourself very useful, far more so than could have been expected from a girl child. Your help with the crops, your knowledge of the lodestone and your suggestions about the boat building—all to the good." Here his dry voice became even colder than before. "But do not forget yourself. Do not forget who you are."

He didn't wait to hear an answer. He was gone when she looked up.

That night the winds rose, and the rain fell. Lightning struck the Tarxin's garden house and very nearly burned it to the ground.

Sweat had caused much of the mud to come off, leaving Dhulyn feeling sticky, and not a little itchy. She had eaten the fish several hours before—it had lasted even less time in this heat than she'd thought. She'd considered keeping at least part of her trousers to use as a sling, but the smell of dead fish convinced her to leave them behind. She was going to die anyway, might as well be as comfortable as possible. It wasn't until afterward she'd realized that she'd left her rocks behind as well. She'd shrugged. No Mercenary Brother was ever really unarmed. The only luck she'd had so far was to find, first another stream at which she'd drunk her fill and rewet her head covering, and then a road.

She frowned. If you could call this a road. It was flat, somewhat smooth, and showed some signs of metalwork at low points. But the few prints she could make out in the dust were puzzling. Bare feet, yes. Sandaled feet, yes. And at least one print that could have been a boot. Thin wheels about an arm's length apart, yes. An animal with four two-toed feet leaving a print something like the Berdanan camel. It took her several hours to figure out what was missing, which she blamed on the heat.

There were no hoofprints. Why were there no hoofprints? She was just too tired, and too hot to consider what this meant.

The sun had lowered enough to get in her eyes when a glint of metal down the road in front of her brought Dhulyn to a stop.

People.

Her first instinct was to find cover, buy time to assess the situation. But she thought better of it. This could be her chance to find a way to shelter, to begin gathering the information she would need to find and kill the Storm Witch.

The glint of metal disappeared into a small cloud of dust, which eventually resolved itself into two guards on foot, one armed with a crossbow, the other a sword, and two larger, huskier men carrying a sedan chair between them. The two guards, deeply tanned and wearing only leather harness above their short kilts, stopped on seeing her, and spread out to flank her. She let them. The noble in the chair tapped on the side of the chair's sunshade and the two carriers lowered their burden to the ground.

Slaves? Dhulyn thought, taking a careful breath and shaking out her hands. *Mutes?* She stood her ground as the man stepped out of the chair and approached her. He wore sandals with soles thick enough to keep his feet clear of the dirt, but even so, he was only Dhulyn's own height. His skin color was much darker than her own, but he was paler than his guards. His clothing seemed eminently suitable to the climate, a long piece of vertically creased and folded linen wrapped around his lower body, topped with a short-sleeved tunic cropped at his navel and heavily embroidered in what looked like gold thread that matched the series of tiny rings piercing the edges of his ears. His sword was slung much too low around his hips, the folds of his skirt contrived in such a way as to make the weapon seem more a piece of jewelry than a method of defense.

The noble stopped a half span in front of her, put his fists on his hips and looked her up and down. Dhulyn knew she hardly looked the part of a Mercenary Brother, naked, unarmed, filthy with mud and sweat, scratched by thornbushes, barefoot, and smelling of old fish.

She tilted her head to one side and smiled her wolf's smile. The noble backed up half a step. The guard on the left, the swordsman, suppressed a smile. The crossbowman on the right and the two chair carriers pretended they hadn't seen anything. Somehow, they all gave the impression of having had plenty of practice at that.

"You are an escaped slave," the noble said slowly, as if he expected her to misunderstand him. He spoke the common tongue, but his accent was one Dhulyn had never heard. "Tell me quickly what House you're from and I promise I won't punish you too severely."

"You are a fool," Dhulyn said, just as slowly and clearly, aware that to him she'd be the one with the accent. "Tell me quickly you won't jump to conclusions again and I promise to stop laughing at you."

The man's face darkened to the point that Dhulyn feared for the condition of his heart. The ghost of a smile on the face of the swords-man standing behind him widened to a real grin, quickly stifled.

The noble lifted his hand and the two guards tensed. "Don't lie again," the noble said, still with great clarity.

Dhulyn raised her eyebrows. "I didn't lie," she said. "You *are* a fool."

"The scars on your back show you are a slave."

"Scars don't make a me slave, just as a sword doesn't make you a warrior."

The noble dropped his hand.

Dhulyn didn't need the signal, having seen from the corner of her eye that the crossbowman was lifting his weapon. As the man's finger tightened she jumped to the left and caught the bolt in her right hand. With her left hand, she pulled off her head covering and threw it into the face of the swordsman, leaped forward, and drove the crossbow bolt into the noble's hand, pinning it to his thigh, jerked his sword free herself—*knew it was belted too low*—as she swept the noble's feet out from under him, and turned to face the two guards.

Only to find them openmouthed, wide-eyed, and staring.

"Paledyn," the crossbowman said, his weapon hanging slack from his hand.

Dhulyn stepped backward until she had all three men clearly in her line of sight.

"What are you waiting for? Kill her!" The stupid noble was pull-ing at his hand, apparently unaware that was the fastest way to cripple himself.

"But, Xar, she is Paledyn." Now it was the swordsman who spoke.

Now the man turned again to face her, and the color drained from his face.

"Your p–pardon, Xara," he said. Dhulyn would have bet her second-best sword it was rage that made him stutter, not fear or awe. "I did not see—I could not have expected a woman."

"I told you not to jump to conclusions," she said.

The two guards looked from Dhulyn to the noble and back again, as if expecting something more. Finally, the noble spoke again.

"I offer you my home, roof, table, and bed. I am Loraxin, House Feld." The underlings, even the slaves by the chair, relaxed.

Again, Dhulyn was willing to bet that the House's gritted teeth spoke more of his anger than his pain.

"I am Dhulyn Wolfshead, the Scholar," she replied equally formally. "I was Schooled by Dorian the Black Traveler. I fight with my Brother—" her throat closed and she had to cough and start again. "I have fought at the sea battle of Sadron, at Arcosa for the Tarkin of Imrion, and Bhexyllia to the westward, with the Great King."

"May we tend the House's wound, Xara Paledyn?" The swordsman stepped forward.

"Lay your sword on the ground and back away from it," she said.

"I assure you, Xara—"

"Just do as I say."

The man nodded, laid his sword flat on the ground, and backed away from it. Dhulyn picked it up without taking her eyes from anyone. Just as she thought. This was a real sword, not the jeweled toy the Noble Loraxin Feld had been wearing. At her nod, the two guards bent over their employer.

"It should come out of the thigh muscle quite easily with a little cutting," she said. "Unless, of course, he's complicated matters with all this squirming about."

The crossbow bolt hadn't penetrated very deeply into the man's thigh, and they detached it quickly and cleanly using the method she had suggested. When it came to removing it from his hand, however, the two guards were clearly beyond their knowledge, though it seemed to Dhulyn that the swordsman at least was contemplating the risks involved in knocking his noble patron out.

"Allow me," she suggested. "I am not a Knife, but it appears I've had more experience with wounds than you." She nudged the crossbowman with her toe. "Bind the thigh wound, will you? And you," she said, turning to the swordsman. "Brace him against your knees and hold his hand quite still."

She'd noticed, in the brief time she'd held the thing, that the bolt itself was metal, but the fletching was the more ordinary feathers, glued to the metal shaft, and stiffened, no doubt, with the selfsame glue.

"Bring me some water."

The crossbowman had finished with the man's thigh wound, and now ran to the chair to fetch a large skin. Dhulyn accepted it with a nod, rinsed out her mouth, spat out the grit that had accumulated, rinsed again, and filled her mouth with water, swishing it through her teeth several times. Handing back the waterskin, she bent over and slipped the whole fletched section of the crossbow bolt into her mouth, losing only a few drops of water in the process.

The man's hand smelled of scent—sandalwood and rose water if she was any judge—and just a little of sweat and old leather. She worried at the fletching with her teeth until the stiffened feathers were free of their glue and she could spit them out. She eased the now clean bolt through the man's hand.

She glanced up. House Feld had fainted.

"Why not soak the fletching loose with just the water?" the swordsman said, as the other guard bound up the wound.

"It wastes water," she said. "And saliva helps to dissolve the glue faster." She picked up the skin again, rinsed out her mouth once more, and took several healthy swallows.

"I'm sure House Feld intended to offer you his chair, Paledyn," the swordsman said. "But . . ." he raised his eyebrows and indicated the unconscious man he held against his knee.

Dhulyn almost smiled. "I would not have taken it," she said. "Are we far from the table, roof, and bed that he *did* offer me?"

"We were on our way to Pont House, but we will return to Feld House at once, Paledyn."

"You will call me Dhulyn Wolfshead," she told him, walking back to the chair as the two guards lifted the unconscious noble.

She hesitated, causing both men to look over their shoulders at her. She waved them on and followed, feeling the slaves' glances flick away from her as she neared them.

Loraxin Feld became aware of the sounds of sandals slapping lightly against the road surface; light voices conversing quietly. The smell of the chair carriers. His eyes fluttered open and what he saw made him struggle to sit up. The sun was at the wrong angle, they were heading in the wrong direction. A sharp pain in his hand, and a throb in his thigh brought everything back to him with a jolt.

The Paledyn.

His heart began to pound, and he forced himself to calm down, to take a deep breath. Could this finally be the opportunity he'd been seeking for so long? He'd been looking for a way to bring himself to the attention of the Tarxin, Light of the Sun. And rumor had it that the Tarxin, Light of the Sun, was looking for a Paledyn.

And now he, Loraxin Feld, had a Paledyn.

If she *was* a Paledyn. He chewed at his lower lip. Could a *woman* be a Paledyn? He had never heard of such a thing.

What if the whole thing was a trick? His neighbors playing some dangerous joke on him? He cursed himself for a shortsighted fool. If only he hadn't been so quick to offer her roof, table, and bed. He was bound now, like it or not. Female or not. She could have been trained. And tattooed for that matter. He would need to devise some way of testing her. He closed his eyes and pretended he was still asleep. *Caids*, his hand hurt.

Eight

XERWIN HAD NOT SEEN a great deal of his sister since her accident. Once Xendra was out of danger, he'd had to rejoin his Battle Wing on the southeastern frontier almost immediately. Somewhere in those foothills were camps that—among other things— were helping escaped slaves make it through the mountains. Xerwin couldn't leave his men for very long; in the Tarxin's armies, discipline was applied from the top down.

And it didn't help that he was now Tar, and had so many more responsibilities. Xerwin had thought he was busy when all he had to worry about was the First Battle Wing and the Nomads. Though his father the Tarxin had taken the trade with the Nomads back into his own hands—and badly, Xerwin privately thought—other, more highly public duties had been added. Regular oversight of the Sanctuaries and the Libraries; inspections of the properties held directly by the Tarxinate; meetings with ambassadors—especially those from the land of his betrothed. He smiled, thinking of the headdress she had sent him, embroidered with her own hands. It would be a few years yet until she would be old enough to leave her father's house.

And now, it seemed, his own sister was not likely to leave *her* father's house. The Tarxin had agreed to break the betrothal to Naxot with very little argument. Had seemed, in fact, to be pleased with Xerwin for suggesting it.

"A very good thought, young one," he'd said, his harsh voice unusually warm. "I begin to think you may actually have the brain of a Tarxin under all that armor. It's not enough, as I've often told you, to be a good soldier."

Maybe not, Xerwin thought. Still, this latest breach with the Nomads hadn't happened on *his* watch—but his father was still speaking.

"A Storm Witch is too valuable a tool to waste in breeding."

"But she'll be sent to the temple of the Slain God." At least, that's what Naxot had told him.

"Ridiculous. Oh, they'll ask for her, of course. Let them. They've no more notion of what to do with a real Holy Woman than my dog has. Old Telxorn is trembling in his sandals at the very idea that someone with higher status than his may come to live at his temple. Besides, I'm still Tarxin here, and she is still my daughter. Let them send whatever priests or attendants she must have. But Telxorn has agreed that Xendra is better left here."

After a hefty donation to the temple. Xerwin was smart enough to keep that thought to himself. His older brother, the previous Tar, had died of expressing himself too freely. Well, probably, Xerwin thought, as he strode down the corridor toward his sister's apartments, delegated to tell her of the change in her betrothal, now that she was too valuable a tool to waste in breeding.

He wondered how his sister would like being such a valuable tool.

The guards at Xendra's door came to attention and saluted him, but did not stand aside, or open the doors to her suite to allow him to enter. He smiled and raised his eyebrows, where his father would have raised his staff.

"Gorn and Tashek, isn't it?" he said, dredging their names out of his memory. It was this kind of detail, his old general had taught him, that made men willing to follow you anywhere. "A reason I should not enter?" He nodded at the door, prepared to be given some girlish excuse.

"No one is to enter, my Tar," Swordsman Gorn said. "Orders of the Tarxin, Light of the Sun."

Xerwin's heart was suddenly in his throat. "Has something happened to her? Has her illness returned?"

The door was suddenly flung open from the inside. "Do you think you're making *enough* noise? I—Oh, I beg your pardon Tar Xerwin, I didn't see you there."

At any other time, or with any other person, the abrupt change of tone would have been funny. It wasn't Kendraxa in the doorway, but Finexa Delso, one of Xendra's newer attendants. And she was giving him the kind of smile women at court had increasingly given him since his brother had . . . died.

"The Swordsmen were just telling me that no one is to enter here, Xara Finexa. On my father's orders. But it's *on* his orders that I've come."

"Oh, Tar Xerwin, surely the Tarxin, Light of the Sun, couldn't have meant *you*." Finexa fluttered her eyelashes and extended her hand as if she was about to touch him on the arm. Xerwin wasn't averse to female companionship, but he preferred those with considerably more discretion than Finexa Delso practiced.

"I'll just see that the Tara is ready to receive you, Tar Xerwin," the woman murmured in an even more honeyed voice before turning and walking to the inner door, hips swaying.

Since her back was turned, Xerwin permitted himself a small sigh and did his best not to grimace when the door opened again and Finexa beckoned him in with smiles and demure looks.

He stood blinking at the state of the room while the woman closed the doors behind him. Much of the furniture had been pushed against the walls, and Xendra's usual pastimes—her sewing, her collection of costumed dolls, and her box of vera tiles—showed evidence of neglect. Large maps had been spread across the center of the room, where a little grouping of padded chairs and small tables had always stood. Ornaments of glass, metal, and stone had been taken down from the shelves and ledges to keep the edges of the maps from curling up.

In the center of this, on her knees, was his sister Xendra. She sat back on her heels as he came in, still frowning down at the maps in front of her.

A bruise darkened her right cheek, and Xerwin felt instant rage, clenching his hands into fists. Almost immediately, he realized that there was only one person who could have struck the Tara of Mortaxa. The one person against whom even the Tar of Mortaxa could take no vengeance.

Their father. The Tarxin.

When Xendra finally raised her eyes to his, he'd had enough time to relax his fists, take a deep breath, and smile, though he found he was still angry.

And then his anger was gone, vanished like a drop of water hitting a blade being hammered at the blacksmith's forge. In the instant that their eyes met, Xendra had looked at him as though she did not know him. And while she was now smiling, and nodding, and getting to her feet, Xerwin still had the uneasy feeling that all her recognition was on the surface.

"I expected Kendraxa," he said, grasping at any thought that might explain his sister's oddness. "Is she ill today?"

"I don't know," Xendra said. Her tone was curiously flat, and her answer definitely unexpected. Xerwin would have wagered his best short sword that Xendra had known her nurse Kendraxa's exact whereabouts ever since she was old enough to toddle after the noblewoman.

"The Tarxin sent for her yesterday morning, after the thunderstorm," his sister continued. She was standing now, but still frowning down at her maps. "I haven't seen her since."

"You didn't ask?"

At this question, Xendra looked up. "I assumed the Tarxin had other duties for her."

Xerwin swallowed, temporarily speechless. What could possibly have happened that would lead Xendra to speak of her dearest companion in that cool, matter-of-fact voice? And did it have anything to do with the bruise on Xendra's face?

Kendraxa had never had any other duties in this House but attendance on Xendra. She had come to the capital with Xendra's mother for the express purpose of looking after the children of the royal marriage. Unless Xendra herself sent the woman away, their father would probably not even remember Kendraxa existed.

And Xendra had never before called their father "the Tarxin." Never. When they were alone together she had always called him "Father."

Xendra *was* changed, he thought, and in more ways than even Naxot had suggested.

That reminded him. "I have news from our father," he said. "I don't know whether it will be welcome to you."

She looked up again, eyes narrowed, face set like stone. Whatever it was that had passed between his sister and his father, Xendra at least had not put it behind her.

"You are no longer betrothed," he said—and stopped. He could have sworn that an expression of relief had flitted over Xendra's face.

"I'm sure the Tarxin, Light of the Sun, had his reasons," she said.

Xerwin licked his lips. What was happening? A suspicion began to form in the back of his mind, one that he studiously ignored.

"It was Naxot," he said. "The Scholars of his House told him that you were a Holy Woman now, and that Brides of the Slain God didn't marry in the ordinary way."

"I see," she said. "Well." She looked around her at her maps. "I do expect to be quite busy with my other duties. You might tell the Tarxin that I'm working very hard, when you see him."

"Do you have any message for Naxot?"

"Who?"

"Naxot. Of House Lilso. Your former betrothed."

This time it was her turn to stand, blinking. "Please say whatever you think appropriate," she said finally.

The floating, hazy uneasiness that had been with him since he'd come into the room suddenly solidified. There had been that moment when it seemed Xendra hadn't recognized him. Then her total lack of concern for Kendraxa. Now she appeared not to remember a man she'd been making moon eyes at her whole life.

Who are you? Once again, hard-won caution kept him from speaking his suspicions aloud. In fact, it might be better to pretend that he had noticed nothing unusual, at least, until he had a chance to find out more.

Which begged the question. Did his father know? Xendra's accident seemed to have done more than give her the powers of a Storm Witch. But was this simply memory loss that was being concealed, or—Xerwin could hardly form the thought—was this in some way no longer his sister?

He made what excuses he could—it wasn't hard, she was already focusing on her maps—and almost ran out of his sister's rooms. When he found himself heading for the Tarxin's wing, he slowed. He needed to know more before he confronted his father—if he did so at all. Xerwin tapped his fingers on the leather-wrapped hilt of his formal sword. He needed more information. Who would be likely to have it?

He nodded slowly, lower lip between his teeth.

Kendraxa.

The swordsman Remm Shalyn had been assigned as her guide and servant—and her minder and jailer, Dhulyn Wolfshead suspected, though *he* at least was under no illusion that he could stop her from coming and going as she pleased. She'd been given other servants as well, among them a personal maid, a woman to bathe her, and a little page boy to run errands. They were all, as far as she could tell, terrified of her. She'd refused the voluminous skirts, constricting bodices, and teetering shoes laid out for her in her suite—fashions obviously designed to show that the wearers' husbands, fathers, brothers, or owners were rich enough that their wives, daughters, sisters, or concubines need not perform any actual labor. But as Dhulyn had learned in the courts of the Great King in the West, such dress also prevented any serious physical exercise, any running away, or even any simple walking, for Sun and Moon's sake.

Dhulyn had insisted on carrying a dagger, and wearing a version of the kilt and tunic that Remm himself was wearing, although hers was slightly longer and fuller for modesty's sake—his, not hers, Mercenary Schooling being sufficient to do away completely with body shyness. Good thing she'd had some recent practice in walking with skirts. Loraxin Feld could not actually restrict her to the women's quarters, Remm had told her, though she guessed the Noble House would certainly have liked to. According to what Remm was telling her, "roof, table, and bed" was a very specific offer, and couldn't be modified.

"So the Tarxin is your ruler." Earlier conversation had established that this land was, indeed, Mortaxa. In that, Mother Sun had smiled on her.

"Exactly, though you should say 'Light of the Sun' when you say his name or title. The Tarxina, his wife. A Tar, or Tara, son or daughter. And all of their names will begin with the most noble letter 'X.'"

Frowning, Dhulyn tried to catch the accent, the "x" sound being somewhere between a "k" and a "z."

"At present, there's Xalbalil Tarxin, Light of the Sun. His heir, son of his second Tarxina, Tar Xerwin, and Xendra the young Tara, daughter of the third Tarxina. The children of the first Tarxina have all perished."

Was it Dhulyn's imagination or did Remm's voice falter a bit when he said the Tara's name?

"The Nomads who were bringing me here spoke of a Storm Witch."

"She is part of the royal household." Again, Remm Shalyn hesitated, but said nothing further. Dhulyn nodded as though her question had no significance.

"And where does Loraxin, House Feld, fit in?"

"He's one of the least Nobility, though it wouldn't please him to hear me say so. He's entitled to be called 'Xar,' and his wife 'Xara,' but you'll notice the noble letter doesn't appear until the third syllable of his name, so that marks where he stands."

Dhulyn nodded. Remm, she'd noticed, had a proper surname of his own, not just "Feld" like the House.

"You've got some very interesting scars, if you don't mind my saying so, Dhulyn Wolfshead."

It had taken some doing to get even Remm to stop calling her "Xara Paledyn." She'd had to give up with the servants—even in her own mind, she refused to use the word "slaves."

"I was a very stubborn student, and often disciplined," she said, having learned the hard way that in some places it was best not to admit you had ever been a slave.

"And the, uh . . ." Remm Shalyn gestured at a spot on his own upper lip.

"The tip of a whip that flicked 'round and caught me on the face," she said. And so it had, though it was her then master's Steward of Keys who'd been on the other end of the whip, and not her Schooler, as she was letting Remm Shalyn believe. And a lucky thing for her it had been, for the facial scar had ruined her for her master, who'd sold her to a passing slave merchant and it was while she was in that slaver's ship that Dorian the Black had rescued her.

She'd been eleven years old, and a Mercenary ever since.

"Are you a free man, Remm Shalyn, if you don't mind my asking?"

"I don't know what things are like where you come from, Dhulyn Wolfshead, but here we don't put weapons into the hands of slaves."

"Where I come from, slavery is considered a false economy at best, and an abominable practice at worst."

"Well, for the Slain God's sake, don't mention that to House Feld, whatever you do. It would give him apoplexy, for certain."

"You never know, apoplexy may suit him."

Dhulyn took mental note that Remm Shalyn called the nobleman by his title, and not more formally as "my House." A hired guard, then, who did not consider himself a member of the Household.

They had been walking through the village that had grown up around, and indeed was mostly an extension of, Feld House. The walls of town and homes alike were whitewashed stucco, such as Dhulyn had sometimes seen in the Galanate of Navra, and covered the small prominence which some long-ago Feld had chosen as the site for his House. They were at the southern end of the village when the narrow alley they followed dead-ended in a rectangular terrace enclosed by house walls on three sides, and a low balustrade on the fourth. The terrace was featureless except for weeds growing up through the cracks between the flagstones, and what looked like two large, stone chimney tops, pierced along the sides and stoppered shut with large slabs of wood at the top like corks in a bottle.

"Ah, the cistern," Remm Shalyn said. "Would you like to see it?"

Dhulyn's shoulders were already twitching upward when she stopped the shrug and took a deep breath. "Why not?"

They retraced their steps halfway back along the alley, the ground inclining away from them as they walked, until Remm indicated an archway to their right. The entrance was recessed into the wall, and guarded by a metal grille, pocked and marked with rust, which stood open. Remm stepped back in an attitude of respect, but Dhulyn waved him in ahead of her. The temperature dropped almost immediately as they cleared the threshold and began to descend the worn stone steps. At the bottom, there was barely room for them to stand on the ledge that ran along the width of a long, narrow chamber with an arched and vaulted ceiling into which were set the stone openings they had seen from above.

"There are another seven ledges identical to this one below the surface," Remm said. He squatted down and dipped his hand into the water, shaking off the drops as he stood again. "Rain's collected from all over this quarter. They tell me the cistern's never been this full before, but we've had so much rain in the past three months . . ."

Remm went on speaking, but Dhulyn was watching the ripples of water that moved outward from where he had touched the surface as they caught and reflected the tiny slivers of light that found their way into the cistern from the terrace above them through the pierced openings of the small stone chimneys.

Ripples. Tiny waves.

Dhulyn became aware that Remm Shalyn was no longer speaking. She cleared her throat.

"So the water collects on the terrace above?"

"Mmmmm." Dhulyn glanced sideways. Remm Shalyn was studying her with his head tilted to one side. "Do they mean anything?"

"What?" She heard his voice as if from far away, and her own, equally distant, answering him.

He gestured at his own temples. "Your tattoos. Is there significance to the color or pattern?"

Dhulyn swallowed, blinking. "They show where you have been Schooled. Blue and green are the colors of Dorian the Black Traveler."

"And the black line is his mark as well?"

Something squeezed her heart and her throat closed. She took air in through her nose and released it through her mouth. Forcing her hands to relax and open. "No. The black lines show that I am Partnered. My Partner has . . . *had* an identical pattern marked on his badge. He was killed in the storm that threw me into the water."

"A great loss."

Dhulyn nodded and turned away. Remm followed her back up into the outside world.

The wind had risen in the short time they were below ground, and the sky was dark with clouds.

"It appears your cistern will be overflowing by morning." When she glanced at him, Remm was staring at the sky, eyebrows drawn sharply down. He tilted his head to look sideways at her.

"You said earlier that slavery was a false economy. What did you mean?"

Dhulyn looked up but could see nothing in the sky that would have prompted such a question. She sighed. "Everything that I have read tells me that, though slavery has been practiced by many since the time of the Caids, invariably the society which depends upon it fails."

"Again, I'd keep that to myself, if I were you."

Remm started off down the alley but Dhulyn stood still, waiting until he stopped, looked over his shoulder, and came back to her.

"Which one of us is supposed to turn in the other?"

"Pardon, Xara?" From this angle, and in the light of the overcast sky, it was hard to be sure, but Dhulyn thought the man had paled under his soldier's tan.

"That's twice you've implied that you and your employer don't see things the same way; twice you've led me to do the same. So which of us is expected to run telling tales?"

Remm pressed his lips tight together, the muscles in his jaw jumping. "Dhulyn Wolfshead. You are a Paledyn. Loraxin Feld has no power over you. Even now messengers are being sent to prepare your journey to Ketxan City, to the Tarxin himself." He glanced away and then back, his expression grim. "Me, House Feld can destroy."

"And yet you speak so freely?"

He lifted one shoulder and let it drop. "You are a Paledyn."

And you are testing me. Though it was reckless of him to do so. Dhulyn closed her eyes. She should feel something, she knew, something besides this sudden exhaustion, this hollowness. The man's danger was real. Without work as a guard he would very likely starve, or, worse, have to sell himself to feed whatever family he had. He was trusting her, depending upon her as would a soldier under her command in the field. She should care.

But before she could follow that thought, however reluctantly, she was stopped by the sound of approaching footsteps.

"Xara Paledyn, the House sends for you." In the young page's voice and eye was his awareness of what might have happened to him if he had not found her—or what might still happen if she did not come with him now.

"Is there some urgency?" she said, indicating even as she spoke that she would follow the boy.

"He has some livestock he would like your opinion on."

Horses. She began to run. Horses to take her to the Tarxin. And where he was, the Storm Witch would be.

Dhulyn was several spans ahead of her escort by the time she reached Feld House, and was through the gate and into the large inner courtyard without stopping. She had woken up that day meaning to ask where the horses were kept, and had somehow forgotten about them. Horses would help her; she was always clear-minded with a horse under her. She was three paces into the courtyard when the gates slammed shut behind her, and she dove to one side, rolling as she hit the ground and came up crouching with her back against the baked mud wall, pulling the dagger from the back of her sash.

Quickly, she scanned the open space within the gates. It was completely deserted. No guards, no servants going about their daily chores.

The sedan chair which had been standing to the right of the gate when she and Remm Shalyn had gone out for their walk was gone. As was a small handcart full of melons that had been awaiting the attention of the cooks. The gates were closed, but not, so far as she could see from this angle, barred. The main House doors were likewise shut as were the smaller gates that led to the garden and rear quarters where the animals were housed.

Pounding and shouting came from the gate and Dhulyn eased herself to her feet, though she stayed with her back to the wall. That would be Remm Shalyn, and either the gate would open to admit him, or it would not. One way or the other, this strange silent courtyard would be explained.

She smiled her wolf's smile. Her blood was running, her muscles warm, her breathing soft and easy. If something was coming to kill her, she was ready.

A sound like muffled hooves came from the inner gate leading to the animal compound and Dhulyn looked up. Was it horses after all?

But the beast that came thundering through the gate swinging its heavily horned head was no horse. It had the coloring and light hindquarters of an inglera, but was massively thick through the shoulders, and its neck supported a rack of horns as thick as her arm and as sharp as her second-best sword. Its shoulders were easily as high as her own, and the look in its red-rimmed eyes spoke of something more than normal fury.

"*Blooded* demons." Anger washed over her like a tide, setting her blood pounding in her ears and drowning her in heat. Trying to kill her, were they? Just like they'd killed her Partner, the Sun-blasted toads. Well *she* chose when she'd die, thank you very much. Not a bunch of cowards who hid behind drugged animals. What? Was her death supposed to look like an accident?

"Over here, meat pie. That's right, I'm talking to you." At the sound of her voice the beast looked in her direction, lowered its head, and began to paw the ground.

Dhulyn kicked free of the kilt wrapped around her legs and shifted her knife until she was holding it like a sword. She would much rather have had a sword, even the dainty one she'd taken from Loraxin the previous afternoon, but the dagger was all she'd found in her room when she'd awakened.

She began inching sideways toward the gate, not that she thought it would open to her hand, but in order to see if the beast would follow her. She racked her brain, trying to remember everything she could about the bull jumping she'd watched one sunny spring afternoon on the Isle of Cabrea. And the Python *Shora*, for a fighter on foot against someone armed and mounted. Surely that would help.

"Come on, stew meat, what are you waiting for?"

Much faster than she had imagined possible, given its weight and size, the beast charged and Dhulyn jumped, throwing herself up and forward, twisting and arching her body. She reached for the horn to help in her vaulting, as she'd seen bull jumpers do, but the beast hooked right, and she only brushed the horn with her fingertips as she began to fall. Twisting again, she jammed the dagger in deep, high in the animal's shoulder, and managed to control her fall long enough to avoid the worst from the flashing hooves.

She hit the ground on her own shoulder and grunted, rolling away minus one knife and plus one blow on the left thigh. Lucky thing it *wasn't* a horse, she thought. An iron-shod hoof might have broken her leg. As it was, she'd have a bruise the size of her hand and be limping for a week, though she felt little pain now.

But the beast hooked to the right when it charged. Its right, not hers. Which told her where the horns were likely to be when it tried to gore her, and gave her a chance to be elsewhere.

She rolled to the left as the beast passed through the space she'd just occupied and crashed against the wooden doors of the gate, which shivered, but held. Dhulyn got to her feet, tested her weight on her left leg, and grinned. She'd had worse in training. As she watched the beast pace around the courtyard, she kept her weight forward on her toes, knees slightly bent, arms and hands relaxed from lowered shoulders. If she really were a bull jumper, there'd be others in the yard with her to distract the animal, tire it out for her.

She would have to do that herself. Outlast the thing.

She shrugged, aware of the wolf's smile that stretched her lips, and braided the fingers of her right hand against ill luck.

The sounds of a scuffle almost made her look up. "Paledyn!" came the strangled cry, and a short, businesslike sword with a worn leather grip landed point down in the dirt next to her.

Dhulyn had barely enough time to grab it up when the beast

charged again. This time, trusting that the animal would hook again to the right, Dhulyn ran toward it on tiptoe, gauging her timing carefully, and when the great, horned head lowered at the last moment, she stepped up onto the beast's forehead, ran lightly down its spine and jumped clear just as it crashed against the stuccoed wall and sank to its knees, shaking its great head.

Confused, it spun around, almost chasing its tail in rage. Dhulyn found herself back where she had started, and caught up her kilt where it lay trampled into the dirt against the courtyard wall. Dangling the fold of cloth off to her left, she approached the beast slowly.

It was breathing hoarsely, its great barrel of a chest heaving, flecks of blood showing around its nose and mouth. Whatever drug they'd given it to drive it mad was having a worse effect. Unfortunately, Dhulyn couldn't count on it dropping dead soon enough.

Sun and Stars blind you. She gritted her teeth, knowing what she had to do, and hoping that Remm Shalyn's sword was long enough to do it.

"Come on, come you." On her toes now, she twitched the trampled kilt as far to her left as she could hold it, preparing to run forward as the beast charged, hoping that it would try for the cloth rather than her. Dhulyn eyed the spot she wanted, high on the animal's left side, where the angle should let her reach through the cage of bone and find the heart.

As the animal moved, she ran toward it, calling out to it as she would to a favorite horse, arching her body and sucking in her stomach as the horns swung round. In the last possible instant she thrust in the sword, turning from her heels to put her full weight behind it. Blood gushed from the beast's mouth and she was dragged to her knees still pushing down on the hilt of Remm's sword. When she felt the great heart stop, she stood up and stepped back, pulling the sword free.

Suddenly there were people around her, a strong arm around her waist, and her knees began to buckle. Remm, blood in the corner of his mouth, and a bruise forming on the plane of his left cheek.

An inner door swung open and Loraxin Feld came running out to her side.

"I'm so sorry, Paledyn, so sorry." And he was, too, Dhulyn could tell. Sorry enough that he spoke like a child, from the heart, no formal and meaningless mouthings of apologies and forgiveness. His hands trembled, he was white as the stuccoed walls behind him, and there was sweat on his upper lip, guilt as well as remorse in his face. He had thought the beast would kill her, and would now have to deal with the fact that it had not.

"You'd have had some explanations to give the Tarxin, I think, had I died in here." Her voice sounded rough and remote through the blood that still pounded in her ears.

"Please, Tara Paledyn—" It seemed she'd been upgraded from a Xara. "I don't know how this happened—an accident in moving the kinglera, I will have the slaves responsible killed. And you—" Loraxin turned on Remm Shalyn. "You are dismissed, how could you let the Paledyn come into such danger?"

"You will kill no one," Dhulyn said, blinking. "After all, this was an accident." *I should sit down, and quickly.* As if in response to her thought, Remm lifted her right arm and swung it around his shoulders, bracing her. Her knees steadied. "Remm Shalyn, you are now in my employ."

"Yes, Tara Paledyn."

Nine

AT FIRST HE COULDN'T breathe, and his lungs hurt, and his head pounded, and that part of the nightmare seemed to last forever. He knew it was a nightmare because Dhulyn was not there. He thought he saw her once, her pale face and her steel-gray eyes, the scar that made her lip curl back when she smiled in a certain way, her hair the color of old blood, held back from her face in loops of tiny braids, thick with ribbons, feathers, and hidden wires.

"My soul," she said, trailing her fingertips over his face before disappearing once again into the dark that was the whole world for him now.

An immeasurable time later he felt he was not alone.

"Dhulyn?"

#Calm# #Well-being#

Parno fell asleep.

He woke up to damp darkness. His eyes were sticky and his mouth strangely dry. Great rushing gusts of air swept around and past him; deep creakings and groanings throbbed like the skin of a drum and made his bones shiver. The skin crawled on the back of his neck. He was not alone, but he couldn't pinpoint any specific life around him. He blinked for what seemed like hours and achieved nothing but sore eyes. Parno forced himself to focus on the Lizard *Shora*, feeling the warmth of sun on rock, until he stopped twitching and even the muscles of his face relaxed.

As if it had been waiting for this, glimmers of light began to form around him. Soft luminescence illuminated a small cavelike chamber, the size of the cheapest private room at an inn, with smaller tunnels leading away from it in several directions. The substance of the walls and floor was damp and spongy, but dark as basalt. The air smelled of fish, brine, rot, and some unidentifiable musk.

#Stay#

He recognized the mind touch of the Crayx. Were they asking him, or telling him?

"Where am I? Where is my Partner?"

Parno sensed a shift in the consciousness around him, feelings and sensations that were just short of full thoughts, and once, the fleeting image of Dhulyn preparing herself by meditation and focus to read an old book in a foreign tongue.

#You were the only Pod sense in the water# came the answer to his question. A small part of Parno felt the exhilaration of knowing that he was sharing full thoughts with the Crayx for the first time, but he pushed it away. He had more important things to consider just now.

Dhulyn had gone into the water. Parno was sure of this, though he didn't know how. He had confused memories of tumbling through raging waves until his sense of direction—even his sense of up and down—had deserted him; of great winds, and of holding his breath until it seemed his lungs would burst. Like all Mercenary Brothers, Dhulyn had superb breath control, but Parno's had been augmented by years of practice with his pipes.

He rubbed at his upper arms. He was cold and his hands felt as though they didn't belong to him. He understood with acid clarity what had happened. Dhulyn *had* gone into the water after him. But she wouldn't have been able to hold her breath as long as he could, and the Crayx wouldn't have noticed her; they wouldn't have saved her as they'd saved him. Nothing, no one, could have survived the water-spout without such help.

Dhulyn was gone.

#Calm# #Let the pain flow through and past you like a cold current# #Do not hold it within#

Parno took a deep breath of salt-and-seaweed–flavored air and felt the calmness pass through him, pushing his loss before it, sweeping it like dust from his heart and soul.

"Don't," he said. His sorrow might be the only thing he had left of her. "Leave me my grief."

#Should you not release it# #Do not allow the despair you feel to kill you#

"Why not?"

#*Wavetreader* Pod awaits you#

Parno shrugged, wondering if the gesture would translate mentally. "I'd just as soon die." *In Battle and in Death.* That was more than a mere salutation. It was a promise.

#Very well# #Resignation# #If this is what you wish, you may remain with us# #Release your self, let your awareness float as though you were about to sleep# #We thank you for the nourishment, and we welcome you to ourselves#

Suddenly, as if his mind were a dark room and someone had thrown open a curtain, he saw, felt, *knew* what he was really speaking with.

The Crayx were not just the creatures that could be seen from the ship's rail, they were hundreds, perhaps thousands, of consciousnesses, all sharing, all one, a vast storehouse of memories, of . . . personalities? Of souls? Neither word seem to quite fit what he could sense. This was what Darlara had been trying to tell him. He had an impression that these beings occupied an enormous space, but not like an arena crowded with people crammed into seats, rather like a vast sky full of stars, or an endless meadow full of flowers. With a little effort, he could come upon, contact, speak with, any one individual. Or he could simply share with all. And he was being offered a place in this garden of beings.

"Wait." Parno struggled to sit upright; the material on which he was lying gave under his hands. "Am I injured? Am I dying?"

#We understood you wished to die# #If your grief is too heavy a burden, and you will not let us lift it . . .#

Was it too heavy? Parno rubbed his face with his hands. How could he live without her—easy to know how he didn't *die* with her, the Crayx had saved him, unknowingly interfering with the natural process that would have allowed them to die together.

#Sorrow# #Regret#

"You couldn't have known."

#Your soul may rest with us, if you wish it# #As long as the seas have salt and the currents flow#

What about Dhulyn's soul?

#She will go to her own place#

"Without me?"

#Should you stay with us, then without you, yes#

Parno's hands formed into fists. Partners were Partners, "in Battle and in Death." And this death wasn't going to part them, not if he had anything to say about it. He tried to stand, but found his bare feet sinking into the softness around him.

"Then I won't stay, thank you just the same."

#As you wish#

Malfin Cor was on his knees, head down over the broken foresail stay when he felt Darlara closing in on his port side.

"Can't be fixed," he said without looking up. "Not to hold any kind of strain anyway. Have to save the bits for something else. 'Least the rudder's all right." He glanced up and frowned, though he'd known she hadn't been paying attention. "What's more important than the ship?"

"Not *more* important. But, Mal, he's found."

"Not—the Lionsmane?" Mal dropped the pieces of wood to lie unnoticed on the deck and straightened, resting his hands on his thighs. That meant that one would return, at least, of the thirteen missing from the *Wavetreader* and the even more damaged *Skydancer*.

Dar nodded, barely able to speak, licking dry lips that still showed edges of salt. They had both of them been wet to the skin for the hours it had taken the winds and waters of the spout to finally pass and settle, and their clothes, hair, and skin were still coated with a fine dusting of dry salt. They would wash it off the first chance they got, but the ship came first.

"Blown so far by wind and wave that *Skydancer* Pod found him and is passing him back to us," Dar said, gripping him by the shoulder. "Mal. They offered him a chance to one with them, and he refused, wanted to come back. Told you I'd have him for my own, told you he'd stay."

"But you didn't—"

She cuffed him on the back of the head. " 'Course not. How could I? They can't find to save her, so they can hardly find to drown her."

Mal blinked at the serenity in his sister's tone. " 'Course not, no. But seeing you were so set on it . . ."

"Not *that* set on it." She cuffed him again. This time he raised his arm to block it. "How could you think it?"

"Don't really."

And he didn't, not really. He didn't really think Dar would ask the Pod to kill for her.

"Wouldn't have asked for it, no," she agreed, squatting down on her heels next to him. "But not sorry for all that." She shrugged. "Without Pod sense after all."

"All thinking life's important." That was the real lesson of the Crayx, what made them all different from the landsters.

Dar nodded, but in her mind she was shrugging, and Mal knew it. Of course, all thinking life was important, it was just hard sometimes to remember that the others, those without Pod sense, *could* think.

"She wouldn't have wanted to stay," his twin said finally. "And he might not have stayed without her. Have our new bloodline, for certain. A good wind and a fair current, for us at least."

Mal nudged her with his shoulder. "He'll feel her loss, remember that."

"I'll help him."

"If he wants it."

#We are ready now# #Move as we show you# #Patience#

The lambent patches in the chamber where Parno had waited as patiently as he could dimmed and died out as he got to his knees and was ready to crawl. He waited, having been warned what to expect, and when finally one of smaller passages began to glow, Parno moved into it. Following that cold luminescence, he crawled for some time in a direction he felt as "forward" before he began to go "up." The colors of the tunnel walls varied from the almost black of the place in which he had regained consciousness to a rich dark pink. The air was an even temperature, hot enough to make him sweat now that he was moving, and as humid as the jungles north of Berdana. Twice, as he crawled, his ears popped, as though he were climbing in the mountains. Just where was he, exactly? A system of underwater caves where some magic of the Crayx kept air to breathe?

Finally, he arrived at a pale green tube in which he could stand upright.

#Are you ready#

Somehow Parno must have said he was, for the next thing he knew he was slammed by a wall of moving air and water, and propelled upward, as an arrow from a bow. He tumbled once, and before he could right himself, he shot out into daylight so bright it stabbed his eyes before he could squeeze them shut. Then he was falling, and felt water around him again, and the rough, scaled hide of the Crayx.

Parno was alone when he woke up. Really alone, no one in the room with him, no Crayx sharing the mental space in his head. The first night after his rescue, after he'd shut the door in Darlara Cor's face when she'd tried to come into the cabin with him, he'd tossed and shifted until he'd finally gotten up and gone on deck. There the *Wave-treader* Crayx had spoken with him, gently, and finally he had allowed them to smooth the sharp edge from his grief at least enough to allow him to sleep.

Last night, he hadn't even tried to sleep in his own bunk but had rolled himself in Dhulyn's bedding—and fallen asleep almost immediately. Her blankets still smelled of her, that unquantifiable essence that told the deep layers of his mind that she was still here, that he did not need to stay awake and keep watch. He had not dreamed of her again, not after surfacing from the belly of the Crayx. He wasn't sure whether or not he wished to.

He noted the amount of light that entered through the larboard shutters and briefly considered simply rolling over again and going back to sleep. But something told him that if he did, he'd find his dreams invaded by the Crayx. For all that he didn't wish to succumb to the offer made by *Skydancer* Pod, for all that he wasn't ready to die until he could figure out how that would allow him to join Dhulyn, he couldn't just lie here. He had to do *something*.

But when he finally rolled out of the bunk, straightened the clothing he'd somehow neglected to take off, and pushed his fingers through his hair, sweeping it back from his face, he found that his determination had deserted him. There would be people out on deck, and they would speak to him. And even if they did not, he would see that look on their faces. The look that said "We are sorry," "We are here for you," "We understand." When they couldn't possibly understand.

And not just the looks. If he went out and joined them, he could *feel* them, their compassion, and their pity echoing his own sense of loss back to him. And underneath it, a sense of puzzlement, as some in the Pod wondered why so much fuss was being made over what they saw as a temporary loss. To the Nomads, their afterlife was concrete and real—it swam beside them every day, and in some sense shared their lives. Oddly, it was only the young man Conford, the one who'd been tricked into jumping him that first day, who looked at Parno with any real understanding in his eyes.

No. Much better to stay in the cabin. His glance fell on Dhulyn's packs, neatly placed, ties tied, straps strapped. All according to the Common Rule and the dictates of her own personal neatness. Carefully not thinking too deeply about what he was doing, Parno opened the pack nearest him. Much of their heavier gear had been left behind in Lesonika with the horses—Parno grimaced. He wasn't looking forward to what he would say to Bloodbone when the mare realized he had come back without her mistress.

If he made it back. He might figure out how to join Dhulyn before that. In Battle and in Death. That's what he was counting on.

He smiled, lifting out Dhulyn's second-best sword. Its balance was off by a hair—not enough to bother anyone else, but enough that any Mercenary Brother would notice it. He laid it to one side. A short sword with a very elaborate guard. Seven throwing knives. Her spare dagger. Two wrist knives, one of Teliscan make. A dozen steel arrow shafts. Two dozen crossbow bolts. A short double-recurve bow, taken to pieces for traveling, and the tools to reassemble it. Likewise a crossbow.

And a small olive wood box in a velvet bag so old much of the nap had worn away. Typical that Dhulyn kept it in among her weapons.

"Sun, Moon, and Stars," he said, unconsciously using his Partner's favorite expletives. He slipped off the velvet bag and stroked his fingers along the wood grain. Dhulyn's vera tiles. Not the ones she would use for gambling, but a set with extra tiles. The set she used to focus her Sight.

Parno sat back on his heels. *That* was what had been nagging at him since he'd regained consciousness in the belly of the Crayx. Dhulyn was a Seer, why hadn't she Seen what was coming? She'd even used the vera tiles several times on board without his prompting her. Usually he had to nag her.

Had she Seen this outcome? Was this the *real* reason she'd tried to stay off the *Wavetreader*? Had she Seen her own death?

But then, why hadn't she told him? Parno scratched at the beard growing in along his jaw. *Demons and perverts.* He would have let Huelra die, and his blooded crew along with him—

Why didn't she tell him?

Parno picked up the box and threw it across the cabin. It bounced against the wall with such force that it popped open, scattering tiles all over the floor.

The full horror of it swept over him in one clear wave of comprehension. What was the one thing he had made her swear, over and over, on their Brotherhood, on their Partnership, *never* to tell him? It hadn't been her own death Dhulyn had seen, but *his*. And somehow, she had *not* Seen that the Crayx would save him.

And that meant that Dhulyn had saved Huelra and his crew, had jumped into the sea herself, rather than break her oath to him. Just for that, nothing else. Parno let his head fall into his hands. This was too much. How could he live having caused her death?

But had he? Now he knew the reason for her odd behavior, her watchfulness, and her occasional abstraction. They'd seen the outcomes of Visions change before—perhaps this one, too, might not have come to pass.

Except for the Storm Witch.

Parno knew the storm that had killed Dhulyn Wolfshead was no natural occurrence—and he knew who and what to blame for his Partner's death. And what to do about it before he joined her.

He was just placing the last tile back into the box when Captain Malfin Cor knocked—and Parno grimaced when he realized he'd known who it was without asking. He didn't want this, any of this. He just wanted to be left alone to take his vengeance. But he was beginning to realize that among the Nomads—as part of the Pod—you were never alone.

"Lionsmane," came Malfin's voice. "Sit in council. Join us, please." Now Parno could hear all the missing pronouns, the "we," the "you," that the Nomads took for granted, since they could not mistake one another. He heaved another great sigh, placed Dhulyn's tiles in the center of her bunk, and opened the door, blinking at the light, though the day was still gray with cloud that hung heavy and hot overhead.

Familiar as Parno was with councils both political and military, he was unprepared for how quickly the Nomads came to order, and how thorough was the silence which fell over the crowded deck. As before, younger children were sent below, out of the way, but this time Parno could sense that their minders were linked through the Crayx with the rest of the crew.

Crews, he realized. *Skydancer Pod was also present, though he could see neither Crayx nor what was left of the damaged ship. Skydancer* itself was on its crippled way south and east, Parno picked up the thought, to be repaired in one of the havens where the landlocked Nomads lived.

His Pod sense was much stronger now, and Parno could hear and follow the buzz of thoughts much more easily than he could when the two ships had come together before the waterspout had struck. Before Dhulyn had been swept away and drowned. Parno took that thought and pushed it deep. He wasn't going to share that with anyone. Trying to focus outward instead of in, as if he was pushing notes through the chanter of his pipes, Parno found he could make out individual thoughts, as well as individual people such as Darlara and Malfin. He caught a warming glimpse of the great Crayx who had saved him. Behind these surface thoughts was a buzzing, a hum that tickled at his brain, as though he brushed up against a giant purring lion in the dark.

Darlara motioned him to a seat near her, and he nodded his thanks as he took it. It was not her fault that he was alone. She laid her fingertips lightly against his wrist, and he forced himself not to flinch away. Fortunately, at that moment, there was an unmistakable call for attention, and all the Nomads became even more focused and more silent than they had been a moment before, like an audience when the prologue stepped in front of the curtain.

#Three currents flow from this spot# came the clearest thought, giving Parno the impression of great age and size. #First, we can complete the original passage, bearing the Paledyn Parno Lionsmane# here, Parno sensed a picture of himself that was partly visual, partly the sound of piping #to the Mortaxa as we said we would#

#Second, the Treader Pods can abandon that portion of the land entirely, and attempt to establish new spawning grounds, and new trading treaties, perhaps with the landsters of the other side of the Long Ocean in Boravia or the northern continent# There was a feeling of unrest from the greater group, but no one else spoke. #This would be difficult, but it can be done# the first voice acknowledged.

#Finally, we can hold the Mortaxa to account for what they have done, and somehow carry the offensive into their currents#

The hum returned, as arguments and counterarguments crossed, as support for each of the three ideas and suggestions for the final one flowed back and forth through the shared consciousness. Parno stopped paying attention. Regardless of what the Pod decided, he knew which course of action he would follow. Finally, the tension of the buzzing changed, as the argument swelled, pulling Parno out of his own thoughts and back into the collective.

Not enough to leave the lands of the Mortaxa, we must go farther This was a human speaking; the thoughts felt younger and smaller. #We could withdraw entirely, leave the land to the landsters#

Demons and perverts, Parno thought, shaking his head, not caring who could hear him.

#What says the Paledyn Parno Lionsmane#

"Think you heard me," he said, reinforcing the uncertain power of his Pod sense by speaking the words aloud. "If you'd read any history, any politics, you'd know they're both filled with the stories of people who were exiled—or who exiled themselves. Withdrawal doesn't solve this kind of problem, it just postpones it. The Mortaxa won't leave you be, even if they agree to do it, which they haven't. They're not even abiding by the agreements you have with them now."

#Parno Lionsmane is correct# came the thought from that oldest presence. #When the landsters did not know of, or did not believe in our existence, they hunted us like animals# #We were in great danger from them, and it would be that way again# #In turning away from the land, we turn away from The First Agreement and our troubles will increase rather than decrease#

#Nor is it right and fair to our human parts to turn away entirely from the land# came another thought. #What of our kin in the havens—do we abandon them as well#

Parno felt a wave of bewildered confusion, touched through with despair.

"There's a current you haven't thought of," he said. The right thing to do was so obvious to him he was surprised that no one else had suggested it. From first meeting them in the hold of the *Catseye*, he had found the Nomads ready to fight, and they'd often spoken of their skirmishes and even their wars with the landsters over trade issues. They'd been quick enough to challenge him and Dhulyn in Lesonika, and the Crayx were ready to destroy ships that trespassed on their oceans. But then, that was all defensive thinking, wasn't it? Perhaps it took a Mercenary Brother to suggest how they could go on the offensive.

"What do you propose?" It was odd to hear Malfin's voice echo in both his ears and his mind.

"Kill the Storm Witch."

The beings around him fell silent again.

The new discussion continued well into the afternoon and evening, though most of the group had found Parno's suggestion to their liking. The general feeling seemed to be that once the Witch was removed, their relationship with the Mortaxa would return to what it had been before her coming.

Parno did his best to show them that wouldn't be true either. "They're already building ships," he pointed out. "And thinking about travel and trading on their own accounts. They claim they can produce a lodestone. These are the types of ideas that don't merely go away." The fox had been shown the henhouse, and it would be very difficult to make it forget what it knew. But his words went unheard, and eventually he stopped, keeping any further thoughts or suggestions to himself. *What does it matter what they do?* he thought, eyeing the door to his cabin and thinking of his bunk with longing. Truth was, he found it blooded hard to care what the Nomads and the Crayx decided. Or whether this would solve their present problems, or give them entirely new ones to worry about.

Parno Lionsmane had his own reasons for wanting the Storm Witch dead. Reasons that had nothing to do with the Nomads, the Crayx, the Mortaxa, *or* their blooded trading problems. The Storm Witch had killed his Partner, his soul, and for that, she would die.

Parno rubbed his face, massaging the crease that formed between his eyebrows while Darlara uncurled the map and adjusted the woven straps that would hold it flat on the table. The Pods had finally decided to accept his idea. And when Malfin and Darlara had suggested he lead them, the assent was close to unanimous.

"Choose someone else," he'd said, weary beyond thinking. But they had persisted, and finally he'd asked for maps. He'd said neither yes nor no, but the first thing any commander would need was information.

The shutters of the cabin's two windows were closed against the gusts of wind that threatened to put out the lamps. The parchments Mal was pulling out of the cupboard under the bunks were very old, much older than the charts kept available on the wall shelves. Their inks were faded, and many showed a dark mark along one edge, as if they had at one time been kept next to a store of oil. When Parno had declared the nautical charts useless for his purpose, it had taken Malfin a moment or two, and a nudge from the Crayx, to remember that these seldom-used maps were even on board.

Does this show the detail you need? Darlara tapped an area of shoreline marked with green dots. *This is the spawning ground—*

Parno held up one hand, still massaging his eyes with the fingertips of the other. "Can you stop that, please?"

"Don't want to exclude the Crayx."

"Not asking you to exclude them." *Blood, now I'm doing it.* "I'm just asking you to exclude me. My head's banging like a drum. And is there anything to drink in here?"

He felt the other two look at each other before the link connecting them all was abruptly severed. A queer emptiness echoed in his head.

"Didn't practice this morning," Darlara said with the air of someone diagnosing a problem. "Nor yesterday."

Parno gripped the edge of the table with both hands and let his breath out slowly. "My Partner's dead," he said, the words falling like lead from his mouth. "Who do you suggest I practice with?"

Darlara opened her mouth, but Parno never learned what her answer would have been. Malfin straightened from digging into the storage cupboards under his bunk and put his hand on his twin's arm.

"Who'd you practice with before Partnering? Or, say, when a Mercenary Brother's alone, who'd they practice with?"

Parno shrugged one shoulder and turned his eyes back to the faded lines of the map on the table.

Lionsmane As much as he wanted to ignore it, the touch of minds with the twins standing together so close to him was stronger than he could push away.

"Lionsmane, if you grow soft and weak, how will you lead us? How

kill the Storm Witch?" Parno looked up to see the two strangely similar faces staring down at him. For a moment, he wasn't sure which of
them had spoken. They were out of his mind again, now that he was
paying attention.

"Your plan, isn't it? *Your* suggestion that all agreed to and follow.
Will be of no use to us, or to yourself, if go on this way."

He went on looking at them, a sour feeling in his belly. He knew
they were right. Whatever else had happened, he was still a Mercenary
Brother; *that* he had not lost. The Common Rule still held him, still
guided him. He looked down at the map again, back up at them, and
unclenched his jaw. "I'll sleep now." He slid himself out from the table.
"Tomorrow, first watch, you get me three fighters."

He made his way out the door, staggering across the heaving deck to
his own cabin, and fell into Dhulyn's bunk like a dead man.

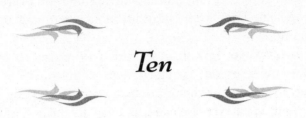

Ten

"**N**o."

"But, Dhulyn Wolfshead, this is the only proper way for someone of your status to travel." Remm Shalyn was so agitated that for an instant Dhulyn considered giving in. Then she remembered that the two sturdy bearers standing next to the sedan chair were slaves and her resolve hardened.

"What is my status, exactly?"

Remm and the Feld House Steward of Keys—it was unclear to Dhulyn whether this man was slave or free—eyed one another, each clearly hoping the other would speak.

"I would say very high, Tara Paledyn," the Steward finally said. "The Paledyns are Hands of the Slain God, and in the old chronicles sat only under the Tarxin, Light of the Sun, himself."

Like a Jaldean High Priest, Dhulyn thought. "If my status is truly as high as this," she said, "then surely I may do as I please, since you could not be expected to stop me. And I tell you for certain, I will not ride in *that*." She eyed the sedan chair and its waiting slaves with distaste. She'd already learned that there were no horses available. Not here in House Feld, nor anywhere else this side of the Long Ocean. Oh, the Mortaxa knew what horses were, but there hadn't been any in these lands since the times of the Caids. Something, some illness or some act of the Slain God had destroyed them all generations before. When attempts had been made to bring horses from Boravia, they would sicken and die within days of arrival—those that survived the trip at all. Dhulyn had let the subject drop.

Remm Shalyn and the Steward were still hovering between her and the chair.

"Remm Shalyn and I will walk," she said. "It can't take any longer than being carried."

The two men remained silent, Remm carefully looking past her and the Steward examining the ground next to her feet.

"What now?" she said. "Surely even the Tarxin—" she paused to allow them time to say "Light of the Sun," "—occasionally walks?"

"But Tara Paledyn," the Steward finally choked out. "You must take *some* servants with you. Otherwise, how will you be known for what you are?" His eyes flicked at her Mercenary badge and quickly away. "From a distance, I mean, Tara, of course."

"He's right," Remm said. "Walking you can excuse as an eccentricity, but to be otherwise unaccompanied—" he shook his head. "We'll be stopped by every guard, to say nothing of every Steward and lesser noble, between here and the city."

Dhulyn let a heavy sigh escape through her nose. It was all she could do not to roll her eyes to the Sun. "What is the minimum number I must take," she said, only to spark off another debate between Remm Shalyn and the Steward. At least, with Remm to advise her, Dhulyn was able to limit her entourage to those servants healthy enough to keep pace with her, even with her sore leg.

Finally, Remm judged that they were ready to leave. Besides Remm Shalyn himself there were the two chair men who would now function as load carriers, a young boy to use as page and runner, and two women who could serve her as maids, cook her food, and carry the shade that would protect Dhulyn from the sun.

"No," she said again. "No sunshade." They couldn't possibly carry it and keep up. When she explained to the older of the women what she wanted instead, the younger was sent off and returned with a large square of linen, rather too heavily embroidered for the purpose, but serviceable. With a silk sash Dhulyn knotted and wound, she fashioned the linen square into a draping headdress such as was worn in the Berdanan desert. She touched the embroidery on her tunic where she'd hidden the lockpicks she'd taken from her ruined vest. She'd transfer some into her headdress as soon as she was alone.

When she saw the size of the packs the men were expected to carry, she shook her head again.

"I understand there are no horses, but surely there are other beasts which can be used as pack animals? What about that thing in the courtyard yesterday?"

"True, the kinglera are large enough," Remm said. "But only the males are both large and strong enough, and unfortunately, as you saw yesterday, they lack the temperament—they can't be broken to household use. The females are more docile, but they are much smaller and weaker."

Besides, Dhulyn thought. *When you have slaves, why should you breed better animals?*

Finally, the Steward, after requesting permission, presented her with a small handcart. This, too, would slow them down, but Dhulyn agreed because most of the load the two men and the boy would carry was food. They would bring all they needed with them, since it would be unheard of for them to hunt on what was, after all, private property.

"All the way from here to the city," Dhulyn said. "All the land is owned?"

"Whatever isn't part of House or Holding belongs to the Tarxin, Light of the Sun, of course."

"Of course." Dhulyn tried to keep the sarcasm from her voice. Technically, the whole of any country belonged to the ruler, Tarxin, or Galan, or King. But in practice, very few rulers tried to enforce their control over vast regions of empty land. Apparently, the Tarxin of the Mortaxa felt differently.

Loraxin Feld came out himself to bid her a formal farewell.

More likely to make sure I'm really going, she thought. The man was still white around the eyes from the "accident" of the day before. Dhulyn had let him know that under no circumstances was he to accompany her to her audience with the Tarxin.

"Remm Shalyn tells me you are ready to leave us, Tara Paledyn." Loraxin licked his lips.

When Dhulyn did no more than incline her head, the man swallowed and looked ill. "Let there be shade on your journey and cool water, and may you arrive in good health." The words were barely whispered.

Dhulyn decided to take pity on the man. "I will give the Tarxin your best wishes, and tell him that you have treated me well." Her voice must have carried some sincerity at least, for Loraxin began to look less as though he would lose his breakfast. "These servants," she added, "they are mine?"

The man turned so pale as to show a tinge of green. "Of course, Tara Paledyn, of course."

Lucky I don't ask for the rest of them, she thought, smiling her wolf's smile.

Despite the delays, they still had most of the morning ahead of them when they finally set out. Their general heading was northeast, away from where Dhulyn had come out of the water, but toward, as Remm Shalyn explained it, the shoreline of another sea. It was clear, however, when she questioned him more closely, that he had very little idea of the oceans that surrounded the land, and how they connected. The land, on the other hand, he knew well.

"We'll be until midafternoon walking through the plains that surround House Feld, and then we'll see the Arxden Forest in front of us. Feld maintains a guesthouse there just as the trees begin where we should spend the night." Remm eyed the servants with them. "It'll take us most of the day tomorrow, maybe longer, to get through the forest."

"It seems a hot place to find a forest."

"Trees more than you can number, taller than buildings, what else would you call it? These are all old growth trees, preserved for the production of fressian moss, from which House Feld derives most of its income, as you may imagine."

Dhulyn nodded without saying anything more. She had more experience than many with the properties of the expensive drugs made from fressian moss.

"Tell me what I can expect at the court of the Tarxin. The ruler himself, of course . . ."

"And Tar Xerwin, the only surviving heir. The last Tarxina, the third wife, died a year ago, trying to produce a son of her own, it's been said, and the Tarxin, Light of the Sun, hasn't remarried . . . yet. But rumors have it that his health's beginning to fail. It was Tar Xerwin who was betrothed last year, not his father."

Dhulyn smiled. Wherever he got it from, Remm's irreverent attitude was a relief compared to the constant bowing and fussing of the others. He seemed even more relaxed now that he was working for her, and readier to talk.

How and what do I pay him, she wondered.

"Tara Xendra, she's the third wife's daughter. Rumor has it that, since her accident six months ago, she's become a Holy Woman, or a Weather Mage—though who knows really. Some say *she's* the one behind the discovery of the lodestone, but I don't see how *that* could be. Maybe she's Marked and they're just trying to keep her out of the Sanctuary. No official announcement's been made in any case. But you'll probably have the most to do with the Council of Houses, and the Priests of the Slain God."

Dhulyn nodded, but her thoughts had run down another path. So it was the Tarxin's own daughter, Xendra, who was the Storm Witch. That would make a hard job even harder.

"The Marked live in Sanctuaries?" she had the presence of mind to ask when she realized Remm had stopped speaking.

"How else could we be sure their talents are kept available for all and are being used wisely?" Remm gave her a wide-eyed innocent look and Dhulyn found herself smiling before she remembered she had nothing to smile about.

"And the Slain God?" she said.

Remm Shalyn became instantly serious and moved closer to her, lowering his voice. "As a Hand of the Slain God, you're obviously not a heretic yourself, Dhulyn Wolfshead. Heresy is technically legal, but unbelievers generally find themselves losing status. Most guards and the military and the Tarxin, Light of the Sun, follow the Slain One. We go to him when we die, ready to rise with him when the need comes. Some say the Nomad crisis will cause him to rise, but I say they should stop smoking fresa."

But Dhulyn had already relaxed. "We call him the Sleeping God," she said. "Soldiers and Mercenary Brothers follow him in Boravia as well. You mentioned the military—what of them?"

"The Battle Wings are stationed at outposts along the frontiers, with two training camps in the east. The Tarxin is the official Commander, but it's been Tar Xerwin's responsibility since he came to manhood. He's very popular with the men, so it's said, but they can't come closer than ten days' march of Ketxan City, so much good that would do him if he fell out with his father."

"No military in the capital itself, then?"

"The Light of the Sun's personal guard is the only official armed force in the City. The Houses have guards and escorts, naturally, but there are strict limits as to how many, and how they can be armed."

Shortly past midday, with the Arxden Forest in sight, Dhulyn called a halt for food. An outcropping of rock was tall enough to give them shade, and there were several boulders of a convenient size for sitting. Once she'd chosen the spot, however, she found she had to allow the servants to set up her own seat first, with Remm allowed—somewhat grudgingly, it seemed—to sit near her. No other seats were prepared, and at first it seemed the servants intended to stand for the whole time. When she couldn't persuade either the women or the two men to sit down with her, Dhulyn finally ordered them to sit apart in another section of shade to get at least some rest while they enjoyed their own meal. Even then there was some shuffling of feet and uncertain glances from the young page.

"If you don't rest, you won't be able to help me later on," Dhulyn pointed out finally. That did the trick, and she was able to sit down comfortably and drink her juice mixed with wine and eat smoked duck legs.

"What about a leasr House, like Loraxin Feld?" she said, after washing down the first of the duck. "Would he have a seat on the Council?"

Remm snorted, speaking around a mouthful of duck. "Not likely. Even though it's called the Council of Houses, it's really limited to the Great Houses, and they are very watchful over who belongs. Under them would be the lesser Houses, then least, the plain landowners, merchants, and so on—and it's not always easy to tell which is which. Loraxin Feld, for example, his family started out as merchants. They've only been a House for five or six generations, and believe me, no one forgets it. Finally, there are the tradesmen, usually family connections of a least House or landowner, or soldiers such as myself."

"And then, below everyone else, the slaves." He nodded.

"Speaking of which, what is the process for freeing them?" she asked.

Remm paused, a dried date stuffed with cheese halfway to his mouth. "Freeing them?"

"Yes, what documents do I need, what clerk do I bribe. You know, the process by which I can free these people, for example?" She gestured with her free hand to the other patch of shade.

"You want to free them?"

"Yes."

"Why?"

Dhulyn studied Remm Shalyn's face. He watched her with a measured expression. "I disapprove of the practice of slavery," she said finally.

To her surprise, Remm burst out laughing, slapping his knee with the hand that didn't have a wine cup in it. "You remind me of my great-aunt Tella. Married above herself and made up for it by having just that prim way of speaking. 'I disapprove.' " He laughed again.

Dhulyn lifted one eyebrow. No one had ever called her prim before. "You haven't answered my question."

Remm leaned forward, elbows on knees, turning the empty cup around in his fingers. Dhulyn waited. She knew a man thinking when she saw one. And she'd wager her second-best sword she knew what he was thinking about. Trust her, or not? Nothing she could say would help him decide. He'd have to come to his own conclusion, based on whatever he already knew about her.

"It's highly illegal to help a slave to his freedom. Or her freedom, for that matter." Remm stopped turning the cup, but he did not look up. "The penalty for doing so is—"

"Let me guess, slavery." At least he looked at her then, if only fleetingly. "There are no freedmen, then, in Mortaxa?"

"*Freed*men? Who would feed them? How could they live?"

"Having prepared me with this warning, what is your true answer?"

"There are those who feel as you do. They . . ." Remm looked directly at her, grinning. "They disapprove of the practice. There is a group. Runaways are helped. Some go by sea—though none of those by my hands, mine all go by land. There are lands to the south, beyond the mountains, where men can live free." He shrugged. "It's said Tar Xerwin's latest campaigns have been to the foothills, trying to find the source of the help that's been coming to the slaves."

Dhulyn eyed him carefully. "That's what *you're* doing, hiring out to these Houses, here in the outlands, helping slaves escape."

He shrugged again, grinning at her.

"My arrival, my taking you away, must be upsetting your plans."

Remm straightened, looking around at the plate of food, and offering Dhulyn the last stuffed date. "We can't free slaves everywhere we go, or it would be noticed. I don't mind going somewhere I haven't been before. I can renew old acquaintances, perhaps make some new ones."

"And you have a way to recognize one another." She waved the food away.

"We do." Remm popped the date into his mouth and chewed. Slowly.

And he obviously was not going to tell her anything more. Dhulyn began to laugh—only to stop short, her breath stopping in her throat. How could she be laughing? Only hours ago, it had seemed impossible that she would ever laugh again.

She nodded once more in the direction of the other patch of shade, where the servants—no, the slaves—waited for her to finish her lunch. "And these? How badly are they *really* needed to maintain my status?"

"We could manage," Remm said. "A Paledyn, with one sword servant—but not everyone wishes to be freed. And they *all* must agree."

Dhulyn shook her head. "Don't tell me you didn't give that careful thought when you were picking out which ones would come with us. When would it have to be done?"

"Tomorrow. There are ways out of the fressian forest. We can arrange it tonight."

Xerwin found it harder than he'd expected to find Kendraxa. He'd been able to establish pretty quickly through his own servants that the woman was still in the House, but her exact whereabouts had not been so easy to pinpoint. It was not until the next afternoon that the Royal House Steward himself brought Xerwin the information that Kendraxa was now to be found in the Tarxina's apartments, empty since the death of the Tarxin's last wife. Xerwin had not been in his stepmother's rooms since the woman's death the year before. He found Kendraxa at a northern window, embroidering a red headdress with golden thread.

"Please, do not trouble yourself," he said as the woman hastened to rise to her feet as he entered the room. When had she become so old? He'd always thought of Kendraxa as no older than his stepmother had been, perhaps ten years older than himself. Today she looked thinner, more tired, and with more lines around her eyes than she should have. He took the seat across from her, noting that even when she was alone in the apartments, Kendraxa had taken the lesser chair.

"Are you comfortable here? You've been so long with my sister."

"I am. I thank you, Tar Xerwin. You won't remember, no reason you should, but I lived in these rooms with the Tarxina before the Tara Xendra was born, so they're familiar to me, you might say." Still, there was something subdued in her tone.

Now that it came to the moment, Xerwin hesitated. How could he ask what he'd come to ask?

"I don't think my father has ever punished Xendra this way before," he said finally, trying to keep his smile sympathetic. "Though it's hard to say which of you would feel the more deprived."

"Indeed." Kendraxa's eyes had returned to the work in her hands. The needle gleamed in the sunlight streaming in the window.

Xerwin leaned forward, his elbows on his knees. "I saw my sister yesterday," he said. "Or rather, I saw the Tara Xendra."

Kendraxa's hands stilled, the needle halfway though a stitch. *She knows*, he thought.

"How long?" he asked. "Come, you can tell me." He saw her consider it, and thought it a mark of the woman's desperate isolation that she chose to answer.

"Since the accident," she said, her fingers pulling the thread through the stitch. "Or rather, since the Marked saw to her, the Healer and Finder. When she finally came to herself . . ." Kendraxa's lips trembled.

"She was not herself."

The woman inclined her head, just once. "At first, I couldn't be sure; after such a fall, some confusion was only to be expected. So the Healer said. And I so hoped—" Kendraxa pressed her trembling lips tight for a moment before she continued. "But she only became more watchful, more cautious in what she said. Xendra was always ready to talk about herself, the Slain One knows." Kendraxa's smile was hard to see. "And her smile, so ready, so joyous. But this one," she shook her head, "this one asked too many questions, and studied the answers to things Xendra knew very well. And once or twice, in the night, she called out in a language I have never heard."

Xerwin stared at his clasped hands, saw the knuckles standing out white.

"What do you think happened?"

"Can I know? I'm a lady page, Tar Xerwin, you can guess what my education has been." She shrugged, half holding out the embroidery in her hands as evidence of what she said.

"I know you for nobody's fool, whatever your education might be," he said. "An emptyhead is not chosen as companion for a Tarxina, nor as nurse for a young Tara. Tell me what you think."

Something in his tone—or in his face—must have convinced her. She licked her lips. "How much do you remember, did you know, of your sister's illness?"

Xerwin thought. "She fell from the wall around the palace precinct, injuring her head. She was unconscious for many days. I remember you crying." He glanced up. There were tears in Kendraxa's eyes now. "The Healer came from the Sanctuary, and then she was getting better."

"You didn't know about the Finder?"

Xerwin shrugged. "I knew the Healer had come with both a Mender and a Finder. I assumed that was part of their normal practice."

"They told your father the Tarxin, Light of the Sun, that your sister's spirit was missing from her body. Your father told them to find it."

"And the Finder Found . . ." Xerwin didn't really need Kendraxa's nod to answer him.

"Someone's spirit, that's certain. But Xendra's? Not so far as I can see."

Xerwin's hands formed into fists. "How can I tell my father?"

He felt Kendraxa's fingertips on his arm. "Tar Xerwin, your father already knows."

"Put up your swords!"

As the man to his right stepped back, Parno flicked out with the point of his right-hand sword and opened a cut the length of his first knuckle in the man's right pectoral muscle, where it would bleed but do no harm.

"Lionsmane, stop. You will kill someone at this rate."

No voice but Darlara's would have reached him through the concentration of the Mirror *Shora*. Parno blinked, licked away a trickle of sweat that neared his mouth. There was another voice that could have reached him, but he would never hear that one again. He stuck his left-hand sword into the wood of the deck and smoothed his oiled hair away from his face.

He glanced around at the three fighters Darlara had chosen for him. A man of his own age, Deniss showed a white swatch of hair from an old scalp cut and wore the scaled jerkin. The other two were women, Tindar and Elian, clearly twins, as alike as two grains of sand. And now even more alike as he had given each of them identical cuts, on their right collarbones. All three were pale and sweating, breathing hard.

A chink of metal to his left and Parno spun, both swords up, and took a step toward the sound before he realized it was unarmed crew who backed away from him, wide-eyed people with the money they'd been wagering in their hands.

"Can't have you killing people, Lionsmane," Darlara said.

"None of them are dead." Parno looked around, but she was alone. Her brother must be off watch. He lowered his swords again and straightened.

Dar shook her head. "Nevertheless. Teach them to move as you do, or find some way to even the match. Five people? You unarmed?"

Parno took in a great lungful of air and let it out slowly. He was tempted to say he wouldn't bother with the sparring at all, that they should leave him alone. He couldn't face another day of staring at the maps and drawings Malfin Cor had found for him and seeing nothing more than colored lines and meaningless shapes. He rubbed the bridge of his nose between thumb and forefinger. What was so difficult about this decision? What was so important? What matter of life or death hinged on it?

His gaze dropped to the hilt of the Teliscan blade he had in his left hand. In his mind he saw Dhulyn's face when she'd given it to him. Just after Arcosa, it had been, when they'd decided to Partner. But the expression he saw her wearing now wasn't the one she'd had then. Now she was showing him her wolf's smile. His hand closed tightly enough that he could feel the steel tang under the corded grip of the sword. He had a score to settle. A reason to stay alive. He'd almost forgotten.

The Storm Witch.

Darlara and Malfin were right. To get to the Witch, to defeat her, he needed a clear head. If nothing else, a workout would help him sleep, and sleep would clear the clouds and cobwebs from his brain.

After a moment, he said, "Get me a blindfold, then."

At the edge of his senses, Parno could feel the communication going on between the crew members as those watching used their Pod sense to summon those still below.

"Captain." It was the older man. "Done for this morning. Be excused."

Darlara nodded. "Done, Deniss. You two?"

The twins grinned, showing identical gaps in their front teeth. "Like to try him blindfolded," said one, as the other nodded. Parno felt an answering grin on his own lips.

"Deniss," he called the older man to him. "Hold this for me, will you?" He handed Deniss his sword and pulled the long dagger from the back of his belt. Two swords *or* a blindfold he could manage. Just now he had his doubts about two swords *and* a blindfold.

The Hunter's *Shora*, one of the basic twenty-seven taught to all Mercenary Brothers, was a little *too* basic for this fight, Parno thought. It taught you to feel the direction of the wind on your skin, to move without making noise enough to frighten a mouse. But to be blindfolded he needed something more than that. He needed the Stalking Cat *Shora*. In addition to stealth, the Stalking Cat would give him heightened senses beyond what the basic Hunter's could do. If he was blindfolded, he would need to locate each opponent by their smell, feel every shift of air, hear the movement of clothing, of weapons. Dhulyn said that, properly done, the Stalking Cat would allow you to feel the beat of your opponent's heart.

And in addition to the Stalking Cat, the Crab *Shora* for the shifting of the deck, and for, Parno bared his teeth, the large claw he had in his right hand and the smaller one in his left.

A third fighter had stepped forward to replace Deniss, a tall, clean-shaven youth with the marks of frostbite on his cheeks. He carried a shorter sword than the twins did, Parno noted automatically, one with a slight curve which would be sharp along that edge.

"Conford, isn't it?" Parno said, recognizing him. "Hope you're not as angry as you were. Anger's no reliable ally in a fight."

Conford inclined his head. "Keep that in mind, Mercenary Brother."

Darlara pulled a silken sash from around her waist and approached him with it held up in her hands. Parno went down on one knee.

"Give me a moment," he said, loud enough that all could hear him.

"Keep the watchers well back. I'll stand when I am ready to begin. Attack from any direction, but be so good as to come at me one at a time." He waited until his three opponents had nodded before closing his eyes and tilting his head up for the blindfold.

Darlara's fingers were cold on his skin as she wrapped the sash around his eyes twice, tying it at the back of his skull. As she moved away, Parno began to repeat to himself the trigger words of the Stalking Cat *Shora*. The first thing he felt, even before he began to breathe slowly, was the presence of the Crayx, like the hum of a crowd in the distance. Parno shut them out of his conscious thought as his heartbeat slowed, and he pricked up his ears, flared his nostrils. His skin shivered as the hairs on his arms and the back of his neck stood up.

The deck rose and fell beneath his feet. The wind came from . . . there; with it on his left cheek, he was facing aft. The twins Tindar and Elian stood to his left, their drying sweat making them easy to locate and identify. They were slightly closer together than they were to Conford, who was behind him and to his right. From the gurgle of his stomach, the man had not eaten yet this morning.

Parno rose to his feet, and in the same movement, feeling the rush of air, raised his right arm, sword in the guard position and heard/felt the jar as his blade met Conford's and the blow's weight shivered through his arm bones. He heard the man's grunt, and the drawing in of a dozen breaths. Parno pushed off with his left foot, spinning, and bringing his left hand around to where the other blade must be, to catch it with the guard of his dagger, twisting and pulling it out of his opponent's hands.

There was a gasp from the crowd of watchers as the sword fell free and clattered to the deck. From the sound, several had had to step back out of the way.

The twin sisters smelled different now, their sweat was fear sharp. They had moved apart, but thanks to the wind, and the Stalking Cat *Shora*, Parno was able to point to the right-hand one with his sword, and the left-hand one with his dagger.

"One down," he said. "Two to go."

Apparently, the twins felt that the loss of one for their side freed them to attack together, or perhaps, Parno thought, they simply could not break themselves of the habit. In either case, it worked in his favor. Even sightless, he knew that anything he struck was an enemy, and even sighted, they had to take care not to hit each other. There was no movement of air, so they ran forward with blades raised. In the last possible moment Parno ducked, rolled forward, and heard with satisfaction the sound of their bodies colliding.

An unexpected calm fell over Parno as he rolled to his feet and spun around to face in the direction of the twins. Even as he trusted to his timing, lunging forward and kicking out, knocking one of them over and apparently—judging from the sound—into the other one as they tried to get up, he could feel the *Shora* working through him, calming him with its familiar touch. A tightness he had not been aware of loosened, and he felt freer, more alive, and somehow more himself than he had done since the storm.

A shift of air, a rasp as a foot slid along the wood of the deck before being lifted clear. Conford had found his weapon again. Parno spun toward the noise, his own sword at high guard, dagger at low. Conford's sword was a slashing weapon, and the chances were he'd bring it down, or across from . . . there! Parno parried, stepped quickly within the man's reach and elbowed him in the face. He felt the contact, and smelled the blood as it burst from Conford's nose. A shuffle behind him, he ducked, bringing Conford down with him as the swords of the twins sliced through the air where he'd been standing.

"Enough," Darlara said.

Parno pulled off the blindfold and wiped his face with it. He touched his forehead to each of his opponents, just as if they had been Mercenary Brothers, and set off across the deck.

Parno looked up as the door of the cabin swung open, letting in cool sunlight filtered through streaky clouds. Darlara Cor came in and closed the door behind her, leaning against it and folding her arms across her chest. Parno almost smiled, reminded of one of his sisters. He was wiping the swords he'd used with an oiled cloth.

"Was a good workout," he said. "Thank you for suggesting it. Ready whenever you are to examine those maps."

Darlara stayed silent and, except for the tapping of her left index finger against her right elbow, she didn't move. Parno stowed the extra sword and turned to meet her eyes. They seemed darker than usual in her heart-shaped face, her full mouth set in a thin, firm line.

"Promised me a child."

Parno felt the muscles in his jaw tighten as he gritted his teeth. *Demons!* The woman couldn't be serious. In the face of his loss—his Partner and, in a very real way, his future, since he could not imagine surviving his vengeance. No. Some of the calm that the *Shora* had brought him melted away. It was too much that he should be asked to consider the future of others. But he could tell from the set planes of her face that Darlara was very serious indeed.

"Can't," was all he could finally bring himself to say.

"Say you can't. Mean you won't."

"At the moment it's the same thing."

But she was already shaking her head. She let her arms fall to her sides and stepped forward enough to lean against the table. "Not so. Gave your word, to me, to the Pod. Is it worth nothing? That's not what we've come to believe."

Demons and perverts. Parno slammed his open hands down on the table. Darlara blinked, but did not back away.

"Anger changes nothing."

And the worst of it was, she was right. His anger would not bring Dhulyn back, would not restore the world to rightness. In fact, much as he hated to admit it, it might even get in the way of the things he needed to do. Using the *Shora* to spar just now had shown him that he needed to regain his equilibrium, no matter how brightly his loss still burned within him.

He sat down and thrust his hands through his hair. He felt the feather touch of Darlara's fingertips on his arm.

"Promised me a child," she said. "Doesn't mean you stay, doesn't mean we wed. A child, a new bloodline for the Pod. *You* promised."

She was in her rights to ask, to remind him. And she was tactful enough, and smart enough, not to remind him that Dhulyn, as Senior Partner, had given her permission.

"Now?" The word was bitter acid as it left his mouth.

Darlara smiled, but it was a small, sad, companionable smile, not a smile of triumph.

"Lie down," she suggested. "Just lie down for now. Need warmth and a heart beating close to yours. Come, let's lie down."

It was not until hours later, when they had done much more than lie down, that he remembered they were in Dhulyn's bed.

Eleven

"I F MY SISTER HAS become a Storm Witch, well and good. But if a new being has taken over her body—how can we know it doesn't mean us harm?" Xerwin had met Naxot on the peldar court, but they hadn't yet begun their match. He'd needed to speak to someone, this was a safe place to talk—and Naxot's interests ran sufficiently close to his own, Xerwin considered, to make him a safe companion to talk to.

Naxot stopped bouncing the rubbery pelot on his racket, catching it in his hand. "She's done nothing but good so far. She's helped with some of the crops, and has explained the magic of the lodestone."

"If she has no evil intent, why has she not declared herself?"

"Perhaps she thinks to test us in some way?"

Xerwin paused in his pacing. *I wish I could believe the way Naxot believes*, he thought, and not for the first time. But it was hard to grow up as he had and believe that his father really was the Light of the Sun.

"I suppose that's possible," he said to his friend. "But this feels more like a plot of my father's than the suggestion of the Slain God."

Naxot waved this away. "Not even your father, Light of the Sun, acts completely alone." He spun the racket in his hand and looked up. "The Priests of the Slain God have authority over the Mages and Holy Women. When Telxorn comes to invest your . . . I mean the Storm Witch, surely he will know whether there is cause for concern? And, Xerwin, let's not forget. Whether this is your sister or not, she *is* a Storm Witch, a Holy Woman. Whatever her purpose here, should we be questioning it?"

Xerwin picked up his racket and put his hand out for the pelot.

Naxot was such a good man, straightforward and orthodox. Perhaps, after all, he was a little too orthodox for this particular problem.

Naxot Lilso took the long way back to his own House when his peldar game with Xerwin finally ended. He needed time to think. He wasn't happy with the Tar's attitude. Xerwin had always been his friend, but there were higher issues at stake here—and more than one way to favor and power at court, if it came to that. However upset Xerwin might be about his sister, and he'd always had a soft spot for the girl, a Holy Woman was a Holy Woman. Xerwin might be willing to set the religious questions aside, but Naxot could not.

Naxot's route would take him past the Tarxin's audience chamber.

RAIN HISSES DOWN ON SLICK DECKS AND DHULYN CURSES AND TRIES TO LOOK AWAY. NOT THIS VISION, PLEASE GODS, NOT *THIS* ONE. IF SHE MUST SEE THE PAST, LET IT AT LEAST BE SOMETHING USEFUL. SURELY THERE COULD BE NO REASON TO SHOW HER *THIS* PAST. BUT EVEN AS SHE TURNS HER HEAD, TWO GIGGLING FORMS RUN TOWARD HER. TWO STURDY CHILDREN, NAKED AND CLEARLY ESCAPED FROM THEIR BEDS TO PLAY IN THE RAIN. THEY ARE ABOUT THREE YEARS OLD, TODDLERS REALLY, BUT AS FIRM AND STEADY ON THEIR BARE FEET AS THOUGH THEY'D LEARNED TO WALK AT SEA. AS THEY WOULD HAVE, SHE REALIZES WHEN THEY GET CLOSE ENOUGH FOR HER TO SEE THEM CLEARLY.

GIRLS THEY ARE, TWINS, SQUARE-BUILT, WITH A MOST FAMILIAR CHIN BELOW AMBER EYES. LUCKILY, THEY HAVE THEIR MOTHER'S NOSE. BECAUSE, IN ALL ELSE, THEY APPEAR TO BE THEIR FATHER'S CHILDREN. EVEN THE COLOR OF THEIR HAIR, WET AS IT IS, IS UNMISTAKABLE. THESE ARE PARNO'S CHILDREN.

"BACK HERE, YOU TWO TERRORS," THE VOICE SOUNDS ODD TO DHULYN, BUT IT'S CLEAR. "BACK IN BED THIS MINUTE, OR THERE'LL BE NO GREAT GATHERING FOR YOU! NO PONY RIDES!"

A FUTURE FOR THEM IS POSSIBLE. DHULYN'S HEART LEAPS WITH JOY AS HER TEARS FALL. . . .

THE SLIM WOMAN, HER SANDY HAIR STILL TOUCHED WITH GRAY, IS BACK AT HER CIRCULAR DESK. HER HAZEL EYES ARE CLOSED, THE PATTERN OF LINES THAT SURROUND THEM SMOOTH. THE WOMAN MURMURS, CHANTING UNDER HER BREATH. OVER HER HEAD THE MIST FORMS, SWIRLING AND BRIGHT WITH SUN. SHE THRUSTS HER ARMS INTO IT AND DISAPPEARS . . .

TWINS AGAIN, BUT OLDER, AND VERY OBVIOUSLY NOT THE SAME GIRLS. THESE

ARE PALE AS MILK, EVEN THEIR LONG HAIR COLORLESS AS NEW CHEESE. THEY ARE
BONE-THIN, CLINGING TO ONE ANOTHER AS IF THEY LACKED THE STRENGTH TO
SIT UP ALONE. THEY SIT IN A DOUBLE CHAIR, ALMOST A THRONE, WHOSE CUSH-
IONS AND WELL-PADDED, RED VELVET SEAT ONLY SERVE TO MAKE THEM SEEM
PALER BY COMPARISON.

THEY CONCENTRATE ON SOMETHING OFF TO THEIR LEFT. THEY TURN THEIR
HEADS AT PRECISELY THE SAME MOMENT, WITH PRECISELY THE SAME MOVEMENT,
TO LOOK AT DHULYN WITH THEIR RED EYES.

"SISTER," THEY SAY. . . .

SHE KNOWS THIS WOMAN VERY WELL, HER LONG FACE, HER STONE-COLORED
EYES, AND HER BLOOD-RED HAIR. "GO NOW," SHE SAYS. "UP INTO THE TREES," SHE
SAYS. "REMEMBER WHAT I TOLD YOU, MY SOUL?" "KEEP MY EYES TIGHT SHUT,"
DHULYN ANSWERS HER MOTHER. "DON'T LOOK NO MATTER WHAT I HEAR."
"THAT'S RIGHT, MY HEART. OFF YOU GO NOW."

AND THE WOMAN WHO IS HER MOTHER WATCHES AS THE CHILD WHO WAS
DHULYN RUNS AWAY TO THE TREES, TO THE PLACE IN WHICH SHE WAS TOLD TO
HIDE. HER MOTHER THEN TURNS TO THE DHULYN WHO SEES ALL THIS, AND
SMILES.

"MOTHER," DHULYN SAYS, TAKING A STEP TOWARD THE WOMAN OF HER VI-
SION, THINKING NOW ONLY OF THE QUESTION SHE HAS LONGED TO ASK. "HOW,
MOTHER?" SHE ASKS. "WHY? HOW DID YOU NOT SEE AND PREVENT THE BREAK-
ING OF THE TRIBES?" BUT EVEN AS HER MOTHER PARTS HER LIPS TO ANSWER, HER
HEAD TILTS AS SHE LISTENS TO OTHER SOUNDS, AND TURNS AWAY. SHE HAS ONE
HAND LIFTED, ONE FINGER EXTENDED AS IF TO SAY "WAIT."

BUT THE VISION IS GONE.

Dhulyn sat down on the wide lip of the courtyard fountain and rubbed
at her eyes, moving her fingers up and out, to massage her forehead
and temples as well. Thank Father Moon there'd been no Vision of
Parno. That would have been more than she could stand. *I cannot do
this again*, she thought. She had never deliberately avoided Visions in
the past, but she would from now on. The possibility of having to live
through Parno's loss again and again—Dhulyn took a deep breath, and
tried to slow the beating of her heart.

The night air was markedly cooler than the day, a phenomenon
Dhulyn had always associated with deserts rather than cultivated land.
When she'd first come out of her room, there had been thunder and

lightning off in the distance, but that had stopped now. Whatever its source, the coolness was welcome. Not that she had a headache; it merely felt as though she *should* have. Experience was making her better able to recognize Visions of the past, and that same experience had taught her that such Visions always gave useful information. But she'd Seen the episode with her mother before, why would she need to See it again? Why her mother, and why that particular moment, the last time she'd seen her mother alive? Dhulyn shivered, suddenly cold. *I'm the only one left. Again.* She had escaped alive that time, when the Bascani had come and the Tribes were broken. And she'd escaped alive this time as well. She braided the fingers of her right hand in the old sign against ill luck.

"Are you trying to tell me something, my mother?" All the women of the Espadryni, what the rest of the world called the Red Horsemen, were Marked with the Sight. Which did not explain to Dhulyn's satisfaction how and why they had allowed the Tribes to be broken, leaving only Dhulyn alive.

Was she somehow *supposed* to survive Parno? As she had so evidently been meant to survive the breaking of the Tribes? Was this yet another plan to which she did not have the key? She blew out her breath through her nose. This would be the second time that she'd lost the people most important to her, her family—

Except that the Mercenary Brotherhood was her family. Parno was her Partner, certain sure. But his death did not leave her entirely alone in the world. She touched her Mercenary badge with the tips of her fingers. She still had her Brotherhood, and the Common Rule.

"Pasillon," she said, invoking the part of the Common Rule that called all Mercenary Brothers to come to the aid of—and to avenge—any other Brother. Vengeance for Parno was her first goal, she reminded herself. If she survived the killing of the Storm Witch—by no means a certainty since she was the child of the Tarxin and therefore well-guarded—then she could think about what came next.

Footsteps along the gallery on the far side of the courtyard brought her head up and her hand reaching for the knife in her belt. But it was Remm Shalyn, returning from his scouting trip into the forest.

"Dhulyn Wolfshead, are you well?" Remm saw her and stepped out from under the gallery. "The Holding Steward will be concerned that your bed is not to your liking."

Dhulyn shrugged. "I take it your expedition has been successful?"

"It has. We'll hardly have to go off our own trail."

Remm came closer, and as he passed through a shaft of moonlight, his kilt sparkled white. Dhulyn sat up straight, remembering another part of her Vision.

"Tell me, Remm Shalyn. Are there Seers in Ketxan City's Sanctuary?"

Parno shifted the straps on Malfin's table and let the yellowed parchment roll closed. With his fingertips, he massaged the skin and muscles around his eyes and along his temples. He leaned forward, his elbows on the table, his head in his hands. Strategy, that was the problem. They were limited in their tactics. Couldn't swarm, for example; there simply weren't enough of them. Hard to lay siege to a place from the sea—not that they had the numbers for that either. For a moment, while studying the map, he'd had a glimmering of an idea. If the map was still accurate—and both the captains assured him that it was—he had seen the shadow of the answer, and then it had gone, before he could put his finger on its tail. He put his hands to the edge of the table and started to push himself away before he remembered that the furniture was bolted to the floor.

The cabin door creaked open, and Malfin stuck his head into the opening.

"Lionsmane, Crayx ask for music, would you . . . ?"

Parno had to allow that the Crayx had been scrupulous about staying out of his head, and for that, if nothing else, he should honor their request and play for them. Besides, music had been known to clear his head in the past.

He slid sideways off the bench and started to the door.

But once he'd fetched his pipes from the cabin—the heavy drones, the war pipes, better for the Crayx to hear directly—he found himself leaning on the rail as he filled the air bag, unsure what to play. He attached the chanter and began to noodle, just letting his fingers float over the sound holes. He let his eyes close, shutting out the deck, the crew, the now-blazing sun, and the fitful wind that made what sail there was flap, and the rigging creak. This is what Dhulyn used to call his pipe *Shora*, the tuning up that prepared him to play.

With that thought, he found his fingers playing once again the children's song that had such special meaning to Dhulyn. As he coaxed the skipping notes from the chanter, he began to complicate them with the music of the drones, adding seconds and thirds, intricacies that built upon the basic notes until the children's chant became once again the hymn to the Sleeping God it had originally been.

Slowly, note by woven note, the hymn began to change, to take on specific imagery. A run of higher notes, with a sharp drone behind them, became Dhulyn's swordplay, masterful and sure, deadly and bright. Chords were her throaty laugh. The lament became more sure, more steady, as Parno realized what he was doing. He played Dhulyn, the way horses seemed to speak to her, the way weapons sang in her hands. The wolf's smile she showed to others, the smile she saved for him alone. The way she smelled after she had not bathed for many days.

Finally, not really sure how much time had passed, he lowered the pipes, and, blinking, looked around him. The watch was the same, the same faces looked back at him, though some had tears in their eyes.

#We see her now# #The music shows her to us# #Sorrow# #Compassion#

"Have not seen one tenth part of her." Even though he muttered under his breath, Parno was all too aware of the others on deck, now studiously ignoring him.

#You are unjust to your talent and your skill# #Your song of her will live with us always now# #Is this not she#

In his mind an image he hadn't called there. Dhulyn with her right hand on the neck of a horse, the animal shadowy and unclear, turning to look over her shoulder at him, smiling, her gray eyes alight with laughter.

Parno coughed, clearing his throat, wiping away his tears with the back of his hand. "Yes," he said. "That is she."

#The image is yours, you will be able to call it whenever you wish, it will be clear and crisp# #A small thing, but strengthening your memory is a part of what we can do#

#Do not fear# This was another voice. #No other will share this image without your consent# #It is not our way, but we know that humans have private things#

#Darlara did not share you with us, for example#

Parno felt a hot flush rise up through his cheeks and dropped his eyes to his pipes. He hadn't even thought of that. Hastily, he changed the subject.

"Are those images how you keep the souls of those who go to you when they die? Like portraits?"

#Not at all# #The soul itself joins us, becoming part of the Great Pod#

"What about new Crayx? Where do their souls come from?" One by one, Parno removed the drones and began to bleed the remaining air out of the bag.

#There are no new Crayx# #We are the same, always#

"But the spawning grounds?"

#We grow always, larger and larger# #We would grow too large for the oceans, so as that time approaches, we prepare smaller bodies# #In the spawning grounds we emerge in our new bodies, leaving the old behind, as we leave behind each old layer of skin and scales#

"Then you don't produce young?" Parno restored the last piece of his disassembled pipes into their bag and looked over the side. There were several Crayx within sight. *Which of these speaks to me?* he wondered. *And how old is it?*

#We do not#

"But the Nomads . . ." Parno looked toward the cabin where Darlara was sleeping.

#Have young, though not so many as land-based humans# Parno caught an undercurrent of thought that substituted "no Pod sense" for the phrase "land-based."

"And you have room for all of them when they die?"

#Amusement# #Souls do not occupy space#

Parno blinked. That had never occurred to him. Of course, he'd never had reason to think about souls in this way before. Which reminded him of his other question.

"How old are you? How far back do you remember?"

For the first time, the answer was not immediate. #Time is not the same for us# #We know what it is for you, we have seen the effects of its passage# #Watch#

#This is Ketxan City when we made our first treaties with humans, in the before that you humans call the time of the Caids# #Before the Great Chaos# #Before the first coming of the Green Shadow#

Before Parno could interrupt, another image came into his mind.

This time he was looking across a large bay of water toward a city built up on the islands of a flat sprawling delta. A city like Tenezia, without roads, but rather canals and bridges. Unlike Tenezia, however, this long ago Ketxan boasted airy towers.

#This is Ketxan City as we see it now#

Where the broad delta had been was a massive cliff face, taller than the tallest tower Parno had ever seen. There were openings, windows, balconies, and even doors cut into the living rock, with ladders connecting some of the lower levels. At the foot of the cliff, like a ruffle on a skirt, wharfs, jetties, and piers were built out into the sea.

#This is time, yes# #There is duration, change#

"But surely you also change? You're not the same beings that you were then?"

#There is no then# #For the Great Pod, there is only now# #We thank you for the music, Parno Lionsmane#

And suddenly, he was alone.

At first he stayed where he was, enjoying the quiet sounds of the ship around him, the sun on his face. He hadn't realized he was so curious about the Crayx. Dhulyn would have been interested by what he'd learned, as she was—had been—interested in everything. He hugged his bag of pipes closer. He missed her, Caids knew how much. But somehow, whether it was the steady familiarity of the *Shora*, or of his music, Parno realized that the sharpest edge of his grief had been blunted.

He pressed his lips together in a tight smile. In order to do what he wanted to do, in order to find and kill the Storm Witch, he needed to be at his very best. If the patterns and discipline of the *Shora*, and his music, restored him to his best self, it was a thing to be welcomed.

He stood, and was halfway back to the cabin to put away his pipes when a thought slowed his steps. He was almost certain that Malfin had mentioned attacking Ketxan City. But, given the cliffs he had seen in the Crayx's image of the place . . . Parno turned and made his way back to Malfin's cabin. When he entered, he found Darlara sitting across from her brother at the cleared table, a bowl of cooked grains in front of her.

"Tell me," Parno said. "These attacks on Ketxan City, how did you manage them?" So far as he could see from the image the Crayx had shown him, there was no landing place at Ketxan. He had not seen siege weapons on the *Wavetreader,* nor could he see any way to equip even much larger ships with such things. How could the Nomads, armed only with swords, garwons, and crossbows, mount a serious attack on the cliff city?

Darlara was swallowing, so it was Malfin who answered. "The Crayx push them back, enough so that we can land."

"But Mortaxa have no Pod sense, how do the Crayx push them?"

"With their water bolts," Darlara said. "May we?" She tapped her forehead. When Parno nodded, he felt the Crayx again, and the image that appeared in his mind made him laugh aloud.

"I think I see our plan," he told them.

Carcali was on her knees by the toy shelves. She didn't know who had last put these dolls away, but she could tell it had not been the little girl who loved them. They'd been shoved in any which way, back to front, facedown, even piled on top of one another. The dolls varied considerably in their dress, Carcali noted, as she straightened and rearranged them. There were elaborately dressed nobles and more simply dressed servants, and more than one soldier doll, all with tiny weapons. The favorites appeared to be one soldier in particular—an officer judging from his armor—and a little girl doll whose painted face was quite worn, and whose hair had been frequently rebraided. It wasn't until she heard the lock engage that Carcali looked up, this last doll still in her hands. Her stomach rumbled, and she pressed her lips together as saliva began to flow. Were they bringing food this time, or only water again? She cursed her caution now for keeping her from saying something to Tar Xerwin when he came, but he hadn't sounded all that friendly. For all she knew, the man was just another spy for the Tarxin.

When the two guards entered and stood one to each side of the door, Carcali rose, unwilling to be caught on her knees. In the last moment, she realized she was still holding the doll, and thrust it hastily behind her. She wasn't going to look any more childlike and vulnerable than she could help. Not to the man who had first struck her, and was now keeping her prisoner. Though she would have felt more confident if she wasn't sure that the Tarxin had seen her quick movement, and had correctly interpreted it.

What happened next did nothing to boost her confidence. At a signal from the Tarxin, the Honor Guard accompanying him stepped back out of the room and closed the door. Carcali waited, unsure what she should do, but determined not to be the first to speak. The Tarxin looked around the room, taking in the daybed with its gaily colored cushions, and the closed and barred door of the sheltered balcony that looked out on the sea. Finally, he turned away and appeared to study the maps on her table.

Automatically, Carcali went to stand on the other side of her worktable, though she made no move to cover the designs she'd made on the maps. The Tarxin had no Art, and wouldn't understand the meaning of the symbols she'd drawn, but she felt stronger there, close to her work.

When she glanced up, he was looking directly into her eyes. He indicated her chair, and waited until she was seated before he took the chair across from her, lifted off his gold-chased headdress and placed it to one side. With his eyes still fixed on hers, he leaned back, patting the arms of the chair with the palms of his hands.

"I think we have seen that we each can hurt the other," he said, his voice rough as the gravel paths in the upper gardens. His eyes were large, but dark and cold. "We have each tried our strengths, and we are well matched. You have the weather Art, and can use it against me, but I am the Tarxin, and have the power to starve you or put you to death if I so choose."

Carcali's hands formed fists on the arms of her own chair.

"I can leave this body, and still control the weather."

The man across from her spread out his hands. "Then why have you not done so?"

The pain in her hands reminded Carcali to loosen her grip. Oh, how badly she would have liked to call his bluff. But he wasn't the one bluffing.

She hadn't fully disconnected since she'd reawakened in this body, it made her shiver just to think about it. What if she lost the connection again, to spend who knew how long before she somehow reconnected? If she ever did. There were so many things about this life, this world—this body—she didn't like, didn't know, and didn't understand. But it was better by far than the impersonal emptiness of the weatherspheres. She wouldn't go back there. She wouldn't. . . . But.

"If you kill me," she said, in her light child's voice. "I'd have no reason *not* to leave the body."

He just nodded and leaned back again, raising his hands and looking at her over the tent he'd made of his fingers.

"We can each of us harm the other," he repeated. "Shall we see if there is any way we can help each other?"

"I am ready to hear your proposal." Carcali leaned back herself, consciously trying to imitate his air of relaxation. But it was pretense, and she doubted he was fooled.

He might be sincere about his offer—he'd agreed to keep the Healers away once she'd shown him what she could do, and he'd kept his bargains so far. But she had to be careful. He was the one with all the power here, and he wouldn't hesitate to use it. She raised her hand to her bruised cheek.

"I will undertake never to strike you again," he said, as if in response to her gesture. "But in return you must in public treat me in all ways as your Tarxin and your father."

"Agreed," she said. "If by 'strike' you include any and all physical discipline, including imprisoning me and withholding food."

This time he did smile, but it was, she thought, a smile of admiration.

"Agreed." He leaned forward. "You have satisfied me that to allow the Healers to treat you will destroy your Art, as you call it. There are two ways in which this Art can be useful to me. As a weapon against my enemies, and as a tool for the benefit of my people. That is what you can give me. What can I give you in return?"

Carcali tried to keep her face as impassive as the Tarxin's, fighting not to show the surge of triumph and excitement that flowed through her at his words. She had to be very careful; he was experienced and tricky. She had to be sure to ask for *exactly* what she wanted.

"I will help you in the ways you've outlined." She was pleased that her voice sounded so calm, so reasonable. "But I must be able to practice and develop my Art without interference. I need more authority as myself," she said. "As the Tara Xendra."

The Tarxin frowned, but not as though he meant to disagree with her. "That is difficult," he said. "Women do not rule here, as they do across the Long Ocean, and many will find it hard to have a woman in authority over them." He pulled at his lower lip. "It has been many generations since there was last a practitioner of the Art among our people, and the Scholars tell us that such Mages and Witches were wards of the Slain God, going to serve at his temple. In fact, Telxorn, the Chief Priest, has already asked for you."

He's trying to scare me, Carcali thought. "Perhaps I should be having this discussion with him."

"Perhaps." The Tarxin didn't look nearly worried enough. "But I remind you that whatever the common people may think about your holiness, Telxorn is a man grown old in the service of the Slain One, and to him you are still the Tara Xendra, a young girl he has known since she was born. He will expect you to be biddable and you will have to force him to give you what I offer you freely. Meanwhile I, and the rest of my people, would suffer at the weather along with him until he finally sees what I have already seen." The man frowned, and then his face lightened as he snapped his fingers. "Of course. There has never been a practitioner of the Art with Royal Blood. We can refuse him on that basis. If you do not serve in the temple, then you will have both your status as Tara, and your status as a Holy Weather Witch. We can base your authority on that."

There was something in his tone, or the crinkle of his eyes, that told Carcali the man was being tricky, but she still found herself nodding in agreement. He wasn't being strictly truthful about the temple, but she was grateful to be kept out of the hands of the priesthood with their superstitious nonsense about the Slain God. Interesting what he'd said, though, about others seeing her only as the Tara Xendra.

"Tell me, Tarxin Xalbalil, how do you see me? Who do *you* think I am?"

He looked at her a long time, his eyebrows raised over his coal-dark eyes. "My dear child, what does it matter?"

Twelve

THE CLOUDS HAD BROKEN up sometime before dawn, making the last leg of the journey from the final guesthouse somewhat hotter and sunnier than Dhulyn would have liked. The forest was far behind them now, and for some time their road had been taking them past cultivated fields.

"This close to the capital, these are all market gardens," Remm Shalyn said, seeing her interest.

"I recognize some of the plants," Dhulyn said. "Those are artichokes, and those potatoes. They are cultivated in Boravia as well. But here, I see, harvesting has already begun. Back there, most of these crops won't be ripe enough to harvest for a moon at least."

"Why would that be?"

Dhulyn looked across at him, but Remm seemed to be perfectly serious. "You are much farther north here," she said, keeping her tone as neutral as she could. "The farther north you travel, the warmer it is, the longer the growing seasons, the earlier the sowing, and therefore the earlier the harvests."

"And are the harvests very late, then, in your homeland?" Remm was interested, Dhulyn could see, but only just enough to be polite. He had a soldier's practical grasp of things, and *that* she found familiar. A little irritating, but familiar and, in a strange way, comforting.

"In my homeland there is only grass for the horses, and then snow, and ice. It is civilized people who plant crops."

"Ice, I've heard of, packed in straw and brought by riverboat from the mountains to the south to cool the drinks of the rich, but snow?"

They had walked several spans by the time Dhulyn gave up trying to describe snow.

The fields they passed now were changing. Up ahead were what looked like grapevines. Recent rains meant the fields were well watered, but it also meant there had been a growth of weeds, and that some of the new plants needed restaking. Dhulyn noticed that for the most part the field hands did not look toward them as they passed. Slaves, of course. Each field was being supervised by an attendant who stood at one end, under a planted sunshade, watching the progress of the others.

"Are the watchers slaves as well?" Dhulyn asked following the nearest one with her eyes.

"Usually," Remm Shalyn said. "Only the very rich can afford to pay for this kind of work. In the free lands on the other side of the mountains, the farms and fields are worked by groups of free men who hold everything in common." Remm looked sideways at her, one eyebrow raised in puzzlement. "Tell me," he said. "How did you know that there would be runaway slaves?"

"Loraxin thought I was a runaway," she said. "It followed. And it also follows that there must be some place to run to."

Remm shook his head, his mouth twisted in a smile. "Are all Paledyn such deep thinkers as you?"

What answer can I give him? she thought. There were Mercenary Brothers who did not think beyond the *Shora*, for certain. She knew many such. But Dorian the Black had told her many times, "The more you know, the more likely you are to stay alive," and she'd believed him.

"So the servants I meet now will all be slaves?"

Remm Shalyn rubbed at his chin. He'd been careful to shave every morning. "Well, no. Especially not in the palace. Oh, I don't mean there won't be slaves in the kitchens, or among the cleaners, but some of the very rich live in the City, the Noble Houses—"

"The very ones who are rich enough to pay for service, and who use that method to show off their wealth."

"Exactly." Remm focused his attention on the vines they were passing. Dhulyn looked in the same direction but saw nothing unusual. Then Remm looked down at his feet. And cleared his throat.

Dhulyn decided to wait him out.

"I am thinking, Dhulyn Wolfshead." Dhulyn raised her eyebrows, but Remm was not looking at her, so the effect was lost. "Perhaps it would be best if you uncovered your head," he said finally. "Now that we have no servants with us, it would be best if the people we will now encounter see your," he gestured at his own temple, "your Paledyn's tattoo."

"Have we much farther?"

"By midmorning, we will be at the walls."

Dhulyn squinted upward, judging the strength of the sun. Parno had often teased her that the sun did not brown her, and it was true that next to the rich gold of his own coloring she never looked darker than old ivory. But pale as she might seem, she did brown, nevertheless. She pulled off her headdress, turning it back into a linen scarf and a knotted sash, and tying both around her hips.

"Will there be a problem since we have no runner to send ahead to tell the guards we are coming?" she asked Remm Shalyn.

"The palace guards are already expecting us," he said.

Dhulyn pressed her lips together and barely stopped herself from rolling her eyes to Mother Sun. This would by no means be the first time that knowledge at the palace didn't find its way to the ordinary soldier. "And the gate guards will have been told as well?"

"The gate is not guarded."

No guards? Dhulyn pursed her lips in a silent whistle. She'd understood from what Remm had told her that the country of the Mortaxa was large, larger than any of the realms in Boravia, with the capital, Ketxan City, on the coast. But Battle Wings or no, were their enemies so far distant that the walls of the capital did not need guards? These were remarkably complacent people, and history had often told her what usually rewarded such complacency. Dhulyn knew how she would attack the city, if she were ever given the task.

The walls, when they finally arrived at them, impressed her even less. They were built of the same white-washed, stucco-covered mud bricks that she had seen used for building material in Berdana, but these walls were no taller than she was herself, and only just wide enough to allow someone to walk comfortably on the top.

And just as Remm Shalyn had said, the gates stood wide and empty.

Dhulyn looked at the gardens, walkways, and pavilions to be seen within the gates, and back at the cultivated fields without. "It seems that the primary purpose of these walls is to keep the fields separate, rather than to enclose and protect the city."

Remm frowned. "Certainly, it's considered a sign of status among the Noble Houses to have winter places in the Upper City. I think it was the present Light of the Sun's father who declared there could be no more building here."

"Naturally. It would be in the interest of those same Noble Houses to make sure the precinct was as small and exclusive as possible." She looked around her, but there was nothing but gardens and the single-story pavilions as far as she could see. "And the palace?"

"There's no direct entrance from the Upper City, but do you see those pillars?"

Dhulyn looked where he was pointing and saw that there were indeed a set of five pillars to be seen to the north and east.

"That marks the official entrance to Ketxan City itself."

"The entrance?"

Remm gestured with his hands. "To the Lower City, of course. Ketxan City is built into the rock cliffs that face the Coral Sea."

As they approached the entrance to the Lower City, the buildings became more impressive, many of them built of stone. The same stone, Dhulyn guessed, which had been carved out and removed to form the rooms and corridors of the city below them. The entrance itself consisted of the five pillars they had seen from a distance, which flanked a descending ramp of polished terrazzo leading down to enormous open-worked double doors made from metal bars, like a portcullis. Dhulyn stopped, fists on her hips, and looked upward to examine the gates more carefully, disbelief making her shake her head.

As if to confirm her worst fears, the guard was actually a porter, an elegantly robed man whose round eyes and widened nostrils showed exactly what he thought of a Paledyn who turned up on foot, bare-headed, wearing a short kilt, and with only one attendant. He looked as though he wished to turn them away, so Dhulyn gave him her wolf's smile. As he backed away from her, she stepped forward.

"The Tarxin, Light of the Sun, has sent for me."

Dhulyn kept her attention on the man on the throne, without in any way losing sight of the pikemen stationed along the walls, and in particular the two who stood one to each side of the Tarxin. Was he another Loraxin Feld? Would he feel the need to test her? But the guards did not move, did not even, as far as she could tell, shift their eyes to follow her as she approached the throne. She could not be sure, never having met the man before, but she would wager her second-best sword that something about her pleased the Tarxin Xalbalil very much indeed. How best to keep him that way? She had been given a chance to bathe—in fact, the Steward of Keys who had met them at the entrance to the palace itself had insisted on it—and once again she had turned down women's garments in favor of what Remm assured her was appropriate clothing for a young man of a high Noble House. Only the absence of jewelry and perfume distinguished her from many in the audience room.

Now Dhulyn ignored everyone else, took a stride forward, and, bending from the hips, placed her palms flat on the floor in front of her. Such was the bow one gave to the Great King in the West, though she suspected no one here would recognize it. It was very impressive, however, to anyone who hadn't seen it done routinely. She straightened.

"I greet you, Tarxin Xalbalil, Light of the Sun. I am Dhulyn Wolfs-head, called the Scholar. I was schooled by Dorian of the River, the Black Traveler, and I have fought with my Brothers at Sadron, Arcosa, and at Bhexyllia with the Great King to the West. I have come to serve." She inclined her head again.

"I had not thought to see a female Paledyn." Though, from the evenness of his tone, the Tarxin had been warned what to expect. His voice was cold and rough, like a knife dulled by hard use drawn across a stone.

"The Slain God chooses whom he wills." Dhulyn touched her fingers to her forehead in salute. Nothing a great ruler liked more than plenty of respect.

"That he does." The Tarxin touched his own forehead, as did everyone else in the room.

Interesting. Dhulyn kept her own face from showing any reaction, seeing the Mercenary salute used here as an acknowledgment of the Slain God.

"I have heard tales of your prowess in my land, Paledyn," the Tarxin said. "You have already fought and defeated many with your bare hands."

Did the man's eyes flick toward Remm Shalyn, still down on one knee behind her? She inclined her head. "You are too kind, Light of the Sun."

"Go now, and rest from your journey." The Tarxin flicked his hand and another Steward, not the one who had met them at the entrance, stepped forward. There was a vertical frown line between this man's gray brows, but Dhulyn had the feeling it was permanent, and had little to do with her.

"There will be feasting tonight," the Tarxin continued. "It would please me that you join us, if you are rested."

"I will attend." Dhulyn bent forward once more to touch her palms to the floor and turned to follow the Steward.

A feast? Just the place one could meet with the Storm Witch.

❦

"But, Lionsmane, we know nothing about attacking on land."

"These maps are accurate? These bluffs here no higher than is shown?"

"Believe so." Malfin caught his sister's eye even as he nodded.

#Yes#

"Then should be able to land small forces here—" Parno tapped a spot on the coast to the west of Ketxan City that showed where the mouth of a large creek cut into the coastal bluffs. "And here." He tapped another spot to the east where there was a rocky beach. "Reading the symbols correctly? There's depth enough there and the ships can get close enough?"

"At high tide, in those two areas, yes," Malfin said. "But still don't see . . ." His voice trailed off as his sister wrapped her hand around his upper arm, her eyes fixed on Parno's face.

"Let him explain, Mal," she said. Parno wasn't sure that he was entirely comfortable at the confidence in her voice—nor at the glow in her face. He turned his eyes back to the map.

"If land here, and here," he said, once again laying his index fingers on the maps. "Should be able to make our way overland to the walls of the city here, and here." He moved his fingers. "Avoiding the cliff face of the city entirely. From what you tell me of your usual tactics, no one will be expecting an assault from the land, and there will be minimal guards along the walls. To make doubly sure of that, after dropping off the assault teams, the ship will return to sea, enter the harbor in the usual way, and bombard the city front with water bolts." He looked up at them. "See now? Will concentrate their soldiers against what they believe to be your usual frontal assault."

Mal was nodding. "But how will we coordinate the attacks?"

Parno smiled. Amazing how people couldn't see a tactical use for something they'd had their whole lives. "Pod sense." He saw the light dawn over both their faces.

#Amusement# Parno felt not only the amusement of the Crayx, but of Mal and Dar as well. #Pod sense or no# the Crayx continued #You cannot lead both expeditions and no one on board the *Wavetreader* has sufficient knowledge to maneuver on land, to tell directions for example# #You must have only one landing party, or do you wish us to summon other Pods#

Darlara nodded. "True, won't take the city with just our crew, no matter how well you train them."

Parno looked from one captain to the other. It was lucky they had him. "Don't want to take the city," he reminded them. "What would we do with it? Want to kill the Storm Witch."

With a sinking in his stomach, Parno wondered if either of *them* had noticed he'd said "we."

It was not the first time Dhulyn had attended a feast of this exalted kind. It was not even the first time she had been seated at the high table. But it was the first time she had been alone, without Parno. She forced herself to push those memories away, not to wish for his familiar grin and his ingrained knowledge of the manners of Noble Houses.

Not that even Parno's knowledge would have been of much use here, since the court of the Tarxin bore little resemblance to that of any other court Dhulyn had ever seen. It was the first time that Dhulyn had ever seen the seating order determined not merely by rank, but by gender. Here the women were seated at a separate table, set centrally and perpendicular to the high table, and presided over by a young girl who could not have seen her birth moon more than ten or eleven times.

The Stewards must have received special orders to treat Dhulyn as though she were a man, since she had been seated at the same table as the Tarxin. There was an empty chair on either side of him, something Dhulyn had never seen done in any court in Boravia, but she had been given what amounted to the place of honor, the next seat at his left hand. On her other side was his son, Tar Xerwin, the heir.

The Tar had inclined his head, a little grimly, when the Hall Steward introduced them in the anteroom, and Dhulyn had given him exactly the same degree of bow in response. She'd had the sense that his grimness had nothing to do with her, however—or at least not directly. She wondered whether she should try the Two Hearts *Shora*. The Tar would make a useful ally.

Once at table, Dhulyn was careful to observe the manners of the others, and to copy them insofar as it was possible. Everyone at the high table had their own attendant standing behind them, and though Remm Shalyn stood behind her chair, he had very little to do besides signal to the servers when he saw her plate or glass empty. The service at their table was done by young girls, their hair covered with veils and much bedecked with bangles and pendants. The ladies' table, Dhulyn was amused to see, was served by young boys, severely dressed in a manner that mimicked the uniform of the guards.

A nervous reflex caused Dhulyn to smile at the first girl who approached the table in front of her. The girl's hand shook, almost dropping the small tidbit she was placing on Dhulyn's plate with a long pair of silver tongs. Dhulyn glanced sideways and saw the Tar lifting the morsel to his mouth with his right hand. She did the same.

A slice of cured ham so thin it was like the finest parchment, wrapped around a sugared date. Her mouth watered and she wondered whether there were any more. But what the girls were bringing now were tiny cups of clear glass, filled with a bright green liquid. Wiping her hand on the napkin to the right of her plate, as she saw both the Tarxin and Tar Xerwin do, Dhulyn lifted the glass and tossed the contents down her throat. She covered her mouth politely and coughed.

"It's unexpected, isn't it?" Tar Xerwin said. Though his tone was just as cool, his voice was a warmer, more musical version of his father's. "Pureed apple, olive oil, vinegar, and garlic."

"We are allowed to speak, then?" The man was slim, and well-muscled, not at all the type to be so precise about his food. Then again, the Tarxin himself was also slim which, given his years, meant that great attention and care were being paid to his diet.

"Indeed, though most women are more likely to faint than to talk to me."

Dhulyn cut short her laugh. "Oh. Your pardon, Tar Xerwin, I assumed you were joking."

"And yet, you are not afraid." He did not look at her when he spoke, however. His gaze appeared directed toward the ladies' table.

"Why would I be?"

"Because you see now that I was not joking."

Dhulyn shrugged. "What is the worst you can do to me?"

Now he turned to look at her. He lifted one shoulder and let it fall. "I could have you killed, or worse."

"Possibly." She looked him directly in the eyes, and smiled her wolf's smile. He did not move, only blinked, but for a moment Dhulyn thought she saw something more in his face than a bored and offended noble. "Possibly you *could* have me killed. But I'll tell you what you cannot do, Tar Xerwin. You cannot frighten me to death."

The Tar didn't exactly smile, but his eyes brightened, and his countenance seemed warmer. "To answer your question, then, yes, we are allowed to speak, but my father prefers to eat his meal in peace. If and when he wishes to discuss something with someone, he will call them up to sit next to him."

"A great honor." Dhulyn eyed the platter of thinly sliced cold meats that had been placed between her and the Tar. Evidently they were to be shared.

"It is. Don't be surprised if you're called over yourself. My father is very pleased with you."

"I saw that at my audience with him." Following Xerwin's lead, Dhulyn rolled up a slice of meat and popped it into her mouth. A cured sausage, spicy and piquant in its flavors. "Tell me, Tar Xerwin, is your father, the Light of the Sun, pleased with me as a man is pleased with a woman?"

Tar Xerwin looked startled and, for a flashing instant, younger than his polished manners and self-assured air had made him seem.

"You are direct," he said finally, with his first genuine smile. "I forgot that you are a Paledyn. To be equally direct, my father's tastes in women run differently. You would be too tall, too thin and," here his smile widened, "too dangerous for him." He waited while the platter was removed, and individual dishes set down in front of them bearing toasted slices of bread no bigger than the palm of Dhulyn's hand, covered with thin slices of something pale, and decorated with loose berries.

"Don't tell me," Dhulyn said, lifting one to her mouth and taking a bite. "Mmmm. Goose liver. I've never seen it so pale."

"Try some with the berries." When her mouth was full, Xerwin continued. "No, I would say my father thinks of you as a Paledyn, not as a woman. Note that you are seated here, and not at the women's table with my sister."

"He *is* pleased that I am female, however," Dhulyn pointed out. It seemed that the Tar, at any rate, was excused from the constant repetition of "Light of the Sun." Without turning to study the women's table more carefully, it was impossible to know which woman was the Tara Xendra.

"He is, but I think that is because the Storm Witch is also female." He glanced toward the women's table, and Dhulyn thought his lips might have hardened a little.

She nodded. It was difficult to be sure; all the seated women had their hair covered in the same type of veils worn by the serving girls, though of much richer fabrics and more expensive colors. There were several of the right age, but Dhulyn was fairly certain she had not seen the fair-haired woman of her Visions. Caution and Schooling told her it might be best, for the moment, not to ask after her. Better that she not show too much interest just at first.

"And what of you, Tar Xerwin?" she asked, careful not to let her lip curl again as she smiled. "How do you think of me?"

As she had been talking to him, Dhulyn had been careful to control her respiration, until the breaths came slower, and deeper. Slowly, her skin had grown warmer. Now she looked directly into Xerwin's eyes, parting her lips, and his breathing also slowed. The color came up into his face, and then he paled again.

"In whatever manner you would wish me to think, Dhulyn Wolfshead."

It was the first time he had said her name, and Dhulyn thought she could let it rest there, for now. The Two Hearts *Shora* had done its work.

They kept up their dance of words through the rest of the feast. Through the fish, grilled with melon sauce and mushrooms, through the inglera tenderloin topped with more goose liver and pureed apple, through the tiny individual legs of lamb, whose creamy sauce had still more apple and garlic in it. Each dish had come accompanied with a decorative edible, potatoes cut to resemble lace and deep fried, or miniature tarts of a pale yellow color and buttery taste that Xerwin told her were made from corn.

Xerwin slowly became a different person from the one who had sat down, and Dhulyn found his attitude strange altogether. Unlike the behavior she had seen in the court of the Great King to the West, Xerwin now appeared to treat her as in every way his equal. She had gathered from the Long Ocean Nomads that the Mortaxa revered Paledyns, but she had not understood that the reverence was sufficient to outweigh the ingrained prejudices of the culture. At the same time, the Two Hearts *Shora* had made her certain that Xerwin was aware of her as a woman. His heart rate had remained faster than normal, and he had managed to brush against her several times.

Dhulyn eyed the latest platter as it was set down between them. It appeared they had at last arrived at the sweet course, and the end of the meal was in sight. There were two small bowls of almonds, chocolate and ganje beaten into egg whites, a torte of chocolate layered with a green nut, and another made of quince jelly layered with fine slices of a sharp sheep's milk cheese.

As the young servers came around with tiny cups of ganje, black and hot, Xerwin, and others at the head table, were taking out small jeweled boxes. Xerwin used the point of his dagger, equally jeweled, to add a tiny amount of powder from the box to his ganje. Others were doing the same, though the young man on Xerwin's left side was sniffing the powder off the back of his hand.

Fresa, Dhulyn thought. Or some other form of the fressian moss, powdered for easy consumption. In Boravia, fressian drugs were so expensive and rare no one ever used them recreationally. There was no way of knowing what such use might bring. Dhulyn had just raised her hand, palm out, to Xerwin's offer of his jeweled box when the closer of the two young men who had stood behind the Tarxin's chair for the entire meal approached them and bent to speak quietly into Xerwin's ear.

Xerwin nodded, waited for the guard to return to his station before standing up and offering Dhulyn his hand. She stood, and let him lead her over one seat to sit down again next to the Tarxin. His ganje was untouched, and there was no sign of any type of fressian on the table in front of him. Quiet fell over the room as people stopped their conversations and looked toward the high table.

"My people." Rough as it was, the Tarxin's voice was pitched to be clearly heard throughout the dining chamber. "I have the pleasure to present the Paledyn, Dhulyn Wolfshead, escaped from the ships of the Nomads. We are greatly favored by the appearance of another who has been touched by the Slain God." He gestured toward the women's table.

"We know that the Paledyn is here to help us in our dispute with the Nomads of the Long Ocean. Like the Paledyns of old, Dhulyn Wolfshead will see fair dealing, and our rights confirmed."

Will I now, Dhulyn thought. *That's confident of you.*

"I would like to ask the Paledyn, here in front of you all, for an additional boon. I would ask her that she extend her protection over my other child, the Tara Xendra, in whom has recently manifested the Art of a Weather Mage. Come, my dear, meet the Paledyn."

It was the child, Dhulyn saw with a cold shock, who stood and crossed the short distance of floor to stand in front of her father on the far side of the table.

This wasn't possible. Dhulyn had Seen the Storm Witch several times, a tall, slim, fair-haired woman. Not a small, stocky girl with the same jet-black eyebrows as her father and her brother. She would not become tall and slim no matter how much time passed. The child raised coal-black eyes to meet Dhulyn's, and Dhulyn shivered, steeling herself to touch her forehead in salute, in recognition of the Slain God's servant.

Those eyes did not belong to a child. Those eyes were a good deal older than eleven years.

Dhulyn bowed, and smiled, and at one point touched her forehead again, all without consciously hearing anything more that was said. She found herself back in her seat next to the Tar Xerwin. His eyes were turned toward where his sister was sitting down once more at her own table. His face showed no emotion whatsoever, but Dhulyn saw that his hand gripped his cup of ganje so tightly that his knuckles stood out white.

He knows, she thought. *Whatever is happening here, he knows what it is.* And he wasn't happy about it.

Looked like she was right to use the Two Hearts *Shora*.

Thirteen

"**W**ILL YOU COME IN?"

Tar Xerwin had escorted her to the door of the rooms Dhulyn had been given. They were only one level down from the apartments of the royal family, no doubt kept set aside for important guests and visitors. Remm Shalyn, carrying a lamp, was already at the door, waiting to open it for her. Xerwin's attendants stopped a span down the corridor, and waited for him there. This would not have been the first time, Dhulyn thought, that they had accompanied their master to some lady's door.

Though it might have been, judging from the frown on Xerwin's face.

"Dhulyn Wolfshead, I thank you for the honor, but I fear I must decline. Business of my father's will have me rise early tomorrow."

Dhulyn tilted her head toward his ear. They were almost exactly the same height. "I did not invite you to my bed, Tar Xerwin," she said, so softly that she knew only he could hear her. "I know what I saw when I looked at Tara Xendra, and from the look on your face, you are not happy with it. I ask you again, will you come in?"

The frown was startled away, to be replaced almost as rapidly with a perfect imitation of a warm smile.

So, he can *control his features when he wishes to.*

"As you wish, Dhulyn Wolfshead." He signaled to his attendants and, faces carefully impassive, they took up stations along the corridor.

"Remm Shalyn, I thank you for your service today. I hope that you will rest well."

His left eyelid quivered, as if he longed to wink at her, but all he said before he bowed and turned away to his own rooms was, "An honor and a pleasure, Tara Paledyn."

Upon entering her sitting room, Dhulyn smiled at Xerwin and indicated the best chair before she checked that there were no attendants waiting for her in one of the other rooms. As Remm Shalyn had told her, it was minor nobles rather than slaves who acted as body servants in the Tarxin's palace, and she had taken full advantage of this to limit her own attendants as far as she could. When she returned to the sitting room, Xerwin was still standing next to the large armchair, staring down at it as if there was something fascinating on the seat. Dhulyn checked the minuscule balcony that was the only other exit to the suite of rooms and turned back to him.

"How do I know I can trust you?" he said without looking up.

Dhulyn sat cross-legged on the divan, tucking her kilt and her feet under her. She shrugged. "You must trust someone. Why should it not be me? The chief advantage of a Paledyn, so far as I can see, is that I belong to no one, am of no faction, and can judge with clear eyes."

"The Tarxin takes it for granted that you will argue on our side."

"He's an intelligent man. As such, he would be sure to at least pretend to believe his cause is just. And you, Xerwin?"

He sighed, pulling out his little box of fresa, and placing it on the table, his eyes straying to the wooden tray on the low table to his right. Dhulyn pulled off the linen cloth to reveal a jug of water, and one of wine, along with cups of different sizes, a plate of pastries and a bowl of fruit. "I have learned to take nothing for granted," he said.

Dhulyn smiled her wolf's smile. Spoken like the true son of a shrewd father.

"How long has the Tara Xendra been . . . not herself?"

Xerwin lowered himself into the chair and rubbed at his eyes. "Thank you for not calling her my sister."

Dhulyn poured out a cup of wine and handed it to him.

"What I saw is real, then? Whatever it may be, that child is not, or is no longer, your sister?"

Xerwin paused in the act of adding a tiny portion of fresa to his wine, hesitated, and returned it to the little box, snapping it shut. "How were you so certain? So quickly? You have never even met my sister."

Dhulyn drummed the fingers of her left hand on her knee. "I have seen such things before." She tried to keep her tone matter-of-fact, as if she were merely describing a horse she'd once seen, or a dog. The man's situation was a horrible one. She would prefer not to make it worse. "I'm sure that possession by spirits, even by gods, is not unknown even here."

He nodded. "There are tales. But, if it is a god, do they not usually make themselves known?"

Dhulyn decided there was no good end to that line of questioning. "Do you know how this occurred?"

She listened as he told of the Tara's fall, how she had hit her head and not regained consciousness.

"A Healer was not sent for immediately?"

"You understand, there seemed no need at first. Her attendants were not anxious to explain how they had allowed the accident to occur in the first place. Her head ached, and she had been frightened by the fall, but it was thought that rest alone was needed. When they could not rouse her, then they grew frightened and sent word to the Tarxin."

Dhulyn noticed that he did not call the man "my father."

"Even then," Xerwin continued, "it took time for the Tarxin to come, and he thought it best to wait another day before calling in the Marked."

"For blood's sake, *why?*" The words were out before she could stop them.

"The Tarxinate must not seem weak." Now Xerwin sounded as though he were quoting someone else's words. "I was told none of this until long after," he added.

"And when the Healer finally came?"

Dhulyn let Xerwin finish his tale uninterrupted. How the Marked never ventured out of their Sanctuary except in groups, what the Tarxin had told them to do when they informed him that the girl's spirit was lost.

"Clearly, the soul Found and Healed to the body was not that of your sister." Dhulyn poured out another glass of wine, waited until Xerwin had taken a sip, shaking her head at his offer of fresa. "When did you first suspect?"

"Only a few days ago. She was too ill at first for me to be much with her." He shrugged. "I had to return to my Battle Wing. And my duties have been increasing as well . . ." His voice trailed away, but his face grew thoughtful, so his distraction did not seem a likely result of the drug. "Do you think that was purposefully done?"

Dhulyn tilted her head, lifting one shoulder. "What told you then, when you finally saw your sister?"

"She did not know who Naxot was."

"I fear I can say the same."

"You saw the man sitting to my left? He's the heir to House Lilso, once next in importance to the Royal House, and hoping to be as important again." He'd been the one who sniffed his fresa, Dhulyn recalled. "He is—or was—Xendra's betrothed."

"She wouldn't be the first woman to forget she was betrothed," Dhulyn said with a smile.

But Xerwin saw no humor in it. "This is not some foreign prince, whose name might be knocked out of her head. Naxot is my closest ally at court, and Xendra has known him her whole life. She used to follow us around when she was a toddler, climbing into his lap and begging for sweets and kisses. She adored him."

Dhulyn noticed Xerwin's use of the past tense.

"And he was always kind to her, never brushed her off, as another of his age might have done. As I frequently did." Xerwin blinked and looked away.

Suddenly, sharp as a knife, Dhulyn felt an almost overwhelming desire for her Partner. Parno was so much better at dealing with people and their feelings, their regrets and their guilt. With a hand that trembled, just a little, Dhulyn poured out a cup of wine for herself, and took a swallow.

"What will you do, then? Destroy her?" she asked when she knew her voice would be steady. Xerwin, eyes still fixed on the wine jug, nodded, but very slowly. "Whoever it is that now occupies your sister's body is obviously a Storm Witch. She can do much good for your people."

"Naxot says the same thing, and I'm sure that's how my father thinks, though not for the same reasons. He thinks only of the power a Storm Witch brings him—principally over the Nomads at the moment, though he won't stop there. She's no more than a tool to him, as my sword is to me." He looked up, frowning. "But she isn't a tool, any more than my officers or my soldiers. She must have her own thoughts, her own plans. She is wearing Xendra's body like a glove, pretending to be my sister. If she is innocent, why the pretense? If she is evil, what can she bring to us but evil? Can I take such a chance?" He sat up straight, rested his hands on his thighs. "But you are a Paledyn, you will have your own view of these matters."

Dhulyn almost laughed aloud. "As it happens," she said, "my view is not so different from yours. It was the Witch who caused the storm which almost killed me, and did kill my Partner, another Paledyn." For a moment Dhulyn's throat closed. This was the first time she had spoken the words aloud. "If we are to destroy this spirit, we must first learn as much as possible. Will destroying the body kill it, for example? We must speak to the Marked who were there when Tara Xendra was Healed."

"Will they tell us the truth?"

"Only one way to find out. And, Xerwin," Dhulyn paused, but he did not correct her form of address. "You must remember that if we are successful in destroying the Storm Witch, it does not follow that we will be able to restore your sister."

The bleak look in his eyes told her that Xerwin had already thought of this.

"Come," she said, getting to her feet. "Sunrise comes quickly, and you must be ready to meet with the Tarxin."

Xerwin turned back at the door.

"These are strange and complicated times, Dhulyn Wolfshead. My friend Naxot says we are in the age of miracles. Mages, Paledyns." His smile was bittersweet. "And who knows what might be next. Some say the Slain God will rise."

"Oh, I think that is most unlikely."

Long after Xerwin had gone, Dhulyn was still awake, sorting through the weapons that Remm Shalyn had found for her. The swords were all of the shorter, heavier variety she had already seen, best used to slash and cut. That told her much about the style of fighting she might have to face.

She sat back in the chair. She was stalling and she knew it. It would be a simple matter to kill the girl. Nothing simpler, given that the Tarxin had put the child under her protection. All Dhulyn had to do was ask to meet with her, kill her—using bare hands if necessary—and then die fighting her way out. That had been her plan all along, sketchy though it might seem.

But would killing the body kill the Storm Witch? Or would the spirit merely be freed to inhabit some other helpless person? Because that was not part of Dhulyn's plan at all. Before she could act, she had to know. She wanted to be sure that the thing was destroyed.

Darlara usually enjoyed her time on watch. Through the Crayx she could see the whole ship, feel/taste the waters around it, sense the presence of the whole Pod, touch them lightly as they slept, performed their duties, ate, played with their children, hummed a soft lullaby, made love. And for the last few days, she put her hand on her lower belly, there had been a new life she could not yet sense directly. Or so the Crayx had told her.

But tonight, instead of joyful, Darlara felt edgy, distracted, unable to follow any one path of thought or feeling. She left her position by Ana-Paula at the wheel, and went down to the main deck, hoping that activity would clear her head, but finding her feet leading her toward the door of her own cabin, where she had left Parno Lionsmane asleep when she came on watch.

As soon as she realized where her feet were leading her, she went to the rail and leaned her elbows on it, letting her head fall into her hands.

#He still grieves# #You must have more patience#

How long

#Even now, his grief is less sharp# #There is something, a patterning, that he uses when he fights, and when he makes music, that helps him# #It restores him to himself# #Yes#

Should I tell him about the child *Would his current then flow more closely with ours*

#His current now carries him toward his revenge# #He believes he will die in taking his vengeance#

But would the child not show him that there is another current *It may be, that if knows there will be a child, might make a greater effort to live*

#It may be#

This time Darlara had her hand on the latch of the cabin door before she turned aside and went to the rail again.

Some time later, Mal, yawning and rubbing the sleep from his eyes, came and nudged her with his shoulder.

Your watch already

Jesting *How can I sleep with all this turmoil* *Will, won't, might, shouldn't, what if* *Think I can't feel that, even if don't have your thoughts*

Darlara rested her cheek against her brother's shoulder. *Sorry* *Don't know what to do*

Guessed that

Darlara butted him with her head, somehow eased by his chuckle. *Serious*

Know *But tell me what it's about* *This way, losing sleep for nothing*

It's the child

He slipped an arm around her shoulders and pulled her close. *Know for sure then*

Crayx say so *Certain*

Wonderful *The best news*

Darlara knew she should feel that way, too. And the greater part of her did. Would feel that way for the rest of her life, regardless of what Parno Lionsmane might do. But now that she had part of what she wanted, why should she not try to get all of it?

Crayx say Lionsmane might not be seeking hard to live, now that his Partner's gone *He'll get his revenge, but not carefully, thinking he might as well die*

But if he knows about the child, won't he want to stay *Won't he want to see it grow*

Darlara nodded. Of course Malfin thought the same as she did herself. They were twins, after all.

But see, what if, knowing that his promise is filled, what if that's what lets him decide to die Malfin began to frown and Darlara rushed to finish her thought. *If don't tell him, he'll still have his promise to fulfill, perhaps take better care*

Don't tell him *Are you crazed* *When you show, he'll know*

But by then he'll be with us for moons, he'll be better, he won't want to die anymore He'll stay with me, she hadn't quite the courage to form the thought clearly, though she knew Mal picked it up.

Mal, openmouthed, shook his head slowly from side to side. *He'll know you lied, and that's if Crayx don't tell him* Mal's anger could not have been plainer if he was shouting from the Racha's nest.

But he'll be alive, he'd forgive

Mal turned to look her squarely in the face. He took a step back from her, and Darlara swallowed hard. Mal had actually taken a step away from her.

"What are you thinking?" he said aloud, as if he didn't want to share her thoughts anymore. "Isn't some landster, we don't care if the shell knife we sell him falls apart in six moons. Lionsmane is Pod-sensed. Crayx know him, saved him. He's part of us." Mal tapped his chest with his closed fist. "Lie to him, lie to *all* of us." He pointed his finger at her in a way that suddenly reminded Darlara of their mother. "Tell him, or I will."

#Or we will#

"There. See?"

Darlara felt the tears spring into her eyes. Mal was right, could she *really* have been thinking about lying? The Pod did not lie to each other—could not lie, really, since the Crayx always knew the truth. And yet, she'd been thinking . . . her face fell forward into her hands and she felt her brother's strong arm once more around her shoulders.

Sorry she wept. *So sorry*

#Forgiveness# #Understanding#

Darlara straightened, wiping off her tears with the sleeve of her shirt. She patted Mal in response to his worried look and turned away.

This time she went all the way to the cabin and went in, closing the door behind her.

Carcali sat on her little balcony, the stone cold beneath her, her arms wrapped around her knees. Watching the clouds through the balusters. Something about the way that woman looked at her at the feast had taken her aback, just a little. Carcali had shrugged off the idea of these Paledyn—this Artless culture had so many superstitions. Like their Slain God and the animal worship of the Nomads, and the creepy *otherness* of the Marked. Carcali shuddered, skin crawling, remembering the six-fingered touch of the so-called Healer. Why didn't he fix his hand if he was so good?

Carcali stood up and went inside, rubbing the outside of her arms with her hands. That woman. That Paledyn, had looked at her as if she could see right through her, as if she already knew everything there was to know about her, and didn't like what she knew.

Carcali felt the warmth of rising anger. What right had that woman to look at her like that? Tattooed like a Master Artist, and no more Art about her than there was about this chair. Carcali kicked it away from the table enough to sit down.

There was no reason for her to second-guess her arrangement with the Tarxin just because some painted barbarian—*scarred*, no less— looked at her like all her aunts, her mother, and both grandmothers rolled into one. After all, making an alliance with the Tarxin was the smart thing to do. He was the most powerful person around here. If her own people had only sided with her, backed her, she wouldn't be in this mess, she—

Carcali stopped, breathing hard, tears threatening. The Tarxin was the most powerful, but that didn't make him *right*. She'd learned that lesson the hard way.

Maybe she needed other allies. Better allies. What about the brother, Xerwin? He at least made you feel you were talking to a real person when he looked at you.

Xerwin had dreamed of the Paledyn in the night. What little sleep he managed in the few hours before dawn brought the sun to his window had been broken up with images of what they had talked about the night before. Storm clouds turning into people he had not seen in years, his old guard sergeant, his mother. Images of his sister showing him the dances she had learned. Images of Dhulyn Wolfshead's smile. He dreamed that she took his face in her hands and kissed him with her cool lips.

Xerwin pushed the empty cup of ganje away, snapped his box of fresa shut and rubbed his hand across his mouth. Well, *that* could complicate things considerably, couldn't it? It wouldn't mean the end of his betrothal—that was a purely political alliance, the girl was still a child, and he had in fact never met her. A private bonding with a Paledyn, known to all but never spoken of . . . it could be acceptable to even the most orthodox and conservative, even Naxot's House couldn't find fault. It would be the same as a bond with a Holy Woman, something only she could choose.

Such a bond as Naxot might have hoped for, if Xendra were really a Storm Witch. Or if the Storm Witch was really Xendra . . . or . . . Xerwin shook his head. No good thinking about that. It was almost time to meet with his father.

As Xerwin navigated the corridors between his own suite and his father's morning room, he found that he felt better than he had for days. Even if what he fantasized about her was not likely to come to pass, the fact that Dhulyn Wolfshead, a Paledyn, saw the situation the same way he did, gave him confidence. Before speaking with her, he'd been unsure whether to confront his father on the subject of the spirit that had usurped his sister's body. Now he knew it would be the correct thing to do.

A small gathering of people in the Tarxin's anteroom made him slow his pace. He did not immediately recognize the child emerging with her escort of two lady pages and an armsman as the Storm Witch. Instead of her usual child's white clothing, she was dressed in a robe of sky blue, embroidered over with gold. Not unlike the colors he wore himself, Xerwin realized.

"Xerwin." The Storm Witch made an abortive gesture, lifting her arms awkwardly as if she meant to embrace him, but didn't know how. A hand squeezed his heart. His sister would have known, would have run to him, regardless of protocol.

"Tara Xendra," he said, formally inclining his head to her.

"Tar Xerwin." She inclined her head also. Did he imagine it, or was there something different about her voice?

Xerwin waited until the Storm Witch and her attendants had turned into the corridor before presenting himself at the Tarxin's door. When he was admitted, he found his father standing at one of the two tables in the room set at right angles to the windows. Where the Tarxin stood were large scrolls, some held open with weights, some curled and waiting. The other table held only the plates of a solitary breakfast.

"Well done, my boy," the Tarxin said, lifting his eyes from the maps he was studying and gesturing to a chair.

"My lord?"

"You spent most of the night in the Paledyn's rooms. Well done, indeed. I've reason to congratulate you on your good thinking yet again, it seems. And it appears that women will always succumb to a pretty face, even such women as that."

Xerwin's lips parted, but something made him hold his tongue before he could explain to his father just how wrong he was. He hesitated, lowering himself into the chair slowly. It seemed wrong somehow to let his father say such things—think such things—but whether he was defending the Paledyn or himself, Xerwin didn't know.

"F–father," he said, stumbling over the word. "The Storm Witch that inhabits Xendra's body." Xerwin glanced up and found his father looking at him. The man's eyes were bright, but his face was a stone mask. Xerwin tried to remember how confident he'd felt in the corridor only moments ago.

"The Storm Witch," he said again. "Should we not find some way to rid ourselves of her?"

The Tarxin pushed the charts and scrolls on the table to one side and took the seat across from Xerwin. He leaned back in the chair, resting his elbows on the arms. Xerwin tried to keep his gaze from faltering.

"Is this the advice of the Paledyn?"

Again Xerwin hesitated, trying to see all the consequences of his answer. There was something in the way the man had said the word "Paledyn," coupled with the way he'd just spoken of her that told Xerwin his father did not think as highly of the Paledyns as he would have people believe. Caution made Xerwin change his answer.

"No, sir," he said finally.

"I should think not. What brings this thought to you, then?"

Xerwin hoped he didn't look as relieved as he felt. He made himself shrug. "If it should turn on us, it might be as well to know how to kill it."

"That is a good thought, my son. A good thought, but a poor ploy." The Tarxin shook his head. "You have much left to learn, I see. You do not destroy a useful tool because it is dangerous. You use its strength against it. This one is such a tool. A sword to the hand, nothing more. She can be dealt with, bargained with, and used."

Xerwin blinked at the Tarxin's use of his own metaphor. "What of Xendra?" he asked.

"She is gone." The Tarxin's voice had a note of finality Xerwin had heard many times before. "There is nothing we can do for her which will justify losing the services of the Storm Witch. Do you understand?"

"Yes, sir. Of course." *He'd do the same if it was me,* Xerwin thought. *We're all just tools to him.* To use and discard. He was right to be careful, and he should try to be more careful still.

"When do you go next to the Sanctuary?"

Xerwin blinked, glad to think of something else. "Not for some days yet, seven or eight I would say."

Tarxin pulled the nearest scroll closer to him and began to unroll it. "Go today. They foretold the coming of the Paledyn—though the Caids know they might have warned us she was female—now she is here, we must see what more they can tell us."

It took Xerwin a moment to realize that he had been dismissed. Careful to take his leave in the correct manner, whether the Tarxin appeared to notice or not, Xerwin let himself out of the room and nodded at the servants waiting outside. He turned toward the stairwell as he reached the main corridor, and started walking faster as he realized he was heading toward Dhulyn Wolfshead's rooms on the lower level. They should visit the Marked, she had said. And this made as good an opportunity as any.

Parno climbed high into the rigging. He needed time, and privacy, to think. The Crayx would stay out of his thoughts—or at least pretend to, which amounted to the same thing—but even though they could not read his mind without the help of the Crayx, it was more than he could stand to see Dar's and Mal's faces hovering at his elbow.

Parno had not expected it, but the knowledge that a child was coming did change things. Everything that he had been taught, both in his Noble House and later, in the Mercenary Schools, told him that you stood by your word, that you did not walk away from your commitments and your obligations. It was always possible that he would not live to fulfill his obligation to his child—that might happen to anyone and Mercenary Brothers, in particular, were always prepared to die—but if he survived his attempt to destroy the Storm Witch, would his obligation to the child outweigh the demands of his Partnership?

He grinned, squinting his eyes into the rising wind. If Dhulyn were here, she would have an opinion, but if she were, her opinion wouldn't be necessary. He knew what the Common Rule required, and what it said about Mercenary Brothers who abandoned or did not provide for their children.

"Demons and perverts," he said.

#Do you require us# He could sense a warm humor in the question.

"Just debating with myself."

#Debate with others may be more fruitful#

"Perhaps, but I'd like to sort out my own thoughts first, if you don't mind."

#Acknowledgment#

Parno sighed. When Darlara had approached him to remind him of his promise, he hadn't been thinking clearly—hadn't been thinking at all, he saw now. The reality of a child, what that would mean, simply had not occurred to him. Almost as if, without realizing it, he had simply assumed no child would come. And now? Dhulyn had agreed to this, knowing, as she'd thought, that he would die. What would she wish him to do now? Now that she was the one gone?

"Death doesn't part us." As he said the words, he found he felt stronger, more confident. "We are still Partners, in Battle, and in Death." Dhulyn, if she *were* here, would be bringing her Scholar's training to bear on the argument.

"The child will live, or it will not live," he said, trying to remember how the lines of logic worked. "It will be Pod-sensed, or it will not." That was a very logical approach, and not something that Dar would want to consider.

If the child is Pod-sensed, he thought, *no better place for it than here on the* Wavetreader. But if it was not . . . He trusted what he had been told, that those children went to the Nomad havens, carefully hidden and safe. But in his case that was not the only option. Mercenary Brother or no, he had a family in Imrion who acknowledged him, and the child could be sent to them.

Fourteen

"THIS IS WHERE we part company."

Dhulyn brought her gaze down from the lofty ceiling of the Sanctuary Hall bright with torches and reflected daylight, and turned back to Xerwin. He shifted his eyes away from her, almost as though he were embarrassed.

"It's likely that they will answer your questions more easily than they will mine," he said. "You *are* a Paledyn, and they would trust in your fair dealing and discretion. Me, they will see as the representative of the Tarxin, and I already know what answers they gave him."

Dhulyn nodded. That made sense. "And you?"

"An errand for the Tarxin that I must perform alone."

That wasn't strictly true, Dhulyn thought as she watched Xerwin cross the hall toward the far end. An errand for the Tarxin, now that she'd believe. But whether he had to perform it alone, or whether he merely wished to—she shook her head. Xerwin did not give the appearance of regretting their alliance of the evening before, the Two Hearts *Shora* had done its work, charming him enough to listen to her, and to value what she had said. But something was troubling the young man, making him shift his eyes, and until she knew what it was, she had to treat it as a possible danger. Better cautious than cursing.

As Dhulyn waited for Remm Shalyn to return with a Sanctuary Guide, other petitioners began to trickle into the Hall. Gradually, Dhulyn became aware that many of these others were circling closer to her as they waited. Several caught her eye and smiled, inclining their heads and murmuring, "Paledyn," when they saw she was looking. Finally, an older woman in the veils and bangles of an upper servant came close enough to stretch out a hand holding a dark purple flower. Dhulyn took the blossom in her left hand, touching her forehead with the fingers of her right. As if the woman had somehow opened a door, others now came closer, two more with flowers, and a little boy with a carved wooden warrior—clearly a favorite toy from the wear—that Dhulyn held to her forehead and then returned, to the child's evident delight. As she did this, two other women came close enough to touch her outstretched arm. Dhulyn tensed, but they both backed away, touching their own foreheads.

"Tara Paledyn?"

Dhulyn had already been aware that those crowding around her to her left had parted to allow the young woman's halting approach, so she was not surprised to be addressed. And since she'd known the approach was halting, she wasn't surprised to find the girl leaning on a staff. The shoe on the left foot had been built up, and there was clearly something wrong in the way that foot was attached to the ankle. The young woman's only other distinguishing feature was that she wore no veils, her dark brown hair, pulled back and braided, was uncovered.

"If you would come with me, Tara Paledyn, the Marks you have asked to see are ready for you." There was some whispering among those watching, but though they stayed back, none seemed inclined to leave.

The Sanctuary Guide turned and led the way across the cold tiled floor toward the plain wooden doors at the closer end of the hall. Glancing sideways, Dhulyn could see the crowd following at a discreet distance as Remm Shalyn fell in at her left side.

"I am Dhulyn Wolfshead," she said to her guide. "What are you called?"

"I am Mender Fourteen," the young woman said.

Dhulyn slowed to a halt. "Your pardon if I am ignorant and offend. But do you not have names?"

The girl smiled, clearly not offended. "We do, but they are generally used only within the Sanctuary, among ourselves."

"I would prefer to use a name, if it is allowed."

"Then I am Medolyn."

Medolyn led Dhulyn and Remm Shalyn out of the vast public entry hall through a set of double doors into what was clearly an anteroom. Another bareheaded young woman stood pressing her hands together behind a large table on which were scrolls, pens, and bottles of ink.

Dhulyn smiled to herself. Clerks were clerks, it seemed, wherever one might go.

"This is the Paledyn Dhulyn Wolfshead," Medolyn said. The other girl scrambled to her feet. "This is Coria, a Finder."

"All of us clerks are," the other girl said with a grin. "Only a Finder could figure out where all the records are. You're to see the First Healer, aren't you, Tara Paledyn? And the First Mender and Finder as well, I think? They're waiting in the Blue Chamber, Medolyn. Your sword servant may remain here," Coria said to Dhulyn. "Or return to the main hall."

"I didn't think to see women being used as Stewards or clerks," Dhulyn said, as they left the anteroom and started down a long corridor lit by tall glass lamps standing in front of polished metal squares.

"There aren't so many of us that we can be particular about these things. Is it different, then, across the Long Ocean?"

Was there something more than mere curiosity in the girl's voice? Something wistful? Parno would have known, Dhulyn thought.

"It is. Men and women share all tasks and all things equally. Nor do the Marked live in Sanctuaries."

Medolyn stopped in front of a broad wooden door, inlaid with blue tiles.

"But where do they live, and how?"

"Where they choose, and by selling their services."

"But our service belongs to the Tarxin."

They're slaves, Dhulyn thought, a chill creeping up her back. *Well-treated, carefully looked after, but slaves nonetheless. He sells their services to others, I'll wager.* Thank Sun and Moon she'd told no one, not even the Nomads, of her own Mark.

"And if they don't live together, how is it ensured that the children are Marked?"

The chill spread across Dhulyn's shoulders and up the back of her neck. Were the Marked here being bred for their talent? And not as carefully as the Nomads handled their breeding. That would explain Medolyn's deformed foot. "It is not. The Marked marry whom they choose, and sometimes the children are Marked, and sometimes not. There are Guildhalls, for training—" And this was probably one of those, once upon a time. "But the Marked don't live there beyond the time they're trained."

Medolyn shook her head, her lower lip between her teeth. "It sounds . . . but perhaps I would be afraid, living on my own."

Dhulyn was spared an answer by the opening of the door. Medolyn led the way through, bowed to the three people sitting around a cold central fire bowl, and left.

"We welcome you, Tara Paledyn." The man who spoke was clearly the oldest of the trio, hawk-nosed, with pale green eyes and dark hair receding from his forehead. "I am Ellis, First Healer. This is First Finder Javen and First Mender Rascon." The Finder was a middle-aged woman whose graying hair was pulled tightly off her lined face. The Mender was the youngest of the three, a pretty woman with a heart-shaped face surrounded by dark curly hair escaping from its combs.

Dhulyn touched her forehead. "I am Dhulyn Wolfshead, called the Scholar. I was Schooled by Dorian of the River, the Black Traveler."

"If you would sit?" He indicated the fourth chair. Clearly, Dhulyn thought, the best chair in the room.

When they were all seated, and ganje had been offered and poured, the Healer spoke again.

"In what way can we serve you, Tara Paledyn?"

Dhulyn had thought of several ways to open the discussion she wanted to have, but the girl Medolyn had given her an opening she could not ignore. "Tell me," she said. "Why do you not Heal that young woman's foot?"

From the tightening of lips and the narrowing of eyes, all three of the Marked were at least somewhat offended by her question. *Good. Get them off-balance.*

"For the same reason I don't Heal this." Ellis Healer held up his left hand. There was an extra finger between the thumb and first finger. Ah, Dhulyn thought, *this* was the Healer she'd been seeing in her Visions.

"Medolyn's foot is not the result of injury. She was born with it. As I was born with my extra finger. There is no Healer living who has enough life energy to Heal a defect of birth, at least not on this side of the Long Ocean." His tone was not quite sharp enough to be disrespectful, but the intention was there.

"I have not heard that Healers could not heal birth defects," Dhulyn said evenly. Her words surprised them, that much she could see. "But I have never seen a Mark with such a defect—though I admit, I have not seen more than a few dozen in my lifetime."

The Mender, Rascon, threw her hands into the air. "We've been telling the cursed Tarxins for generations that we can't be bred like cattle without harm being done, to our Marks as well as to ourselves, but they've never listened."

"Have you tried refusing your services?" Dhulyn was sure she knew the answer, but was curious as to how they would phrase it.

"There's a limit to how much we can defy the Tarxin," Ellis said bluntly. "According to our agreement with the Tarxinate, we are given the privileges of home, roof, table, and bed. In return we owe our services. Theoretically, we have neutrality and privacy, self-government within the shelter of the Tarxinate. However . . ." The three Marked exchanged a glance. "In recent months, the present Tarxin has been . . . encroaching on our privileges."

"Perhaps you could help us?" Rascon Mender sat forward in her eagerness, hope in her eyes.

Dhulyn did not know what to answer. Her task here was to kill the Storm Witch and avenge the death of her Partner. The Common Rule, and her own heart, demanded it. She couldn't let the plight of these people deflect her from her goal. But the Marked were, in some measure, her people as well. If they were in need, could she turn her back on them? Normally, the Common Rule kept the Mercenary Brotherhood politically neutral, but surely she could speak to Remm Shalyn. Perhaps some of his contacts . . . ?

Dhulyn gave herself a mental shake. "I have come, as you know, with my own tasks to accomplish." Their faces, which had begun to relax, tightened once more. "If I am successful," she continued. "It may be that I can advise you as well." That would have to satisfy them, and herself, for now. Further than that she could not go.

"Tell us, then, how may we serve you?"

But even now, Dhulyn found she was unwilling to let the question of their abilities lie.

"You'll forgive my pursuing this question," she said. "But it may touch on my primary task. How is it that you would have life force enough to restore a spirit to its body, but insufficient to Heal yourself?"

"If I may answer." The others nodded and let Javen Finder continue. "Each Mark uses the life force of the Marked one," she said. "The harder the task, the greater the amount of life force used."

Dhulyn stifled her impatience. She'd asked, and now she had to listen.

"Life force is restored in the Marked one by eating, by sleep, and in some cases by singing, or playing music. But to Heal, for example, a defect of birth, that would require an amount of life force equivalent to the birth itself."

Dhulyn leaned forward, a thought having occurred to her. "I have seen Finders use scrying bowls, and Menders as well, use some tool symbolic of what they do, to focus their concentration. Would this not help you use less life force?"

Javen Finder leaned forward as well, eagerness plain on her face. "Do you know where we could find these things, Paledyn? Scholars have told us that such items were once used, but even working to-gether, none of us Finders have been able to locate such a thing."

"The Nomads aren't able to trade for them, no matter what we offer in exchange—or so they say," Rascon Mender said, nodding.

"They say truly. The ones I have seen were the property of the Marked ones who used them," Dhulyn said. "In all my travels I have never seen them for sale, or trade." Though she had seen, in a Scholars' Library, an ancient text describing how a Finder's bowl was made—but best to say nothing of that now. No point in giving false hopes; this would be something else for Remm Shalyn to investigate for her.

Ellis Healer stared off into the middle distance. "If we were able, if we could increase our powers, we'd be able to save the pregnancies that do not come to term, and Heal the babies that do not live. There'd be more of us, more Healers, more Seers for that matter. It's all we can do right now to keep the White Twins healthy, the Slain One knows, and when they die, we'll have no more Seers." Ellis blinked, drawing in a deep breath and looking around at his colleagues.

Rascon Mender tossed back her ganje and frowned down at her empty cup.

"Are they barren, then?" Dhulyn was asking as much for herself as for them.

"As good as. You know that only women are Seers?" Dhulyn nod-ded. "With Seers, the Mark itself consumes the life force that they would use to produce a child. They can either See or bear children, not both. In order to produce a child, there must be enough Seers that the others get all the Visions, while each in turn produces a child."

Well, so many of her questions answered, Dhulyn thought. Here was why the Visions seemed to be linked to her woman's cycle, stronger and weaker as the blood came and went. And here was the reason she had never borne any children of her own.

"How many must there be?"

Javen Finder spread her hands. "Who can know? The White Twins were born of two Healers, maybe twenty years after the last Seer died. So far as our records go, there have never been more than three Seers at one time."

"And no Marked appear in the outside population?"

Here the three Marked exchanged a look among themselves. "Sometimes, among the slaves, yes," Ellis Healer said. "It's our right to inspect any child when they reach the correct age, but we rarely obtain such a child from a Noble House."

"Unless the child is female." All three lowered their eyes, and Rascon Mender fussed with the jug of ganje, refilling cups.

Dhulyn was not surprised. A handy way to rid yourself of an unwanted child, and the female children would be the most unwanted.

"You have given me much to think about," she said finally, setting her cup of ganje down on the table to her right hand. "Now tell me, how did the Storm Witch come to inhabit the body of the Tarxin's daughter?"

Shock, and something like awe rippled across their faces before the Marked ones regained control of their features. *Good,* Dhulyn thought. *They'll be more likely to tell me the truth if they think I already know.* Still, at first it seemed they wouldn't say anything at all; each looked at the others, as if no one wanted to begin.

"Oh, for Sun and Moon," Dhulyn said, rubbing her forehead with the fingers of her left hand. "Speak freely, I beg you. I give you my oath as a—as a Paledyn that you will not suffer because you have told me the truth."

Rascon Mender looked at Javen Finder, and both turned to Ellis Healer. Finally, clearing his throat, he began.

"You must consider, Tara Paledyn, that we were not summoned for some two or three days after the Tara Xendra fell."

"How did she fall, exactly?" Dhulyn realized she had been thinking along the lines of a fall from a horse, but of course, without horses . . .

"She had been playing in the gardens above, and slipped while running along the top of a wall," Javen said.

"There is no doubt that she hit her head, the swelling and discoloration were still quite noticeable when we viewed her," Ellis continued. "We were told that she lost consciousness for only a very short period at that time, and while she complained of headache, she did eat her supper that evening, and fell asleep normally."

"You understand," cut in Rascon. "All this is what we were told at the time; we've no way to know whether any of it's true. The lady pages wouldn't have wanted the Tarxin, Light of the Sun, to know that they'd let his child hurt herself, so they might not have told soon enough, you see? They might have said she was fine at first just to save themselves."

"In any case, when we examined her, we found that while the body lived, it was empty, the soul was gone, and we so informed the Tarxin, Light of the Sun."

"Then I made the mistake of saying the soul was 'lost,' you see, meaning to speak it softly like, and the Tarxin, Light of the Sun, told Javen here to Find it." Rascon shook her head, and still another curl fell loose from her combs.

"And the thing was, I did Find a soul almost right away." Javen gestured with her hands. "And it was so eager to get into the body that I took it for the Tara's own soul, else why so eager?"

"So you Found, Healed, and Mended," Dhulyn said. "You have placed this soul into the Tara's body. Can you take it out? Will taking it out destroy it?"

Again, the exchange of looks between the Marked ones. Finally, Javen spoke up. "Tara Paledyn. What we tell you now no one else knows, not even others here in the Sanctuary."

"We trust in your goodness, and in your word, you see." Rascon evidently felt she needed to make things clear.

"You may do so," Dhulyn said.

"Four days after the events we tell you of, we came again to the Tara Xendra's apartments, to make sure she was feeling no further ill effects," Javen said. "It was obvious to us that she was no longer the Tara Xendra. We feared then what the Tarxin, Light of the Sun, might do."

"It's one thing not to heal his daughter, you see. It's another entirely to set some foreign spirit masquerading about in his daughter's body." Rascon's brisk tone was thinly spread over a very real fear.

"What did you do?" For it was obvious from their shifting and throat clearing that they had done something.

"We expelled the spirit from the body." Ellis Healer's voice was low.

"What?"

"We were trying—we thought we might Find the real Xendra after all, you see, since we knew this one wasn't her. But it didn't stay expelled, that was the problem. We could push it out, but we couldn't keep it out."

"So even if the real child's spirit is out there to be Found . . ."

"It can't get back into its own body, no, because the body's occupied, isn't it?" Rascon slapped her hands on her knees.

"Tara Paledyn, there is more." The Healer laced his fingers together. "Three times we tried to expel the strange spirit, and each time there were great storms, with winds and lightnings. Once, even ice fell from the sky. It was clear to us that the spirit possessing the child's body was a Weather Mage, such as the old books speak of. We made no further attempts."

"But you *can* expel the Storm Witch, you *can* put the real child's soul back?"

"Very likely, the true soul would be easy to Heal and Mend quickly, but Paledyn, we do not have the real child's soul."

Dhulyn tapped her fingers on the arm of her chair. "Find it," she said. "Perhaps now that the stronger soul of the Storm Witch is no longer," Dhulyn waved her hands, "distracting you, you can Find the real soul more easily."

Javen Finder frowned, looking inward before she spoke. "Well, if you say so, Tara Paledyn. I'll try."

Had she made the right decision, Dhulyn wondered? Would the Storm Witch be easier, or harder to destroy outside of the body? Instinct told her that if the spirit wanted so desperately to stay in the body, expelling it was the right thing to do. Would that be the same as destroying it?

Dhulyn sighed. At the very least, she would know more. And knowledge was always like a good sword in the hand of someone who knew how to use it.

The Seers' section of the Sanctuary was well apart from the areas of the other Marked, and unlike them, the White Twins never came out of their rooms. Petitioners, even the Tarxin himself, had to go or send to them. Xerwin felt his skin crawl and forced his shoulders to stop creeping up around his ears. This was the real reason he hadn't wanted Dhulyn Wolfshead to accompany him on his errand. How could he let her see his reaction to the Seers?

As usual, he was met beyond the Seers' door by one of the elderly women who served as the White Twins' attendants. He had sent ahead to let them know he was coming. Early on, he'd learned that when he didn't, he wasn't likely to get a useful Vision, if he got one at all.

"Right this way, Tar Xerwin, if you please," the woman said the same way she always did. She kept her hands folded at her waist and toddled in front of him on her short legs like a self-important hen.

The White Twins had one of the innermost rooms of the Sanctuary, where no sunlight could find them, even by accident. Nor were their personal rooms lit by use of the mirrored panels that brought true sunlight into the inner rooms of many of the Noble Houses. This did not mean the Twins had no light in their rooms, however. The sisters were said to be afraid of the dark, and so there were always lamps lit and candles burning, dozens of them, set into cloudy glass bowls or covered with colored glass shades.

The two women were playing a game with chalks and vera tiles on the floor when he was ushered into their day room. Drawing contorted stick figures and images of the Slain God knew what strange things. As always when they saw him, they ran squealing to touch his clothes and his hair with their long white fingers, exclaiming over its color and darkness, and holding up the ends of their own white braids to compare.

"Now then, now then," he said, as he always did, sounding in his own ears like some wise old uncle from a play. "If you sit down and behave yourselves, I've got chocolate for you."

"We know you, don't we," said one, while the other nodded, and nodded and kept on nodding. They had names, but since they never answered to them, no one used them, calling them only "girls" or "my dears."

Sometimes it was hard to remember that these women were older than he was, and that though their faces were unlined, there should perhaps be some gray starting to show in the hair that had always been whiter than the sands of the beach.

"Of course you know me, I'm Xerwin," he said. They wouldn't remember his rank, or anyone else's for that matter, which Xerwin had always suspected was one of the reasons the Tarxin did not like to come. They nodded, only twice thank the Slain God, but their pink eyes were empty.

"Xerwin, Xerwin, Xerwin," sang one, sinking back to the floor.

"That's right, and now you're going to answer some questions for me, aren't you?"

"You said you had chocolate," the first one said, and the other nodded again.

"Are you sitting in your big chair? Are you behaving yourselves?" He arched his eyebrows and put his hands on his hips, as they giggled and ran for their chairs. He'd learned that if he treated the Twins as he'd treated Xendra when she was five or six, he'd get the best response.

"Now, can you sing your song for me?"

"We know lots of songs," the twin on the left said.

"But for chocolate you'll sing your special song, you know the one I like?" Xerwin began to hum a simple, repetitive tune. The twin on the left clapped her hands and begun to hum as well, while the twin on the right began to sing. Soon, her sister had joined her.

The words were nonsense as far as Xerwin could tell, though when he came for a Vision they always sang the same words, and as they sang, their voices grew stronger, deepened. They sat very still, clasping hands, breathing in unison. They reached the point in the song where they always stopped, and sat, quietly, their faces relaxed, older, their eyes focused to some great distance, true, but *focused* in a way they had not been moments before.

Recognizing his moment, Xerwin had his question ready. "What does the coming of the Paledyn mean for the Mortaxa?"

"We see a tall woman, a warrior, hair like old blood, scarred of face, but clean of soul and vision. She leads a small, dark child by the hand.

They are singing." Both white women smiled, identical smiles, and Xerwin's breath caught in his throat.

"They sing a song we all know, though you never sing it with us," the twin on the right said.

Xerwin shuddered. This woman, the woman who was speaking now, and her sister—assured, confident, smiling at some secret humor—why did they appear only when the twins were Seeing? Where were they when the Visions were gone?

"When the Paledyn comes, rain will fall in the desert; the hind chase the lion; the creatures of the sea will walk the beaches."

"What does this mean?"

"Who is simple now? Who the child?" The twin on the left looked directly at him and smiled. "Should we speak more plain? The Paledyn changes all. Nothing will be as it was. The world as you know it will be gone, forever."

"For better or for worse?" But now they no longer listened.

"Trees will flower in winter; the sea will rise, the land ripple and flow."

Their voices slowly faded, and the twin on the right began singing once more. Their faces slackened and their pink eyes unfocused.

The Vision was gone, the Sight finished, and the Seers were children again. Xerwin chewed on his lower lip as he left the White Twins to the care of their attendants. He knew poetry when he heard it, and the extremity of what they'd said didn't frighten him. Change was what they meant, great change. That was what Dhulyn Wolfshead was bringing. He stepped out into the main hall and checked the people waiting there, but he saw no sign of her.

There was one change he definitely wanted, and that was to get that Storm Witch out of his sister's body. Dhulyn Wolfshead had said she would help with that, and the White Twins had definitely seen her leading a dark-haired child by the hand. But if he told his father what he'd learned here today . . . Xerwin let out the breath he hadn't realized he was holding.

"What weighty Vision brings about such a sigh, Tar Xerwin?"

Xerwin looked round to find Naxot at his elbow.

"Naxot, thank the Slain God." Xerwin took his friend by the arm and led him to an uninhabited bench near the door through which the Paledyn would have passed earlier into the inner Sanctuary. Xerwin's own attendants would keep any others out of hearing distance.

"The White Twins say that the Paledyn will bring changes, great changes." He closed his hand around Naxot's wrist. "I think she may bring Xendra back."

"Can she do this?"

"Who knows? Perhaps she will persuade the Storm Witch to return to her own place."

"But the Storm Witch is a Holy Woman."

Xerwin bit down on his impatience. Naxot's orthodoxy was becoming irritating. "And Paledyns are the Hands of the Slain God."

"What will you tell the Tarxin, Light of the Sun?" Naxot said.

That is a very good question, Xerwin thought. "What if I don't tell him anything at all?" He looked at Naxot from the corner of his eye.

"Leave everything to the Slain God, Xerwin," Naxot said, patting him on the shoulder. "Do nothing rash before prayer."

"Perhaps you're right," Xerwin said, standing up as he saw the door to the inner Sanctuary opening.

Fifteen

THE SANCTUARY HALL WAS NOTICEABLY darker now that the sun had set, and the great mirrors of polished silver and glass no longer had daylight to reflect. Remm Shalyn escorted Dhulyn across the wide expanse of floor, impossibly huge now that it was empty except for them.

"I stop out here," he said, twisting up his lips and looking around him with bright eyes. "It was you they sent for, not me," he added to her raised eyebrow.

"And you'll give some thought to what we discussed?"

"I could do more than think about it, if I ask to see the First Marks, while you're with the Seers." He smiled and looked over her shoulder as a middle-aged woman appeared in the Seers' doorway. She touched her forehead to Dhulyn as they neared her, and nodded to Remm Shalyn. Remm stepped to one side, leaned his shoulder against the wall next to the door, and grinned.

"I'll be here when you come out, Dhulyn Wolfshead."

The Seers' portion of the Sanctuary was darker than even the almost deserted main hall. This was the section of the Sanctuary farthest from the cliff face, deep into the rock that formed the city. As Dhulyn followed her guide, her Mercenary-Schooled senses automatically noted the direction of each turning. If for some reason the lighting failed, Dhulyn would have no trouble finding her way back to the entrance—or to any other spot in the city she had already been.

"Are you Marked yourself, lady?" she asked the attendant who was guiding her.

"Well, I am, then," the woman said, looking back over her shoulder.

"But it doesn't go deep, my Mark. I can Heal small things—scratches, sore throats, and such. I mostly look after the little ones, and for the last while I've been helping with the White Twins. They don't like change, you see, it upsets them and throws off their Visions. If they see me around them more and more, little by little, I can help with them more."

"Is their present attendant getting older?"

"You're a sharp one, then. Though, seeing as you're a Paledyn, I suppose I shouldn't be surprised. Right this way, please, Tara."

They turned yet another corner and the light dimmed even more. The single door in front of them had raised panels, but was otherwise unadorned. The attendant noticed Dhulyn's interest.

"The old Seer, the one before the Twins, she was blind, they say, so you don't see the kind of decoration we have elsewhere."

"And the White Twins, they do not care for decoration?"

"Ah well, they're children, aren't they? Their tastes are going to run a different way. You'll see, Tara."

The woman hesitated with her hand on the door latch. "You've been told what to expect, then, Tara? It's not just what they look like, you see, it's that they're really like children, and if they've a Sight for you alone, well, then I have to leave you with them, you see."

"I have been told, yes."

Nodding, the woman opened the door and stepped through, saying "Here she is, then, my dear ones, the Tara Paledyn come to see you." Dhulyn stepped forward, and heard the door shut behind her.

The room was full of soft light, candles in glass jars and lamps with colored shades. Two women, skin so white it almost glowed, sat at the farthest of three tables, spoons in their hands, bowls of porridge in front of them.

Even though Remm Shalyn had warned Dhulyn what to expect, her breath still faltered in her throat when she saw them. An Outlander, and a Red Horseman, Dhulyn was well used to being the palest person in any gathering, but these women made her look like a Berdanan. She had seen a horse once with the White Disease, and she knew that it happened occasionally with other animals, but to see these women, white as the finest parchment, their eyes red as coals—at first her mind simply rejected the image. She remembered what Parno had said about twins, that some could make their livings traveling with players. But these women could not have done such a thing. Like the horse Dhulyn had seen, their skin would not tan, and exposure to the sun would eventually kill them.

They had leaped to their feet as soon as Dhulyn cleared the doorway, flinging down their spoons and rushing to her with their arms outstretched. They ran without heed across chalk drawings of stick figures and round, four-legged beasts on the floor. One had a smear of jam on her cheek. And a fleck of gold in the pink iris of her left eye. Dhulyn braced herself as they flung themselves on her, wrapping their arms around her tightly enough to make her uncomfortable.

"Careful, careful of the blades, my hearts," she said, working her arms free as gently as she could. The hilts of sword and daggers were digging into her hipbones, and undoubtedly into the rib cages of the women hugging her.

"We Saw you coming," the one said. "We Saw you. You don't know us, but we know you, Sister. Welcome, welcome, welcome."

"Come, come." They dragged her forward, not to the table that held their suppers, but to one closer to the long row of candles. "Come see our things."

These were the toys of princesses. Wooden dolls with articulated joints, finely dressed and with little veils covering their hair. Small wooden animals populated a farmyard made with a miniature fence and stacks of vera tiles. Dhulyn pressed her lips together and looked away from the chanter that lay to one side with other musical instruments. It was altogether too much like the one Parno attached to his pipes.

"Very beautiful," Dhulyn said as one of the women held up what was obviously her favorite doll. It was hard for Dhulyn to show more than courteous interest; her own childhood had been short, and she'd had little experience with children in her Mercenary's life. She found herself hoping, as they continued to present her with their toys and precious possessions, that her smiles and exclamations were satisfying to the Twins. Oddly, she found the contrast between their behavior and their apparent age less distracting than their illness.

"We have a secret," said the golden-eyed one in a whisper. "You need to See," she said. "Come, we can all See together."

Dhulyn's heart froze in her chest. Would they understand what it might cost her, if they told anyone else what they knew? Almost as if they had read her mind, the other Twin put her finger up to her lips. "Secret," she mouthed, nodding her head over and over.

Another thought struck Dhulyn, even more dreadful than the first. "Wait, wait now." She tried to be gentle pulling back from them. "What if I don't want to See?"

"But why?" "But you must." They spoke simultaneously and then looked at each other with brows drawn down.

"I'm afraid."

The Twin on the left snickered and the one on the right elbowed her. "What of?"

"I might See my Partner's death again," Dhulyn said simply. "And I don't want to."

"But we're together." The girl seemed to be puzzled. "Together, we can choose."

"We can choose what we See, because we See together," the other explained. The other one rolled her eyes in a manner so reminiscent of a child beginning to be impatient with an adult's dimness that Dhulyn almost laughed.

"Come, come." This time they led her over to a smaller, round table which had been cleared of a great deal of chalks, pens, tiny paint brushes—and more loose vera tiles Dhulyn saw with a shiver—now lying scattered on the floor. Three chairs had been set around the table, and the Twins made her sit in one, taking the others for themselves.

"Hands now." Dhulyn took their hands, still sticky with the jam from their suppers.

"Clear your mind," said the one with the golden fleck in her eye. "Clear, clear. Clear as sky."

"What's your question? Make your question clear."

They began to sing, a tune familiar to Dhulyn, but with words she had never heard. Not nonsense sounds, she realized, with a shiver, she *had* heard words like them. This was the language of the Caids. How close to the original, she wondered, could this be?

"No, silly," the Twin on her right tugged at her hand. "That's not your question."

Dhulyn felt herself blushing. Here, all alone, was not the time for her attention to slip so easily from her task. She began by humming along with the Twins, finally singing the words she knew, the words to a children's song, to the tune.

How could she destroy the Storm Witch? That was the question she needed answered.

SUDDENLY, SHE IS STANDING IN A TINY CLEARING IN THE WOODS, WHERE SNOW LINGERS IN THE HOLLOWS, AND IN THE DEEPER BRANCHES OF THE PINES. WHERE SHE STANDS, WITH THE TWINS BESIDE HER, THE GROUND IS CLEAR.

"NEVER FEAR, DEAR ONE," SAYS THE TWIN ON HER LEFT. "WE WILL NEVER TELL ANYONE YOU ARE MARKED."

"THERE IS LITTLE WE CAN DO FOR OURSELVES," THE OTHER ADDS. "BUT WE CAN CERTAINLY DO THIS MUCH FOR YOU. YOU MUST KNOW THAT WE HAVE BEEN WAITING ALL OUR LIVES FOR YOU TO COME."

"YOU DON'T KNOW US, BUT WE KNOW YOU, AND LOVE YOU LIKE A TRUE SISTER. I AM AMAIA," THIS IS THE TWIN WITH THE GOLD-MARKED EYE. "AND THIS KERIA."

"BUT YOU ARE . . ." DHULYN FALTERS, NOT KNOWING HOW TO FINISH HER THOUGHT WITHOUT GIVING OFFENSE.

"NOT WITLESS?" THE TWO SISTERS SMILE AT EACH OTHER. "NOT NOW, NO. SO YOU SEE WHY WE SPEND AS MUCH TIME IN VISION AS WE CAN."

DHULYN LOOKS AROUND HER. SHE CAN FEEL THEIR TOUCH, THE HARDNESS OF THE COLD GROUND UNDER HER BOOTS, THE CHILL OF THE AIR, THINGS SHE DOES NOT ALWAYS FEEL IN VISIONS.

"THIS IS WHAT IT MEANS TO SEE WHILE IN COMPANY?"

"PRECISELY," AMAIA SAYS, NODDING. "IT'S NOT ONLY TO HAVE CHILDREN, AS THE HEALER TOLD YOU, THAT SEERS BAND TOGETHER, IT IS FOR THE STRENGTH OF THE VISIONS, THE CONTROL WE HAVE OVER THE SIGHT, WHEN WE ARE TOGETHER."

"AND SO WE ARE STRONGER IN VISION," KERIA ADDS. "CLEANER, MORE OUR-SELVES, AS YOU ARE MORE YOURSELF, SISTER."

DHULYN REALIZES FOR THE FIRST TIME THAT SHE IS DRESSED IN HER OLD QUILTED, MULTICOLORED VEST, HER SOFTEST LEATHER TROUSERS, AND THE SEMLORIAN BOOTS SHE'D LEFT IN HER CABIN ON THE *WAVETREADER*. AND HER HAIR IS LONG AGAIN, ITS FINE BRAIDS KNOTTED AND TIED BACK OFF HER FACE.

"THIS IS YOUR VISION," KERIA SAYS. "WE ARE HERE ONLY TO HELP YOU, TO MAKE IT STRONGER."

"DO YOU KNOW THIS PLACE AT ALL? HAVE YOU SEEN THIS BEFORE?"

"NO, I DON'T THINK . . ." DHULYN PAUSES, SURELY THAT SMELL IS ONE SHE KNOWS. SHE TURNS TOWARD IT, AND A PATH OPENS IN THE FOREST. ALL THREE

STEP INTO IT, AND AS THEY FOLLOW IT, THE FOREST CLOSES ONCE MORE BEHIND THEM AND THE PATH DISAPPEARS. VERY QUICKLY, THE PATH AHEAD OF THEM OPENS UP INTO A CLEARING, AND THERE DHULYN SEES A REDHEADED WOMAN, WIPING THE HAIR OUT OF A SMALL CHILD'S FACE.

"MY MOTHER," SHE SAYS TO THE TWINS. "AND MYSELF."

DHULYN SHAKES HER HEAD A LITTLE, THE SMALLEST OF MOVEMENTS SIDE TO SIDE. WHY THIS VISION AGAIN? HOW WILL THIS HELP HER DESTROY THE STORM WITCH? SHE HAS ALWAYS SEEN THIS VISION FROM A DIFFERENT ANGLE, AND FROM MUCH CLOSER, TOO. SHE LOOKS TOWARD THE SPOT WHICH WOULD GIVE HER THE FAMILIAR POINT OF VIEW, HALF EXPECTING TO SEE A SHADOW OF HER SEEING SELF, BUT THE PLACE IS EMPTY. FROM WHERE SHE STANDS NOW, THE TWINS TO EITHER SIDE OF HER, DHULYN CAN SEE MORE OF THE CAMP BEHIND HER MOTHER, THE OTHER FIRES, FIGURES RUNNING, HORSES LOOSE, AND THE UNMISTAKABLE RISE AND FALL OF WEAPONS IN THE NEAR DISTANCE.

"USUALLY, I CAN HEAR MY MOTHER SPEAKING," DHULYN SAYS WHEN SHE REALIZES THEY COULD HEAR NO NOISE OTHER THAN THE WIND IN THE TREES.

KERIA PUT HER HAND ON DHULYN'S ARM. "THIS IS CLEARLY ANOTHER PART OF THE STORY." AS THEY WATCH, THE CHILD KISSES HER MOTHER AND WALKS TOWARD THEM. EVEN THOUGH THEY KNOW THEY DON'T HAVE TO, ALL THREE OF THEM STEP BACK OUT OF THE CHILD'S WAY AS SHE PUSHES THROUGH UNDERBRUSH AND LOW BRANCHES. THE PATH THAT EXISTED FOR DHULYN AND THE TWINS DOES NOT EXIST FOR HER.

"DO YOU REMEMBER THIS NIGHT?" AMAIA LOOKS BACK OVER HER SHOULDER AT DHULYN'S MOTHER, WHO IS REMOVING THE LAST TRACES OF THE CHILD FROM HER CAMPSITE.

DHULYN SHAKES HER HEAD. "UNTIL I FIRST HAD THIS VISION, NOT SO LONG AGO, I HAD NO MEMORIES OF MY MOTHER AT ALL. I COULD NOT EVEN PICTURE HER FACE. I HAVE SEEN HER IN SEVERAL VISIONS SINCE, SOMETIMES WITH FRESNOYN, SOMETIMES USING THE VERA TILES."

"BEST WE TELL NO ONE OF THE FRESNOYN," AMAIA SAYS. "THINGS ARE BAD ENOUGH WITHOUT THAT, AND WE WOULDN'T BE ABLE TO STOP THEM."

"ANOTHER SECRET," KERIA AGREES.

A PART OF DHULYN WISHES TO STAY AND WATCH WHAT HAPPENS TO THE HORSEMEN'S CAMP. SHE KNOWS THAT THIS WAS THE NIGHT IN WHICH THE TRIBES ARE BROKEN BY TREACHERY AND DECEIT, BUT SHE HAS ONLY MET ONE OTHER SURVIVOR, AND KNOWS VERY LITTLE OF WHAT OCCURS ON THIS NIGHT. STILL SHE FINDS HERSELF TURNING TO FOLLOW THE CHILD SHE WAS INTO THE HIDING PLACE HER MOTHER HAD PREPARED FOR HER.

IT IS CLOSER THAN DHULYN WOULD HAVE THOUGHT, BUT THE CHILD IS CAREFUL, PLACING HER FEET ONLY ON CLEAR SPOTS WHERE SHE WILL LEAVE NO PRINT, DUCKING UNDER SNOW-LADEN BRANCHES THAT A GROWN PERSON WOULD HAVE TO AVOID ENTIRELY. FINALLY, THE CHILD GOES TO HER KNEES AND CRAWLS INTO THE SMALLEST GAP BETWEEN THE BOUGHS OF A PINE THICKET. AS BEFORE, A PATH CLEARS FOR DHULYN AND THE WHITE SEERS. HERE IN THE THICKET THERE IS ALREADY A SMALL WATERSKIN, A POUCH WITH TRAVEL BREAD, A CLOAK, AND A PILE OF SOFT INGLERA HIDES.

BUT THE CHILD THEY FIND ASLEEP ON THE SKINS IS NOT THE YOUNG DHULYN, BUT AN OLDER, DARKER CHILD, HER THICK BLACK HAIR BRAIDED INTO A CROWN AROUND HER HEAD, HER VEILS SET TO ONE SIDE.

AMAIA BLINKS HER GOLD-FLECKED EYE AND CROUCHES DOWN ON HER HEELS, HOLDING HER HAND OUT OVER THE SLEEPING CHILD.

"THIS IS THE TARA XENDRA," SHE SAYS. "WE KNOW HER. HER BROTHER BROUGHT HER ONCE TO PLAY WITH OUR OTHER SELVES."

Parno clapped his hands and the six members of the crew he was watching held up their swords and stood back from each other. Two of them, he noted, acted with some degree of sharpness and precision. He didn't have time to School them in the Mercenary manner, but he and Dhulyn had twice taken untrained civilians and turned them into reasonable fighting units. He was confident he could do the same here, with half-trained Nomads, even without her.

"What do you think?" Malfin had come up on his left side, and Parno was certain he'd *felt* the man's approach seconds before he'd heard him.

"The second on the left, and the first on the right. They'll do. The two farthest from me fight as though the sword has only a point." Parno looked across his folded arms at the captain. "Been trained only with the *garwon*, I expect?"

Mal nodded. "Would it be better if gave you only those with some sword training?"

Parno grinned before patting Mal on the shoulder. "Would seem logical, wouldn't it? The fact is some are suited to fast training and some aren't. Those who are . . ." he shrugged. "It doesn't seem to matter whether they're already swordsmen or not."

Mal nodded. "Sar and Chels, you're on the list," he called out. "The rest of you are excused." He turned back to Parno. "Gives you seven. Be enough?"

"It will. Remember, not trying to take the city, or even to breach the walls, just to get in. The fewer the better, so long as they're the right ones."

"Still wish could come with you myself."

Parno knew the sentiment was a real one, the man was sincere. But captains had special duties, and were bound in a way that other Nomads were not. Even with a twin to share the captaincy, Malfin could no more leave his ship for this than the Crayx could leave the ocean.

Parno had spent the better part of two days drilling the weapons handlers aboard the *Wavetreader*. Almost every adult had some experience with sword, arbalest, or *garwon*—Nomad life required that all had at least a basic training—but he had found only these seven showing the aptitude that would respond to accelerated training. He wasn't surprised that the group included the twins Tindar and Elian who had sparred with him that day, as well as Conford and Mikel the bosun. But he was a little surprised at how good Conford was, all things considered. And how ready he was to listen, and learn.

Parno set his squad up in pairs, directing Conford to take his turn with the winner in each pair. "Remember what I've shown you," he said. "The first seven movements, only, until one of you is touched. Then Conford will step in. I'll be watching, so stay sharp."

"Dar told me about your family in Imrion." Mal found a place to sit on the rail. "Would really accept a connection with Nomads? Know you're a Mercenary and all, but . . ."

Parno kept his eyes on the pairs sparring in front of him as he answered. "According to the Common Rule, a Mercenary Brother has no family but the Brotherhood itself," he said. "But my family chooses to acknowledge me, regardless of the Common Rule, and what I might think." And they'd acknowledged Dhulyn as well, though that wasn't something Parno wanted to say aloud. "And at that, I'm not the one who's had the strangest time in my family, just the one who's managed to stay alive." He glanced at Mal. "And my cousin, the House now, is a very practical man. Will see this as an alliance worth cultivating."

Parno stepped across to where the fighters had begun to spread apart, within the confines of the section of deck they'd been given for their workout. He touched the elbow of the twin Tindar and waited until the swords stopped. "Don't look just at the tip of her sword," he told Tindar's opponent. "Try to see the sword, her shoulders, even her eyes, all at once. Each movement will give you a clue to the next one." He turned back to Tindar. "Vary your strokes more, if use only third and fourth, will be very easy to stop you."

"Is that how *you* got me?" But she was grinning as she said it, blinking the sweat out of her eyes. The day was warm, but windy.

"Not going to tell you *all* my secrets." When they'd resumed fighting, Parno turned back to Mal, and found Dar standing beside her brother. Parno glanced at the sun, judging from its distance above the yardarm that Mal's watch was almost over.

Dar's eyes were shining, and her smile was at once brilliant and gentle. Parno thought she had never looked so beautiful.

"Good news for us," she said. "And for your cousins." She placed the palm of her hand against her belly, in a gesture Parno had seen many a pregnant woman use before her. "Crayx say twins."

Parno blew out his breath. "Can you . . . ?" he gestured awkwardly, not knowing exactly how to word what he wanted to ask.

"No," she said. "Too early. But Crayx can, through me. So Pod-sensed for certain, the little ones."

Parno nodded. "But will keep in mind what I said about my family, won't you? They'll acknowledge the connection. And there might be others," he added, when he sensed what he knew was a shade of doubt pass through them. "If I'm Pod-sensed, there might be others in my family as well."

At that, their faces brightened, and the tiny shadow of doubt passed from their eyes.

"Off to rest." Dar cuffed her brother on the shoulder with the back of her hand. "My watch now."

Grinning, Mal slapped Parno on the back and walked off to his cabin. Darlara slipped her arm through Parno's and he did not pull away, telling himself there was no need. There was only crew around them, only Nomads. There was no reason to keep watch, and besides, since Dar was on his left side, his best sword hand was free.

By this time most of the matches were over, and the recruits were standing in a rough circle, watching Conford spar with his latest opponent. The young man had taken his shirt off, and while there was a red stroke across his upper left arm, he seemed otherwise untouched.

"That one, Conford? Seems to stand apart," Parno said. "More skilled than the others, but there's something else."

"He's an exchange, thought you knew." Dar's face changed. "No, it was your Partner he spoke to most, remember now."

"So came from another Pod?"

The two fighters were clearly slowing down, their blades still moving, but falling lower and lower as inexperienced wrists and forearms tired.

"*Windwaver* Pod. Comes once a year from the Round Ocean, far to the east of here."

"Or far to the west, depending on where you start." It was odd to think that from the land of the Mortaxa, the Round Ocean was to the east, when children in Boravia grew up thinking of it as to the west.

Dar grinned, tucked loose hair back into the scarf she was wearing. "The Round Ocean is always where it is. It's only the Pods that move."

A shout declared the bout over, and the two fighters stood in identical postures of exhaustion, bent over, chests heaving, hands braced on thighs.

"Well done, all of you," Parno said. He drew Dar with him as he inserted himself into the group, looking at a bad bruise here, and giving an encouraging slap there.

"All are excused watches until your training finishes," Dar said. "Go clean up now, and get ready to eat."

"Conford." The younger man turned to Parno and smiled, wiping his face off with his shirt. "Come see me when you've cleaned up."

Parno waited until the man had gone to join the others before turning back to Dar. "So Conford comes from another Pod entirely?"

Dar nodded. "Good to exchange with Nomads from the other oceans, keeps the bloodlines clean, but usually happens at our Great Gatherings every five years. Conford's a special case."

"How so?"

"Usually must have four generations of unconnected blood for an exchange to be made. But Conford needed to leave his ship, and *Wavetreader* was the only Pod close enough."

Halfway up the gangway to the aft upper deck Parno stopped, and looked back along the lower deck to where his recruits were sloshing each other with water pulled up from over the side.

"He doesn't have the look of a troublemaker," he said, before following Dar the last few steps to the top.

"Oh, no. His twin had died, and he couldn't stay where she no longer was."

"Died? Some kind of accident?" Except for the frostbite they'd seen when he and Dhulyn had first come on board, Parno had observed no signs of illness among the crew. Even without the assistance of the Marked, the Nomads seemed to enjoy good health.

"She was lost overboard." Dar frowned and sat down on the pilot's bench behind and to port of the wheel. "When the moment came, wouldn't let the Crayx swallow her, as you were swallowed, and so wasn't saved." Dar waved her hand toward the sea where the Crayx were. "Doesn't live still."

Parno stayed upright, leaning his elbow against the rail, remembering his own experience inside the Crayx, and the offer they had made him. "Why wouldn't she?"

"Don't know. Some say she had the enclosure sickness, and couldn't bring herself to enter such a small space. Don't know, though, never knew someone with it. Have you heard of such things?"

"Yes," he said. "Yes, I've heard of it." It had been on the tip of his tongue to tell her that he had a mild form of the horizon sickness himself, but habit, and the Common Rule, held it back. "It must have been difficult for her in any case. So much of a ship is enclosed and small."

Dar shrugged. "Slept on deck, I imagine."

"And the Crayx could not have forced her to be saved?"

"Of course. But how could we live that way? Knowing they would force us against our will?" She turned her face toward him, her dark eyes shining though her face was somber. What she said confirmed Parno's own experience. The Crayx would not force their human partners—not even to save them.

"Too hard for Conford to stay." Dar had gone on with her story. "So took first chance of exchange that offered. Fits in well enough, but hard, very hard to be one where were always two." She rested her fingertips on his wrist. "Hard for you, too?"

Parno's jaw clenched against the wave of grief that washed through him, and it was all he could do not to clench his fists as well. From the clouding of her eyes, Darlara clearly saw this in his face, but she did not turn away, or remove her hand. At least his child—children, he corrected—had a brave mother.

"Was not Partnered my whole life," he said when he thought his voice was steady enough.

"No, but best part, most important part."

Somehow, it was easier, knowing that Dar understood.

Before he needed to say anything, Conford came up the gangway and presented himself, hair wet, clothing brushed and shaken out.

"Asked for me, Paledyn."

"Conford." Now that he knew what to look for, Parno could see the marks of strain around the younger man's eyes. The telltale signs of sleepless nights and loss of appetite. "Know what I intend to do?"

"Aye, sir. Kill the Storm Witch."

Carefully, not giving so much detail as to overwhelm, Parno explained his strategy, the landing party, the coordinated attack on the frontage of Ketxan City. At first, Conford followed him with brow furrowed and frown, but as Parno finished, the young Nomad was smiling.

"So I'm for the land?" His eyes sparkled.

"Fight well, and have good instincts, and this is the more dangerous part."

If anything, Conford seemed happier. "Aye, sir."

"Conford, I need a second. Both the captains would like to go, but you know why they can't." Conford nodded. "A second isn't someone who's there for glory, or even someone who's there to give his life for his fellows. He's someone I can count on to get the job done if I fall. And if possible, be there to bring his comrades back. Understand?"

Now he had stopped smiling, his lips pressed together in a line, but Parno felt optimistic when the younger man did not answer immediately, and without thought. It seemed that Parno had judged his man correctly. In a manner of speaking, Conford was the closest person on board to another Mercenary, in that he understood death in the depth of his soul and, in his way, was ready to die. He shared that understanding, and that readiness with Parno. Could he also share the understanding of duty and obligation?

Conford gave a short nod. "Aye, Paledyn. Understood. I can do that."

Sixteen

"**Y**OUR FATHER THE TARXIN, Light of the Sun, has sent the Paledyn to see you, Tara Xendra."

Carcali put down the tiny finger harp but didn't turn from the toy shelves. She often found herself, instead of studying her maps and making calculations, rearranging the small wooden animals, wondering if the jewels in their harnesses could possibly be real. She sighed and turned to face the other woman. She'd already learned there wasn't much point in arguing with Finexa. Supposedly, she was only a new lady page, now that the Tara Xendra was acknowledged as a Storm Witch, and no longer a mere child whose old attendant Kendraxa was more nurse than page. In fact, Carcali suspected that Finexa reported to the Tarxin every day—or at least when there was anything to report. And refusing to meet with the painted barbarian woman would probably come under that heading. Things had been going well since her last meeting with the Tarxin. He'd seen to it that she had the supplies she needed, and had sent for one of the globes in the Scholars' Library, where they were on notice to assist her when she sent for them. She had to be careful not to do anything that would jeopardize that.

"Just taking a short break," she said, hoping she didn't sound as defensive as she felt. "Why is the Paledyn here?"

"The Light of the Sun did not say, Tara Xendra. But he has asked her to watch over you. Perhaps that explains it."

"Very well, I will see her."

Finexa's eyes narrowed, but all she did was give a shallow curtsy and turn back to the door.

Somehow, the Paledyn, when she entered, looked taller, rougher, and more dangerous standing in what was still, for all intents and purposes, the day room of an eleven-year-old girl. She had managed to find, or have made for her, a pair of pale gold linen trousers and over them she wore a green sleeveless jerkin trimmed with satin ties, and with a bright red patch sewn on one shoulder. Her blood-red hair had been knotted into several tiny braids, short enough to stand up around her face, but somehow, there was nothing remotely funny about the style. Her granite-gray eyes looked at Carcali as though she were measuring her.

The woman wasn't very old, Carcali realized, maybe only four or five years older than she was herself—her real age, not the age of this body. Something in the Paledyn's face reminded Carcali of her Wind Instructor in her first year at the Academy. The same mixture of patience, knowledge, and focus.

Carcali swallowed and stood up, coming out from behind her table. She wasn't going to be intimidated by a woman so close to her own age—a woman with tattoos and a scar on her face. The Academy, the Artists who were her superiors, all were long gone, and the Tarxin was the only one here she needed to be afraid of.

"What shall I call you?" The woman's voice was like raw silk, rough and smooth at the same time.

"I am the Tara Xendra," Carcali said as sharply as she could manage. The woman's raised eyebrows did nothing to help her keep her composure. On the contrary, the Paledyn's gesture seemed calculated to rattle her, perhaps even goad her into losing her temper. Well, she wasn't going to fall for that.

"Have you no other name that you might prefer me to use?"

For a second, Carcali's lips actually parted, as the sudden temptation to tell the Paledyn the truth was almost irresistible. Part of her wanted to see the shock and awe shake the composure of that scarred face, but a part of her simply wanted to tell someone, even this woman, everything. She let the moment pass, saying nothing at all, and the Paledyn inclined her head, all the while keeping her eyes fixed on Carcali's face.

"I am Dhulyn Wolfshead, called the Scholar. I was Schooled by Dorian of the River, the Black Traveler. You may call me Wolfshead."

Carcali gritted her teeth. She certainly wasn't going to call the woman "Scholar," no matter who else might. She turned away, crossing behind the table again to resume her seat. She froze, one hand on the arm of her chair. The Paledyn was already sitting down in the guest chair. How had she moved so quickly, so quietly, in the few seconds Carcali's back was turned? Deliberately, as if she hadn't been shaken by the Wolfshead, Carcali sat down, moving the pen and inkwell to one side, squaring them up with the edge of the worktable.

"My father the Tarxin, Light of the Sun, sent you to meet with me." Let that remind the woman who she was dealing with.

The Paledyn tilted her head to one side. "He has asked me to extend my protection over you."

"What protection can you give me, that he cannot provide?"

The woman spread her hands, palms up. For the first time she smiled, her lip curling back from her teeth in a snarl. Carcali blinked and sat up straighter, then blushed as she realized the woman had seen—and correctly judged—her reaction.

"Could he stop me from killing you myself?" the Paledyn said.

The horrible thing was the Paledyn asked this question in the same even tone that she had used all along—not in a manner intended to frighten or threaten, but as if Carcali's every answer was being weighed in a balance.

"You would never leave the city alive." Carcali's lips were almost too stiff to speak.

The woman shrugged, and her disinterest was somehow more frightening than anything else she might have done. "There are larger things," she said in her rough silk voice, "than my life, or yours."

There *were* larger things. Carcali swallowed. There were whole worlds, civilizations like the one she had destroyed with her arrogance and her pride. Carcali waited, frozen, but the Paledyn continued to sit, perfectly composed, elbows on the arms of her chair, fingertips placed together. Carcali managed to loosen the grip of her own hands.

"I have work the Tarxin has given me," she said, reaching for her stylus with a hand that trembled only slightly. "So if you're not going to kill me just at the moment . . ."

The woman's eyes brightened, and Carcali had the crazy feeling that she had almost smiled.

"Why do you not return to your own place?"

Carcali froze again, her fingers on the stylus. The Paledyn couldn't possibly know. "What do you mean? This is my place." She glanced up, but the Paledyn's face was impassive once more, the hint of brightness gone. She moved her head to the left and back again, just once.

The nape of Carcali's neck prickled as the hair stood up. For the last few days, since news of the Paledyn had arrived in the Tarxin's court, Carcali's servants and attendants had been telling her all kinds of strange tales of them—their invincibility, their honor, how it was impossible to trick or lie to them. She'd dismissed it as primitive superstition, but—*Don't be so silly*, she told herself. *What else could it be?*

"I watched you walk up to the Tarxin's table, and you do not walk like a girl who has seen her birth moon only eleven times," the woman said now. "You are developing a line here," she indicated her forehead between her brows, "when you frown, that a child of that age would not have. You do not school your expressions as carefully as a child brought up in the Tarxin of Mortaxa's court would know how to do. Even now, you look at me with a face that says you have been caught sneaking sweets. In other words, with the face of guilt. And I know," she said finally, leaning forward enough to place her hand on the edge of Carcali's table. "That the natural powers of Marked or Mage come with the maturing of the body, and I doubt very much that the body of the Tara Xendra has yet reached the beginnings of her woman's time. So, where do you come from, and why do you not return?"

"You couldn't possibly understand." The words were out before she could stop them.

"Perhaps you're right. Full understanding comes with full knowledge, something one person cannot give to another. But you could give me enough knowledge to understand how to help and protect you." The Paledyn leaned back again and Carcali took a deep breath for the first time in what felt like hours. "Come. I have told you what I know, what I see with my own eyes. Let me tell you also what I suspect. I believe you are a Caid, though how you find yourself here is more than I can know, I admit."

"What could *you* know about the Caids?" Too late, Carcali realized she hadn't denied the suggestion.

"I have spent more than a year in a Scholars' Library. I know things that the common sword-wearer does not know, even across the Long Ocean, where I think such things are better understood than they are here. I know that the Caids were not gods, as some people think of them, but people like ourselves. And I know that among them were many powerful Mages, some powerful enough to manipulate even the fabric of space and time. And some who were foolish enough to do it. So if you are, as I suspect, one of these, why do you not go back?"

"I can't." The words were out before Carcali could stop them, pushed by the guilt that was always hovering in the back of her mind, no matter how much she tried to ignore it. She would have given anything for the words to be unsaid—even she could hear the longing and despair that informed them.

"Can't or won't?"

"Can't. It's not possible." Carcali spoke through clenched teeth. Did the woman think she hadn't *tried*? Would she have suffered all that time trapped in the weatherspheres if there had been a way home?

The Paledyn's eyes narrowed. "What did you do there, that you can't go back?"

Carcali's heart stopped in her chest, her breath in her throat. She closed her mouth tight against the desire to tell her, to blurt it out. *I destroyed the world. Tell her, say it.* But then reason reasserted itself. The Paledyn *couldn't* know. That would be impossible. This was just good intuition, nothing more. She could tell that Carcali felt guilty about *something*, and was using that knowledge like a sharp knife to probe deeper. Maybe there was something to this Schooling of hers after all, if it led to such perception.

"It is a reasonable question," the woman said, when Carcali did not answer. "Considering the evil you have done here. Do you not, even now, occupy the body that belongs to another, forcing a child's spirit to wander alone and afraid? There is cold in summer, rain in the desert. Lightning cracking the sky. Hailstorms, hurricanes, and tempests. Grain dies flooded in the field, snow and ice fall on the ocean. There will be famine and there has been—" Here the Paledyn's voice caught. "Shipwreck."

Carcali grasped the edge of the table to help her stay in her seat as the room around her swayed. "I didn't do any of those things!" She looked down at her maps, at the lines she'd drawn between mountain range, shoreline, and valley. "My changes have all been local. You're lying."

The Paledyn seemed genuinely surprised, even to the extent of turning pale enough for her eyebrows to stand out like bloodstains. "Are you not a Storm Witch—*the* Storm Witch? Even I, in my Schooling aboard a fast ship, learned that where weather is involved, there is no such thing as 'local.' If you did not do these things, who did? If you believe I lie about the ravages of your storms, why do you not go, find out?" She lifted her arms in an unmistakable way, in the way a Weather Mage did to enter the spheres, and Carcali's stomach dropped. How could the woman know these things?

"I can't. I can't." Carcali put her face down on the backs of her clenched hands. How could this be happening? But she knew how, even if no one else did. Without leaving her body and entering completely into the weatherspheres, she had less control, and with less control, even the small changes she'd been making could cause damage elsewhere.

"You speak—and you act—like the child you are in appearance, rather than the woman I know you to be," the Paledyn said. "You have power, but you have no discipline. Power without discipline is dangerous."

Carcali stared at the woman on the other side of the table. How could she *know* these things? Those were almost the very words that the Artists had said to her.

"Help me." Only a few minutes ago, Carcali could never have imagined asking this woman—tattooed and scarred barbarian, she'd called her—for help. But somehow the Paledyn knew and understood things no one else here seemed to know. "Please, can you help me," she repeated. "It's the Tarxin, he's threatening me. If I don't do what he says . . ." Carcali let her words die away. The Paledyn was sitting rigid in her chair, her eyes icy, her face a mask of stone.

Carcali pulled herself up straight, hardening her own face. This woman wasn't going to help her, Carcali thought, shocked at the depth of her disappointment. "Please leave," she said. Inside she was screaming *GET OUT*, but she managed to control herself. "I don't know what you want. I can't help you." She heard the bitterness in her voice. Just for a moment she'd allowed herself to hope.

There was an odd look on the Paledyn's face as she stood and looked down at Carcali. Her eyes were narrowed, a muscle bunched at the side of her jaw. She was very pale, but somehow her eyes were not so cold. As soon as the door was closed behind her, Carcali ran over and threw the latch, leaned with her hand against the door, breathing hard.

She wasn't going to let the Paledyn Dhulyn Wolfshead make her feel guilty—at least, no more guilty than she already felt. She wrapped her arms around herself. The weather changes—they were the Tarxin's fault. If he'd left her alone, or at least given her more time . . . She was doing the best she could, but after so long without a body—she'd been so confused at first—her Art was still just barely up to apprentice standards. And as for the child, well, Carcali couldn't be responsible for what had happened to her. She never knew the child, never encountered her at all. As for the idea that she might be lost, trapped in the weatherspheres the same way Carcali had been—

Carcali suddenly bent over at the waist, unable to stop the spew of vomit that gushed out onto the tiled floor. *No*, she thought, gasping for air against the spasming of her diaphragm. She scrubbed at her mouth with a corner of her head veil before pulling the garment off and dropping it over the vomit. She forced her mind back to that immeasurable time just before she was pushed into the young Tara's body.

Her idea had worked so beautifully at first. She'd launched herself alone—and why not, she'd thought. Everyone soloed eventually, and she was so much more powerful than any of the other Crafters and Apprentices, she'd been sure that she could do it. And she'd seen right away that her solution would work. It hadn't been easy, but finally her patience and concentration put all the colors and temperatures right. She'd finished, or so she'd thought. It was only then that she'd realized she'd lost the connection with her body—and, with it, any chance to check and revise errors.

Then she'd panicked. And by the time her panic was over, it was too late, the thread connecting her to her body was well and truly gone.

Carcali did not know how long she'd been lost, floating in the spheres—time, space, even her own awareness of such things, became twisted and uncertain when the connection to the body was severed. When she'd felt a tugging at her formless self, she almost hadn't responded, almost hadn't recognized it for what it was. The feeling was so unfamiliar. Recognition had finally come, and she'd thought the Artists had found her at last, had come to save her, and she'd rushed forward, ready to admit she'd been wrong, she'd been arrogant—anything to be restored. Anything to leave behind this formless despair. A sense of great urgency had swept over her, bringing joy and relief with it.

Even when the body didn't feel perfect, Carcali hadn't worried. Of course it would feel strange after so long in the weatherspheres. By the time she realized what had happened, by the time she knew that she didn't wear her own body, that it and her friends and teachers—her whole world—were gone, mere legend to these people . . . by that time she knew she would do anything, tolerate anything, rather than to return to the nothingness of the spheres.

But there hadn't been another soul. Carcali swore there hadn't been. Whatever she may have done to her own people, and her own time, with her arrogance and haste, she was sure she had not condemned an innocent child to the torment she had experienced. The child was not a Mage, her soul could not have survived leaving her body.

Carcali was sure.

Dhulyn leaned against the wall next to the Storm Witch's door and rubbed her face with her hands. Thank Sun and Moon the lady page was nowhere to be seen. Never, never since Dorian the Black had found her standing over the body of the dead slaver, had she come so close to simply killing someone out of hand.

To think it was all an *accident*. That selfish coward—that *parasite* of a stone-souled WITCH, had killed Parno, had destroyed their lives *by accident*. She hadn't even *known*.

But that didn't make her innocent of Parno's death. That wouldn't save her, the very next time the Witch—

"Did it work? Does she trust you?"

Dhulyn had Xerwin by the throat before she registered who it was and let him go. "Sorry," she said. "You startled me."

The Tar rubbed his throat and tried to smile. "I promise not to do it again." Still rubbing his neck, he peered into her face. "You're very white. What happened in there?"

"How much has the Storm Witch been told about recent events? About the Nomads and their claims?"

Xerwin shrugged, drawing her to follow him with a tilt of his head. He glanced around him, and Dhulyn realized he had somehow freed himself of his usual attendants. "Since the Tarxin replaced me as liaison to the Nomads, I've had no say in our contacts with them. So *I* certainly haven't discussed anything with the Storm Witch. And I wouldn't think any of her maids have much head for politics."

Dhulyn refrained from correcting him. In her experience, the higher up the ladder of nobility, the less people understood that the people below them knew far more about what was happening in their lives than they ever let on. As they turned into a wider corridor, she stayed silent, fairly sure she knew where they were heading. Sure enough, Xerwin led her up a flight of stone steps, down a corridor whose latticed walls opened into a tiny courtyard, and finally up another staircase and out into the sunlit and walled garden that was the precinct of the Tarxin in the Upper City. Dhulyn let her lip curl up. In any other place there would have been a guard at the steps, but here in Ketxan City, things were done differently.

"We can talk here," Xerwin said, indicating a stone bench covered in densely woven cloths in the royal colors of gold and green. The bench sat in the shade of a trimmed willow, next to a pool where water tinkled over rocks. "This is the Tarxin's private precinct. No one is allowed up here without either the Tarxin or myself."

"What about Tara Xendra?"

Xerwin looked at her sideways, as if thinking of something for the first time. "No," he said. "Now that you mention it, even she has to come with either me or the Tarxin." He shrugged. "Of course, women aren't supposed to wander about without escorts anyway."

"No, I suppose not." If Dhulyn's tone was a little dry, Xerwin did not notice.

Obviously, rock and earth had been moved here to create the pond, and with it a small elevation from which almost the whole garden could be seen, and the low wall which surrounded it. Beyond she could see the Upper City itself, and some of the more prominent landmarks. She drew up her feet to sit cross-legged. One of the maps she had seen on the Storm Witch's table had been of the Upper City.

"I saw this enclosure when I entered the City," she said. "I was surprised that the Upper City itself had no guards or gates."

"Why would we need guards here? The Battle Wings patrol our borders, and the only trouble we've been having is from the south." Xerwin paused, his face thoughtful. "I wouldn't be surprised if trouble comes from the Nomads, with the Tarxin's new policies, but they attack only from the water."

"So you have no defensible walls, and keep no guards here?"

"There are Stewards at the City entrance, of course, you saw them." He turned to lean his back against the side of the bench, placing himself farther into the shade. "And I suppose some of the Houses might keep Stewards in their pavilions. But you were telling me why it would matter if anyone had been talking to the Storm Witch about our current situation with the Nomads."

Dhulyn studied Xerwin's face with some care. Like anyone who had trained others, and led soldiers in battle, she'd had every trick tried on her, and seen hundreds who were trying to lie. Xerwin showed none of the signs she was familiar with. Which either meant he was very good, or he was being truthful.

"The Witch seemed to be unaware that there had been storms at sea, that the Nomads are claiming they've been attacked through the medium of her magic."

Xerwin shook his head. "So far as I know, she's only been asked to adjust the weather here in Mortaxa. Little things, rain for the fields, a warm wind when frost threatened the wine grapes. Perhaps a few things farther afield, but nothing more that I'm aware of. Do you mean the Nomads have been lying all along?"

Dhulyn drummed her fingers on her knee. "You forget, Xerwin, I was myself shipwrecked. The Nomads on that vessel were sure they were attacked specifically to prevent our—*my* arrival." How much did Xerwin, or any of the Mortaxa, understand about the laws of Sun and Moon, Wind and Rain? Anyone who lived, or had been Schooled on a ship understood firsthand the connections between wind in one place and rain in another. "I mean that the Storm Witch *is* responsible for the weather the Nomads complain of, but she seems to be unaware of it herself. Is it possible that she was not told of the Nomads' complaints?"

Xerwin turned up his palms. "Who would tell a young girl of such things? And if such things are possible, how could the Storm Witch not know?"

"I assure you such things are possible. Heavy snow and rain in the mountains cause flooding in the valley; hurricanes in one place can mean days of high winds and rain even a moon's march away. As for how the Witch did not know . . ." Dhulyn shrugged. "It has always been true that a little learning is a dangerous thing."

Xerwin closed his hand around her wrist. Dhulyn froze, looked at his hand, and looked up, meeting his eyes. He swallowed, kept his eyes on hers, but took his hand away. "What do you mean?"

"The Marked can do damage, especially Healers or Menders, if they are not well trained. Even Finders may Find every horse in a town, and not the precise animal sought. So it is possible that the Storm Witch has talent and power, but insufficient training. It is also possible that in order to perform her magic well, she needs to be given information that has been withheld from her."

"How were we to have known?"

Dhulyn refrained from shrugging again. Two things had worked against the Storm Witch. First, she had wanted everyone to think she was the Tara Xendra, so she hadn't asked many questions. And second, as Xerwin had said himself, who in this place would have thought to tell a young girl—Tara or not—anything of importance?

"But if she is not guilty of the acts of malice the Nomads accuse her of—" Xerwin was frowning, not, as Dhulyn could see, because he could not follow the thought through to its logical conclusion, but because he could not see use in the conclusion he found.

"Will that make a difference to your father? He already sees his dominion spreading over the Nomads and their oceans." Dhulyn decided to keep silent, for the moment at least, about the Crayx. "You've said yourself the Storm Witch is a sword to his hand. Will he stop himself from using it?"

Xerwin's face had settled into the impassive mask that in itself was a sign he was hiding his thoughts. Not for the first time Dhulyn thanked the Mercenary Brotherhood from keeping her out of this kind of life. If she hid things from people, it was because they were strangers, not because she was afraid.

"We might reach the Storm Witch, if she is really just unpracticed and not evil," Xerwin finally said. "But the Tarxin will never be persuaded to give up an advantage he's long sought, that's certain."

"Then we must stick to our original plan," Dhulyn agreed. Though whether she was trying to convince herself or Xerwin was something she did not want to examine too closely. "The Storm Witch is a danger to anyone who might cross her—still more so if she cannot control her magics. She is like a mad dog, or a child in a temper who sets fire to the house and kills his whole family. And if we speak of children," she added. "There is the child your sister to consider."

At this Xerwin looked up, and quickly looked away again, as if embarrassed. "I did not tell you. The White Twins, the Seers, told me they had had a Vision of you leading a young child by the hand. Could it be that you will restore my sister?"

"It could be." Dhulyn nodded slowly. "It's hard to be sure of the meanings of isolated Visions—or so I have read," she added. "It certainly appears the possibility exists." If nothing else, she thought, her own Vision showed her that the child Xendra was still alive, that her soul still existed, somehow, somewhere, in hiding. "And your sister deserves what chance she can have to be restored. That the Storm Witch refuses to consider the harm she does to your sister tells us much of her natural temperament—to say nothing of her honor. But it also points us to the way to overcome her."

"How is that?"

"She is in a terror of leaving your sister's body," Dhulyn said, remembering the adult horror and desperation in the childish face. "Such terror leads me to think that she will be destroyed if we expel her from the body."

"How can we do such a thing?"

"Can the Marked ones be brought secretly into the palace?"

#Lionsmane#

Parno set the bow he was oiling down on the tabletop, wiping his fingers clean on the scrap of rag. "Hear you," he said. He still spoke aloud when talking with the Crayx, even though he knew he didn't have to. Somehow, it kept things feeling normal for him. He supposed that one day, he would simply forget, and speak to them only with his Pod sense, as everyone else did.

#We have found someone who can tell you of the City# #We know you do not like to listen to another's thoughts# #But Oskarn is of the *Sunwaver Pod*, their current is now in the Round Ocean, and he cannot be brought to face you# #He has been through the City of the Mortaxa more than once#

Parno winced. They were right, he didn't like receiving someone else's thoughts, or knowing that his were being sent. But that, too, was something he would have to get used to. He hadn't known that the Crayx could convey the thoughts of someone as far away as this Oskarn was. Did this mean that any Crayx could talk to any Crayx, anywhere in the world?

#Yes#

"Let me get out parchment and pens," Parno said, shaking his head and getting to his feet. The other cabin was still being used by whichever captain was not on watch, so Parno had had all maps and documents transferred to the one he increasingly shared with Darlara. The Crayx waited until he had fetched clean scraps to make notes on, and was seated once again.

"I'm ready."

This is many years ago Somehow, the man's thoughts, his voice, sounded differently in Parno's mind than that of any Crayx. He could tell that he was conversing with another human, that the human was male, and even that he was very old. *When the Mortaxa were better disposed toward us* *The Crayx had told us of a Pod-sensed one to the south, inland, and our Pod was the only one near* *You know that they keep slaves*

"I know," Parno said, wondering if the face he made was somehow transmitted to Oskarn along with his words.

The slaves are many, especially away from the City, and the one we sensed was a slave child *I volunteered to fetch her* *There was no other who would go so far from the sea, not even for a Pod-sensed child, but I was young, and felt myself invincible, and as it is, I was not harmed* *I hired guides who helped me find and buy the child, and I returned to my Pod with her*

"But you passed through the City to do so?"

Twice *And waited there while the sale was registered and sealed, lest there be some difficulty after*

"And you can describe the City to me? Particularly the land side?" Parno took up his pen in preparation.

I can *You have seen great palaces and buildings, such as might be seen in the vast cities of the Great King*

"I have."

From the sea, the City seems to be a palace, carved from the living rock of the cliff face, span after span, layer upon layer, showing windows and balconies, and here and there a staircase *Docks, wharfs, and piers are built, floating upon the sea, and it is here that we dock, and hold markets* *There are four entrances, two at the dock level, and two others in the third level* *But the City itself extends past this facade, deep into the bluff behind it* *Wells and shafts, cut vertically into the heart of the rock from the summit far above, carry air and light into the lower levels*

What Oskarn described as Parno took notes and made drawings, did indeed sound like a huge, many-storied palace, with innumerable corridors that functioned as streets and alleys, and large open spaces that served the purpose of public squares and buildings. Parno learned that the seaward part of the rock held the homes of Noble Houses, with the Tarxin's palace at the very top. The poorer or less important people lived lower down, and deeper into the rock—some might never see true daylight for weeks at a time, if ever.

"And the land approach? The entrances from the top?"

The Upper City is laid out like a formal garden within a decorative wall, but instead of plots of flowers and trees, the High Nobles have winter houses out in the air *At this time of year, there would be too much heat for these to be much occupied* *Few have permission to build* *The largest precinct is that of the Tarxin's palace, and is truly a garden, with its own wall for the privacy of the ruler and his family*

Parno continued to draw as Oskarn described the Upper City. Particularly the parts around the public entrance to the Lower City, and the Tarxin's walled garden. It soon became apparent that, extensive as the man's knowledge was, and as detailed his memory, he had only seen limited parts of the city. Two items stood out. First, the Upper City was like an unfortified town, with low walls and no guards. Second, the wall of the Tarxin's precinct was not high by Boravian standards. Nor was it ditched or moated. Nor, he was surprised to learn, was it usually guarded.

The guards are all the Tarxin's men, and keep to the inner City Oskarn said.

"What can you tell me of the rooms in the palace itself?"

Alas, nothing *There was no reason for me, a common Nomad, neither captain nor chief trader, to be received by the Tarxin*

No help for it, Parno thought shrugging. Once he was in the palace precincts, it would be a question of capturing someone and persuading them to tell him where the Storm Witch might be found.

Amusement

Seventeen

DHULYN KEPT ONE EYE on the movement of shadows across the jewel-bright patterns of the tiled floor in her sitting room, and the other on the pocket of thin leather she was sewing into the back of her new vest. The pocket would hold one of the daggers she'd picked out and had sharpened to her specifications. She'd asked the palace seamstresses for scraps of cloth and leather, waving aside as politely as she could their offers to do any sewing she might require with the declaration that Paledyns were required to do certain ceremonial things themselves. People would think that she had used these scraps to create, on the back of her vest, a larger version of her Mercenary badge. And so she had. What they wouldn't see was how much she'd thickened the material, and what she had hidden there.

Dhulyn bit off the thread, slipped the vest on, and reached over her shoulder, first with the left hand, then with the right, to make sure she could reach the pocket. She then repeated the whole business with the dagger in place.

Satisfied, she took the vest off once more and began to work on four shorter, wider straps that she would attach lower down on the vest, closer to her waist. These would hold the small hatchet she'd liberated on her tour of the kitchens and honed herself on the edge of the stone window ledge. Unlike the dagger, the hatchet would be sewn into the vest, and be ready to hand when it was needed. Experience had taught her that unlike a hidden dagger, once a hatchet was out, you rarely had a chance to put it back.

As the last stitch went into place, Dhulyn looked up and, her head tilted, slowed her breathing, letting herself fall into the Stalking Cat

Shora, the better to listen. Quickly, she stood, pulled on the vest, and did up the ties. The scraps of cloth, needles, and other sewing tools, along with the old vest she'd been using as a pattern she gathered up and thrust into the inner chamber. She was leaning against the worktable, sword in hand, when the expected tap came at the door.

"Come," she said.

She'd expected Xerwin to be first through the door, but it seemed the Tar had some sense after all. Instead, it was Remm Shalyn, a wide grin on his pleasant features, who led the three Marked ones in, and Xerwin who waited in the outer corridor in case questions had to be answered. Not that there were many errands being run at this time of day, when most people were preparing for the midday meal.

"The Tar's plan worked like a throw of loaded dice, Dhulyn Wolfshead," Remm said. Though it didn't seem possible, his grin grew even wider.

"No one above, then?" She looked at Xerwin.

"Exactly as I thought," he said, unable to keep the satisfaction out of his voice. "Much too hot up there at this time of day for anyone, even the servants." By which he meant, Dhulyn knew, the garden slaves who kept the pavilions of the High Noble Houses clean and their flowers blooming. They would have gone up early in the morning to cover over valuable plants against the glare of the sun, but by this time Xerwin had expected the place to be deserted—and it seemed he had been right.

"Your pardon, Tar Xerwin," Remm said, though he had, in fact, waited until the Tar had finished speaking. "But if there is water available, the Marked ones are in need of it."

Dhulyn gestured her permission at a tray on the table to her left, which held cups and a water jug beautifully glazed in black and red, and turned back to Xerwin.

"Is this heat natural?" She could tell by the way he raised his eyebrows that he hadn't even considered it. A Storm Witch could cause a great deal of mischief if she went about it carefully.

But the Tar was shaking his head. "I'll be looking askance at the morning sea breezes next," he said. "And they've been constant my whole life. For the season and time of day, this heat is normal. Though," he added, "only last evening I overheard my attendants gossiping. Apparently one of the High Noble Houses—I didn't quite catch which—has been wondering whether perhaps the Tara Xendra could be persuaded to create cooler air for some party they're planning." It was Dhulyn's turn to raise her eyebrows, and Xerwin grinned. "I hope I'm there to see the look on the Tarxin's face if the House actually asks him."

"Don't be too sure of his answer," Dhulyn said. "If the House is important enough, the Tarxin might very well allow it."

As Xerwin pursed his lips in a silent whistle, shaking his head, Dhulyn once more checked the angle of light on the floor.

"Tar Xerwin," she said. "I believe you are eating with the Tarxin today?"

"Surely you're not trying to be rid of me?"

Dhulyn rolled her eyes and waved him toward the door. "Of course I am. I don't want anyone to come looking for you."

"With your leave, Dhulyn Wolfshead," Remm said as soon as Xerwin was gone. "Speaking of food, I should go order us some."

"Fetch it yourself," Dhulyn said. "That way no one will see how much you bring." She glanced at the Marked ones and looked back at Remm, who was nodding.

"Back shortly." He touched his forehead to her and left, pulling the door shut behind him. Dhulyn followed him to the door and listened as his footsteps and his light whistle died away. She threw the bolt, and turned back to face the Marked.

All three had put aside their veils, and except that she was seeing them in daylight, they looked much the same. Ellis Healer, a linen bag hanging over his shoulder, was still leaning on a staff, but the two women were recuperating from their journey more quickly.

"You have spoken with the White Twins," Ellis said. Rascon Mender still had her cup of water to her lips, and Javen Finder was mopping the sweat off her face with a clean corner of her veil.

Dhulyn sheathed her sword and strode back to the table, propping one hip up on the edge. Closer together, they would be less likely to be overheard. "Who else knows?"

"No one *we've* told, that's certain," Rascon Mender said.

Ellis Healer frowned at her and she blushed, turning away to refill her cup. "Not many within the Sanctuary besides the three of us even know you were sent for. Kalinda, of course, the one who showed you in, the White Twins themselves, but . . ." he fixed Dhulyn with a watchful eye. "You will have noticed that they are fully aware only when they are Seeing."

Dhulyn nodded.

"So you will realize that they could tell no one, and as for the rest of us." He shrugged. "We make it a practice not to talk about our own affairs to the unMarked."

"And as for them—and there're some—who don't think as we do on these subjects, why, we don't tell them anything." Rascon seemed to have recovered her cheery equilibrium. "What about your man, that Remm Shalyn," she continued. "Is *he* to be trusted?"

"So far as I trust anyone, yes." Dhulyn ran her fingertips along her sword hilt. She didn't know whether it was the company of the Marked—or the number of weapons she now had hidden in her clothing—but she was beginning to feel relaxed for the first time since the storm at sea. "And do you know what the White Twins told me?"

The was a general shaking of heads, but this time the two younger Marked waited for Ellis Healer to speak. "Likewise, who would tell us? The Twins?"

Dhulyn relaxed even more. It seemed that the secret of her own Mark was safe. Now the trick would be how to tell these three what they needed to know to Find the Tara Xendra without giving away that she'd had the Vision herself.

"The White Twins have Seen the Tara Xendra, that much is clear from what they told me," she said. The others looked at one another and nodded. "The child's spirit is safe, but it is in hiding."

The Finder was shaking her head, frowning. "But that shouldn't make any difference. It's things that are lost or hidden that I Find."

"But if she were nowhere near, Javen," Rascon said. "And if the Storm Witch's soul was in the way . . ."

"Did the White Twins say anything else? Was any clue given?" Javen Finder asked.

This was the dangerous part of the path. "They spoke of a grove of trees," Dhulyn said. "A thicket in which the child lay concealed."

"A spirit child hiding in a spirit wood?" Javen Finder's face, so eager a moment ago, had fallen, and she was chewing at her lower lip. "It's not like I can Find a Vision, you know. Otherwise we'd *all* be Seers."

"I have something here that may help you." Dhulyn went to the end of the table nearest the window and folded back a piece of silk cloth to expose a small bowl, sturdy and perfectly round, glazed a deep blue on the outside and a pure white on the inside. All three Marked gathered close, looking down at it.

"Remm Shalyn had it made to my order—by a master, as you can see. The glaze both inside and out is perfect, without mar, flaw, or shadow. No hand but the maker's has touched it, neither Remm's nor mine. The water it holds is brought from a spring, and passed three times through a piece of pure undyed silk."

"How did you know what's needed?" Javen said, her voice trembling.

Dhulyn shrugged. "The two I've seen were old, passed from generation to generation. But once, many years ago, I read a fragment of an ancient book which described the making of a Finder's bowl. Much of it would make no sense unless you'd actually seen one." Dhulyn indicated the chair she'd had placed near the bowl. "Will you try?"

Javen sat down, wiping the palms of her hands dry against her skirt. She pressed her palms together, fingers against her lips, eyes closed. She took a deep breath, opened her eyes, and looked into the bowl.

"Oh, what beautiful colors," she exclaimed.

Dhulyn exchanged glances with the other Marked. Rascon was just giving a small nod, confirming that the rest of them saw only the white interior, when a knock came at the door.

"The food?"

Dhulyn drew down her brows in a frown. Would Remm knock? Or was he too burdened by food to manage the door. She jerked her head toward the doorway to the inner room and waited until the Marked had gone through it. She shut the door on them, tossed the loose piece of silk back over the bowl and threw open the door as if she was in a great temper.

But she swallowed the tart words she would have used to greet Remm Shalyn. A young girl, correctly veiled, stood in the open door, her eyes as round as the bangles on her wrists.

"Your pardon, T–tara P–paledyn," the girl stammered. "But the Tarxin, Light of the Sun, has asked for your presence."

For a moment Dhulyn stayed where she was, right hand gripping the edge of the door. Was the girl frightened at meeting the Paledyn? Or was it the errand itself that frightened her?

"Wait for me, young one," she said in as soft a voice as she could manage. "I will accompany you in a moment." Dhulyn shut the door in the girl's face and stood leaning against it. If this summons was Xerwin's doing, he'd have something to answer for when she caught up with him. She pushed away from the door, turning toward the inner room, and the Marked. They should be safe enough here when Remm Shalyn returned.

She wished she could say the same for herself.

Everyone who could find a clear space on deck was out taking advantage of the warm rain to refill every water cask, bag, and bottle, and to rinse off whatever clothing, skin, and hair had last been washed in salt water.

Parno Lionsmane was in the forward section of the deck that under more regular circumstances would be the designated bathing area. He'd found that while he had become used to the smell and taste of salt on his skin—and on the skin of others—he was just as pleased to be able to rinse it off. The Nomads, living together so closely, had no great feelings of body modesty, and almost his entire squad, both male and female, were in the bathing area with him. In a way, it was like being back in his Mercenary School.

More and more, except for the presence of so many children, Parno found himself reminded of his own Schooling, especially since the intensive training of his strike force so closely resembled the constant drilling and practice that Schooling required. He'd found that he was even teaching his squad versions of some basic *Shoras*, modified only to take into account the shortness of the time they had for training.

Once or twice, watching the squad practice, he'd looked around, unconsciously expecting to see Dhulyn off to one side, getting a different angle on the recruits. Grief still came when he thought of her, but it no longer stabbed him to the heart, or took his breath away. She had always wanted to start her own School, to do for others what Dorian the Black had done for her. It wasn't impossible, Parno thought now as Conford passed him a towel, for a School to be started on a Nomad ship. After all, the Nomads had taken him in, just as the Brotherhood had done, all those years ago, when he had been cast out by his House.

#You have a place here, should you want it# #As you did in your Brotherhood#

As I still have in my Brotherhood For the first time Parno spoke directly mind to mind with the Crayx, without speaking his thoughts aloud. But this was something he wasn't ready to share with the Nomads around him. Not even with Darlara.

#Does no one ever leave the Brotherhood then#

Parno stopped his fast answer. Of course, there were other ways to leave the Brotherhood than death. There was that Cloudwoman who'd gone back to her tribe when a Racha bird had needed her. He had himself been asked to return to his own place, for that matter, by the new head of his House. But he'd refused. Even if he'd wished to—and he hadn't—he was Partnered, and the decision was as much Dhulyn's as his own.

Partners never leave was the thought he sent the Crayx.

#Of course#

Were they aware of his unexpressed thought, he wondered. *I'm not Partnered any longer.*

He shrugged the thought away as he pulled his shirt on over his head. "Off to your meals now," he told his squad. "Left-hand drill afterward, and don't be late."

He turned back toward the rear cabin, combing his wet hair with his fingers. For the last few days he'd been taking the midday meal with his squad, but today Dar had asked that he share the meal with her. He entered the cabin to find her seated with her back to the window, plates of grilled fish, stewed beans, and flatbreads already on the table. Dar glanced up and smiled as he came in, and Parno found it easy to smile back.

"Have been giving thought to the naming of the children," Darlara said, passing him the platter holding the flatbread.

Parno froze with the platter in midair. "Early, isn't it?"

"Not really. It's a hard life on ship, and must give them every advantage. Are there family names you would prefer to use?"

Parno thought at once of his own father. But the form of names in Imrion—he shook his head. Too complicated, and too loaded with meaning for someone who didn't actually live in that society. He could easily imagine the explanations that would be required if the children became chief traders or captains of a ship—as they well might—and were asked why their names came from a Noble House. Besides, he knew what he really wanted.

"Could one of them be called Dhulyn?"

Darlara took so long to answer that Parno was ready to be disappointed. But she was only waiting until she had chewed and swallowed the piece of honeyed bread she had in her mouth before answering. "A beautiful name," she said. Suddenly she smiled, and rested her hand on his forearm. "Have a wonderful idea. Should name them Dhulyn and Parno."

Now it was his turn not to answer right away.

Darlara tightened her grip on his arm. *It's all right, isn't it?* *Would be brothers, or sisters.*

Somehow, speaking mind to mind made it easier.

Yes

The door of the cabin swung open and Malfin leaned in. "Told him yet?"

"Just getting to it." Darlara gave his arm a final squeeze before shifting in her seat, swinging her legs out until she was turned toward the door.

Parno looked from brother to sister, marveling once more how alike they looked when they were both smiling. A smile began to form on his own lips. *What are you up to*

Hold your breath a bit Malfin turned to look over his shoulder and made a beckoning gesture with his hand.

"We've something for you, Lionsmane," he said aloud. "Just ready now."

Conford came in with a cloth-wrapped bundle in his hands. Parno helped Dar clear off a space on the table so Conford could put his burden down. He backed off a step, touched his forehead to Parno, looked sheepishly at his captains, and shrugged, smiling.

Captain Mal laughed and touched the crewman on the shoulder with his fist.

"Go on."

Still smiling, Conford unwrapped the cloth, exposing a Crayx-skin cuirass, identical to the ones both Mal and Dar were wearing, except that this one was a pale green with a curious coppery sheen.

"Yours, Lionsmane," Mal said.

"Try it on," Dar said. "See if it fits."

Parno knew what the skin felt like from helping Darlara take hers off. To the touch, it was like well-tanned leather, soft and giving.

To a sharp blow, it was as hard as good steel, and would turn away a blade.

"Why?" he said, looking up at the three smiling faces.

"Heard from *Dawntreader* Pod," Mal said. "May be in sight of Ketxan City tomorrow."

"Thought you could use it," Dar added.

Parno nodded. "What does it mean if I wear it?" he said, bluntly. "I know it's more than just armor."

"Are bound to the *Wavetreader*," Mal said.

"As we," Dar added.

"And what does *that* mean?" Parno's voice was harsher than he'd intended. The two captains exchanged worried looks, and the smile faded from Conford's face.

#You are part of this Pod# came the answer from the Crayx. #You cannot be exchanged to another Pod# #No matter what happens, where you are, you are part of us, of *Wavetreader*#

It was like the Mercenary Brotherhood, Parno realized. You didn't need to live in a Mercenary House, or even with other Mercenaries—you could even retire, though not many lived so long. Once a Brother, always a Brother.

#Acknowledgment# #Agreement#

Mal, Dar, and even Conford were nodding.

Parno picked up the cuirass and slipped it on.

#Satisfaction#

There was a guard at the door the young woman led her to, and Dhulyn handed him the sword on her hip and the knife on her belt before he could ask. After all, she still had the dagger and hatchet hidden in her vest. She saw as soon as she entered the room that those, and her hands, would be all she needed, since there was no one else there but Xerwin and the Tarxin Xalbalil. As Dhulyn entered, Xerwin was on his feet, his hand on the back of his chair. Xerwin's face was calm, there was even a slight smile on his lips. Dhulyn felt herself relax ever so slightly.

"Ah, Dhulyn Wolfshead." The Tarxin indicated the chair to his left. "Please, join us. Xerwin told me that he had left you just as you sent your servant for food, so I know you have not yet dined. This would be an excellent chance for us to confer informally."

"I thank you, Light of the Sun. It is an honor." Dhulyn touched her forehead and pulled back her chair, taking her seat. No servants, the Tarxin's manner of addressing her, his calling even Xerwin by name rather than by title, all emphasized the informality of the meal. Still, Dhulyn had some experience dealing with Noble Houses. So long as she kept to the minor formality of never using the Tarxin's name, she should be fine.

As she sat, she rapidly scanned the table, taking in the platters of fruit, fish in simple sauces, and small rolls of bread. This was the diet of a person in shaky health, she thought, perhaps with a bad heart. Was the Tarxin, then, at the point where even Healers could do little for him?

"Tell me, my dear, what do you think of my city?"

So that was how the horse was supposed to jump. Dhulyn offered the Tarxin a basket of warm bread before taking a piece for herself. If the man really expected small talk, he'd chosen the wrong Mercenary Brother.

"It's not unusual for cities of this size, located as this one is on a natural cliff face, to have no walls. But I am surprised that there is no patrol of guards at the outskirts of the Upper City."

"Guards?" From the look of his rounded eyes, the Tarxin was genuinely surprised. "Guards have not been needed since my great grandfather's day. It was he who pacified the lands from the Long Ocean in the west, to the Crescent and Coral Seas to the north, and to the Eastern River."

For pacified, substitute conquered. Dhulyn kept her thought away from her face.

The Tarxin spread a smoked fish paste on a thinly-sliced, twice-baked piece of bread and presented it to Dhulyn. "There are bands of so-called free slaves roving in the southern mountains, but the Battle Wings are there to deal with them." The Tarxin smiled at Xerwin. "The Nomads have attacked us, naturally, but only from the sea," he said while she chewed. "It seems very unlikely that *their* strategies would change now."

"When I was Schooled, I learned that 'unlikely' is a highly dangerous word. One should always prepare for what *can* happen, not for what *might* happen."

Tarxin Xalbalil paused in the spreading of another morsel of fish paste and looked with a frown at Xerwin. "Excellent reasoning, do you not think my son? See to it."

Xerwin put down the leg of fowl he had in his left hand and began to stand up. His father let him get all the way out of his chair before speaking.

"Oh, not now, Xerwin, please, we have a guest. After the meal will do."

"Of course, Father." When the younger man glanced across the table at her, Dhulyn gave him her best smile, careful not to let the scar turn back her lip. He lowered his eyes very quickly back to his plate.

"And how did you find the Marked in their Sanctuary, well-cared for?" At least the old man had waited until she'd served herself a slice of meat and filled her wineglass before he continued.

Dhulyn drew down her eyebrows and sat straighter in her chair, as if giving the Tarxin's question serious thought. Sun and Moon, but she hoped he didn't think to unnerve her by demonstrating that her movements were being reported. He didn't strike her as a fool, and only a fool would have let her—Paledyn or no—wander around unwatched.

And since he wasn't a fool, she had better see to it that she didn't relax *too* much.

"It was an unusual experience for me," she said finally. "To see so many Marked in one place. It is done differently in Boravia, and in the lands of the Great King as well."

The corners of the Tarxin's mouth crimped just a fraction, as if he did not care to be reminded that there was somewhere a king greater than himself, even if so far away. He was irritated enough, Dhulyn saw, that he did not notice his question hadn't really been answered.

"And your visit to my daughter, that was satisfactory?"

"Indeed, my lord. She will need a great deal of support, as I'm sure you have already realized. A child so young, with such powers." Dhulyn shrugged and took a sip of wine. "She might be easily manipulated, and you must choose the people around her with great care. The Tara Xendra might do a great deal of damage if she is left in the wrong hands."

The Tarxin nodded vigorously, as if he was pleased to find that they were both in such accord. *Talk of being manipulated,* Dhulyn thought. She glanced at Xerwin, he blinked at her, face straight. His father appeared to accept that she believed the Storm Witch was a child, but did she really trick him? It was hard to judge. Blood, what she wouldn't give for Parno's opinion. She did not fool herself, sharp as she was; the only advantage she had in this contest was the old man's habit of power. He was so used to holding all the good tiles, it might well have caused him, over the years, to stop looking closely at other people's hands.

And he could be reasoning that he need not fool her for long. Once she supported his side in the argument with the Nomads—as she was clearly expected to do—he might well decide that he had no further use for her.

Mouth full, she inclined her head toward the Tarxin, as if to concentrate better on his words.

"I'm gratified that you both understand the problem so clearly, and that you feel free to advise me. Like the Paledyns of old, your presence will guide us back to the balance we have so sorely missed."

"What has caused the conflict between you and the Nomads? In Boravia, it is understood that your arrangement was well considered, and of long standing."

The Tarxin leaned back in his chair, dipping his fingers into a bowl of water to his left, and drying them on a small napkin. "We are not the same peoples," he said in a measured tone. "We are the children of the Caids, followers of the Slain God. The Nomads are animal worshipers, following—literally—those sea creatures they call the Crayx, using them as living pathways across the ocean." He shrugged. "I have seen them, they are magnificent creatures, supremely useful to navigation as any can realize, but they *are* animals. It would be as though a herdsman began to worship his cows, or the wild kinglera. Diplomacy between our two peoples has always been difficult, no treaties can be solidified with marriages, for example." He spread his hands. "Enough. I am no priest or farmer, for that matter, to let myself be distracted by this. Their women have too much power, but for traders and animal worshipers they are honest enough."

Once again, Dhulyn thought he was being sincere. "What has changed, then?"

"A year ago—or was it more, Xerwin?"

Xerwin paused to finish chewing, and swallowed. "It was more . . . Father. Almost two years, I'd say."

"A pair of Scholars came to us with documents, newly translated, which you can see for yourself Dhulyn Wolfshead—*can* you read?"

"I can."

"Excellent. Well, as I say, this was almost two years ago."

Dhulyn listened as the Tarxin, with the occasional help of Xerwin with details, told her the story she had already heard from the Nomads, but from the Mortaxan point of view. What a shame, she thought, that she was not actually here to arbitrate between them. Mediators were rarely given such full information to help them form their decisions.

She learned that over the centuries, the land-based Mortaxa had tried several times to redress what they saw as their subordinate position in world trade. Attempts at formal partnerships, up to and including marriage into Nomad trading families had always been refused. As had the purchase of ships with which to follow the Crayx—and for no good reasons, from the Mortaxan point of view. Their histories told of attempts to build their own ships and to find their own herds of Crayx, but both times the ships had left Mortaxa never to be heard from again.

And it was very clear, from what the Tarxin was saying, that they simply did not believe in the Nomads' explanation of Pod sense.

Since the consolidation of Mortaxa under the present Tarxin's great grandfather, the land had been enjoying a long period of peace and stability. *Stagnation,* Dhulyn thought, the typical outcome of entrenched slavery. And Tarxin Xalbalil began to think that now was the time to try again.

To make his own mark before he dies, she thought. He wanted to be remembered in the same way his great grandfather was.

"Xerwin, as Battle Wing Commander, had been acting as liaison with the Nomads, but for what I had in mind, a greater authority was needed." Meaning, Dhulyn guessed, that Xerwin had not agreed with his father's ideas. "I began by putting a stop to all trade," the Tarxin continued. "But even as that tactic was beginning to make itself felt, I was distracted by the terrible accident to my dear child Xendra."

Dhulyn put a solemn look on her face and nodded her sympathy. Distraction, the man called it.

"But the Slain God and the Caids have both shown me their favor, not only in restoring my daughter to health, but by making her their instrument in my dealings with the Nomads. Not only have they blessed her with the Weather Art, but they have given her other knowledge, the knowledge of the lodestone. Do you know what this is?"

"I have read of it," Dhulyn said. "A device, whether magical or not I cannot say, that can be used as a guide when there are no other signs, stars, or landmarks."

"Or when you are at sea."

"The Tara Xendra awoke with this learning?" Dhulyn said.

"This and other knowledge, yes. We saw immediately that this gave us a stronger position in our talks with the Nomads."

You would, Dhulyn thought.

"We had now something to offer them, something that would free them from their dependence on the Crayx. But when we spoke to the Nomads of this, the Nomads threatened us, saying that they would destroy any ship that attempted to cross the Long Ocean, or any other oceans or seas. That these places belonged by ancient treaty to the Crayx, as if animals can have treaties with humans."

Dhulyn fought not to let her distaste and skepticism show on her face. Of course, the Mortaxa would think the Nomads were lying, she thought. Lacking Pod sense—or the ability to see even their own slaves or the Marked as human beings—it would be inconceivable for these people to believe that the Crayx were sentient. "And did you, in your turn, threaten the Nomads with the wrath of the Storm Witch?"

The Tarxin's expression set like stone, and Dhulyn was careful to keep her eyes wide open with innocent curiosity. After a few moments the Tarxin relaxed.

"That would have been to answer their bad faith with bad faith of our own," he said.

Which doesn't mean no, she thought. "Of course," she said aloud. She leaned back in her chair, picked up her own napkin to wipe her hands. "So what, precisely, would you wish these negotiations to bring you?"

"At the least, they should allow us to build our own ships, to begin our own trade routes. We are not asking them to starve. There is trade enough for all. It would be better still for us to become partners. Using the lodestones, we could extend trade to those areas where the Crayx herds do not go."

Partners. Mentally, Dhulyn snorted, even as she nodded in apparent agreement with the Tarxin. "Would you be willing, as an opening to the bargaining, and to show good faith, to limit your preliminary trading ventures to those areas where the Nomads do not go?"

Just for a moment, Dhulyn saw again that telltale crimping of the corners of the Tarxin's mouth. "We do not know what might be found there, whether there would be any profit going to new places."

"That might be something you could learn from the Nomads. If you show yourselves to be willing to make concessions now, you might gain all the more in the future, as the Nomads learn to work with you."

"Of course. I see now why the Paledyns of old had such reputations for sagacity."

Dhulyn was spared any need to respond by the entry of a flustered noble servant.

"Your pardon, Tarxin, Light of the Sun, but Nomad ships have been sighted from the north watchtower."

Ships? Dhulyn thought.

Eighteen

"TAR XERWIN, PLEASE ESCORT the Paledyn Dhulyn Wolfshead to the north watchtower."

Xerwin got immediately to his feet, relieved to observe that Dhulyn Wolfshead had also noted the change back to formal titles, now that they were no longer alone in the room. The Paledyn bowed deeply, not quite touching the floor, before turning to follow old Harxin Slan out the door.

Xerwin had to walk around the long end of the table, so as not to pass behind the Tarxin's chair, but as he turned to take his formal leave, his father beckoned him closer. He approached his father's chair and went down on one knee.

"Do I need to tell you not to bother with the patrols she wants?" His father's voice was well-modulated and would not carry into the outer room.

"Of course, my lord Tarxin, Light of the Sun."

The Tarxin patted him on the shoulder, and made shooing motions with his hands.

Even though no one could have seen it, Xerwin's ears still burned hot with embarrassment. His father, the Tarxin, shooing him away as a farm slave might shoo away chickens. As if he would not be Tarxin one day. As if the old man thought he would never die.

"Your pardon, Paledyn," he said when he found Dhulyn Wolfshead and Harxin Slan waiting for him in the outer room. She was rearming herself with the blades she'd left there, while Harxin watched, smiling. "My father had last minute instructions."

She nodded briskly. "He is your superior officer, and his orders must be obeyed," she said.

"And you must obey them as well, my dear." It was clear from his tone that Harxin Slan's words were kindly meant, even flirtatious. The tone, Xerwin realized, that he himself might have used to a noble lady full of her own importance.

And from the look on Harxin's face, the man was just discovering what kind of mistake he'd made.

"I am a Paledyn," Dhulyn Wolfshead said, her rough silk voice somehow sharp and cutting as a knife. "I obey the Common Rule of my Brotherhood. It is for that reason I am here."

Harxin's white face flushed red, and his lips parted, but before he could dig his grave any deeper, Xerwin decided to take pity on him.

"Since the Tarxin, Light of the Sun, has asked me to escort the Tara Paledyn—" There, let the old fool be reminded that she outranked him as well. "You may return to your interrupted duties, Harxin."

"Yes, my lord Tar."

There, Harxin's color was subsiding, and he was able to speak. His short bow was carefully aimed at the space between Xerwin and the Paledyn, thereby insulting no one, before Harxin turned and left the room. Xerwin grinned. There'd be no need to call for the Healer, or for any of the lower servants to clean up the old man's blood.

"The north watchtower's not far," he said to Dhulyn Wolfshead as he led the way out of the room. As soon as they were out of earshot of the guards at the doors to the Tarxin's personal suite, he lowered his voice and spoke. "You must be quite used to that type of treatment, but I apologize for it, nevertheless."

"Are you apologizing for yourself, or for House Slan?"

Xerwin stopped in mid stride, then moved quickly to catch up. "Your meaning?"

She glanced at him sideways. "You just reminded that poor idiot that you and I have the same rank, and yet you walked out of the room before me. If I were another Tar, instead of a Tara, would you not at least have offered to let me go first?"

He couldn't tell whether she was smiling. He opened his mouth several times before finding the words he wanted.

"In your land, in Boravia, would the heir to a Tarxinate allow you to precede them out of a room?"

This time it was Dhulyn Wolfshead who stopped dead in the middle of the corridor, and waited for him to turn back to her. Her left hand was tucked into her sword belt, her right hand rested on the hilt of her sword.

"If I were guarding him, I would insist upon it," she said. Her head was tilted to one side, and Xerwin felt as though her cloud-gray eyes were measuring him. "And in my area of expertise, I would expect to be obeyed, as your father pretends that he will obey my will as Paledyn. But that isn't what you're really asking me, is it? You're asking me whether in Boravia—in Imrion or Navra, Nisvea or any other country there—a woman and a man can be of equal rank, *really* equal rank." She stepped closer to him, close enough that he could smell the wine on her breath. "Let me tell you, *Tar* Xerwin. In Boravia, it is the oldest child who inherits, male or female, so women own businesses and farmland. They are Houses, Scholars, and, yes, even Paledyns. And what's more, they are Tarkins."

A cold wave of anger washed through him, leaving his hands tingling. How dare she, how dare she speak to him in that tone. Not even his schoolmasters had ever used that tone to him. He knew his anger must have shown in his face, but the Paledyn did not back away, did not lower even her eyes, let alone her face. In fact, she seemed to be smiling to herself, as if she had tested something, and found the result she expected.

And suddenly it was as if all his anger evaporated in an instant. She was not afraid of him. It was fear that he saw in the faces of other women, he now saw. Not admiration. Perhaps not even respect. Dhulyn Wolfshead spoke the truth. Everything about her, her tone, her attitude—her very existence, proved that she spoke the truth.

"Women are all these things in Boravia." He waited until she nodded. "And slavery is not practiced there."

"No, it is not."

"And our treatment of our women—I mean, *the* women—that would be seen as a kind of slavery."

"It would."

"And the Nomads, they think as you do in Boravia. So they look at us here in Mortaxa as people they trade with, but not people they respect. Not people they will marry with. Not people they view as they view themselves. They think as little of us as we do of them." It was an uncomfortable feeling, to see this. "I see it now. It explains much that I did not understand in my dealings with them. Why, then, do they trade with us?"

Dhulyn Wolfshead merely shrugged up one shoulder and moved away. "Diplomacy between states is always rather more complicated than less," she said. "Trade is one thing, political alliance is another."

"The Seers said you would bring change. I am beginning to understand just how much."

"I bring new ideas, perhaps. If there is to be change, it is you who will do it."

"And perhaps you will help me."

Dhulyn was happy to let Xerwin keep his own silence as he led the rest of the way to the watchtower. He appeared to be taking her words to heart, and she found she was more than a little uncomfortable with the things she had said, and the way she had said them. She had not been aware that she had so much anger in her—and that was dangerous for a Mercenary Brother. Get angry, get stupid. Get stupid, get dead. That's what the Common Rule said.

One of the other things the Common Rule said was that Mercenary Brothers stayed neutral when it came to politics. They could refuse to take an offer of employment for personal reasons—up to and including having no liking for the politics, or the mustache, of the potential employer. What they weren't to do was interfere unasked with how a given country managed their own peoples.

But they have asked me. Nor did she think she was just splitting hairs. The Tarxin had asked for Paledyns, no matter how much he had intended to use them rather than be guided by them. He had asked. He'd been told by his own Seers that Paledyns would come, and offer a solution to the conflict with the Nomads. And if the solution that was offered did more than that?

There were also the Marked to consider. Did the Common Rule tell her she had to leave them in the condition she found them? Could she not do for them what she would be expected to do for any Mercenary Brother she found in the same straits?

She was glad to get to the watchtower, and the distraction of the viewing glass, a type she'd never seen before. Xerwin dismissed the regular lookout, who seemed happy to go. The sunshine was bright enough to blind.

Xerwin motioned her to use the viewing glass first, half-shrugging and with a smile.

"It looks like two ships at least," she said. "Possibly three, if there is one behind them."

"They will not be bringing Paledyns with them, since you are already here."

"They may not even be the Nomads with whom I traveled. We cannot know where the storm might have blown them."

"Now that they are here, what do you think?" he asked her. "Are my father's suggestions for dealing with the Nomads at all reasonable?"

"They would be a reasonable place to begin," she said. "If they were not based on an entirely incorrect premise."

"My father is wrong about yet another thing? You surprise me."

The words were sarcastic, but the tone, and the look on his face showed only resignation. She gave him a long, measuring glance. Or perhaps there was more than that, perhaps there was some determination as well. She might as well see what he was made of. It seemed to be a day to tell him things.

"The Crayx are not animals," she said. "They are beings as intelligent as we are ourselves, and with a longer history."

Xerwin squeezed his eyes shut, putting both hands to his forehead. "This is too much. How is this possible?" He lowered his hands. "How do you *know?*"

"They speak mind to mind, and not everyone has the ability to hear and speak with them."

"The Nomads must be lying to you. How could such an ability be limited?"

Dhulyn shook her head. Once again, his tone did not match his words. "Is the Mark not limited? Even among the Marked, is not one Mender better talented than another? You've seen the White Twins, how they are like two different sets of people. For the Sun's sake, Xerwin, a Storm Witch inhabits your sister's body!" Dhulyn leaned against the battlement, feeling the heat of the stone through her clothes. "You, yourself, have seen stranger things than sea creatures who can speak to humans. Your deciding that they are nothing more than animals does not make them so. Any more than your confining and breeding the Marked makes them animals. And the people you enslave, they *are* people, and not dogs or cattle." *Shut up. Shut up*, she told herself. Sun and Moon, what was wrong with her?

Xerwin sat down heavily on the lookout's perch, as if Dhulyn Wolfshead's words were each as heavy as the block of stone he was sitting on. She was not looking at him now, he saw, somewhat relieved. She had turned away to face the ocean, and was looking into the middle distance, as if she were thinking of something else entirely. Xerwin was glad of the respite.

Animals who are people. People who are not animals. He rubbed at his face. His head spun so much he was afraid it would come off. *"The Paledyn changes all. Nothing will be as it was. The world as you know it will be gone, forever."* That's what the White Twins had said. Their eerie, adult voices echoed in his head. *"Rain will fall in the desert; the hind chase the lion; the creatures of the sea will walk the beaches. Trees will flower in winter; the sea lose its salt, the land ripple and flow."*

It was coming. An entirely different world. He looked over at Dhulyn Wolfshead. A better one?

His father would never stand for it. Never let it happen.

Well, then, I must do something about my father.

"Dhulyn Wolfshead," he said. "As you say, the Tarxin may only pretend to heed your suggestions, but I will listen to you." *And to begin*, he thought, *I will set up the patrol of the Upper City.*

Carcali let her woman Finexa drape her veils properly, making sure that her face and torso were not obscured, and that the cloth hung neatly and evenly down her back. The Tarxin had summoned her.

"Leave it," she said finally, her skin fairly itching with impatience.

"It cannot be left, Tara," Finexa said. "You go to your father, Light of the Sun, but you must pass through public corridors to reach him, and you must be properly dressed."

She'd speak to the Tarxin about this, Carcali thought. If the Paledyn could go about dressed as she pleased, surely the Storm Witch could as well. The thought of trousers almost made her mouth water.

There were two guards outside the door waiting to escort her to the Tarxin's hall. They were called attendants, but they were more than that, just as Finexa was more than a lady page.

This time Carcali noticed that as she passed through one of the public squares Finexa had mentioned, even a few of the men who saw her acknowledged her, not just the women as before. So it did mean something to be the Storm Witch.

The Tarxin was waiting for her in his private room, off to one side of the audience chamber. Carcali bit at the inside of her lower lip. The last time she'd been in this room, the Tarxin had struck her.

"Good," he said, without looking up. "I thank you for coming so promptly."

Fine words, but a formality only. When he looked up, his face changed. He tilted his head to on side, actually looking at her now, seeing her.

"What would you like to be called?"

A shiver went up her spine. Those were almost the very same words the Paledyn had said to her. And even though the woman had meant to challenge and shake her, Carcali found she would rather have the Paledyn's distrust and challenge, than the Tarxin's false warmth.

"It would be better if I was always called the Tara Xendra, don't you think?"

His face hardened, but whatever his expression had been, it was gone quickly. Carcali steeled herself and went to one of the chairs near the wall and pulled it forward, placing it across the table from the Tarxin. She concentrated on straightening her skirts and veils as she seated herself, not looking up. She couldn't wait for him to ask her to sit down. If she meant to be treated like an equal partner, she needed to act like one.

Suddenly the Tarxin smiled, like a wolf showing all its teeth, and Carcali wished that he would frown at her again.

"I forget. Looking at you, I forget that it is not a little girl, not quite marrying age, sitting before me. I forget that you are something else, something entirely different."

Carcali tilted her head to one side and raised her eyebrows slightly, in imitation of one of her professors when he wanted to show that more of a response was expected.

"You'd do well to remember that others will only see the child, and act accordingly."

"Others will see the Storm Witch, soon enough. Nothing so easily remedied as youth." One of the same professor's sayings. "May I ask why I'm here?"

The Tarxin leaned back in his chair, elbows resting on the arms. "The Nomads have been sighted, two ships at least, out beyond the arm of the western shore. I want you to send a storm that will either put them upon the rocks, or push them far out to sea."

"Why?"

The silence was so profound that Carcali thought she could actually hear the drop of sweat that trailed down the center of her back.

"They are our enemies." His voice was cold enough to drop the temperature of the room.

"When do you want it?"

"Now. Immediately."

Carcali shook her head. "Can't be done, not without more notice. I don't keep the kind of winds you're asking for in my pockets, you know. Air pressure has to be changed, temperatures, humidity . . . these aren't things that can just be conjured up out of nowhere." *Well, they could*, she thought. *But not by me, not anymore.*

He looked at her from under lowered lids. "What is it you fear?"

Carcali thanked the Art that she'd practiced controlling her face, otherwise she didn't know what else he might have picked up from her expression. "I'm afraid you're going to lose your temper with me, and forget what our agreement is," she said finally. "It seemed pretty obvious that I was telling you something you didn't want to hear."

Whether it was the reminder of their bargain, or whether he really was much more pragmatic than she gave him credit for, the Tarxin relaxed.

"How much time do you need?"

"All I can give you this minute is a guess. With a few hours of calculations, I should be able to tell you more precisely."

"And your guess now?"

"At least two days."

"Then you have two days."

He looked down at the pages in front of him. Carcali frowned and kept her seat, pretending she hadn't noticed the dismissal. She had to say something. She *had* to. Her guilt already weighed her down—heavier, if anything, since the Paledyn's visit—she couldn't take any more.

"If the Nomads get too close to shore," she said, "Whatever I do to them will affect the shore as well."

"Can your storm melt rock?" he said, looking up.

"Well, no." Carcali blinked. "But it can destroy homes, crops."

He nodded. "Very well. Warnings can be given to those exposed. If that is all, I must return to my other work." Now he was also pretending he hadn't dismissed her already.

"Of course," she said as she rose to her feet.

"Let them know they may send the Scholar in."

She nodded, turned her back on him, and walked out.

Her guards were waiting for her in the outer room. She gave the Steward the message and watched him approach a blue-robed Scholar before setting off back to her own quarters.

So that's the way it was going to be, was it? He would tell her what to do and she would do it. Some partnership. What gave him the right—*don't be naïve*, she told herself. Power gives him the right. He dictates and others obey. Carcali sucked in a sharp breath, loudly enough that the guard walking ahead of her half turned his head to look at her over his shoulder. Carcali lowered her eyes and kept walking. Was she any better than the Tarxin? Hadn't she thought power was all it would take to solve the problem facing the Academy of Artists? Look how that had ended.

That was why her friend Wenora had been so angry with her; Carcali *had* been bullying people, in a way, since her talent was so much more powerful than anyone else's. Would she have become like the Tarxin if one day, as her ambition was, she'd become the Head Artist? Her footsteps slowed as she reached a wooden bench looking out over a balcony that let onto the sea. She sat down, pulling her veils closely around her.

She'd been using her power to help, back then, when everything had gone so horribly wrong. The Tarxin wanted her to hurt people. Hadn't she had enough of that? How much more? How far was she willing to go before she said stop, enough? She shivered. Xalbalil wouldn't be Tarxin forever, but how many people would be hurt while she waited for him to die? She needed an ally, and she needed one now. If the Paledyn wouldn't help her, then she had to go back to her original idea. Xendra's brother, Tar Xerwin.

She looked up. Would it seem peculiar to the guards if she asked them where Xendra's brother was to be found? Surely this was something she would be expected to know.

Finexa would know. There would be fewer questions raised if she asked Finexa.

Remm Shalyn was waiting for her when Dhulyn got back to her rooms. A waggle of his eyebrows indicated that the Marked were still there, hidden once more in her bedroom. The scrying bowl was no longer on the table, but there was a shoulder bag on a chair that didn't belong to her. She pointed to it.

"I am likely not the only person who has seen that bag hanging from the Healer's shoulder."

Remm blushed and pressed his lips together, nodding. "An oversight, I admit. Won't happen again."

"Was the Finder successful?"

He glanced at the door of her bedroom in such a way that she read the answer on his face. He'd been hoping someone else would be the one to tell her.

"The bowl worked beautifully," Javen Finder said once Remm had let them back into the sitting room. She was trying to be properly downcast and contrite, seeing they'd had no success. But her delight in the bowl was strong, and it showed in the sparkle of her eyes, despite her other feelings. "I saw colors, as I usually do, but much brighter, much clearer than usual. I Found you, Dhulyn Wolfshead, and a toy of the White Twins that's been missing for months." She lowered her eyes, glancing at the bag hanging on the chair. "If I could keep the bowl, I could try again. I'm so sorry to have failed you."

Dhulyn grinned. If the bowl was already in the bag, they'd anticipated her answer. "The bowl is yours, and we haven't failed yet, Javen Finder," she said. "That was only the first of my ideas. There may be another way, but to try it we must return to the Sanctuary. We will need the White Twins."

All three Marked looked at each other, and Rascon Mender's lips actually parted, but she closed her mouth again when Ellis Healer gave a tiny shake of his head. Clearly, they wanted to ask how the Seers could help them. But Dhulyn had no intention of telling them yet—possibly never, if the Seers could re-create the Vision of the hiding child without her.

"We'll need time, and that we may not have. The Nomads have been sighted."

"From where?" Remm handed the shoulder bag to the Healer.

"The north tower."

"The earliest point at which they can be seen. That buys us some time." His brows drew down in a vee. "The Tarxin will call for his Council, and he'll want the Tar with him. And at the right moment— when they've decided what to tell you—they'll call for you, as well. That means the upper gardens will be clear. We'll go as soon as the summons comes for you."

"Should they wait here? We could go together to the Sanctuary after dark."

But Remm was already shaking his head. "No one would call to see them now, during the meal hour, and the midday rest. But as soon as the worst of the heat passes—and word of the Nomads gets around, as it will—there will be people in the Sanctuary, and many will ask for the senior Marked. I can take them back through the gardens, Dhulyn Wolfshead. I know the way now. No need to disturb the Tar Xerwin."

"And if you're found there?"

"With all due respect to the Tar, it's only he or his father can find us there. If it's he, then no problem, if it's the Tarxin, well." Remm Shalyn shrugged. "I confess I was curious as to what story the Tar was going to give his father to explain our presence earlier. Me, I'll just say you sent me, and I was afraid to disobey."

"Very well." Dhulyn rubbed the line she could feel forming between her brows. She looked up at the Marked. "At the end of the third watch, when the Moon has set. Expect me."

It was odd to see such a promising inlet so deserted, even at this time of day. But they had wanted a high tide to take them as far in as possible, and the fact that this was the hottest part of the day simply meant there would be fewer landsters about. The bluffs here were not as high as they were at Ketxan City, but they were cut by a narrow creek. The sun had just passed its highest point when Parno and his squad had taken one of the *Wavetreader*'s boats and set off. The Nomads knew this section of coast well, having put in often for fresh water, and though Parno hadn't felt much wind, they'd been able to use the sails on the small craft to get them almost to the beach.

Seems an odd place to be so familiar with *Is there a village nearby*

There's good fresh water upstream, above the tidal washes That was

Conford. *Can beach the boat there as well, then it's a short climb to the top of the bluff*

*But have *you* been here before, Conford* Surely not, if his exchange had been so recent.

Amusement *No need* *Others have, and their knowledge is my knowledge*

Looks different in the day That was one of the twins. Tindar, Parno thought. *Only ever been here at night*

They doused the sail and took out oars as soon as they were far enough up the creek to lose the wind. In moments the prow of the boat grounded, and Sar and Chels jumped out to haul it as far up the tiny beach as they could. Parno jumped out also, still in his bare feet. His boots were tucked down the front of his tunic, he carried two swords, his daggers, knives, and even a throwing quoit. The others bore the weapons he thought they'd do best with. Swords for the most part, but Tindar's twin, Elian, also had a small ax, and Conford had his *garwon*.

Amusement *Nervousness* *Fear* This last very small.

Parno stayed off to one side while the Nomads pulled the boat far enough up the beach that the movement of waves would not trouble it. Sails and masts were stowed, and the boats turned over. With luck, they would make it back in time to catch the next high tide.

Ready

Agreement

Follow, and keep as quiet as you can

That was one thing that Pod sense gave you, he thought. You knew exactly where everyone else in your squad was, and if necessary, you knew what they were thinking. Instant communication—and completely silent. Better than the nightwatch whisper of the Mercenary Brotherhood, since it could be used over any distance.

#Not any distance# That was the unmistakable voice of a Crayx. Deeper, somehow, and more resonant, though the terms meant nothing when no real sound was made. #Go far enough inland, and we cannot hear you#

How far

#Distance on land is very hard for us# #We have heard the voice of a Pod-sensed one as far as two days' travel on foot# #Farther than that, we cannot be sure#

Not that far, then, as things were measured. A Pod-sensed child growing up almost anywhere in Boravia would be overlooked by the few Crayx who came into the Midland Sea.

#We will look more carefully now#

The trees grew thicker as they walked away from the beach, giving them much needed shade. Though they had covered their heads, and were wearing their lightest garments, the heat was oppressive, and the insects would have been a great deal more so, if it were not for the greasy salve that the Nomads used as protection. One of their most popular trade goods, it was made from an oil excreted by the Crayx. Still, Parno found he had to wave tiny insects away from his face every now and then to avoid breathing them in.

The thickness of the trees did expose one flaw in their plan, however. The Nomads were noisier on land than anyone he'd ever led before. Parno called a halt as one of them blundered through a bush.

Not our fault, nowhere to practice

Parno thought for a moment. Not only could they be heard by anyone near them, but the noise of their own movement would obscure the sound of anyone else's approach. Too bad he hadn't thought of teaching them even one of the simpler Hunter *Shoras*.

#Show us#

Startled, Parno thought for a moment before signaling to the others to rest. He waited until the watch was posted before he closed his eyes and took a deep breath. And another. His heart rate slowed, and his senses turned outward. The Stalking Cat *Shora* settled over him like a blanket, and suddenly the whole clearing was quiet, as Parno and the Nomads, linked by the Crayx, all breathed in the same silent rhythm, their eight hearts beating as one. At first it was disorienting to hear with so many ears, feel the shift of air or the pattern of sunlight with so many skins, but suddenly, as if the minds of the Crayx acted like a clearinghouse for all the different sensations, Parno felt everything fall into place.

Nineteen

MARVELOUS* THAT WAS one of the twins. *Like this all the time* she asked.

*When using the right *Shora** he answered.

A buzz of excitement passed through them all. *What a way to School people*, Parno thought. Unfortunately, it would only work with the Pod-sensed.

At first, even with the *Shora*, the Nomads were not as silent as Mercenary Brothers would have been, but they were so much quieter than they had been moments before that it was like leading an entirely different group of people. Parno found that they weren't able to keep up continuously the level of concentration required for the Stalking Cat *Shora*, but he kept them practicing between breaks, and even without it, the awareness of what was possible made them all take better care. Soon, instead of moving like raw recruits, the Nomads began to have the feel of a squad who had been training together for some time.

It was evening by the time Parno and the Nomads were out of the woods and making their way through cultivated fields and groves of fruit trees to within sight of Ketxan City. There was this to be said about a slave culture; in any other place, the lands around them would have been held by free men or tenant farmers, people who would have been up in the night, watching over their flocks or making their rounds. The Holdings would have been smaller, closer together, and therefore harder to pass unnoticed. In this place, the holdings were huge, the workers penned up at night, and the watching eyes turned inward, not outward. All of which helped to make it relatively easy for Parno and his seven Nomads.

Parno had been hoping for moonlight to help him match the Upper City to the description he'd had from Oskarn of the *Sunwaver* Pod, but the afternoon had slowly become cloudier, and the hoped-for moonlight would not now materialize. They could see lights in some of the pavilions of the Upper City, but certainly not enough to give general illumination.

See there Parno picked out what he thought would be the best route over the wall. *I'll go first, follow in order*

Agreement

In moments they were all over the wall, and had moved forward into a lane between two low buildings which showed no lights.

Silence everyone *Three people approach us*

Instantly, the Stalking Cat *Shora* enveloped them once again, precise and perfect.

People out late

Parno shook his head. *That's a patrol* *See the way they move*

Awareness *Agreement*

*Isn't that what *you* said* Conford thought. *You'd set up patrols if was your place to guard*

That wasn't precisely what he'd said, Parno thought. He'd said it was what any Mercenary would advise. But to come here and find it done ... Parno became aware of a creeping unease. Was it possible that there were Pod-sensed among the Mortaxa after all? Could they have listened to his thoughts?

#No# This was the Crayx. #Not without our knowledge# The Crayx had kept the others from feeling his unease.

Heading toward us *Will pass by*

No Parno wasn't sure exactly how he knew. *In the open, they might have missed us, but not here*

Three for certain *Can smell them* A sense of delight as the Nomad who'd spoken—Mikel?—felt the full usefulness of the Stalking Cat *Shora*.

One experienced man leads two recruits Parno felt the agreement as the others all compared the sounds and understood why he'd drawn that conclusion.

Twins, flank left. Conford, Mikel, right Parno felt them move into place, as Trudi, Sar, and Chels moved back, spreading out to cover them all.

The patrol continued to approach. Their manner was relaxed, more like people going for a walk than guards on patrol—so much so that Parno almost doubted what logic and the Stalking Cat *Shora* told him.

Inexperienced he told the others. *Not expecting trouble* *Move with me*

At exactly the right moment Parno stepped out of a shadow and cut the patrol leader's throat with a sharp stroke of the sword in his right hand. He caught the body as it fell, keeping sound to the minimum, and saw out of the corner of his eye Conford plunging his *garwon* into the second man's temple, and Mikel grappling with the third man, one hand at his throat to keep him from crying out.

Parno felt a grin spread over his face as Sar ran forward to help Mikel. They had all moved simultaneously.

All three guards were dressed in short patterned kilts—there was not enough light to show colors. They wore metaled sandals and leather harness over bare skin, and carried short swords. Only one had a crossbow hanging from his belt.

Take the weapons, and move the bodies into the shadows under that wall Parno instructed.

What now

There may be another patrol, or someone may come looking for this one when they don't report It was too late to change plans, but a good Mercenary Brother learned to adapt to circumstances as he found them. And this was a circumstance Parno had planned for. *Have to split up* he said. *As we discussed* *Conford, take Sar, Mikel, and Chels to the public entrance* *The rest of you, with me*

Agreement *Excitement*

Crayx, are you ready

#We await your word#

Dhulyn returned from the Council meeting to find Remm Shalyn alone in her quarters, weapons spread out on the table to be cleaned, oil and a cleaning cloth in his hand. *Her* weapons.

Before he could finish looking up, she was across the room, lifting his hand from the metalwork on her crossbow.

"Don't touch my things," she said. "Never touch my things."

His eyes went round at what he saw on her face, and he licked his lips. "But Dhulyn Wolfshead, it's my job. I'm your sword servant."

"No." She squeezed her eyes shut. How to make him understand? "Among the Mercenary Brotherhood there are no servants," she began. "We are Brothers. Each our own master, and our own servant."

"But if you spend your time cleaning weapons and harness, you don't have time to *be* a Mercenary Brother."

"If I don't clean my own weapons, how can I be sure they have no defects? How can I be sure they are *mine*?"

He seemed about to argue further and Dhulyn put up her hand, palm toward him. "You tell me you're my sword servant."

"Yes."

"You're to obey me."

"Yes."

She slammed her hand down on the table. "Then obey me."

Remm looked at her openmouthed for the time it took to breathe in twice. Then he began to laugh. "Very well, yes," he said when he had caught his breath. "I think I see."

Dhulyn shook her head at him, but smiled. She was finding it hard, very hard, to deal with this form of thinking, this settled condition of the mind. In Boravia, independence of thought and action could be found in many people, everywhere—in fact, much of it often had to be trained out of people to make them good troops. But here, where the common experience was that one set of people oppressed another, even a naturally independent type like Remm Shalyn, who was used to playing a difficult role, showed evidence of a narrow way of thinking.

"So how did the Council go?" he asked her, pushing himself away from the table and her weapons and going to the sideboard, where there were still pastries and a jug of drink from the midday meal.

She smiled her wolf's smile, and was given an answering grin in return.

"That Tarxin's up to something."

"He usually is." Remm poured her out a cup of fruit juice, still cool in its ceramic jug, and handed it to her. Dhulyn took it without tasting it, seated herself in the big chair to one end of the table, and slung a leg over the arm.

"Apparently, there is no cause for immediate alarm," she said. "The

Nomad ships are at least three days away. Currents prevent them from coming directly to the docks from where they've been sighted. They shall have to come around from a different direction. The Tarxin has asked the representatives of the High Noble Houses to make up a small committee—which is to include me—to meet with the Nomads."

"So we can try the plan you have in mind?"

She looked at him. "Can we go openly to the Sanctuary? It wastes so much time otherwise."

Remm came and sat on the edge of the table near enough to touch her if he put out his hand. "What's your plan, Wolfshead? What can the White Twins do that you can't?"

For a moment Dhulyn studied Remm's face. He looked open, honest, trustworthy. But then, he could act a part if needed, and it would be often needed if he were a freer of slaves. He trusted her with this knowledge of himself. But given how the Marked were circumstanced here in Mortaxa, could she trust him with *her* secrets?

"The White Twins know where the spirit of the child Xendra hides. They have Seen her. Javen Finder cannot Find the child—neither by linking with the Healer and Mender, nor through using the bowl. She can't, as she says, Find a Vision. But if she could link with the Seers, experience their Vision firsthand, perhaps then she could Find the child, searching the world of the Vision, as she searches through this one."

"But the White Twins are . . ." Remm's voice trailed away. He waggled his right hand from side to side.

"Yes, they are. But they can See Xendra. The only question is whether they can also link with the Finder."

I can do it, she thought. She had linked with other Marked before, and thought she could do it again. But she was not ready to tell even the other Marked that she was herself a Seer. She could do nothing to help them, if she were locked inside the Sanctuary with them. She couldn't take the chance that their settled patterns of thinking might betray her, that even the Marked would no longer see her as Paledyn. Just as she couldn't take the chance to try a Vision herself, without Keria and Amaia. With them, she could control the Visions, take them where she wished them to go, something she could never do with any certainty before.

Without the Twins' help, there was no knowing what Visions she might See—anything might come, past or future. At the moment there was nothing of the future she wanted to See, and one particular Vision of the past she would give much never to See again.

A woman was talking to the guards at the entrance to his rooms when Xerwin returned to them after the Council meeting. The guards came to attention and when she turned to see why, he recognized her as the Xara Finexa, the Storm Witch's attendant.

"Forgive me, Tar Xerwin," she said, offering a curtsy which displayed her bosom to good effect. "Your sister, the Tara Xendra waits for you within."

Xerwin wrinkled up his nose, not caring if the woman saw it. His first instinct was simply to refuse. He had nothing to say to the Storm Witch, and could not imagine what she felt she needed to say to him. He started to signal the guard to enter before him, to eject her . . . but Xerwin hesitated. Something had brought her here—even if it was merely some trick. Should he not try to discover what it was? And if she *had* something of consequence to tell him, and he missed hearing it out of misplaced caution . . . he could just imagine what Dhulyn Wolfshead would say about that.

He could be tricky himself, if he needed to be.

Carcali was sitting in the window seat when Tar Xerwin came into his sitting room. She had her arms folded across her chest and her hands tucked into the long sleeves of her child's tunic. She'd been watching the sunset, reaching out and feeling the slow gathering of moisture, the formation of cloud. In her lap, cradled in the folds of her skirt, was a soft toy she had found fallen behind the closed shutter, half-formed, made from scraps of leather with raw inglera fleece for stuffing.

"What brings you here?" he said, his voice quite gruff. "What is so urgent?"

He was looking at her differently now, she noticed. He'd frowned before, but his mouth then had been softer, his eyes warmer. That frown had shown concern. Now his eyes were hard, his mouth a thin line. *He knows*, she thought. He might have wondered before, but now it was clear that he knew she wasn't his little sister. Carcali couldn't see the Tarxin telling him, so it must have been the Paledyn. She shut her eyes, suddenly tired, far more tired than the small Art she'd used so far should make her.

He was still waiting for his answer. What *did* she want from him, what *was* so urgent? It had seemed so simple when she decided to come here. Tell him what was going on, and he'd become an instant ally. Now it didn't seem that simple. She lifted the toy.

"This was for your sister, wasn't it? You were making it for her. You must have loved her very much, to do this with your own hands." She turned it over. "It's a horse, isn't it? The legs should be a little longer."

"You know horses? You've seen them?" His eyes were narrowed, calculating. He stood, leaning his hip against his worktable. She nodded.

"In my own time, my own place, yes." She held out the toy like a peace offering. "My name is Carcali," she said. She almost couldn't believe she was telling him. "And no, that's not so urgent, is it?" She rubbed her face with her hands. "I'm just tired of all the pretending. The Paledyn told you, I suppose."

"It was I told *her* you weren't my sister though, as it happened, I had no need." He came closer. "The Nomads approach. Can this wait?"

Carcali nodded out the window. "The Tarxin's asked me to send a storm to destroy the Nomad ships."

For a second he stood stone still, then he pulled out a chair and sat down. "Can you?"

She nodded. "It would take a few days, but, yes, I can do it."

"Why tell me?" His tone was cautious, wary, but with a good sprinkling of plain curiosity. Her eye fell once more on the toy. She'd come here looking for an ally, someone . . . a better man than the Tarxin, someone who cared about people, not power. Someone who would make a toy for his sister with his own hands.

"The storm won't just affect the Nomads. What I'd have to do, to follow the Tarxin's orders, would cause a lot more damage, far-reaching damage, inland as well as at sea. I've told your father this, and he doesn't care. He wants me to kill those people, no matter the consequences, and I don't want to."

"You've already done as bad."

"But not on purpose, not deliberately. It was an accident." She reached a hand toward him.

"And is it an accident that you occupy my sister's body?"

Carcali sat up straight, gripping the edge of the stone window seat. "I didn't do this, the Marked did." She cleared her throat and tried again. "When that Marked person found me and pulled me into this body, there was no one else there. I was alone in the spheres." Carcali swallowed, trying to get her lips to stop trembling. "Your sister wasn't there."

His eyebrows drew down in a deep vee, his lips pressed together.

"Your sister is gone," Carcali said, as gently as she could.

"And if she is found? Would you vacate her body?"

Carcali rubbed at her eyes. "Listen, you want me to be honest? I'll be honest. It's too late for her to be found. Only a Mage like me, trained in the Art, can leave the body for so long and then return to it." And sometimes not even a Mage like her, but she had no intention of telling him that. "And let me say again—" Carcali found she was pointing her index finger at him and quickly dropped her hand, tapping herself on the sternum instead. "I didn't take your sister's body. It isn't just that I don't want to be out there in the nothing again, not ever again. I'm really sorry for your sister, but she was gone before I ever came along. Ask them! Ask those Marked people. Would they have taken me if your sister had been there? No one gains by pushing me out again, not me, not you, not the people we can help if we work together."

Xerwin turned the toy over in his hands, frowning down at it. A fluff of wool fell to the floor, and he stooped to pick it up. "Xendra always wanted to see a horse with her own eyes. Fond as she was of Naxot, I think she secretly hoped to be married to some ruler across the Long Ocean, to see the horses there." He put the half-made toy aside on the table and looked across at her. Carcali wanted to look away, but steeled herself not to lower her eyes.

"Why come to me?" he said finally. "Why don't you just refuse my father? What can he do to you?"

"You remember the bruise on my face?" His eyes widened, but Carcali saw that Xerwin wasn't really shocked. "He took away Kendraxa who at least was nice to me, and replaced her with that Finexa spy. And he locked my doors and starved me. It wouldn't take long for me to get too weak to practice the Art, and that's the only weapon I have. If I can destroy him, well, he can do the same to me." Carcali took a deep breath.

"Your father doesn't want a partnership with me, as he claims. He doesn't want to work with me, just to use me, control me, as he controls everything. He has no intention of negotiating with the Nomads—or anyone else—Paledyn or no Paledyn. *We* could have a real partnership, you and I. We could trust each other, we could create a world that would be the best for everyone."

"We could change the world." Xerwin was looking inward now, and Carcali would have given a great deal to know what it was he was looking at. She'd never seen that look on his face before.

She got down off the window seat and had taken a step toward him when one of the door guards knocked and entered. Finexa was in the hall behind him, wringing her hands.

"Your pardon, Tar Xerwin, it's the Nomads. They are storming the City."

Dhulyn Wolfshead leaned far over the rail of the tiny balcony in her sitting room, craning her neck from side to side. The night was overcast, but the moonlight that made it through the clouds reflected back twofold from the water.

"I see no ships."

Just as she spoke, a great long-nosed head rose out of the water, and spat a jet of water at one of the lower floors. A small sailboat, moored at dockside, was blown upward by the force of the jet and smashed against the cliff face. A flight of arrows came from one of the middle floors, between Dhulyn and the sea, and a second beast directed its water jet upward.

"Sun and Moon, Wind and Stars." Dhulyn turned to Remm Shalyn. "I did not know they could do that."

Remm looked pale, but smiled. "I had heard," he said. "But I've never before seen it."

Dhulyn looked again at the archers. "Idiots," she said. "Those arrows will never pierce their hides, and if they're aiming for the eyes, they need a better angle."

"What about a crossbow?"

Dhulyn nodded, her eyes still on the incredible jets of water. "Can't do any harm." Which she meant precisely. With a good longbow, or a well-made recurve bow, she might confidently expect to do some damage. But with a crossbow, at this distance, "no harm" was exactly what she would do.

In minutes, Dhulyn was running down the corridor with Remm Shalyn at her heels, carrying her crossbow and a soft leather bag full of bolts. In the Grand Square outside the Tarxin's palace, she found the Senior Guard Commander directing soldiers to their posts on the lower floors.

"It's the Crayx," he told her, rather unnecessarily, she thought. "The Nomads' animals. They train them to shoot jets of water at the City face, to cover an attack."

"But what attack? We've already established that the ships are still days away."

"If their beasts are here, then the Nomads are here as well. They use these animal tricks to distract us, while they gain entry at the lower levels."

"Where the animals are, we'll find their masters," agreed the second-in-command.

Not true, Dhulyn thought. The Crayx had their regular migration routes, and for the most part they followed them, but they could and did deviate from them, and in any case, their movements were no more dependent on the movements of the Nomads than the rising of Mother Sun was dependent on a farmer's breakfast hour. And as far as she had seen, there was no one trying to gain entry from the water level.

Not the lower levels, no.

"The Upper City." Had Xerwin had time to assign patrols there as he'd intended? She thought she'd whispered, but she found all other voices stopped, and the commander turning to look at her.

"You are right," she said. "This is a distraction, but the attack will be made from above, in the Upper City."

"Nonsense." In the excitement, the commander seemed to have forgotten who he was speaking to. "The Nomads have never attacked from overland before. They cannot maneuver on land."

Dhulyn knew very well that just because something had never been done before, did not mean it was impossible. But she also knew when she would be listened to, and when she would be wasting her breath. The commander had already turned away from her. This was clearly an example of the latter.

"Commander." She waited until she had his attention. "You will not mind if I inspect the Upper City."

"Of course not, Paledyn." Relief at being rid of her was evident on his face, and had served to remind the man of his manners.

Catching Remm Shalyn's eye, Dhulyn trotted down the passage that would take them to the Upper City. The Nomads had never attacked overland before. Nothing more likely, she thought, seeing what a siege engine they had in the Crayx and their water jets. But an overland sortie—was that something she or Parno had ever discussed with the Nomads? Because it would be typical Mercenary planning, exactly what she would have done herself, if she had known what tactics the Mortaxa expected, and that the Crayx had this ability. She stopped dead in her tracks.

"Dhulyn Wolfshead? Are you ill?"

All those evenings of talk, of singing, of telling tales, was it possible that an overland attack could have been discussed? Or that the Nomads could have worked it out from some tale one of them had told?

It must be. Because there wasn't any other explanation. There couldn't be. Could there?

She took off running.

Appears was only the one patrol

Typical amateurs *Any Mercenary Brother would have known to have at least two patrols*

Lionsmane

Parno automatically looked in the direction Conford wanted him to look. There were another pair of lights. A second patrol.

As if his thoughts had just conjured them out of the air. What kind of trick was this?

Do the landsters have any other Mages he asked. *Anyone other than the Storm Witch*

Not that we know Everyone agreed on that. *There are Marked* pointed out a single individual Parno couldn't identify.

But the Marked can't conjure lights out of air Parno said. *Or read my thoughts.*

Lionsmane Tension and query were equally obvious in the flavor of the thought. Parno made a quick decision.

Won't cross our path if keep to their present heading he said. *Let them go* *Conford, proceed to the public entrance*

Agreement

Parno waited until Conford's group had melted away into the darkness—almost silently—before leading the twins and Trudi Primoh after him, swinging around westward to approach the wall of the palace precinct obliquely.

Briefly, Parno wondered whether they should have stalked the second patrol, taking one of them prisoner to ask where the Storm Witch could be found. But that was too risky. Better to get inside the palace and frighten it out of a servant or slave.

Once away from the Grand Square, Dhulyn let Remm lead her through the palace corridors to the staircase that would take them up into the royal precinct in the Upper City. Once outside, they could head for the nearest wall. As they neared the stairs, Dhulyn had Remm douse his torch, and handed him the crossbow.

"It will be considerably darker in the Upper City than it was even at the cliff face," she said. "There, the sea itself helped to reflect what little light there is. Carrying lights will make us a target, and dull our own night vision." She'd prefer in any case to trust her own *Shora*-aided eyesight.

The top of the staircase opened onto a square landing with an arched doorway to one side. This doorway, in turn, opened into the portico that sheltered the entrance proper, a small roofed pavilion made entirely of green marble. Dhulyn had noticed on her visit with Xerwin that it was perhaps three paces wide by five paces long, and raised three steps above the ground outside. When they reached the outer doorway, Dhulyn could just make out the long, tree-lined avenue that fronted the pavilion. The lighter blotches, evenly spaced, she knew to be the stone or marble benches which were laid out beneath the trees. Remm was about to step out into the avenue, already pointing to the direction of the nearest wall, when Dhulyn stopped him, taking him by the arm. There. Off to the right. A movement, like a shadow changing shape. A scuff, like the edge of a boot against stone. The sound of someone coming over the wall.

Dhulyn pulled Remm closer to her, using the nightwatch whisper. "Call for the patrol," she said. "They won't come for a female voice."

"Armsmen!" he obligingly roared out in a voice that startled even Dhulyn; it seemed impossible that so big a sound should come out of so small and compact a man. "To the palace wall! To the Tarxin!"

There was no immediate response, but Dhulyn thought she heard a soft sound over to the right. The patrol would not bother to be so quiet, were they being outflanked? Well, she knew better than to be drawn away from her defensible position. She took a quick look to the right, and the left. Not as much room as she'd like. She drew Remm with her back to the inner doorway. "Stay here," she said. "Kill anyone who gets past me." She refrained from saying she expected no one to pass her.

Sounded like just one man *Stay out here, engage the patrol if they come, and secure my exit* *Be as quick as I can* Parno ran down the stone path, wishing his boots were not quite so loud. If he'd had more time, he could have gone completely silently, but with the alarm already given, someone had to get inside quickly, and that someone was him. This avenue of trees, with its stone benches, led toward an enclosed pavilion, the only completely enclosed structure he could see, and unless he was badly mistaken, the direction from which the voice came. This was likely the entrance to the palace below. He smiled to himself when he saw a darker, vertical patch that meant a doorway.

There, a man was approaching on the shadowed side of the avenue. Dhulyn considered her strategy again, and backed up. With only one opponent, better if she let him into the relatively confined space of the entryway. There, the darkness would be to her advantage, and she would be able to prevent him from escaping. She took a deep breath. A modified version of the Hunter's *Shora* would help her senses stay alert. She smiled her wolf's smile. She and Parno had once needed to practice *Shora* while blindfolded. This would be child's play compared to that.

There was someone in the pavilion. Parno wasn't sure how he knew it; there had been neither sound to be heard nor movement to be seen, but someone was definitely in the structure. He slowed, drawing his left-hand sword, but continued to advance, both blades at the ready. Better to deal with this person now, quickly, while there was only one of him. The darkness would be helpful.

*   *   *

Her senses enhanced by the *Shora*, the first thing Dhulyn noticed as her opponent passed the doorway into the darkness of the marble-cool entry was that his heartbeat was exactly in sync with her own. A shiver passed up her spine. And there was an odor, an odd, almost spicy scent that she had smelled somewhere before.

His opponent was nothing more than a darker shadow among all the others. But he knew that shadow, Parno thought, as the skin crawled on his back. Knew that shape, that angle of shoulder. That scent, subtly changed and yet familiar. His breath caught as a light seem to blaze in his mind. "No," he told it, not daring to hope. This must be Mage's work, meant to distract and detain him. There must be a Mage among the Mortaxa after all. He took a firmer grip on his swords and stepped forward.

At that single spoken syllable, Dhulyn froze. Shape, smell, and now sound. It was impossible. It could not be. It was a trick. Could she be having a Vision unaware?

"Are you a ghost?" The nightwatch voice seemed impossibly loud in this confined space.

"Come and try me, Mage's phantom."

The voice. Dhulyn began to tremble.

"I am no phantom." Dhulyn's heart pounded, hard and fast, as she lowered her sword. "I am Dhulyn Wolfshead, called the Scholar, and Schooled by Dorian of the River, the Black Traveler. I have fought at Sadron, and Arcosa, where I met my Partner, Parno Lionsmane. Together we fought at Bhexyllia, for the Great King in the West, and later at Limona, against the Tegriani."

"Tell me something no one else could know."

Dhulyn thought, ideas chasing each other hotly through her mind. There seemed so many things, and yet . . .

"I bear a Mark," she said at last. "I am a Seer. Others know it, but no one this side of the Long Ocean."

Suddenly she was crushed in two strong arms, arms she knew well, and she found that she could not breathe, not because of the pressure of those arms, but because her heart was too full, her throat too thick. She was crying. She could not remember ever crying like that before.

"Dhulyn. Dhulyn, my heart. It can't be. You're alive."

"Enemy behind," she croaked out.

Parno released her and whirled, swords raised. "Where?"

"Well, there could have been," she said, taking what felt like the first deep breath she'd had in weeks.

"But how—the Crayx could not find you anywhere."

"But they clearly found you." Dhulyn's raw silk voice sounded rougher, as if she were trying not to cry. She kept touching him, his face, his hands, running her callused fingers along the edges of his beard and lips as if to assure herself that it was really him. "Do we have time for this? I take it those are your people out there."

"Come to kill the Storm Witch." Parno blinked. He hadn't noticed before how much he'd fallen into the Nomads' form of speech.

"My thinking precisely, but there are complications."

Parno took hold of her wrists. "Don't care. I—I'm not even sure I care whether the Witch lives or dies, not now."

Dhulyn butted him in the shoulder with her head, just like a cat. "I think the matter can be resolved to our satisfaction, but we need time. Can you call off the attack?"

Her words warmed him. It was gratifying that she assumed he was in charge. Though in a way, he supposed he was.

Fall back he said to the Nomads. *Fall back, everyone* *My Partner lives* *Dhulyn Wolfshead lives* *She can take me to the Storm Witch with safety for all*

#Rejoicing# came the deeper notes of the Crayx

Are you certain

Certain *Fall back now, before there is further loss of life on either side*

Confusion *Disagreement*

#Parno Lionsmane, our people need further assurance you are well and secure#

And not insane, he thought. *Look in my thoughts* he told the Crayx. *Can you tell that I am not under any magic, that I have found my Partner, alive and well*

#We see this, and will show the others# #We will fall back, as you suggest, and await your instructions# #We remind everyone, this has all along been Lionsmane's plan# #We are at his orders#

Reluctance *Concern* *Agreement*

#We will stay linked, Lionsmane# #Call upon us as needed#

"You were talking to them, weren't you?"

He swept her up in his arms and swung her around as if they were dancing. "I tell you, it's the greatest way to coordinate a two-pronged attack that's ever been heard of." When he put her down, Dhulyn's smile had faded, and her left eyebrow was raised. Parno grinned all the harder. What an Outlander she was, after all, to be embarrassed by his show of emotion.

"Come on, my soul, my heart! We're alive! We're together again."

"Together again," she murmured.

"Dhulyn Wolfshead?"

They'd been talking throughout in the nightwatch voice, as loud as shouts to them, but virtually silent for anyone more than a pace or two away. At this tentative whisper, Parno swung away from his Partner—his Partner!—and faced the inner doorway, swords raised.

"Show a light, Remm Shalyn," Dhulyn said. "There is no enemy here, but the best of allies."

Twenty

"**P**ART OF ME JUST WANTS to walk out of here and go home." Parno stretched his hand across the table and touched Dhulyn on the back of hers. They had started out sitting side by side on the settee in her sitting room, but when Remm Shalyn had returned from a raid to the kitchens they had taken seats at the table across from one another. Dhulyn found herself stealing glances at her Partner, as if she expected at any moment to find he had disappeared. She was afraid to look at him, and afraid to look away.

"We won't get home without the Nomads," she said. "And their quarrel with the Mortaxa is a real one."

"But this Xerwin is the one they've dealt with before, they speak well of him. If *he* can be made to see reason . . ." Parno's voice trailed off as he thought through his idea. Dhulyn tried to concentrate on the food in front of her, but she was tasting nothing. This *was* Parno—she knew it in her blood and bones—but she was still having trouble believing it. It had taken her the whole of the walk back to her rooms, all three of them being careful not to be seen by anyone else, to realize that under her joy was a thin layer of an emotion she could only define as anger, much as it shocked and shamed her. How could she be *angry* with her Partner? Why?

"Xerwin may well see reason," she said aloud. "But he is not Tarxin here, his father is. And Xalbalil has his own firm plans, which include using the Storm Witch—and myself for that matter—to subjugate the Nomads."

Remm cleared his throat. He was sitting to Dhulyn's right, Parno's left, and had been watching them as they talked, turning his attention from one to the other. "So we remove the Storm Witch, as the best and fastest method of ruining his plans."

Parno raised his index finger, swallowed, and spoke. "Do we? No, listen," he said as Dhulyn opened her mouth. "You tell me the storm was an accident. Well, I've no reason to exact any vengeance on the woman for an act of carelessness or ignorance, not now that you're alive. The Tarxin," he shrugged. "There's more than one way to deal with him. As for the Witch, well, a Weather Mage is a very useful thing."

"What you say is true." Dhulyn spoke slowly, a strange reluctance coming over her. "And there's more to consider than just her magics. There's the knowledge she has of the time of the Caids."

"The lodestone," Remm Shalyn said.

"Exactly. What else might she be able to tell us, what might she know firsthand of their knowledge?"

Parno drummed his fingers on the tabletop. "Still, something is bothering you, my heart."

"What of the child?" Dhulyn spoke as evenly as she could. "The Tara Xendra, the real child."

Parno leaned forward. "You've found her? You're sure?"

"As sure as I am that you're sitting across from me." Dhulyn made sure that Parno was looking straight at her, flicked her eyes sideways at Remm Shalyn, and tapped the table with the third finger of her left hand.

Parno sat back in his seat, brow furrowed in contemplation. "If she's safe where she is," he began. But then he shook his head. "Nothing changes the fact that the Storm Witch has taken over someone else's body—can such a being be trusted, however useful she might be?" He looked up. "We must see what can be done."

"It's too late now to go to the Sanctuary," Remm Shalyn said.

"We'd be stopped?"

Remm was already shaking his head. "The Paledyn Dhulyn Wolfs-head may certainly wander about at her will. But the gates to the Sanctuary will be closed. We should wait until tomorrow night."

Dhulyn leaned forward. "But will the gates not be closed then as well?"

Remm grinned at her. "Not if arrangements have been made, ahead of time. We won't be the only people who have ever wished to consult the Marked quietly, in private. Now, it's too late, but tomorrow I can make such arrangements."

"It's late in any case, and we must get some sleep. Even if the alarms of the day are over, we'll be expected to put in an appearance in the morning."

"Not Parno Lionsmane, I take it?"

Dhulyn caught Parno's eye. He moved his head a fraction to the left, and back again. "No," she said. "Let him be our hidden dagger, for now."

Once the Mortaxan had left to spend what remained of the night in his own quarters, Parno sat once more at the table. He'd been itching for the man to leave, but now that he had, Parno found himself unexpectedly uneasy to be left alone with his Partner. He kept wanting to touch her, to reassure himself that she was really there. But at the same time he wanted to act as normally as possible. To reestablish as quickly as might be their old standing with one another.

Dhulyn stood next to her chair, her eyes still on the door. She looked thinner, Parno thought. Her hair had grown and she had started re-braiding it.

"Can you trust him?" he said.

"I have been trusting him." Dhulyn turned finally to look at him. "Can you trust the Nomads?"

"Yes." It was the simplest answer, and the truth. "Within the mind of the Crayx, it is impossible to lie, or even to disguise the truth."

Dhulyn raised her eyebrows and pursed her lips in a silent whistle. "That would certainly make many things much easier."

Parno grinned. Only his Partner would think that the truth always made things easier. Dhulyn yawned, and Parno felt his own jaws tremble in response.

"Do we keep watch?" he said, getting to his feet again.

"There's only the one way in, well, two if you count the balcony." Dhulyn looked around, frowning, as if she'd misplaced something.

"Then I say no."

Dhulyn picked up the lamp and Parno followed her into the bedroom, sat down on the edge of the bed and rubbed his face with his hands. Every one of his muscles, and the grittiness in his eyes, was reminding him of every hour that had passed and every step he'd marched since early that morning.

Dhulyn set the lamp into its niche by the door and stayed there, leaning against the wall. "You look different," she said.

"It's my new armor." Parno glanced up, smiling, and rapped the Crayx scales with his knuckles.

"Yes." Dhulyn nodded. "And your hair is longer, though I've seen it longer still. Your beard's grown in as well." She shook her head impatiently. "It's more than that. I think it's the Crayx. You have a faraway look in your eyes, that you didn't have before. As if you are listening to someone else."

Parno had bent over to pull off a boot, but now he sat up again, feeling the muscles in his jaw tighten. "You're saying I can't? I can't listen to someone else?"

Dhulyn brought her fists to her forehead. She shook her head and in a moment her whole body seemed to shake with it. "I'm so angry with you," she said through clenched teeth. Yet Parno could swear he heard surprise in her tone. "I'm furious."

Parno stood and went to her, hands up to take her by the wrists. "You don't get furious, my heart," he began. "Or, at least—" A sudden glint in her eyes warned him and he stopped, inches from touching her. "What is it? Not your woman's time already?"

She twisted away from him. "I thought you were dead. I've been mourning you for weeks. And all that time, you were alive—"

"You're angry with me because I'm alive?" Parno blew out his breath. This was unbelievable. "And what about me? You think you're the only one who's been grieving?" He gestured around the room. "You look pretty comfortably set up for a person in mourning, I must say."

Dhulyn's face set in hard planes. "I could just smack you."

Parno made a "come here" gesture with his hands. "What's stopping you."

The first blow came so fast that Parno didn't see it, for all that he'd invited it. She'd kicked him in the face, and while his hand was still on his nose Dhulyn swung again, this time with her fist. Part of him, he realized as he ducked and propelled his shoulder into her midsection, hadn't really expected Dhulyn to hit him at all.

He got hold of her elbow and twisted, but the leverage he thought he had disappeared when she turned her hips and almost wriggled free. She stamped on his instep, but he pulled his foot back in time, though it cost him his hold on her elbow, which she drove into his stomach. He caught it again, and this time he managed to throw her to the floor, with the help of his foot behind her heel.

The next few minutes were a concentrated struggle of elbows, knees, fists, arm twisting, and head butts. At one point, Dhulyn almost got him in a classic choke hold, and it would have worked on any one other than a Mercenary Brother, but Parno knew the countermove and used it. At another point he thought he had her trapped, but in the last moment she got her knee up between them and threw him off. Not that he went far. Finally, the wall itself became his ally, and he had her pinned in the angle where the wall met the floor.

"Dhulyn," he said, and she stopped struggling.

"You *died*, you blooded son of a twisted ox. You left me alone. I almost killed myself, and all the time you were alive and well, and making a new life with the Nomads."

Parno rolled off her, wiping his bleeding nose on his sleeve. "I wanted to die, and the Crayx would have taken me—my soul—into their consciousness." He squeezed his eyes shut. "But I would never have seen you again. In Battle." She kept her head turned away. "Dhulyn."

"Or in Death," she finally said, reaching out her hand to him without turning around. Her hand was cold, and there was a scrape along the knuckles.

"I stayed alive to avenge you, to kill the Storm Witch. After that," he shrugged, finding it a pointless business when lying on the floor. "I figured there'd be no 'after that.' "

Dhulyn used her grip on his hand to roll over and face him. There was a line of dirt smudged across her left cheek, but her face was otherwise unmarked. He must have been taking care without realizing, otherwise she might have had some explanations to give. He wondered how many bruises it had cost him.

"I began that way." She cleared her throat, but lowered her eyes, fixing her glance on their entwined hands. "Thinking I'd kill her and not worry about 'after.' Then." She licked her lips. Parno watched, fascinated. He didn't think he'd ever seen her guilty before.

"Then I met the Marked," she said, still looking down at their hands. "They needed my help. I thought perhaps I'd do that first, before I joined you in death. After all." She blinked and swallowed. "After all, you would still be there."

"You're angry with me because you decided not to die right away?"

She shrugged one shoulder and nodded. "Why was it so easy?" she said. "How could it be so easy to live?"

"You call that easy?" Parno could see from her face she'd suffered the same sleepless nights, the same hopeless dreams, the same staggering pain every time the grief hit her afresh. "It was the hardest thing I've ever done."

"How was it we could? Other Partners, they haven't survived."

"We aren't 'other Partners.' We're Dhulyn Wolfshead and Parno Lionsmane."

She managed a small smile.

"I'm not joking, think about it. The Tribes of the Red Horsemen were broken when you were just a child, younger than this Tara Xendra who's missing now. Your family, your Tribe—blood, your whole *race* was gone. And you survived. My death wasn't going to kill you, not after that."

"Dorian of the River saved me," she said. "The Brotherhood saved me."

Now it was his turn to shrug. "And it saved me as well. My story's different only in degree. When I was cast out of Tenebro House, I lost everything. Family, name, friends, position. If my father hadn't been a sensible man, I wouldn't even have had basic skills. I would have starved."

"So your conclusion is that Mercenaries are hard to kill."

"Well, we go down fighting, that's for certain." He stood and pulled her to her feet.

"In Battle," she said.

"And in Death."

What does he mean she's still alive Darlara wanted to thump the rail. *Has he been magicked somehow*

Didn't see her Conford admitted. He and the others had reached the creek without incident, and were pulling the boat into the water. There was no reason now to wait. Either Lionsmane would be successful in dealing with the Storm Witch, or he would not.

#We did# #We saw her# That was the unmistakable voice of the

Crayx. #She lives, it is certain# #Look# And into all of their minds came the image of the Mercenary woman as she had appeared to the Lionsmane. The image was dark and full of shadows at first, and Darlara began to have hopes, but quickly it cleared to reveal the woman they all remembered, thinner perhaps, and with the marks of sun on her face, but unmistakable.

What if she's gone over to their side

#Lionsmane says it is not so# #It is Lionsmane who knows her# #He is to be trusted#

Darlara bit her lip, wanting to continue the argument, but knowing that what they said was right. Mal put his hand on her shoulder and she covered it with one of her own. The other rested on her belly. It was too soon for there to be any roundness, but she touched it nonetheless.

"Dar." That her twin spoke to her, instead of using the medium of the Crayx, showed how thoroughly he understood her need to stand apart, if only for a few minutes.

"Would have stayed," she said. "Was floating into that current. Know he would have stayed."

"Don't hate him for choosing his own life."

Darlara pressed her lips together and shook her head.

"Don't hate her either," Mal added. Trust her twin to go unerringly to the right spot. "She has her rights. *We* have the bloodline. That's what's important."

It took her a long while, but eventually Darlara nodded in agreement. "Just that I started to hope."

#A communication comes from Lionsmane#

"Done?"

Parno opened his eyes and nodded. "What did I look like?"

Dhulyn considered. "As if you were playing a particularly difficult piece of music, and weren't sure you remembered all the notes. You've told them everything?"

"Everything you told me. The White Seers, the Marked, the spirit of the little girl. Oh, and I told them to move the decoy ships back out of sight. Let the Mortaxa think they've been scared away. Once the Storm Witch is dealt with, it will be safe for the Nomads to come back."

Dhulyn lay back on the bed. They had slept in their clothes, and she had only taken off the sashes that held the short Mortaxan swords. She'd be able to have her own weapons back now, if they could return to the *Wavetreader*.

"Parno, my soul, do you think they tell the truth, the Crayx? Are their treaties and agreements made with the Caids of old? Do their tales go back so far?"

"Not their tales, their memories." Parno stretched out beside her, his hands underneath his head. "It isn't some Crayx of long ago who knew and came to terms with the Caids, it is these Crayx, themselves. They spawn new bodies, but they are the same entities."

"They knew the Caids? Before the coming of the Green Shadow and the rise of the Sleeping God? They knew the Caids then?"

"So they say. Though they weren't always known to each other. The Crayx had been creatures of the deep ocean, living their long lives and thinking their long thoughts. Something happened which made the Crayx seek out the Caids, find the Pod-sensed ones who had always lived among them, unnoticed by anyone, and begin communication with the landsters. Once they were aware of each other, they quickly came to accommodations and agreement."

"The Caids must have been a very different folk from what we are now, if that is what occurred. Nowadays we cannot get two groups of humans who live in neighboring valleys to agree so easily."

"And a good thing, too, or we Mercenary Brothers would have very little work. No, the Crayx say they were not so different, but they had more knowledge." He laughed as Dhulyn rolled her eyes.

"That's blooded helpful," she said. "*That* much we already knew. And so awareness of the Crayx became just another piece of the old learning that we on the land lost?"

"Not entirely," Parno said. "Apparently it became customary for those with Pod sense to live at sea for long periods of time. And when the Green Shadow rose for the first time, those who were at sea stayed there, and never returned to the land, except for the havens. Eventually they became the Nomads."

Dhulyn rolled over to face him, propping her head with an elbow. "But then they must still have some of the knowledge of the Caids?"

Parno shook his head. "The Crayx never had that knowledge—nor wanted it, so far as I can make out—eventually, the Pod-sensed Caids would have started to feel the same way." When there was no response Parno looked over at his Partner. "You've gone white," he said, sitting up. "Dhulyn?"

"Sister." "Sister." Dhulyn is in a long and narrow corridor, with walls of paneled wood, and a floor tiled in black-and-white diamond shapes. A long row of sconces each hold three candles that smell warmly of beeswax. This is a fortune in wax, she thinks, as she passes them by. She hears giggling coming from a room ahead of her and picks up her pace. The room, when she reaches it, is full of sunlight, airy draperies in every color of the rainbow blow in a warm breeze. Two young girls, white braids swinging, tiny breasts barely formed under their shifts, squeal with delight when they see her, and run to throw their arms around her.

"Am I dreaming?" she asks them.

"Oh, no," Amaia says, the gold fleck in her red eye sparkling. "We're seeing, and we decided to see you. Come, see with us."

The window looks out onto a broad city street, with tall buildings, some having as many as ten stories, to each side of the thoroughfare. Dhulyn knows it is night, though there is so much light in the street they cannot see the stars. A young woman, slim, with her hair cut in a short cap runs down the street toward them. It's hard to be sure looking down, but Dhulyn thinks she is tall. When the woman looks up at the sky, Dhulyn sees that she knows the woman, she's seen her before. But always older, she thinks.

"That's the Storm Witch, isn't it?" Keria lays her head on Dhulyn's shoulder as she speaks. The Twins are older now, Dhulyn sees, no longer children.

"Yes, as a young woman."

"Oh, she's not so old, not so old at all." Amaia taps the windowsill with her index fingers, as if playing a drum. Dhulyn notices that the girl bites her nails.

The Storm Witch runs into the building below them, and Dhulyn turns away from the window, halfway expecting her to run into the room. But there is no one in the room but herself and the White Sisters.

"Is the child Xendra still safe?

KERIA SHRUGS. "WE CAN'T GO TO THE WOODS WITHOUT YOU, YOU KNOW. THAT'S YOUR PLACE. WE CAN LOOK NOW, IF YOU WISH."

DHULYN CONSIDERS. IS IT BEST TO MAKE SURE NOW, BEFORE SHE COMES BACK WITH THE OTHER MARKED?

THEY TURN BACK TO THE WINDOW AND THIS TIME IT LOOKS OUT ON A FOREST SCENE, A GROVE OF TREES, A SLEEPING CHILD. SATISFIED, DHULYN STEPS BACK.

"WE SEE YOU HAVE FOUND THE LIONSMANE," KERIA SAYS, SLIPPING HER ARM THROUGH DHULYN'S. "WE'RE VERY PLEASED FOR YOU, SISTER. IT IS HARD TO BE ALONE WHEN YOU'RE USED TO HAVING SOMEONE WITH YOU."

"WAIT." DHULYN PULLS AWAY. "DO YOU MEAN YOU KNEW WE WOULD BE REUNITED?"

"OF COURSE, WE SAW IT."

"BUT WHY DIDN'T YOU TELL ME?"

FOR AN INSTANT THE TWO SISTERS HAVE THE FACES OF STRICKEN CHILDREN. THEN AMAIA SPEAKS. "BUT, SISTER, YOU DID NOT ASK."

"It's a little sterile."

Xerwin stood to one side, watching Naxot as his friend watched the Witch Carcali spinning slowly around, taking in as much of the garden as she could from this vantage point. "This is the dry season," he said. "In the winter it's much more lush."

"Oh, I know, I'm sorry. That didn't come out the way I meant it."

But perhaps it did, Xerwin thought.

"The plants are beautiful," Carcali said.

It was still his sister's voice, even if the intonation was completely different. How long, he wondered, until he no longer heard Xendra when Carcali spoke?

"I should have said formal, not sterile," she continued, coming back down the path toward him. "The way everything is laid out in straight lines, squares, rectangles." She gestured at a nearby edging of green hedge. "Even where things are rounded, it's as if it was laid out with compasses."

"I'm sure it was," Xerwin said. "The garden has been this way as long as I can remember."

"Perhaps the Holy One would enjoy the grotto." Naxot was turning out to be tongue-tied now that he was actually in the company of the Storm Witch.

"Ooooh, a grotto, I'd love that. I guess I'm used to something a little rougher, more natural looking. We were always careful not to mess too much with what nature intended." Her voice trailed away, as they followed Naxot, and the adult expression of frowning abstraction looked very odd on her little girl's face. "I can't do what your father wants me to do," she said quietly. "I won't. This time the Nomads went away by themselves, but next time . . ." She looked up at him, squinting her eyes against the morning sun. "Next time it may not be the Nomads."

She was right. Xerwin knew she was right. But what to do? And how to do it?

"Did you have a chance to speak to the Paledyn?" she said.

"The Tarxin wanted her this morning."

"Come, you two, it's much cooler here." Naxot's voice called to them from farther along the path.

It only took the tinkling sound of moving water to make Carcali walk faster and in a moment more they were in the coolest part of the garden. Willows overhung a large pond filled with lily pads and surrounded by mossy rocks. Rough rocks had been built up on one side to create a tiny waterfall, and behind it was a small cave that could be entered using strategically-placed stepping stones.

"How lovely." Carcali squatted down and trailed her hand into the water. "Where does it come from?"

"It recycles," Xerwin said. "I'm not sure how, to tell you the truth, the gardeners look after it. All I know is that it uses the same water, over and over."

Carcali picked out a rock bright with moss and sat down, removing her court sandals and dangling her feet in the water. There was another rock close by, and Xerwin took that seat for himself. He kept his sandals on, however, his feet dry, and his eyes on the Storm Witch. Naxot remained standing to one side. He couldn't seem to relax.

"So you think my sister is gone?" Xerwin said.

She lifted her shoulders and let them drop with a small sigh. "Look, I know what you're thinking. I'd say your sister was gone anyway, wouldn't I? 'How can I trust anything she says?' you're asking yourself. Well, I don't know what will convince you."

"Either you are lying, or the Paledyn lies."

"And you don't want it to be her, I get that. And not just because you want your sister back, am I right?" She was searching his face. "If it's any consolation to you, I don't think she is lying, the Paledyn, I mean. But . . ." Carcali paused, tapping her upper lip with her tongue. "It doesn't seem likely she would make that kind of mistake."

"What if the Paledyn is neither lying herself nor mistaken, but being lied *to*?"

Both Xerwin and Carcali looked up at Naxot. "Why would the Marked not lie?" Naxot said. "If the Golden Age of Mages and Paledyns is returning, the Marked will surely lose their special status. What are they, after all, but slaves with privileges?"

"Sure." Carcali was nodding. "Think about this. Those Marked people dropped the ball, didn't they? They were supposed to heal your sister by finding her wandering mind and restoring it to her body, this body." Carcali tapped herself on the chest. "Well, how good a job did they do? And they tried to fix it you know, afterward when they figured out it wasn't her—I wasn't her—you know what I mean." She didn't wait for Xerwin's nod, she went right on speaking. "And they couldn't do it, could they? So then the Paledyn comes—she's sort of like an official investigator, right? A neutral party who can look into things, arbitrate disputes, and so on?"

"That is the tradition, yes," Naxot said. "Honor and fair dealing. There have not been Paledyn on this side of the Long Ocean for generations. But they existed still in Boravia."

"Well, I didn't believe in any of that until I met her, but you have to admit, Dhulyn Wolfshead doesn't strike me as anyone's cat's-paw." Carcali frowned. "That didn't come out right, but still, you get what I meant." She lifted her feet and watched the water drops fall back into the pond before submerging them once again.

This time both Xerwin and Naxot recognized they weren't being asked anything and simply waited for her to continue.

"All right. So the Paledyn shows up, asks the Marked to explain themselves, and suddenly they claim they can find your sister. They know where she is and can get her back. Why now and not before?"

"Dhulyn Wolfshead says she was Seen by the White Twins."

Carcali looked sideways at him, with her eyebrows raised and her lips twisted. "And who are they? More of these Marked, right? It's not as though Dhulyn Wolfshead saw your sister herself, is it? I mean, I'd be inclined to believe *her*, who wouldn't? But these White Twins . . ." She shook her head.

Naxot had found a rock to sit on. "I have never heard that Seers could be used to Find. They See Visions of the future, that is all."

Carcali was nodding again. "It's too convenient. It sounds to me as if they're just trying to get out from under. You know," she added in response to Xerwin's look of puzzlement. "Trying to make out that none of this was their fault. And maybe it wasn't, not really. I mean it was your father scared them into trying something, anything, to get him what he wanted."

"And what he 'got,' as you say, was something that he wanted much more than my sister." Xerwin took in a deep lungful of air and let it out slowly. "You both make it sound very simple," he said.

"Well, it is for me, you see. That's the point." She twisted, pulling her feet from the pond, until she was facing him directly. He was grateful that she didn't touch him. "I was there. I'm the only one who really knows. I *know* your sister was nowhere near, and she couldn't have survived long outside her body, not without the training I've had. That's why it's simple for me. I *know*."

Xerwin nodded. What the Storm Witch—Carcali—said made a great deal of sense. Especially since it explained how Dhulyn Wolfshead could still be in the right. He made a decision. He would tell them.

"The Paledyn goes tonight to the Sanctuary," he said. "To Find my sister, she said."

"You mean she *believes* so," Naxot said. "If she is being misled, as *we* think. But we should consider that the Marked are capable of any trickery. They could expel the Storm Witch, and this time permanently." Naxot swallowed. "And so? We would lose a Weather Mage, a useful person, and gain nothing—or worse." Naxot looked from Carcali to Xerwin and back again.

Xerwin found himself nodding. Better that some good should come from his sister's loss. For he found he was convinced, his sister *was* lost. He would go to the Sanctuary himself. He would see what kind of trick the Marked had prepared for the Paledyn, and he would put a stop to it.

And then there would be only the Tarxin to deal with.

Twenty-one

"I CAN'T REMEMBER EVER being in a palace—or castle large or small—where there was not more movement than this during the night." Parno kept his voice low, though not quite in the nightwatch whisper. Remm Shalyn, in the lead position two paces in front of Dhulyn, would have no trouble hearing him. Parno would rather have walked point himself, but he was the only one of the three of them who had never been to the Sanctuary of the Marked. So Remm walked in front, sword in his right hand, a shuttered lantern giving minimum light in his left. Dhulyn was second, her hands empty, with her sword in its sheath, her wrist resting on the hilt. Parno brought up the rear, with a bare blade and a shuttered lantern of his own.

They walked quietly, but didn't trouble to keep to the deeper shadows. Back in her rooms, Dhulyn had explained to Remm what the Common Rule had to say about situations like these.

"Attitude is the best disguise," she had said. "If we come upon anyone who has the authority to stop us—"

"Or who think they have such authority."

"Or who think so," she'd agreed, grinning. "You are merely two attendants escorting the Paledyn."

So far, as Parno had pointed out, they had encountered no one to impress with their charade.

"We left the palace as soon as we came down a level," Dhulyn said in answer to his observation. "If you think of this as a city, or of each level as a town, you'd be closer to the mark. We're away from the cliff face here, so this," she waved around them. "This is a public street in an area where the lesser Houses live. They don't have grounds, in the sense that we think of in Boravia, so all they need is porters, or door guards. And they'd have little inclination to look outside their doors once night had come."

"Isn't it always night here?"

"See those sheets of metal?" Remm Shalyn used his sword to point up at a tall wooden pole. "Shafts are cut in the rock, and when the sun rises, its light is reflected down, across, wherever those mirrors are found, lighting up the whole interior of the City."

"So all keep the same schedule of days and nights?"

"Those without windows have to wait upon and serve those with," Remm said. "It follows that they keep the same schedule."

Having been given these insights, Parno had no trouble recognizing crossroads as they came upon them, or even squares, strangely emptier of life than they would have seemed when out under the stars.

"Odd to think of people setting up their barrows and their market carts here," he said.

Remm led them around two huge air shafts. Both were lined with windows and balconies all the way down to the bottom, many levels below.

"See those large openings," Remm said, pointing at several dark areas in the walls of the shafts. "For the circulation of light and air," he said. "It is a capital offense to block them, or impede them in any way. The Tarxin uses a special squad of slaves to keep them clear and clean."

"So it would be the slaves who know these ways best," Dhulyn said.

Remm slowed, looking at her over his shoulder. "And the significance of this?"

"The shafts would be the logical way to get slaves out of the City," she added.

"You are entirely too clever, Paledyn Dhulyn Wolfshead." Remm had turned to face front, but Parno would swear the man was smiling.

They were heading across the largest square they'd yet encountered, angling toward the stairs on the far side which would let them down to the level of the Marked Sanctuary. Parno found his eyes drawn to his Partner. Everything about her, the way she moved, the easy swing of her hips, the relaxed set of her shoulder and elbows—everything was familiar, known. And yet, he felt as if he was seeing her for the first time. For a second he thought he was dreaming, that she couldn't be walking in front of him now as if she had never been gone. He clamped down on his teeth to stop his jaw from trembling, and resisted the urge to speed up and touch her.

"Three men watch us from the shadows to the left," Dhulyn said softly.

She was speaking to Remm Shalyn, Parno realized, never thinking that she would need to tell him. But the truth was he hadn't seen or sensed them until she spoke. He shook himself and took a firmer grip on his sword, hoping that Dhulyn hadn't noticed his abstraction. That was exactly the kind of daydreaming that got people killed—and the kind of daydreaming that was supposed to be impossible for Mercenary Brothers.

#You are well# came a voice in his head. Evidently his uneasiness was sufficient to call the attention of the Crayx.

Just a little embarrassed he answered them.

#Sympathetic amusement#

"So long as all they're doing is watching us." That was Remm Shalyn, responding to Dhulyn.

"Probably think we can't see them," Parno put in.

"Probably hoping we can't," Dhulyn said. "Three men in the dark, no lantern, keeping silent? Up to no good, my heart. Up to no good."

They reached the broad staircase to the lower level without further incident, and from the foot of the steps found their way easily to the gate of the Sanctuary. The gate was shut, but torches in the Sanctuary Hall were lit, as well as the lamps hanging from the ceiling.

"Is this usual?" Parno found the sudden blaze of light unexpected, and anything unexpected had to be treated with suspicion.

"It's not *un*usual," Remm said. "I believe some light is always left burning to help anyone who comes seeking a Healer, and the Marked themselves use the Sanctuary Hall as their own Grand Square. The gate is customarily locked, however, and . . ." his voice trailed off as a human shape was silhouetted on the other side of the bars.

"Is it you, Dhulyn Wolfshead?" came a young girl's voice.

Remm Shalyn stood aside and Dhulyn stepped up to the gate. "It is, Medolyn Mender. Ellis Healer expects us."

The mechanism of the gate was complicated, but silent. Finally, the left-hand leaf of the iron gates swung open, and Parno followed Dhulyn inside.

The three Marked they'd come to meet were standing off to the right, under a grouping of three oil lamps. They waited there as Dhulyn, Parno, and Remm Shalyn approached them.

"Your companions must wait here, Dhulyn Wolfshead," the older man said.

"Ellis Healer," Dhulyn said. "Rascon Mender and Javen Finder. This is my Partner, Parno Lionsmane, called the Chanter. He was Schooled by Nerysa Warhammer. Where I go, he goes."

Parno pushed back his hood, revealing his Mercenary badge. The woman introduced as Rascon Mender grinned broadly, and nudged the Finder with her elbow. The young girl, Medolyn, lifted her fingers to her mouth.

Ellis Healer looked from one to the other of them with narrowed eyes. "Can this be? There is another Paledyn?"

"I thought he was lost," Dhulyn said. "But he has been restored to me."

"We've been restored to each other," Parno corrected with a grin.

Now Ellis Healer was nodding. "The White Twins kept saying, 'Our friends are coming,' 'Our brother and sister come.' We could not understand it, and no matter how we questioned them, we would receive the same answer. Now it all makes sense, though why they should claim kinship with Paledyns is likely more than any of us will ever know. Of course your brother Paledyn is welcome to join you, but I'm afraid . . ." The Healer's glance shifted over to Remm Shalyn.

"Not to worry," the swordsman said. "It was never my intention to attend. I will stay here and help keep watch."

Parno and Dhulyn were spinning around, swords out, a heartbeat before the sounds from the gate registered on the others. Six men entered. The two in front wore their swords slung at their hip, and from the amount of jewelry they wore, and the length of their kilts, these were nobles. The other four were just as clearly guards, carrying their swords in their hands.

Parno glanced at Dhulyn, but she was watching the newcomers. Six against two, he thought. Against three if they could count on Remm Shalyn. And Dhulyn had said they could. Good odds either way.

Dhulyn did not relax when she saw that Xerwin led the intruders. Parno, she was happy to note, had moved away to her right to give her room to move her sword, but not so far that they could not work in tandem if needed. At least his time among the Nomads had not cost him his sharp edge.

"Tar Xerwin," she said, as much to inform her Partner as to greet the Tar. "I did not expect you to attend this evening." She saw Xerwin's friend's eyes narrow as he took in Parno's Mercenary badge. She was weighing the necessity of more introductions when Xerwin spoke.

"I'm not here to join you, Dhulyn Wolfshead. I'm here to stop you. I've changed my mind, I don't want this."

"*You've* changed your mind?" Dhulyn tried hard to keep the surprise out of her voice. Xerwin had been just as inclined to kill the Storm Witch as she had been herself. "And if I haven't? I have my own reasons to expel the Storm Witch." And she still did. Not as strong as they once were, perhaps, not as compelling, but the danger from the Storm Witch was still real.

"Your reason stands next to you." This was the slightly nasal voice of Xerwin's friend Naxot. "Or did I hear badly a moment ago? Is this not your lost Partner? The man you believed was killed by action of the Storm Witch? If he is restored to you, your need and right for vengeance is gone. As Paledyns, you should protect and support the other Chosen of the Slain God."

Dhulyn smiled, deliberately letting her lip curl back. "*You* would tell *me* what my responsibilities are? What of the Tara Xendra? Have you forgotten her? At the very least, we must see if she can be restored before we strike bargains with a being who would occupy the body of another."

Xerwin shook his head as though it were heavy. "My sister is gone. Some good must come from that. The Storm Witch said—"

"Well, I should think she did." Parno's tone showed that he had probably rolled his eyes. "What would you expect her to say?"

Xerwin shook his head again, his lips pressed together. "Who am I to trust?" he said in a voice rough with frustration. "The Storm Witch tells me she did not see Xendra, that my sister was not in the spheres and that my sister could not have survived there without a Mage's power. Is *that* the truth? The White Twins tell Dhulyn Wolfshead that they can See Xendra, and perhaps they can lead a Finder to her. Is that the truth? Who should I listen to? Who can I trust?"

"You must trust someone, Tar Xerwin," Ellis Healer edged forward and Dhulyn shifted to keep him out of her line of attack. "Whom shall it be?"

Xerwin blinked, and swallowed. "I would trust Dhulyn Wolfshead. I would trust you." He turned toward her. "I believe you are neutral, all the more so now that your Partner is with you. What proof can *you* offer me besides the word of the White Twins that my sister still lives?"

Dhulyn's mouth went suddenly dry. What proof indeed. She wished she had time to consult with Parno, but there was only one real answer. She must tell Xerwin she was Marked, regardless of what danger it might bring her. If she expected Xerwin to trust her, she must trust him.

"Your sister's soul lives, Xerwin. I have Seen her myself."

Xerwin's eyes grew rounder, and his mouth softened.

"What does this mean?" This was his friend, Naxot again. "Why not tell us this before?"

He trusts me, I trust him, Dhulyn reminded herself.

"You misunderstood me, Xar Naxot. I mean that I have *Seen* her myself. I do not rely on the word of the White Twins. I have Seen the Tara Xendra in a Vision of my own. I am a Seer."

The murmurs that came from the other Marked present were so soft as to be hardly more than shallow intakes of breath. Naxot's face was statue-still. Xerwin's mouth had fallen open, but he recovered very quickly.

"I am convinced," he said. "You would not say such a thing of yourself if it were not the truth. If you yourself are a Seer, and have Seen my sister's soul, I believe she lives."

"But does that mean Tara Xendra can be found and restored?" Naxot said. He put a steadying hand on his friend the Tar's arm.

"Surely, we should at least attempt it," Dhulyn said. She'd kept her eyes on the two nobles, knowing that all the time Parno would be watching the four guards, ready for any signal, or any untoward movement.

Naxot was nodding now, a slight frown drawing down his brows. "But does it follow that we should throw away the good that can come from the Storm Witch?" His tone was reasonable, as if he merely offered an alternative idea that had no importance to him personally. As perhaps he did, Dhulyn thought. For all she knew, Naxot functioned as Xerwin's privy council, asking the questions Xerwin would not always ask himself.

"The Tara Xendra, your sister, is a sweet girl," the young man continued. "But if she is safe, if her soul is safe in her present location, should we not consider the greater good?"

Oh, no, Dhulyn thought, all but shaking her head. As soon as some noble began talking about the greater good in terms of the sacrifice of an individual—they *never*, she'd noticed, offered to sacrifice themselves. Xerwin's face had hardened, it seemed he was thinking along the same lines.

"No good can come of this evil," she said. "The Storm Witch may be of some use, may even genuinely wish to help you, but if you sacrifice an innocent child . . ." This time she did shake her head. "This is not something the Slain God would look on with pleasure." *And I should know*, she thought. "Is the Storm Witch somehow more entitled to your sister's body than Xendra is herself?"

"Here's a question I've heard no one ask," Parno said. "What's happened to the Witch's own body? How did she come to lose it? For all we know, her own people cast her out. Since she can survive in these spheres she's told you about, we do her no harm to return her there."

Naxot's parted lips indicated that he had an answer for that as well, but Xerwin forestalled him with a raised hand.

"Enough." The Tar's gesture silenced everyone, and made Dhulyn see for the first time what he would be like as Tarxin. "I have made my decision," he said, and the firmness of his voice supported his words. "Evil or not, the Storm Witch misled me for purposes of her own. My sister is alive, and deserves to be restored to her body if it is possible. Dhulyn Wolfshead, please proceed."

"No, I'm afraid that won't be possible."

This time the interruption came not from the gate, but apparently from the air, somewhere to the left of where they were standing. Parno eyed a section of wall, examining its thickly ornamented stonework with suspicion. He'd wager he and Dhulyn were the only ones not surprised when that part of the wall opened, turning as if on a pivot, and the Tarxin Xalbalil stepped out, flanked by two guards carrying pikes, and six others with swords.

"Thank you, Naxot. It appears you were correct in your estimations. You will have your reward when my son the traitor has received his."

"Naxot!" Xerwin's hand, which had gone for his sword hilt when the wall moved, hung limply at his side.

His friend still wore that stone face he'd showed them earlier. "I had to be certain," he said. "You had changed your mind about her once already. I could not side with you against the Holy Woman," he said, crossing the floor to stand near the Tarxin.

"Xerwin, I'm disappointed in you." The older man's dry voice made Parno's skin crawl. "To take the tool yourself and use it against me, that I expected, and even approved, in a way. You would not have succeeded, but at least it would show you were ready to succeed me in another sense. But to take such a weapon as the Storm Witch and to throw it away, to save a child whose only use is to warm the right man's bed—" he shook his head, but his reptilian smile never changed. "I would suspect your mother of foisting another man's child on me, if we did not look so much alike."

These words seemed to stiffen Xerwin's resolve, as his hand went once more to his sword hilt, and he looked much readier to fight than he had a moment before. Parno caught the small signal Dhulyn sent him and moved with her to flank the Tar, eyeing Xerwin's four men as he moved. One was expressionless, except for the narrowing of his eyes. He looked like he'd stand neutral if he could manage it, until he saw who would gain the upper hand. Two were shocked, and clearly unsure what they should do, but they'd likely follow Xerwin out of habit if nothing else. The fourth was positioning himself to fight—and apparently on Xerwin's side. Remm was inching himself into a better spot on Dhulyn's far side.

Seven, perhaps eight of us, ten of them. Parno eyed the two guards carrying pikes. They'd have to go first. That is, if the talking ever stopped.

"This is convenient, very convenient," the Tarxin was saying. "All the pieces on the board at the same time." He looked at Dhulyn in a way that made Parno tighten the grip on his sword—and then loosen it properly again. "Now I see how it is possible for a woman to be a Paledyn. You've had your master behind you all the while, directing your every move."

It was all Parno could do not to laugh out loud. The man was a very poor judge of character if he could look at Dhulyn and think any such thing. But now the man was addressing him, and Parno tried to hang a serious expression on his face.

"So you are my real adversary here—and I can see from your pretty tunic that you are in league with the fish lovers. Your attack was a clearly a feint, allowing you to get more of your people into Ketxan City. Where have you hidden them all, I wonder?" he waved this away. "Never mind. I will be curious to see what else a search of the Sanctuary will reveal."

"My lord Tarxin, Light of the Sun, you cannot." Aghast was not too strong a word to describe the old Healer's tone. "The Sanctuary is neutral ground, ours so long as we provide our services and abide by the terms and conditions of our treaties. Our privacy is not to be violated."

"But you are in violation of your oaths and treaties," the Tarxin said in his cold raspy voice. "You are obviously in league with the enemies of the Mortaxa, so your Sanctuary is lost."

Xerwin was nodding, his expression sour, his mouth twisted to one side. "That is how we deal with everyone," he said. "They bargain away everything to keep their freedom, and then they find themselves without the freedom to say no."

"Never mind, Ellis," Dhulyn said. "If he had not found this excuse, another would have served. He won't live to hurt you."

"You're outnumbered, you silly woman. Do you think you can fight your way through my guards, even with my foolish son on your side?"

"Odds aren't bad," Parno put in, shrugging. "Counting Xerwin and his boys, only seventeen of them against eight of us."

A soft whistling sound, a CLUNK, and one of the pikemen fell to his knees, his weapon clattering to the floor, Dhulyn's dagger sticking out of his right eye.

"Sixteen," she said.

While everyone was still standing around gawking, Dhulyn ran forward, sword in hand, Remm behind her and to her left, like a good sword servant.

Even as he was dashing forward himself to deal with the second pikeman, Parno noticed that Xerwin was not making the amateur's mistake of going for Naxot, the man who'd betrayed him. No, Xerwin was heading straight for his father. Good. It would make things easier all around if he or Dhulyn didn't have to kill him.

Then his first opponent was before him and the time for watching others was over. The Mortaxan blades were shorter, thicker, better for slashing and cutting than the longer sword Parno had. The man lifted his sword to cut down at Parno's shoulder, and Parno ran in quickly and thrust his own sword through the man's throat. As he went down, Parno slashed at the sword hand of another man, and dashed past him to where the man with the pike was holding Remm Shalyn at bay. Remm was already bleeding from a cut on his upper arm—luckily not his sword arm—when Parno came nearer.

"Leave him to me," he said. Remm grinned and moved out of the way before Parno could trample him.

Parno fell automatically into the Striking Snake *Shora*, avoiding, and occasionally parrying the pike's blade, watching the man's shoulders and neck muscles, looking for the telltale shifting that would signal a feint, or a true blow. The pike's sharp blade was clearly intended to slash as well as stab, and the man wielding it knew his job. Parno's single advantage, he knew, was that he had faced this weapon, or its cultural variation, many times before, and unlike the opponents the man was used to, was not afraid of it. In fact, it was likely that Parno had faced it in earnest, on the battlefield, more often than this man had used it. It was a tenet of the Common Rule, that drilling was one thing, and killing another.

Parno saw his opening, trusted in his Crayx armor, and stepped into the shaft, parrying and bearing down on it with the strength of his blade. He kept applying pressure, down and outward, as he slid his blade up along the shaft until he had closed to within striking range. Before the man could reverse the end of the shaft to strike him, Parno had skewered him through the heart. He had moved too quickly for the man to even think about dropping the shaft and defending himself in some other way.

The pole arm dealt with, Parno turned back to the others in time to slash at the raised sword arm of one of the Tarxin's men, just as he was swinging at Remm Shalyn, who had fallen to one knee, having slipped in someone's blood. Parno hauled Remm back to his feet and took stock. Xerwin and two of his men were engaged with three men in front of the Tarxin, who had at least drawn his knife. Dhulyn had picked up a second sword, and had maneuvered herself between everyone and the still open passage through the wall, preventing escape from that direction. One of Xerwin's men was down, as was the noble Naxot.

Eleven enemies dead, six still on their feet. Seven if you counted the Tarxin.

"Help the other guard," Parno told Remm as he headed toward Xerwin. As he reached the group around the Tarxin, the guard on Xerwin's left went down. Parno stepped over him and cut the throat of the man who'd killed him, reached under Xerwin's arm, and put his sword through the lung and heart of the Tar's opponent.

Parno looked over in time to see Dhulyn stepping over the bodies of her two opponents; Xerwin's remaining guard was bent over, hands on his knees, taking deep breaths. Remm was standing with his hand on the man's shoulder.

Parno turned back. Xerwin had stepped over the bodies around him and knocked the dagger out of his father's hand.

"The field is ours, Xerwin," Parno called. "Whatever you're planning to do, do it now."

And the Tar stood still, his blade up in the middle stance, like a man giving a demonstration of swordplay, and did not move.

"Come, boy," the Tarxin said, his voice, if possible, even colder than it had been before. "If you want the throne, this is the only way. This is what it takes to be Tarxin."

Dhulyn laid her hand on Parno's arm, and he shot a glance at her. She had her tongue pressed to her upper lip, and he knew what she was thinking, just as if the Crayx had given him her thoughts. She thought it possible that Xerwin would back away, that at the last minute he would refuse to strike the final blow, rather than admit he wanted the throne, that he was that much like his father. Just as she was thinking about stepping forward to do it herself, Xerwin, shaking his head, lifted his blade and brought it slicing down through his father's neck.

Twenty-two

"I'VE KILLED MY FATHER." Xerwin rubbed at his upper lip.

"You've killed the Tarxin, which at the moment is rather more important." Dhulyn looked around. Remm Shalyn and the other remaining guards, four of whom had come here with the dead Tarxin, were on their knees, holding their fingertips to their foreheads. The Healer was busy over one man, but even as she watched, he straightened, shaking his head. Parno, half-smiling, waggled his eyebrows at her.

"Tar Xerwin?" Dhulyn touched the younger man on the arm and he finally turned away from his father's body, blinking with some confusion at the kneeling men. Then he took a deep breath that shuddered on the way in, and touched his own forehead. The men lowered their hands and stood.

"At your service, Tarxin, Light of the Sun," Remm Shalyn said. Dhulyn saw a gleam—could it be of humor?—in the man's eyes. "Shall we take care of the slain, Light of the Sun, and see that your father's body is prepared for transport to his—to *your* private apartments?"

"Thank you, yes." Xerwin looked around him. "Try not to track blood *all* over the floor."

"Yes, Light of the Sun." That was one of the other guards, Dhulyn saw, one who had come in with Xerwin's father. None of them, she noticed, whether originally Xerwin's men or his father's, seemed particularly upset, or concerned with the death of the older man. She'd had the impression that Xalbalil Tarxin hadn't been a well-liked man, but this equanimity struck her as unusual. As unobtrusively as she could, she retrieved her throwing dagger and picked up a second sword, sliding it into her sash at the small of her back. She caught Parno's eye, flicked the third finger of her right hand, and looked at the guards. He raised his eyebrows a mere fraction, showing he understood her warning.

Dhulyn stepped back to watch as the remaining guards, aided by the Marked, dealt with the bodies. Those of the soldiers were rolled into what looked like old carpets and hangings, while those of the former Tarxin and the Xar Naxot were laid out more formally, awaiting the arrival of litters. Parno made his way around the periphery of those working until he reached her side.

"I don't think we've ever deposed a ruler so easily," Dhulyn said to him in the nightwatch voice.

"Clearly, we've been doing it wrong."

Remm, his instructions to the Marked given, came over to join them.

"Remm Shalyn," Parno said to him. "What will be the consequences from this . . . event?" Dhulyn smile her wolf's smile. Trust her Partner to be diplomatic. She would have said "assassination."

"If there were any other heirs, there might be a problem," Remm said, shrugging. "But Xerwin, Tarxin Light of the Sun, was the only remaining male child of Xalbalil Tarxin. I don't think there are even close cousins." He jerked his head toward where the old Tarxin's body lay. "Xalbalil didn't leave many relatives alive when *his* father died."

"And may we ask how that happened?" Parno asked, his left eyebrow raised.

Remm's grin was quickly quashed. "Hunting accident," he said, his tone suddenly serious. "That's what was said."

"And this one? What will be said?"

"Oh, I don't know. Cut himself shaving?" Remm blinked rapidly, but otherwise his face remained serious. "Xerwin Tarxin, Light of the Sun, will let his Council know tomorrow that his father has died in the night. There will be public announcements, days of mourning, the funeral." Remm nodded his head at Xerwin. "He'll have to be careful, certainly. Those his father made strong will want to keep that strength. He should probably send word to the Battle Wings before he does anything else. His soldiers love him, and most of the High Noble Houses will remember that, and behave accordingly. The rest of Mortaxa?" He shrugged again. "By the time the news gets to them, it will be old, and one Tarxin's much the same as another. The transition should go relatively smoothly, all things considered."

Remm's voice died away and he backed off a few paces with a shallow bow as Xerwin himself came up to them. The new Tarxin's face was more composed now, though Dhulyn thought there was a harder line to his jaw than there had been before.

"Paledyns," he said, with a brisk nod. "I believe we came here with another purpose."

"If you would prefer to delay—" Dhulyn stopped as Xerwin shook his head.

"Things will be complicated enough in the next few weeks. If I deal with the Storm Witch now, it will be one less complication. And besides." His smile was a twisted thing. "I want my sister back. Now more than ever." He brought his hands up to his face, rubbed it, and ran his fingers back through his hair.

Dhulyn nodded, putting as much sympathy and understanding into that gesture as she could. She had noticed, however, that Xerwin had spoken of the political complications first, and his sister second.

The one guard Ellis Healer had managed to save stood off to one side, alone, with his arms wrapped around his chest. When Parno approached him and spoke, the guard shied away, then touched his forehead with his hand. He held no weapon, Dhulyn noticed, and frankly, from the look of lingering shock on his face, did not seem likely to pick one up. Most of the Marked who had come out of the inner rooms of the Sanctuary, summoned by their Seniors, were now working at cleaning the Sanctuary Hall. Young people, some still in their nightclothes, were on their knees scrubbing at the blood on the stone floor. They had brought litters for the bodies of the nobles, and women were coming with fresh hangings and rugs to cover and wrap the bodies. Xerwin left Dhulyn's side and went to them as they approached the litter that bore his father.

Dhulyn gave him a few minutes before approaching him herself. "Xerwin," she said.

Xerwin straightened, and signaled to his men. "See my father properly disposed in his own quarters. Take Naxot Lilso there as well." He looked at Dhulyn. "What should I tell his father?"

"Stay as close to the truth as you can," she said. "Tell him his son died trying to save the life of his Tarxin. Will he need to know more?"

"I'm not sure. Naxot's father has other sons. That may make a difference to him."

"Will he seek revenge?"

"He may ask for a blood price. I may have to make one of Naxot's sisters my second wife." He glanced sideways at her, seeming about to say something else on that subject, but he looked away instead. "I've time yet to think about that."

"And what of the Storm Witch? What if people ask after her?"

"What Storm Witch? That was just a trick of the old Tarxin's, to make the Nomads submit. My sister will be here, evidently nothing more than the Tara Xendra." Xerwin squared his shoulders as Ellis Healer approached. "Xalbalil Tarxin was a shrewd man, who took advantage of coincidences."

Dhulyn nodded. Who could disprove it, once the Storm Witch was gone?

"Your pardon, Light of the Sun. Tara Paledyn, the White Twins are asking for you."

Dhulyn looked back at the soldiers. Xerwin's senior guard was deploying his remaining men, and those of the old Tarxin, to carry the bodies and form a guard of honor. Remm Shalyn was shaking his head and gesturing toward her. Of course, he considered himself her sword servant, he would insist on accompanying her. That left the guardsmen, alone, with the body of a murdered Tarxin. She turned back to Xerwin. "This may not be the moment for you to leave your men leaderless and unsupervised."

He looked at her, lips parted, but did not speak.

"Better cautious, than cursing," she told him. "Go with your men, see to the old Tarxin, and even Naxot's father, if you wish. I will come to you and report."

For a moment it seemed as though he would argue with her, then abruptly he nodded. "I will await you. Come as soon as you may."

Carcali wondered if she should do something about the rain. It had started just after daybreak as a fine mist, hardly even a drizzle, and welcome, really, after the heat of the last few days. It wasn't that she hadn't expected it—after all, she *had* started to collect wind and storm to throw at the Nomads, though she hadn't gone very far when they'd disappeared of their own accord. The Tarxin hadn't told her to stop her efforts, but . . . *how much time is left of the deadline I gave him*, she wondered, trying to count the time backward in her head.

She shivered at a gust of cold air and pulled her shawl closer around her. Something had been bound to come of even those preliminary actions, but this rain didn't seem to be dissipating. It was definitely getting stronger, in fact, and the skies had grown darker even in the short while she'd been sitting at her balcony door.

Another gust, more violent than the first and carrying a load of rain with it, blew into the opening, soaking the side of her gown and making her cough. Carcali jumped to her feet, grabbed hold of the edge of the left door and pushed against it with her shoulder, struggling to close it. Her large maps and sketches fluttered around the floor and the large parchment on her worktable escaped from its weight and blew over, knocking against the oil lamp and sending it crashing to the tiles.

"Tara Xendra, what are you thinking of? Thank the Slain God that lamp wasn't lit." At least Finexa's genuine fear had shaken all the simpering and archness out of her voice. Annoyance struggled with Carcali's relief. Annoyance that she couldn't shut the window herself—when would she remember that she was only eleven years old?—relief that Finexa had heard the crash and come in to help her.

"What were you doing sitting here in the dark?"

"It isn't dark," Carcali said, rubbing at the outside of her arms. "It's the middle of the afternoon."

"Too dark to work, is what I meant. Won't you come into the other room, please, Tara. I'll get the maid to clean this up."

Carcali followed Finexa into her bedroom and threw herself onto the bed, trying her best to ignore the woman's exasperation when Finexa found the windows in there open as well.

"I'm a Storm Witch, Finexa, for the Art's sake," she said finally. "Why wouldn't I have the windows open?"

The woman subsided into a tight-lipped silence at this reminder.

Carcali sat up, her arms straight out behind her. "Has the Tarxin sent any word today?"

Finexa adjusted the mechanism that closed the slats on the shutters and pulled the curtains over them. "Not today, Tara, no. Were you expecting something?"

So she still had time left. Good. "And my brother? Has he sent me any messages?"

"No, Tara." Sound from the workroom drew Finexa to the door, and with a "tchah" of impatience she went through it to speak to the maids, throwing a perfunctory "your pardon, Tara," over her shoulder as she went.

Carcali chewed on her lower lip. She was trusting Xerwin to help her. "Leave things to me," he'd said, and she was doing just that. And she'd stopped her actions against the Nomads—partly because she wanted to, but mostly because he'd said she should. Another particularly heavy gust of wind shook the shutters.

She pulled the pillow closer and hugged it to her. *I really ought to do something about that storm,* she thought. But it couldn't do any harm to leave it a while longer. And it was good cover if the Tarxin needed to be appeased. "Just doing as ordered," she could tell him. "You think this is bad, you should see what it's like out at sea."

Carcali wondered if Xerwin even realized that they would have to kill the old man in order to be safe themselves?

Parno found that even having been warned what to expect, the White Twins were a shock. Their skin was as pale as the flesh of a fish, and their hair was not so much white as it was colorless. Their eyes were pink, as were their lips and gums, and when one of them passed close enough to a light, he could almost see the blood moving under the skin. They fell upon him, giggling, the moment he had cleared the threshold of their sitting room, following closely on Dhulyn's heels. They had touched his Crayx armor, run their cool fingers over the colors of his Mercenary badge, and felt the muscles in his forearms. They were as guileless as children—they *were* children, in all things but their physical age and their Mark.

Once they had finished "making sure he was real," as they put it, the White Twins greeted the other Marked almost as enthusiastically. An older woman stood smiling to one side, and Parno realized, as they exchanged short bows, that she must be the White Twins' attendant or guardian. Remm Shalyn, who was hovering, round-eyed, at the door, they appeared not to notice.

Parno approached him. "Your first time here?"

The younger man nodded. "I have heard about them, of course, who has not? But to actually *see* them." Remm didn't quite shudder, but Parno thought he might have wanted to.

"Would you prefer to wait outside?" he said, expecting a quick negative, as no young soldier would want to risk being thought a coward. To his surprise, Remm nodded.

"But I must stay if Dhulyn Wolfshead wishes it," he said. "For now, I am pledged to her service."

Parno caught Dhulyn's eye and waited until she was close enough to hear the nightwatch voice. She listened, and inclined her head once.

"Remm Shalyn," she said quietly. "Better you should stand guard outside," she said. "We may want warning if someone comes, more warning than you could give us if you stay within."

He touched his forehead with a cheerful smile and let himself out.

"I find it disconcerting to be saluted in that manner by people who are not Brothers," Parno said.

"It has something to do with the Sleeping God, whom they call the Slain God here. As Paledyns, we're considered Hands of the God."

"That's convenient."

"My thoughts exactly." She gave him the smile she saved only for him, and Parno, smiling himself, lifted his right hand and touched her cheek with the backs of his fingers.

Suddenly they were surrounded by dancing white women.

"Come, Brother, come now, quickly."

"Now how can I be your brother?" Parno said, tweaking the long braid of the twin nearest him. She must be Amaia, he thought, seeing the fleck of gold in her eye that Dhulyn had told him about. Now she took his hand and brought him, skipping, to the other side of the room. A jumble of toys lay on the floor, a tiny walled enclosure with a blocky tower made of—yes, those were vera tiles. A moat had been drawn around it with blue chalk.

"Dhulyn is our sister," Amaia said.

"And you are her brother," Keria added.

"So you must be our brother, too," Amaia concluded.

The twin sisters laughed at this, and began singing the words over and over, to a tune Parno knew very well, though to hear it now made the hairs on his arms and the back of his neck stand up. This was the same children's song he often played for Dhulyn, and though not many people knew it, it had a special meaning for the Sleeping God, and for the Marked.

"They sing this song to begin their trance," Ellis Healer said. "Though, truly, they often sing it at other times as well."

"Is there an instrument here I can use? A chanter, or even a small harp?"

Ellis beckoned the attendant over and repeated Parno's request. Smiling, she did what Parno certainly had never expected her to do. She asked the White Twins.

"Girls," she said. "My darlings, can your brother see your instruments, my dear ones? He'd love to accompany your song with music of his own."

At once the twins stopped singing and ran to a table to the right of the door, in darkness now since the lamps there were not lit. Almost immediately Keria came back to him with an instrument more like a syrinx than the chanter that he would attach to his air pipes.

"It's been a while since I played one of these," he said. He raised the instrument to his lips and gave an experimental blow, satisfying himself that he had not forgotten how.

"Will the Crayx hear you?" The sisters were standing in front of him, shoulder to shoulder, staring at him with their huge red eyes.

"I don't know," he said.

"I hope they do," said the one on the left. Keria, he thought, but with the light at this angle he could not tell which one had the gold fleck in her eye.

"Parno, my heart," Dhulyn said. "The Finder and I are ready."

"Do you know what to do?"

"We know, we know, we know," the sisters sang.

"I think that means 'yes,' " Dhulyn said, smiling.

Javen Finder was standing, her lower lip between her teeth, between her fellow Marked. Parno had never seen anyone who looked less like she wanted to be where she was. But when Dhulyn nodded to her, Javen stepped forward right away, giving a wan smile to the Mender, Rascon, who squeezed her shoulder as she went. Ellis Healer held out a canvas bag and Javen took a small blue bowl out of it. It was plain white on the inside, and Parno recognized it as a Finder's tool.

"Stand right here," Keria said.

"Right here," Amaia agreed, shifting from foot to foot in her excitement. Both of them put their hands on Javen Finder and pulled and prodded until they were satisfied that she was standing in exactly the right spot. Giggling, they waved Dhulyn over to them, twirling their hands at the wrists like flags fluttering in the breeze. When Dhulyn was close enough, each of them took one of her hands, and then linked hands themselves, standing in a circle around the blinking Finder. Javen licked her lips, held the bowl at chest height and looked into it.

"Play now, Brother," Amaia said.

"You know the tune," Keria added, already humming.

Dhulyn caught his eye, and mouthed the words he would have expected from her. "And in Death," he mouthed back, before lifting the syrinx to his lips and beginning to play. He played softly at first, and then with more power, as he renewed his familiarity with the instrument. Dhulyn winked at him, and began to sing, her rough silk voice somehow serving as a fitting accompaniment to the lighter, smoother voices of the White Twins.

As they sang, the sisters' voices grew firmer, more mature, and their faces were suddenly the faces of women his own age. At that moment all three stopped, eyes closed, still with hands linked. The Finder, too, was standing perfectly still, eyes shut tight, eyebrows working as though she was in deep thought. All four of them, Parno saw, the Finder, and the three Seers, were breathing as one.

Parno let the music die away, and lowered the syrinx from his lips. This was like watching his Partner use her tiles, she had the same serene look of calm concentration on her face. He'd thought he'd never see that look again. Never see her again. He loosened his grip on the syrinx before he broke it. All was well. A good wind and a fair current, as Darlara and her brother would say. After a moment he smiled, as he noticed that he, too, was breathing in the same rhythm as the others.

#Interest# #Excitement#

Parno was almost knocked from his feet by the force of the Crayx' thoughts. *What is it, what's happening* He had stopped himself from speaking aloud just in time.

#We can feel her# #Not her thoughts# #No, not her thoughts# #But we *can* feel her# #Giddyness# #Fascination#

For the first time, Parno had the sense that there were a great many Crayx, all communicating, all participating at once. *Who* *What are you talking about*

#Through *your* link, we can feel *her*# #Never felt before# #Euphoria# #She has no Pod sense# #But she is there, we feel her#

"Demons and perverts," Parno said aloud. Quickly he held up his hand, palm out, signaling to Ellis Healer and Rascon Mender that all was well.

#How# A blooded good question, Parno thought, as he heard it echoed back and forth.

#Lionsmane is linked to her, blood to blood, bone to bone, heart to heart#

Parno gave a silent whistle. Those were the very words of the Partnership ceremony.

#Why not before, on the *Wavetreader*# #Too many with Pod sense# #Link too delicate# Parno could tell these were questions.

#Astonishment# #She is with the child# #Your Partner is with the child# *You know of the child*

#We know of *this* child# #We sensed her fear#

She's Pod-sensed Parno stood openmouthed. No words did justice to how he felt. Part of him wanted to laugh out loud. The little girl Dhulyn was trying to save, to restore to her own body—the Tarxin's daughter—was Pod-sensed.

#When she became ill, and frightened# #Lost# #We cared for her soul# #Helped her find a place to feel safe#

Is she in a forest thicket

#No, a sandy beach# #Trees come down to the water# #But only where the stream is# #Ah# #Of course# #Each finds the safe harbor they seek# #For your Partner a forest glade# #For the child herself an empty beach, a stream trickling down through a screen of trees#

And you see both places

#No# #YES# #Amusement# #Through the link we know what others know, see what others see#

And you feel my Partner there, with the child

#Amused joy#

AT LEAST THEY DON'T HAVE TO GO BACK TO WHERE HER MOTHER IS, DHULYN THINKS. PERHAPS BECAUSE IT IS THE SECOND TIME, AND THE WHITE TWINS ARE HERE TO DIRECT THE VISION MORE PRECISELY, THEY ARE STANDING IN THE PATH THAT LEADS TO THE THICKET.

"What is this place?" The voice of Javen Finder is whisper-quiet, but Dhulyn has no trouble hearing her. Javen looks around with eyes made wide by fear.

"This is our Vision," Keria answers. "Ours and our sister, Dhulyn Wolfshead." Javen starts, looking sideways, and Dhulyn realizes that the Finder has never heard the Seers speak in their own undamaged voices.

"I think this is why you couldn't Find her before," Dhulyn says. "Somehow, Xendra's soul exists in the same place our Visions exist, somewhere apart from the world we live in. If you can Find her, now that you are here as well...?"

Javen nods and gathers all her courage together, pressing her lips tight, and taking a firmer grip on her bowl. She looks into it, and In a moment she is smiling. "The colors," she says again, as she did when she first looked into the bowl. She looks up, secures the bowl in the crook of her right arm, and points with her left hand.

At first, Dhulyn sees nothing, and then a faint, colored light is spilling out of the bowl, and along the path, a brilliant jewellike green with splashes of gold swirled into it.

"That is the Tara Xendra," Javen says, joy lifting her voice. "She is this way."

And then they are following the Finder as she runs following the colors down the path toward the grove of trees, pushes her way through the thick underbrush, and there, on her knees with a wooden doll in her arms, is the child they are looking for. She is dressed in gold and green, there is a smudge of dirt on her cheek, and she is clutching the doll fiercely, her teeth holding her lower lip. She stands when they come in, and backs away from them. She looks at them, one after another, the whites of her eyes showing clearly. She is terrified, and Dhulyn racks her brain to think what to say to her.

"You know us, Tara Xendra," Amaia says. "Remember, your brother brought you once to play with us."

"You know me, Tara Xendra. I'm Javen Finder. You remember when your dog Biscuit was lost, and I Found him for you?" Javen has stepped forward, her arms held out to the child. In the normal world, she would never dream of offering to touch the Tara Xendra uninvited, but here, it seems natural.

The child is still round-eyed, but she nods.

"WELL, NOW I'VE FOUND *YOU*, AND I CAN TAKE YOU BACK TO YOUR . . . TO YOUR BROTHER, THE TAR XERWIN. WOULDN'T YOU LIKE TO SEE YOUR BROTHER?"

THE CHILD NODS AGAIN. SLOWLY HER SHOULDERS LOWER. SHE LOOKS AROUND AT THEM ONCE MORE, THIS TIME ACTUALLY SEEING THEM. HER EYEBROWS LIFT WHEN HER GLANCE MOVES OVER TO DHULYN, AND HER MOUTH FALLS OPEN.

"PALEDYN," SHE SAYS, HER VOICE FULL OF WONDER.

"GOOD THING I'M SO RECOGNIZABLE," DHULYN SAYS, SMILING CAREFULLY AT THE CHILD. SHE OFFERS THE CHILD HER HAND. "ARE YOU READY TO COME HOME, LITTLE ONE?"

NODDING, THE TARA XENDRA STEPS FORWARD AND TAKES DHULYN'S HAND. KERIA AND AMAIA ARE NODDING, SMILING. *THEY'VE SEEN THIS BEFORE,* DHULYN THINKS. *ME HOLDING THE CHILD BY THE HAND.*

"JAVEN, ARE YOU READY?"

BUT THE FINDER IS SHAKING HER HEAD, LOOKING FIRST INTO THE BOWL AND THEN SEARCHING THE FLOOR OF THE LITTLE SHADOWED PLACE. BUT THERE ARE NO COLORS.

"I—I CAN'T. I CANNOT FIND THE—THE OTHER PART OF THE CHILD FROM HERE. I—" SHE LOOKS UP, ALMOST AS PALE THE WHITE TWINS BEHIND HER. "I'M SORRY—OH, PLEASE—I'M SO SORRY."

Twenty-three

"THEN I HAVE KILLED MY FATHER for nothing." Xerwin sat at the worktable in the Tarxin's study, documents and scrolls spread out in front of him. His glance at them was automatic, but Dhulyn was sure he did not see them.

"Hardly for nothing," Parno said. "You're now the Tarxin."

Xerwin looked up, little marks of white showing around his pinched nostrils.

Dhulyn looked at Parno, and when he shrugged, she spoke. "You likely would have had to kill him anyway," she said, in her most matter-of-fact voice. "He would have started a war with the Nomads and the Crayx, a war which would have cost Mortaxa a great deal, more perhaps than you know."

Xerwin looked at her, clearly wanting to ask whether this was something she'd Seen, and just as clearly unsure what courtesy required at this moment. "But Xendra *was* Found."

"She was." Dhulyn took a deep breath, trying to ignore her feeling of impatience. Since leaving the Sanctuary of the Marked, they'd been aware of the rising noises of the storm—wind, rain, and in the distance, thunder. She raised her voice to be heard over the noise of the wind rattling the balcony doors. The explanation given by the White Twins was the only one likely to make any sense to Xerwin. "This world, and the place of Visions are two different, separate places. Javen Finder cannot Find your sister from this world, and cannot Find your sister's body, nor the Storm Witch, from the place of Visions. Somehow the two must be brought together."

Xerwin squeezed his eyes shut and held both hands up in the air near his ears, as if to shut out any more information. Dhulyn fell silent, glancing quickly to where her Partner stood, arms folded across his chest.

Parno raised the index finger of his left hand. "May I? They want to try bringing the two worlds together. They succeeded in bringing Javen Finder into the Vision place with them, and they'd like to try the same with your sister's body."

"With the Storm Witch, you mean."

"Since she currently occupies the body, yes."

"And you need me for this."

"I don't think there is anyone else she will trust."

Xerwin was silent for so long that Dhulyn was beginning to wonder whether he had changed his mind yet again. And to consider, what, if anything, she could do about it if he had. One thing was certain, she thought. She would not be very happy if that lonely child in the thicket clutching her doll continued to appear in any of her future Visions.

And even if she didn't, how comfortable would Dhulyn be, knowing that the child was out there?

Apparently Xerwin came to the same conclusion.

"Where do I bring her?" he said at last.

"To the White Twins," she said.

Carcali leaned her eleven-year-old forehead against the trembling shutter on her bedroom window, her right hand to her mouth as she gnawed on her thumbnail. The wind had risen alarmingly, and the rain was much worse. There would be flooding by daybreak, she knew, at the very least. She switched to the other thumb. She just had to hope it would be no worse.

She let her hand fall into her lap, twisting her fingers together. She'd left it too long. A stupid apprentice's mistake—something she would never have done in a million years. She should have been watching more closely, and now it was too late.

"Except it isn't." There, she'd said it. The old Carcali, the confident, know-it-all Carcali, could fix this rain in a snap of her fingers. No problem. But not today, not this Carcali. Not the one who was afraid to release herself fully into the weatherspheres. Not her—oh, no.

A noise came from the outer room, and she jumped, banging her elbow painfully on the edge of the shutter. Who could be coming at this hour? *Someone who wants to speak to me about the weather.* And she could guess who. She smoothed back her hair and straightened her shoulders as she got to her feet.

As Carcali expected, Finexa, a robe thrown hastily over her sleeping gown, opened the bedroom door and stepped into the room. But it was a different Finexa from the one Carcali was expecting. There was not the carefully disguised triumph that a summons to the Tarxin usually brought, no smugness, no prim little smile. Instead Finexa was pale, licking her lips. Her attempt at an affectionate look when she caught Carcali's eye would have been funny, if it hadn't been so obviously born of fear.

"What is it?" Carcali said. "What's happened?"

"You are summoned to the Tarxin, Light of the Sun, Tara Xendra." The woman clung to the edge of the door. "The messenger says immediately, please. Do not stop for ceremony. It will be explained."

Carcali's first impulse was to refuse to go anywhere until she had the promised explanation. Finexa clearly knew something that had shaken her—though something that shook Finexa wasn't necessarily something Carcali needed to worry about. She let the woman wrap a robe around her and pin a veil on her hair—apparently that much ceremony was still required—and prepared to follow the three guards who'd been sent for her. She'd stepped into the hallway before she realized she was alone.

"Aren't you coming?" she asked her attendant, but Finexa was already shaking her head.

"The Tarxin, Light of the Sun, asked for you alone, Tara Xendra," she said.

Carcali felt a stab of fear. Was she being arrested? Surely that wasn't possible? She was the Tara Xendra, for the Art's sake. But it was possible, the more rational part of her mind said, even as her fear tried to choke her. Carcali had overheard her attendants talking, when they thought her so absorbed in her maps that she wasn't paying attention. They'd been talking about the first Tarxina, Xerwin's mother, and it was Xerwin's name that had caught Carcali's ear. A sudden illness, everyone had been told, and the whole country had gone into mourning. But that's not what had really happened, the ladies were saying. The Tarxina had displeased the Tarxin, displeased him *severely*, and not just by not having any more children—at least, not any more children by *him*, one of the older ladies had whispered while the others looked on, wide-eyed, frightened to be hearing such a thing, and yet avid for more, like children telling each stories of demons. The Tarxin had sent for his wife, in the middle of the night, and she'd never been seen again. And even her attendants—some of them—hadn't been seen again either.

At the time, Carcali had dismissed the story as the kind of court gossip that ladies with nothing better to do titillated themselves with. Such things didn't really happen. Now, she was not so sure. The man had shown her that he could starve her to death if he chose to. Would it be so much harder for her to have an accident in the middle of the night?

She stopped in her tracks. Especially since she'd had one accident already. Is *that* what had happened? But what was it an eleven year old had done to anger the Tarxin?

"Tara?" the senior guard said. "We should not waste time."

"No, of course not." She resumed walking. She'd done what the Tarxin had asked for—well, not exactly, but he couldn't prove she hadn't. Was he going to upbraid her for the storm that could be heard even through the thick stone that surrounded the passage? Well, if he had any complaints, she knew what to say. "You rushed me," she would tell him. "I warned you there could be dire consequences and you only gave me two days."

Much sooner than she liked, Carcali found herself in front of the double doors that marked the Tarxin's section of the palace. From the chamber beyond these, doors on the right led to the public-use rooms, and on the left to the family's private rooms. Not that any of the ruler's rooms were really private. She took a deep breath and nodded to the leading guard. He opened the right-hand leaf of the doors and stood back to allow her to enter.

Carcali took three steps into the room and froze. There were more guards here, and most of them were wearing that same look of thinly covered pity that she'd seen on the faces of her escorts. One or two, she thought, eyed her speculatively.

"This way, if you please, Tara Xendra." A Steward stood at the set of doors in the left-hand wall. A private audience, then. But her thoughts were spinning so wildly Carcali couldn't work out whether that made disaster more or less likely. The Steward's face told her nothing, but then the man was trained not to react to anything.

Her hand lifted to her mouth, and she started on the nail of her index finger as she followed him through the door, across the ante-room within, and into the Tarxin's private study.

It seemed that every lamp in the room was lit, including those in the wall brackets by the door. All the Tarxin's rooms faced the sea, and the flames of the lamps flickered slightly in the wind that managed to get through the closed shutters of the three narrow windows. Carcali un-clenched her hands and tried to stride forward with confidence, suddenly aware that she was the only person in the room wearing nightclothes.

As she drew closer to the table, the man looked up, and the face he showed Carcali was not that of the Tarxin at all. The man at the worktable was Xerwin. Suddenly, all she could hear was the pounding of her heart.

"Here, here, sit down." Someone with very warm hands was taking hold of her arms and easing her into a chair. Something soft, heavy, and warm was draped over her, and tucked around her feet.

"Thank you very much," she heard Xerwin say. "If you would leave us now? I will call when you are wanted. Thank you."

"What did they tell you? Why are you so frightened?" Xerwin had taken her hands and was rubbing them between his own. Carcali coughed, trying to get the muscles in her throat to loosen.

"The Tarxin sent for me," she croaked.

The rubbing stopped. "And you thought . . . ?" Xerwin shut his eyes and took a deep breath. "Well, you would, wouldn't you?"

"Where is he?" Things couldn't be *too* bad if Xerwin was here, but there still had to be some kind of explanation. Now that it seemed she had less to be scared of, Carcali found she was starting to get angry.

"Through there." Xerwin sat back and nodded toward a door on the other side of the room. He glanced at the door she'd come in by and leaned forward again. Carcali edged to the front of her chair and put her head as close to his as she could manage.

"Carcali," he breathed. "He's dead. I killed him."

Carcali felt her mouth drop open. Was she dreaming? Had Xer-win somehow heard her thinking about it and killed the man? She blinked and swallowed. Time for all of that later. Xerwin was Tarxin now. That's what they'd meant when they'd said the Tarxin had sent for her. That's why they'd all looked at her that way, because her fa-ther was dead. The guards and soldiers were loyal to Xerwin, everyone knew that, but—

"Who else knows?"

Now Xerwin was blinking at her, his head tilted to one side. "Everyone," he said, his voice puzzled. Then a light seemed to dawn. "Oh," and with a flip of his hand he indicated how closely they were sitting. "No, this is just so that we can speak freely about *other* things."

"Should I start crying or something?" Carcali suddenly felt that tears would come easily, she was so relieved not to be frightened any more.

But Xerwin was shaking his head. "No one would believe it, I'm afraid. Look stricken, by all means when we leave the room, but shocked more than grieved is what people will expect."

Carcali nodded. "I can do that," she said. "So what happens now?"

"This is the tricky part," Xerwin said, lowering his voice. "You and I need to get to the Sanctuary of the Marked. Dhulyn Wolfshead is waiting for us there."

"Why?"

He blinked at her. Carcali felt a flash of impatience. "I'm not Xendra, remember?" She shook herself. She'd been more frightened than she liked to think about, but there was no need to take it out on Xerwin. "I don't know all the little rituals and ceremonies that come up when the Tarxin dies and there's a new one."

Now he was nodding. "Of course, of course. You are right, this is one of those rituals. You and I, because," he cleared his throat. "Because we are the only ones of the Tarxin's blood and must go to the Sanctuary and hold a vigil with the Marked. It is, uh, a tradition. Our wound is Healed, our hearts are Mended, and our serenity is Found." He smiled. "Oh, and the Seers give us a Vision for the new reign."

Carcali chewed on her fingernail. "They don't have to touch us, do they? I mean, this is just a formality, right?"

"Oh, yes, absolutely, just a formality. In fact, all the more so because," and he lowered his voice again, "you are not Xendra."

"And the Paledyn will be there?"

"Just in case there are any questions afterward," he said, tilting his head once more in the direction he'd said the old Tarxin's body lay. He stood up and began to draw her to her feet.

"Wait." She looked at the door and leaned toward him. "Wouldn't we get them to come here? The Marked?"

Xerwin sighed and sat down again. "I can see I'm going to need to explain more to you," he told her. "We're not going openly to the

Sanctuary," he said when she was once more seated facing him. "Not yet. We're going to go now, privately, to prepare for the real ceremony, with the Paledyn there to vouch that everything is correct."

"But why the secrecy?"

He shut his eyes and sighed. "Because you're *not* Xendra. And the Marked know this. Because Dhulyn Wolfshead assures them that it is correct to do so, they are willing to perform the ceremony, but there are special preparations that must be done privately. Then, the public ceremony can take place in the usual fashion."

Carcali waved her hands in the air. "All right, yes, whatever you say." That was the problem with primitive societies, she thought. Empty rituals, ceremonies stripped of all meaning because there was no longer any Art to inform them. To say nothing of the silliness that politics was responsible for.

"Then, if you are ready, this way."

Xerwin could hardly believe that anyone, let alone a Storm Witch, would have fallen for the mass of confused nonsense that had just come out of his mouth. Though he had to admit, as he led Carcali through the hidden passage that was the Tarxin's private corridor to the Sanctuary, he liked that bit about Healing wounds, and Mending hearts. That was inspired. He should have taken more time to create a better story, but all had ended well. Carcali was a little arrogant, in her way—as all powerful people were, he realized. Otherwise she would have listened more carefully to him, questioned him more closely. He should take a lesson from this himself.

Even with the woolly shawl still wrapped around her, Carcali found the walk through the hidden passages chilly. She was glad to get out into the main hall of the Sanctuary, and gladder still to follow Xerwin into a more enclosed area, where small braziers warmed up the rooms. The room they finally reached was quite a large one, filled with the soft lights of candles and small shaded lamps. The Paledyn was there, as Xerwin had told her, with someone else, a larger, golden-haired man behind her. But Carcali's eyes were caught almost immediately by the two women on the far side of the room, standing close together, and holding hands. They peered at her as if they were standing at three times the distance.

They had the White Disease. Perfectly colorless, with pink eyes.

Carcali had read about the affliction, but had never dreamed she would ever see such a thing.

"Look toward me, please." Carcali turned her head toward the rough silk sound of the Paledyn's voice, but her eyes remained fixed on the horrible twins. She felt cool fingers where her neck met her shoulder.

And then the world went black.

Dhulyn Wolfshead caught the slight form in her arms as the girl went down. She looked up at Javen Finder, who nodded.

"She's there," the Finder said. "The Storm Witch."

"Carcali," Xerwin said. "That's her name."

"Good," Dhulyn said. "That may help us."

"Dhulyn, Sister?" Amaia's voice trembled and was in a higher pitch than normal. She clung to Keria, and both pairs of blood-red eyes were round. It was easy for Dhulyn to forget, having Seen them so often in Vision, that the White Twins were children themselves.

"Parno," she said, as gently as she could. Her Partner immediately went to the two Seers, standing behind them and putting his arms around them. Amaia leaned into his chest, and Keria grabbed his forearm in both hands and clung to him.

"There now, my hearts, my own ones," he said in a voice that made Dhulyn's own heart skip a beat. "You're tired, I know, but this will soon be over, and then we can all rest."

"Tired now," Keria said, leaning her forehead against his shoulder. True, Dhulyn thought, they were all tired. The twins were tired as children were, more emotionally than physically. Still, the White Twins were *not* children, and they had an adult's ability to set aside the immediate needs of the body, to understand that there were reserves, and that they could draw upon them.

"Come, my sisters." Dhulyn put as much smile into her voice as she could. She laid the child's body down on the pallet they'd prepared for it, and signaled to the other Marked with her eyes. Ellis Healer took his position at the girl's dark head and bent low, his hands on her shoulders. Javen knelt to her left, centering the bowl carefully on the child's abdomen. Javen then took Ellis' left wrist in her right hand, and the child's left wrist in her own left hand. Rascon Mender mirrored Javen's position on the girl's other side.

"Come sing with me," Dhulyn said, holding her hands out to the White Twins. "One song before bed, please?"

Smiling now, Amaia and Keria let go of Parno and ran to Dhulyn's side, taking her hands and forming a tight circle around the kneeling Marked, and the child's body. *Too bad there aren't more of us*, Dhulyn thought. Even she, hardened Mercenary as she was, could feel a great weariness hanging over her. They'd done what they could to restore their own life energies with food and drink while waiting for Xerwin, but it was little enough in the face of what they had yet to do. It wasn't as though they had their pathway laid out for them, to run down swiftly. They would have to improvise as they went. That took time, and time took energy.

Energy. There was no ganje here, but there were other stimulants, other drugs.

"Ellis," she said. "Do you keep fresnoyn in the Sanctuary? Or any of the fressian drugs?"

"Here." Xerwin stepped forward, his hand already reaching into his pouch. From it he drew the tiny jeweled box that held his powdered fresa and held it out to her. Remm Shalyn was already pouring out a cup of the red currant juice on the nearby table. Dhulyn added the entire contents of the vial—not that it was much, and stirred it with her finger.

"Drink." Dhulyn held the cup out to Keria. "Just a mouthful, mind.

"You put your finger in it," the girl said, wrinkling up her nose.

"Ah, but I'm made of sugar," Dhulyn said. "Watch." She took a good-sized mouthful herself and swallowed. "Mmmm, that's good."

"Give it to me, I'll drink it," said Amaia. In the face of her sibling's readiness to obey, Keria took the cup and, still grimacing, swallowed a careful mouthful.

"Now me! My turn!" Amaia finished the liquid that was in the cup and smiled, licking her lips.

Dhulyn handed Remm Shalyn back the cup, nodding to him and to Xerwin. She looked at Parno.

"In Battle," she said, not caring who heard her.

Parno touched the fingers of his free hand to his forehead. "And in Death." He lifted the syrinx once more to his lips.

Dhulyn took hold of the girls' hands again, and this time they smiled at her. The room seemed very bright, the glowing light from the candles appearing almost to throb in time with the beating of her heart.

When she moved her head, however slowly, colors and light trailed behind things, like paint smearing under a brush. The music, too, began to pull at her, and Dhulyn shifted her feet in time. Keria laughed, a deep-throated, woman's laugh, and began to sing. Dhulyn and Amaia joined in. As the music and the dance swept over them, Dhulyn looked down at the body of the child. The child would want to dance with them. Would want to join them in their game.

THIS TIME THE VISION BEGINS WITHIN THE THICKET, WHERE THE CHILD STANDS ON HER FEET. IT APPEARS FROM THE POSITION OF HER HANDS AND FEET THAT SHE *HAS* BEEN DANCING, BUT SHE STOPS WHEN SHE SEES THEM APPEAR. SUDDENLY SHE CRIES OUT WITH DELIGHT AND RUNS FORWARD, BRUSHING AGAINST DHULYN'S THIGHS IN HER HASTE.

IT'S HER BODY, DHULYN REALIZES. XENDRA HAS SEEN HER OWN BODY WITHIN THE CIRCLE AND FAR FROM BEING FRIGHTENED BY IT, IS ANXIOUS TO RECLAIM IT. THE FINDER MOVES HER BOWL TO ONE SIDE AND, STILL PEERING INTO IT, TAKES THE STANDING CHILD BY THE WRIST. RASCON THE MENDER PLUNGES HER HANDS INTO THE CHEST AND INTO THE HEAD OF THE CHILD LYING AT HER FEET, AND STRUGGLES TO PULL THEM OUT AGAIN. SOMETHING RESISTS HER, BUT SHE GRITS HER TEETH AND PULLS. THE MUSCLES STAND OUT IN HER FOREARMS, AND THE VEINS IN HER NECK.

"SING LOUDER," KERIA SAYS. "SHE NEEDS ALL THE POWER WE CAN GIVE HER."

MAYBE WE SHOULD HAVE GIVEN THEM *THE FRESA,* DHULYN THINKS. EVEN AS SHE IS THINKING, SHE RAISES HER VOICE. SHE COULD NOT SAY WHAT WORDS SHE IS SINGING, BUT SHE KNOWS THEY ARE THE SAME WORDS KERIA AND AMAIA SING.

SUDDENLY, RASCON THE MENDER FALLS BACK FROM THE BODY. SHE MOVES HER HANDS TO ONE SIDE, AS IF SHE WERE THROWING SOMETHING DOWN, AND A YOUNG WOMAN APPEARS. THE CHILD XENDRA LEAPS FORWARD, AND DISAPPEARS INTO THE BODY. THE HEALER LEANS FORWARD, THE FINDER AND THE MENDER AS WELL, EACH ONE WITH THEIR EYES CLOSED, THEIR LIPS MOVING.

DHULYN CATCHES THE EYE OF THE NEWCOMER. SHE RECOGNIZES THE CLOSE-CROPPED HAIR, THE FINE-BONED FEATURES. BUT SOMETHING IS WRONG. THIS IS NOT THE MATURE WOMAN DHULYN HAS SEEN WORKING AT HER ART. THIS IS A YOUNG WOMAN WHO HAS SEEN HER BIRTH MOON NO MORE THAN NINETEEN, PERHAPS TWENTY TIMES.

"THIS ISN'T RIGHT," DHULYN SAYS. "SHE'S MUCH OLDER THAN THIS."

Twenty-four

THE CHILD'S BODY GASPED, arching this way and that, but the Marked kneeling and standing around her remained impassive and still. The Mender, Parno couldn't remember her name, perhaps *she* showed some agitation, her eyes moving under her closed lids, her lips pressed more firmly together.

The White Twins stood steady and firm, their skin so transparent that even in this light Parno thought he could see the movement of their blood under it. That same light gave Dhulyn color, made her pale skin a rich ivory, her blood-red hair almost ruby—though Parno couldn't be sure whether this seeming richness was the result of the contrast between Dhulyn and the White Twins, or of his own wonder at being able to see her at all. He still couldn't quite believe it. *Let me not be dreaming,* he prayed, though he couldn't have said which god he spoke to. *Or if I dream, let me never wake.*

The Marked sat back on their heels. The Healer reached up with his six-fingered hand to massage the bony ridge of his brow. The Mender was breathing fast, the Finder looking around her, blinking. The little girl curled over on to her side, the palm of her hand tucked under her cheek.

The Seers did not move.

#She needs help# The thought came from nowhere. #Your Brother, your Partner, she needs your strength#

How Even as he responded, Parno had lowered the pipes and went striding over to where Dhulyn stood, eyes closed, holding the hands of the White Seers, ready to take her by the elbows and support her.

#No# #Urgency# #Keep playing# #Come with us# #Let your mind float# #Follow the music#

Parno set the syrinx to his lips once more, trying not to let his impatience get in the way of the music. How exactly was he supposed to let his mind float when Dhulyn was in danger? And how could she be in danger, for that matter, when she was standing right in front of him?

#Concentrate#

Parno squeezed his eyes shut, and made a better effort, letting the demands of the music control his breathing, letting the words of his personal triggering *Shora* run through his head. He felt himself relaxing, the muscles of his shoulder and neck loosening. He began to hear another tune, not competing with, but running counterpoint to the one he was playing. He began to play *to* that tune, answering it and following it with his own music, until he felt that the new tune carried him, and his music, away with it.

The new tune was the sound of the wind playing in the same vast meadow that he'd sensed before, the vast garden of souls where those who had gone to the Crayx at the death of their bodies could be found. The new tune was the tinkling fall of an unseen fountain, the songs of the birds, and the humming of the minds that lived there.

#Come further in# #This way, look here#

Parno found himself in a cool blue grotto, an enormous limestone cavern with an underwater passage to the sea.

#This is *our* place of refuge# came the thought. #For your Partner a forest, for the child Xendra a sunny beach, for us, this cavern# #Come#
A head broke the surface and Parno looked into the deep, round eyes of a Crayx. It was a pale green, with a copper iridescence to its scales. Parno touched his fingertips to the his scaled cuirass; it was from this Crayx, he realized, that his armor had come. The Crayx extended its long, narrow head, and Parno knew immediately what was wanted, and climbed onto its back. Its neck was only slightly larger than the body of a horse, and he was able to take a firm grip with his knees, and brace his hands on the ridged scales.

#The link to your Partner is very strong now, and her Vision prevails, aided by her White Sisters# #It is there we must go# #Now#

#Fear not# the Crayx told him, and then it dove into the water.

Normal, she felt normal. Carcali ran her hands over her face, hair, body, stunned with what she was feeling, almost frantic with delight. This was her real body, her own body. She seemed to be inside a hedgerow, but there was light, somehow, enough to see by in any case. There were people on their knees on the floor, and three others, standing to one side.

"This isn't right." She heard someone say. "She's much older than this."

And then she feels a sharp displacement of air.

KERIA AND AMAIA ARE STILL HOLDING HER HANDS, EVEN THOUGH THEY ARE NOT CHILDREN HERE, AND THEY ARE NOT FRIGHTENED.

"DOES SHE LOOK YOUNGER TO HERSELF HERE?" DHULYN ASKS THEM. "IS THIS HER MENTAL IMAGE OF HERSELF?"

"THIS IS HER TRUE SELF," KERIA SAYS.

"JUST AS YOU ARE YOUR TRUE SELF," AMAIA ADDS.

"AND WE ARE OUR TRUE SELVES."

"I HAVE ALWAYS SEEN HER OLDER. A MATURE WOMAN AT WORK IN HER LABORATORY." *WHAT DOES THIS MEAN?* DHULYN WONDERS. WHAT FUTURE, OR WHAT PAST, HAD SHE SEEN, IF THIS YOUNG WOMAN IS THE TRUE SELF OF THE STORM WITCH?

THE MARKED ARE MOVING, THE CHILD IS SITTING UP, YAWNING. ALL FOUR TURN TOWARD DHULYN AND THE OTHER SEERS. ELLIS HEALER RUBS AT HIS FACE, EXHAUSTION WRITTEN IN EVERY LINE. RASCON MENDER HAS A HAND ON HER SIDE, BREATHING AS THOUGH SHE'S BEEN RUNNING. JAVEN FINDER LOOKS AS THOUGH SHE MIGHT START CRYING.

THEY WINK OUT OF EXISTENCE.

THE STORM WITCH LOOKS AT THE PLACE WHERE THEY WERE, HER MOUTH OPEN, HER BROWS DRAWN TOGETHER. SHE LOOKS UP AT THEM.

DHULYN ISN'T SURE WHAT TO DO, BUT THE TWINS ARE TURNING AWAY, TOWARD THE THINNER PART OF THE THICKET THAT WILL LET THEM OUT INTO THE PATH OUTSIDE, AND SHE TURNS TO GO WITH THEM. SHE SEES THAT XENDRA'S PLAYTHINGS ARE NOW GONE. THERE IS ONLY A WATERSKIN, A PILE OF INGLERA SKINS, A SMALL PACK OF FOOD. THE SPACE IS BECOMING ONCE AGAIN THE PLACE WHERE DHULYN HID AS A CHILD.

"WAIT, WHERE ARE YOU GOING?" THE STORM WITCH IS ON HER FEET. SHE'S WEARING LIGHT BLUE TROUSERS, A PALE YELLOW TOP WITH SHORT SLEEVES. THERE ARE SMALL GOLD STUDS IN HER EARS, AND HER FEET ARE BARE. HER CROPPED HAIR IS DISHEVELED, SHORT SPIKES STICKING UP IN ALL DIRECTIONS. HER GRAY-GREEN EYES ARE ROUND, THE PUPILS TINY POINTS.

"WE GO BACK TO OUR OWN PLACES NOW," KERIA SAYS. "YOU SHOULD DO THE SAME, STORM WITCH. YOUR RULE OVER THE CHILD'S BODY HAS ENDED, YOU MAY RETURN TO YOUR OWN PLACE."

"YOU CAN'T DO THIS TO ME!" SHE TAKES A STEP TOWARD THEM, HER HAND LIFTED. SHE LOOKS AT DHULYN, AS IF TRULY SEEING HER FOR THE FIRST TIME. "PALEDYN! YOU CAN'T LEAVE ME. I HAVE NOWHERE TO GO." HER HANDS REACH OUT. "I WON'T GO BACK TO THE WEATHERSPHERES, I WON'T. YOU DON'T UNDERSTAND, I'LL GO MAD!"

DHULYN WONDERS IF THE GIRL ISN'T ALREADY MAD. "CAN SHE REMAIN HERE?" BUT THE TWINS ARE ALREADY SHAKING THEIR HEADS.

"THIS IS A REAL PLACE, A VISION PLACE, BUT IT IS TEMPORARY, A BUBBLE," KERIA SAYS.

"IT IS YOUR VISION, DHULYN, AND WITHOUT YOU, IT WILL NO LONGER EXIST," AMAIA SAYS.

"ONCE WE LEAVE HERE, THE BUBBLE WILL COLLAPSE." KERIA TURNS TO THE WITCH. "WE ARE SORRY," SHE SAID. "BUT YOU MUST RETURN TO YOUR OWN PLACE."

"BUT THE WEATHERSPHERES ISN'T MY PLACE, I DON'T BELONG THERE." SHE TURNS ONCE MORE TO DHULYN. "YOU KNOW THAT. YOU KNOW WHAT I REALLY AM. MY WORLD—MY *PLACE*—DOESN'T EXIST ANYMORE. YOU *KNOW* THAT." HER FACE HARDENED. "YOU HAVE TO HELP ME. IF YOU DON'T—IF I GO BACK TO THE SPHERES, I SWEAR TO YOU I'LL—I'LL BRING ON AN ICE AGE AND YOU'LL ALL DIE. I'LL DESTROY YOU ALL. THE WHOLE WORLD. I'VE DONE IT ONCE ALREADY."

DHULYN FEELS A SINKING IN HER STOMACH. THE GIRL *IS* MAD. THAT'S CLEAR.

"YOU DESTROYED THE WORLD?" SHE SAYS, STRIVING TO KEEP HER VOICE REASONABLE AND CALM. " *YOU? IN* WHAT FASHION? THE WORLD STILL EXISTS."

"NOT *MY* WORLD," THE WITCH SAYS. "*MY* WORLD'S GONE. THE PEOPLE, THE BUILDINGS, THE KNOWLEDGE." HER VOICE HITCHES, AND HER EYES STARE. "EVERYTHING. GONE. LITTLE FRAGMENTS, SCRAPS OF STONE, BITS OF METAL. THAT'S ALL THAT'S LEFT."

"AND *YOU* DID THIS? BUT TIME ALONE WOULD DO IT, YOU DID NOTHING." DHULYN LIFTS HER HEAD. THERE IS A SOUND FROM OUTSIDE THE THICKET, A SOUND SHE KNOWS VERY WELL. "A HORSEMAN COMES."

<hr />

The motion of the Crayx under him began to change from a smooth gliding through the water to short, rhythmic movements, like the prancing of a particularly well-schooled horse. Then he saw that it was, in fact, a horse he was riding, a coppery-shaded roan, with an oddly pale mane. They were riding down a hunting trail in a rough forest, thick with underbrush. It was winter here, and he could see old snow drifted up here and there. The horse followed the trail steadily, heading directly for a thicket of pines growing so closely together that their branches formed a kind of wall. The horse shouldered its way into the thicket, and Parno raised his arm to keep the branches out of his face.

The final branches parted, and he saw Dhulyn with the White Twins, and a young, fair-haired woman.

"You are just in time, my soul." Dhulyn's heart swells with the sight of her Partner. She realizes that being parted from him, she had been afraid that she would not find her way back. That somehow the necessity to keep the Storm Witch from the child would keep her from returning. Now that Parno is here, she stands straighter. Whatever comes, they will face it together.

"The Witch is telling us that we should fear her, because she's destroyed the world."

"My name's Carcali, for the Art's sake, not 'the Witch.'" From the hardness of her face, Dhulyn knows that the woman is afraid, and that her fear is taking the form of anger.

"You'll have to explain yourself a little better, Carcali," Parno says, as he dismounts. Dhulyn wonders where the horse came from, and why it is such an unusual color. It turns its dark, very round eyes on her and she suddenly sees the truth. The horse is a Crayx, and that is how Parno is here. At least . . . she squeezes her eyes shut, blinks. she still doesn't see quite how.

"The sun was too hot, and everything was going to burn and die. Carcali says. "All the plans and solutions that people were coming up with were just ways to buy us more time. None of them would have saved the world. I found a way—I thought I'd found a way to cool the sun, to reverse the process that was making it heat. But they didn't agree, they told me I wasn't ready, that they wouldn't help. And when I tried to do it myself, I . . . I lost—" She squeezes her eyes shut, arms wrapped around her body, and Dhulyn glances at Parno. He moves his shoulders in the smallest of shrugs.

"What did you lose, Carcali?" he asks.

"This," she says. "My self. My body. I thought I didn't need an anchor,

BUT I DID. AND WHEN I REALIZED THAT I COULDN'T GET BACK, I PANICKED. THE WEATHERSPHERES—" CARCALI CLUTCHES HER HEAD IN HER HANDS, HER FINGERS DIGGING THROUGH THE TUFTS OF HER PALE HAIR. "IT WAS LIKE I COULDN'T FEEL THEM ANYMORE EITHER, BUT THEY COULD FEEL ME." HER VOICE DROPS TO A WHISPER. "DON'T YOU SEE? MY CONFUSION, MY PANIC MUST HAVE ENTERED INTO THE SPHERES, AND EVERYTHING WAS CHAOS AND POWER AND MY CIVILIZATION WAS DESTROYED."

CARCALI, THE STORM WITCH, SINKS TO HER KNEES, STILL HOLDING HER HEAD IN HER HANDS. KERIA AND AMAIA GO TO HER, KNEELING BESIDE HER, AND PUT THEIR ARMS AROUND HER. AMAIA STROKES CARCALI'S HAIR, AND KERIA MAKES SOOTHING NOISES. DHULYN LOOKS AT PARNO OVER THE TOPS OF THEIR HEADS. SHE CAN SEE ON HIS FACE WHAT HE'S THINKING. THE CIVILIZATION OF THE CAIDS *HAD* BEEN DESTROYED, BUT NOT BY CATACLYSMIC WEATHER CHANGE. PARNO LIFTS HIS RIGHT EYEBROW, AND DHULYN GIVES HIM AN IMPERCEPTIBLE NOD. EVEN AS SHE OPENS HER MOUTH, ANOTHER SPEAKS BEFORE HER.

#We know the time of which she speaks# #The time of the cooling of the sun#

DHULYN LOOKS UP, WONDERING WHERE THE VOICE COMES FROM, WHEN SHE REALIZES THAT IT COMES FROM EVERYWHERE, AND NOWHERE.

"WHAT IS THAT? WHO . . . ?" CARCALI JERKS HER HEAD FROM SIDE TO SIDE, LOOKING FOR THE SOURCE OF THE VOICE. THE WHITE TWINS TRY TO CALM HER, BUT SHE SHIES AWAY FROM THEIR HANDS.

"IT'S THE CRAYX," PARNO SAYS. "CAN YOU ALL HEAR THEM?"

#We use you, Lionsmane, and your link with your Partner, and her link with her fellow Seers#

"AND CARCALI?" DHULYN ASKS.

THE COPPER HORSE TOSSES ITS HEAD. *IT MAKES A BEAUTIFUL HORSE,* DHULYN THINKS.

#She is just consciousness now, and she occupies this space for the moment# #As do we all# #So long as the music plays#

NOW THAT IT IS MENTIONED, DHULYN CAN JUST HEAR A FAINT TUNE PLAYING A LONG WAY OFF. IT SOUNDS AS THOUGH IT MIGHT BE JUST THE WIND BLOWING THROUGH THE TENT ROPES IN THE FAR OFF CAMP OF THE RED HORSEMEN. SHE LOOKS AT THE YOUNG WOMAN IN THE CROOK OF KERIA'S ARM. CARCALI HAS BOTH HANDS OVER HER MOUTH, HER EYES WIDE OPEN ABOVE THEM.

"WE KNOW," KERIA SAYS.

"YOU THOUGHT THEY WERE JUST FISH," AMAIA ADDS.

"MOST PEOPLE DO," KERIA SAYS. SHE PATS CARCALI'S SHOULDER.

DHULYN TURNS TO THE HORSE. SHE FINDS IT EASIER TO ACT AS IF THE VOICE COMES FROM IT. "YOU KNOW OF THIS TIME, YOU SAY?"

#It was before we made ourselves known to the Caids# #The changes in the sun would have brought about the destruction of the world in two generations of humans# #But the sun was cooled, and the world saved#

"NO, THAT'S NOT RIGHT." CARCALI HAS GATHERED HER STRENGTH. "WHAT HAPPENED TO MY WORLD, THEN? TO MY CIVILIZATION? TIME ALONE CAN'T DO WHAT I'VE SEEN."

#The Green Shadow came# #Oh, some time after the cooling of the sun# #After the Pod-sensed joined us# #After our treaties with your people# #A long while after, as humans measure time#

AND CARCALI HAS BEEN WANDERING ALONE IN THE WEATHERSPHERES ALL THAT TIME. DHULYN SHUDDERS. SHE HAS THE FEELING IT WAS ONLY A FEW MOONS AGO, IN THE CRAYX'S WAY OF MEASURING. CAN SHE HOPE THAT THE DISEMBODIED STORM WITCH FEELS THE SAME WAY?

Parno looked with interest at the fair-haired young woman kneeling between Keria and Amaia. So this was the Storm Witch in her real shape. She didn't seem all that formidable. She would be about the age of the younger of his two sisters. At the moment she had her hands over her mouth again, her eyes tightly shut, and tears leaking out of them.

Dhulyn stood to one side, her lips pressed together, drumming the fingers of her right hand on her sword hilt. Parno almost laughed aloud. Those were clear signs his Partner was impatient and uncomfortable—and she'd stay that way until Carcali stopped crying.

Finally, the young woman heaved a great, broken sigh, and accepted the offer of a scrap of cloth from Amaia to wipe off her face and blow her nose.

"I didn't kill them." There was a note of wonder in her voice, but she was still very close to tears. However good the news, it was almost more than Carcali could take in. She had clearly been living a long time with the pain and guilt of what she'd done. It would take time still for her to truly believe she was innocent.

"But you can't make me go back to the weatherspheres, please." She looked from face to face, and her own hardened when she did not see what she hoped for.

#Would you come to live with us# the Crayx suggested. #Join our consciousness# #You are not Pod sensed, but perhaps from here, with the links . . .#

"No, please, I couldn't." Carcali clung to the arms of the White Twins, who *looked at Parno and Dhulyn over her bent head with pity in their red eyes.* "I couldn't live like that. Not like an animal."

#Amusement# #You would not be alone# #Compassion#

Carcali looked away. "I couldn't."

"Sun, Moon, and Stars girl, what can *you do, then?" Dhulyn's voice cut through the air like her own well-sharpened sword.* "You can't have someone else's body, you can't stay here, you don't want to go back to the weatherspheres, and now you don't want to join the Crayx. What* do *you want?"*

"I want to go home." Burst into tears.

Dhulyn threw her hands into the air and stalked off, as far as she could in this small thicket. Parno was torn between laughing at her inability to cope with so much emotion, and his very real sympathy with her feelings of frustration.

#Why should she not go home#

Dhulyn turned and looked at the horse, who was quite calmly flicking its ears back and forth. Keria and Amaia looked at each other, at Dhulyn, at Parno, and at the horse. Carcali once again searched one face after another watched to see where the next blow would fall.

"How can she go home?" Dhulyn said in her rough silk voice. "Her home is gone. It's in the past, hundreds—no, thousands of years."

"We See the past," Amaia said, as her sister nodded. "In the Vision place there is no time."

"Like the Crayx," Parno whispered. Everyone looked at him. "The Crayx," *he repeated.* "They don't experience time the same way we do. There's no past for them, there's only now."

"So Carcali's home . . ."

"Is just another place to them, another bubble like this one."

#But it is her bubble, as this one is yours# #We can take her, if she wishes to go#

Carcali was backing away from them. "It's a trick. You'll hand me over to these animals and they'll wait until you've gone and then they'll drown me."

"Oh, for the Moon's sake." Dhulyn threw her hands into the air. "You stupid little fool."

"Dhulyn." Parno took his Partner by the arm and led her to one side. "Think how alone she's been," he said to her in the nightwatch voice. "I know I went a little mad when I lost you. I could have killed some of the Nomads, just because I didn't care enough to be watchful. She's lost everyone, everything. Can we expect clear thinking from her?"

"Oh, I know." Only Dhulyn could sound sullen using the nightwatch voice. The corner of her mouth twitched. "I'm not saying I'd really kill her, just that I feel like it." She glanced back at the others. "But she doesn't trust us, so what are we to do?"

"I'll go with her."

The grip Dhulyn took on his forearm was painful. "No. I won't lose you again. No."

"Quietly, my heart. And I'd like the use of this arm again, if you don't mind." Her hand relaxed, but she did not release him. "I trust the Crayx. If they say they can do it, they can. Even if they lose Carcali, they would never lose me. Can you think of another solution?" Dhulyn shook her head. "And you and I will never be separated, not really. We know that now."

She nodded. "I've Seen her older. In her own laboratory, but older than she is here. This must be what that Vision was showing me."

"So we succeed. In Battle," he said.

"And in Death," she answered.

Parno turned back to the others, Dhulyn at his elbow. "I'll go with you," he said to Carcali. "That way you can be sure there is no trickery."

"You'll go? You'd do this for me?"

"If the Crayx can take us both."

#We can# #And bring you back again, Lionsmane# #But it must be quickly, while the links remain, and the music still plays#

Was he still playing? Parno wondered. How much time was passing in that world?

#Let the Seers sing# #Mount again, both of you#

Parno swung himself on to the horse and put out his hand for Carcali. Dhulyn stood ready to give the girl a leg up. She looked from one to the other, licking her lips.

"He'll keep you safe," Dhulyn said. "You'll see. He'll take you right to your own door, like the son of a Noble House that he is. And you'll go to work on cooling that sun, now that you know it was done."

"But they said no, they said it wouldn't work."

Dhulyn shook her head. "You really are an idiot, youngster. You did it, don't you see? You must have done it, before you were lost in the weather-spheres. Your people, they didn't say it couldn't be done, just that you couldn't do it alone. So get some help, you blooded fool."

❦

Javen Finder was on her knees, lower lip between her teeth, concentrating on her bowl. But she shook her head.

"Nothing," she said to the others. "No colors will come. I'm sorry, Light of the Sun, I can't Find them."

Xerwin hugged Xendra tighter in the circle of his arms. She muttered but did not awaken, only tightened her arms around his neck. "But they could still be in this Vision place, where you *cannot* Find them, could they not? Where Xendra was?"

"Yes, Light of the Sun, they could be."

The White Twins and Dhulyn Wolfshead still stood, motionless now, holding hands. The new Paledyn still played, but more softly now, barely audible, as if his mouth was drying.

"Shall we stop him playing?" Xerwin asked.

They rode through the forest again, Carcali clinging to him, arms wrapped tightly around his waist. The forest turned denser, hotter, thicker, a real jungle, and suddenly they were in the sea, but that turned into a rainstorm, and either way, they didn't get wet. A village became a town became a city. There were strange smells, bitter, though they made Carcali laugh, and when he looked up, Parno saw the night sky was unfamiliar. All at once they were walking on the smoothest pavement Parno had ever seen, and Carcali ran ahead of him to a door painted the bright blue of a clear summer sky. She threw the door open and a wind rose up, blowing her into a small, tidy room with two beds, one against each wall. Carcali grunted as she landed on the bed to the right of the entry. She sat up right away, looking around her, tears falling down her cheeks, though she didn't bother to wipe them away.

"Paledyn," she said, looking around her through her tears. "Are you still here? Thank you, thank Dhulyn Wolfshead for me. Thank the Crayx." Before she can say anything more, she began to sob, and Parno heard the sound of hooves in the distance, and the sound of the sea. And music was playing, the Sleeping God's tune. Dhulyn was singing. She had a good enough voice, but not one people would pay money to hear.

"Oh, thank you very much," she said, cuffing him on the shoulder. She took the pipes from his cramping fingers. "I'll just stick to killing people from now on, shall I?"

Twenty-five

THE WIND WAS STRONG but steady, making the banners and flags that flew from mastheads, stays, and balconies flap and rattle.

"I never thought I'd see this day," said Remm Shalyn.

"The new Tarxin means to show his people what the new future is," Dhulyn said. "This is a strong beginning, but a good one."

The *Wavetreader* was at anchor in the deep harbor off the cliff face of Ketxan City. A vast floating platform, the size of a city square, had been erected between the ship and the permanent wharfs and piers, and in the center of it stood Xerwin, the Tarxin of Mortaxa, his sister, the Tara Xendra, and as many representatives of the High Noble Houses as could crowd themselves on. The balconies and windows of the City were packed with citizenry, all here to witness the historic betrothal of their Tara Xendra with Tar Malfin Cor of the Long Ocean Nomads.

"You think they realize their Tara is being wed to a mere sea captain?" Parno said out of the corner of his mouth.

"Some do, but those are the very ones who look to profit most from the connection, so they're unlikely to quibble." Dhulyn could hear the amusement in Remm Shalyn's voice.

The High Priest of the Slain God, who was officiating, caught Dhulyn's eye and motioned her forward with a frown. Dhulyn and Parno both stepped into their places at the priest's side.

"We call here to witness this solemn binding the Paledyn Dhulyn Wolfshead, and the Paledyn Parno Lionsmane, Hands of the Slain God, come to us from the far side of the Long Ocean."

They had already witnessed the written documents of the marriage, carried at the moment by Scholars from the Library of Ketxan City who were standing to one side of the bride and groom. Much of the last few weeks had been taken up with the creation of the contracts of the marriage, and at that Dhulyn had been given the clear message that the whole process had been scandalously rushed.

"This marriage to be the symbol of the joining of our two peoples, the first of many such marriages . . ." the priest was saying. And it would be so, Dhulyn knew. That fact that all the marriages would be with Pod-sensed Mortaxans might not be immediately obvious, but eventually, with the royal family leading the way, the whole idea of the Crayx would be taken for granted by the landsters.

"To remain with her family until the age of fifteen . . ."

Malfin Cor was fourteen years older than Xendra, but such an age difference was not significant when it came to political alliances. The Nomads knew Xerwin, and the Crayx trusted in Xendra's confidence in him; all were content. On his side, Xerwin had wanted to establish an alliance between his people and the Nomads as quickly as possible. Malfin was the nearest Nomad of significant rank, something more important at this juncture than his age. As Dhulyn already knew, the relationships between Pod-sensed people were such that physical age really had no significance.

"To spend half of each year with her people . . ."

Malfin Cor and the Tara Xendra both caught her gaze at the same moment, as both rolled their eyes in identical expressions of amusement. Dhulyn stifled her own laughter with difficulty, but managed to look sober enough when the priest shot her a suspicious glance. Through her Pod sense, Xendra could be with the *Wavetreader* Pod whenever she wished to be, and one of the things the young Tara had made clear since her return was that she definitely wished to be—she had started, Parno had said, to privately call the Crayx "seahorses."

"Free access to the Sanctuary of the Marked . . ."

In fact, the Marked were now free to come out of their Sanctuary, if they chose to. Medolyn Mender and her friend Coria Finder had already booked passage to Boravia, bartering their skills for the trip, and a young Healer Dhulyn had never met was going with them. Parno had provided letters of introduction to his noble cousin, DaleLad Tenebro, so the youngsters would have somewhere to go when they reached Imrion.

"Two ships to be built and manned with mixed crews . . ."

Dhulyn inclined her head. Not as mixed as people might think. *Wavetreader, Windtreader* and *Dawntreader* Pods would all provide crew members out of those who liked the idea of starting a new ship, but the Mortaxan element would be made up of newly discovered Pod-sensed.

After what seemed like hours of bowing and nodding at the right moments, the detailing of the contract was finally over. Malfin Cor gave his betrothed her own *garwon,* a rope of pearls as long as she was tall, and a small Crayx leather cuirass, in the same bright blue with golden tones as his own, which she seemed to value more than the jewels. She gave him a jeweled sword, a cloak in the same bright blue as the cuirass, and a miniature orange tree growing in its own tub, and already bearing fruit.

Finally, the two parties prepared to separate.

"Lionsmane," Darlara Cor said aloud. "Tide at the end of the third watch, don't be late."

Parno waved a hand in acknowledgment before following Dhulyn back into the City. There was no shortcut to the palace, not even for the Tarxin, and they took up their position for the procession behind the priests of the Slain God.

"That was for my benefit, I suppose, since Darlara does not need to speak aloud to you," Dhulyn said when Parno caught up to her.

"She's putting what distance she can between us, that's true."

"Would you rather we waited for the next ship?" Dhulyn watched her Partner's face carefully.

"What? Another moon at least?" He shook his head. "If we stay here any longer, Xerwin will find a way to keep us—him or the White Twins."

Dhulyn smiled. "I asked them if they wanted to come with us."

Parno hesitated between one step and the next. "Did they understand you?"

"Oh, yes, I asked them in a Vision."

"And?"

"And they would not live to make the journey."

"They know this?"

"We Saw it."

Ahead of them, the old priest was taking leave of his new Tarxin, and Xerwin signaled for the Mercenaries to join him as he turned to ascend the final staircase leading to the palace. Tara Xendra's face appeared, wide eyes blinking, peering around her brother and Parno burst out laughing. Dhulyn nudged him with her elbow.

"It's Xendra," he said. "She wants me to find out who made your trousers. She's determined to start living like a Nomad as quickly as she can."

Dhulyn looked over her shoulder to where Remm Shalyn walked with the Tarxin's guards. "Maybe I should pass Remm Shalyn's service to her. He could start teaching her weapons."

"*He* doesn't want to come with us?"

Dhulyn shrugged. "He's needed here, he says, until the slavery question is dealt with." Parno raised his left eyebrow and Dhulyn twitched her own in agreement. The Mortaxa would be a generation, at least, dealing with the slavery question, and that would be if they were very lucky indeed.

"Who knows, we may yet see him again, if the Nomads are going to start a passenger service. He'd make not a bad Mercenary Brother, if he lived through the Schooling."

They passed through the doorway into the Tarxin's private sitting room and found Xerwin struggling out of his ceremonial breastplate. He was entirely alone, his pikemen standing at their posts on the outside of the door, and his servants already dismissed.

"I'd forgotten how difficult this thing is to get out of," he said, as Parno gave him a hand with a tie that had knotted.

"You dismissed your attendants too quickly, Light of the Sun," Dhulyn said, careful not to smile too widely.

Now that his armor was off, Xerwin twisted his arm up behind him to scratch vigorously under his shoulder blade. "I'm not used to it yet," he admitted. "Even when I was Tar, I found it cumbersome to be constantly surrounded by so many servants."

"You're in a position to change that now, if you'd like," Parno pointed out. "My advice would be to keep a good personal guard, people you can trust, and know personally. Use them for your body servants, on the occasions you need any. Everything else is your Steward of Keys' problem, not yours."

"As we do in the Battle Wings. Yes, I like that notion." He looked from one to the other. "Are you sure I can't persuade you to stay? As you see, even the smallest advice from you is helpful."

Dhulyn shook her head. They'd been over this already. "You know we have unfinished business of our own, with our own House. Your instincts are good, Xerwin, follow them. Not every one on your father's Council can be a fool, listen to them until you know. Consult the Scholars of history for precedents. And don't forget that Xendra is now linked to a vast network of minds, many of which know far more about ruling than my Partner and I ever will."

Xerwin rubbed at his eyes with the heels of his hands. "Can they help me with the slavery problem? You've told me Mortaxa will collapse if we continue the practice, Dhulyn Wolfshead, and I believe you. So what do I do?"

Dhulyn shrugged. She knew what she would do, but then, she didn't have the welfare of a whole nation to consider. "Start small. Tax them. Tax the owners for every slave they own. Tax them heavily. Use the revenue to help the slaves who are turned loose."

"Dhulyn," Parno's voice had that listening-to-the-Crayx tone. "The tide turns. The *Wavetreader* is ready for us."

A little over a moon later, the Long Ocean ship *Wavetreader* arrived in the harbor of Lesonika, accompanied by a small Crayx who kept out of sight.

"I don't see *Catseye* anywhere," Dhulyn said when Parno joined her on the dock, with the last of their packs.

Parno took a quick glance around. "I didn't expect it, did you? Huelra might be anywhere along his usual route just now."

"And our horses? And the rest of our baggage?" He could tell that Dhulyn was disappointed. "At least the sun's shining. And here come the captains."

They had taken the last few days in the Midland Sea to say their good-byes to the crew, but the captains were doing them the honor of actually leaving the ship to say farewell in private—or in as much privacy as Nomads ever had.

#As much as they wish# #Amusement#

Parno grinned. Dar had no difficulty yet with the gangway, though she came down it with a hand to her belly. To Parno's eye, there was nothing yet there to see of the twins she was carrying, though both Dar and Dhulyn had sworn that he was blind.

Good wind, fair current came the Nomads' voices in his head, as they exchanged embraces.

Fair current, good wind he answered.

"Be near the sea in seven moons' time," Dar said aloud, so as to include Dhulyn. "You can be present when your girls are born."

"I will be," Parno said. "Expect me."

Dar suddenly stepped forward and hugged Dhulyn, who did her best not to shy away.

"Would have liked to keep you both," she said.

Dhulyn patted Dar's shoulder, knowing that the sentiment was sincere. But she had never again managed a Vision in which she could link with the Crayx, not even using her ancient vera tiles to help her concentrate. Without the White Twins, her Mark simply wasn't strong enough.

They shouldered their packs and, Dhulyn in the lead, headed back down the street toward the Mercenary House.

"We've missed the summer," Dhulyn said, pulling the throat of her red cloak closed. "But at least the sun's shining today."

"It's good to be back," Parno said.

"Let's see how good it is once we've been to Mercenary House."

Parno took her by the elbow. "What kind of problems can they give us? What could be worse than what we've been through already?"

Dhulyn shrugged one shoulder. "You're probably right."